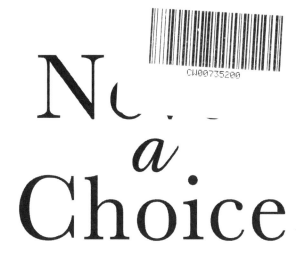

Not *a* Choice

THE CHOICES TRILOGY, BOOK ONE

DEE PALMER

Dedication

For My Husband—All My Love, Always

Prologue

Four Years Ago

"YOU'RE AN IDIOT!" John jerks me further up his back to get a bit more comfortable, and I grip a little tighter with my thighs to prevent me slipping back down before he repeats. "You're an idiot for working with a busted ankle tonight."

"Says the idiot carrying me half a mile home at one in the morning." I kiss the soft hairs on the back of his neck and smile against his warm skin. He smells of fresh cut wood and mint from a recent shower.

"It's bad enough you have to work on a school night, but you needed to rest. It looks like a freaking balloon now." He lifts my leg, but the dim street lamp fails to highlight his argument as my ankle is covered by my jeans and hidden in the shadow of the dark night. He's not really mad. he's never really mad, and he sighs as I rest my chin on his shoulder and my arms hug him just a little tighter.

"I need to work and it looks worse than it is." He grumbles under his breath and continues to walk me home -- well, carry me home. He meets me each night I work late at the local pub. It's a small village pub, and I do a little cooking in the evening, serve food, and help behind the bar. It's not strictly legal, but I'm not likely to tell; I need the extra money and the late nights pay better. It's the only thing John and I ever argue about, I won't take his money and he thinks Kit, my sister, should contribute more. He gets no argument from me there, but he works just as hard. His money is going toward a place of his own because his Dad has given him notice to quit like some troublesome tenant. He needs every penny and at least I still have a home. He shifts again and I can feel the tension in his shoulders. This is the second time he has carried me today. The first was when the injury happened, when I decided to throw myself off the eight foot stone wall.

For the last seven years when my mum was happy enough to let me wander a little further afield, John and I would do just that. Miles and miles of footpaths and bridleways, fields, riverbanks, and woodlands we explored together, and I only ever had the vaguest sense of where we were. I was always in a state of constant surprise that we had managed to find our way home. John would tell me I shouldn't really leave the house without a ball of string tied to my front door, but I didn't need the string. I had John, who always knew where we were and where we were going. He had given me a leg up so I could grab the top of the wall, and using his shoulders I just manage to pitch myself up and sit on the top. He told me to wait, not to jump, and that he still loved me even though I had hopped off and twisted my ankle so bad he had to carry me home. After nearly three miles across the fields he also told me I was a dumb-ass.

For the second time in less than twenty-four hours, John carefully lowered me to my feet by the back door. The house is quiet but my mum has left the kitchen light on, which filters a warm glow across his soft dark features. He is frowning, and I know it has nothing to do with how much his back is probably hurting. "I hate that you have to work, Boo. I hate it might affect your studies." He is holding my gaze, his eyes serious and pained.

"I know, but it won't, I won't let it. I know how important-" I don't finish because he huffs in frustration. I reach my hand to his cheek, his smooth skin hidden beneath his evening stubble. I try to ease his tension and get a smile from his lips by covering them with my own. I am bolder with him now and the tender touch is quickly consumed with pent up passion that is slowly destroying me and driving me insane. I turned sixteen at the end of the summer, it's nearly Christmas and he is almost seventeen. I kind of thought he would be just as eager as me to experience each other in the way we had promised. I had the briefest meltdown when I thought that at best he had the patience of a saint, or at worst he just didn't think of me that way. I was very wrong on both counts and he assured me he thought of me like that every second of every day, but he wanted to wait. He wanted to make sure I was ready and not just because I had reached a legal age, and I know he knew I *was,* but he also wanted it to be perfect. He had saved his wages over the months and had bought the raw materials to fashion a unique promise ring. A smooth band of silver looped in a heart, which was beautifully distorted to look like the symbol for infinity, and had two shiny blue stones set where the metal crossed. He gave this to me on my birthday, his promise to me, and I was ready to give myself to him as my promise to him. This weekend he was moving into his own place and had a special day planned. With no expense spared he promised, but said we would play the rest by ear, adding that he'd had enough self-restraint to last him a lifetime.

He groans against my lips, and I can feel his smile against my mouth as he pushes my shoulder back trying to break away, but I stretch my neck to try and keep the sweet contact a little longer. I let out a heavy sigh and mourn the loss of warmth when he finally succeeds with the separation.

"I'll meet you after college tomorrow, now go get some sleep so you can study hard." He kisses me once more, but with tight lips. It's a definitive dismissal, and I pout, but he laughs and shakes his head at his own personal struggle to leave.

"I can't wait for the weekend," I whisper and grin when I hear him draw in a sharp breath.

He flashes his bright white smile, "Why? What's happening…Ow!" He grips his ribs as I retrieve my finger from jabbing it in his side.

"You're an idiot!" I try to hold my narrowed eyed scowl but end up laughing with him. He steps back to me, his body all hard heat and muscle. He cups my face, and his mint fresh breath kisses my skin when he whispers back, "Me, too," and with one last kiss he starts to walk backwards down the path.

"I saved for this because although I know it's just for one day, I want it to be special. I want to treat you like a princess." His eyes are darker now because his face is in the shadow of moonlight, but I can feel his fire.

"It better not be just for one day." I choose to misinterpret his meaning and am rewarded with a deep laugh as he chooses to misinterpret me.

"Well, in that case, I'm gonna need a second and third job, princess." He quips.

"Dumb-ass," I call after him. It's not about the money. He treats me like a princess every day, but I'll wait for him, because as crazy as I might think it is, it's important to him. It was the worst choice.

Chapter One

Today

"OH, GOOD GOD, Bets, what are you wearing?" Sofia practically screams at me as she bounds into my bedroom only to freeze with a look of complete horror on her face.

"What?" I ask with genuine surprise as I look down at my ensemble.

"I'm supposed to be a 'mature student' remember?"

Sofia has been my best friend since college. She sat next to me at the induction meeting and within five minutes of break time I knew everything. She told me she had recently moved to the area, had four brothers, many, many more cousins, and worked in one of her family's restaurants. She loved dancing, loved drinking more, though, and she had a small angel tattooed on her butt that would have her shipped to the mountains of Italy if her father was ever to find out. We were both aged sixteen starting college, and since John had decided not to go the college route, I was grateful she decided we would be friends. I had only known her four years, but the events of that time irrevocably changed my life, and Sofia, her brother, and her family were my lifeline, and I couldn't repay their kindness if I had a thousand lifetimes. I immediately liked her openness and quickly fell in love with her energy for life, her confidence, but above all her honesty. This is why I had asked for her assistance in creating the 'appropriate' first impression for my first day at University.

"Well, yes, but mature doesn't mean dead. I'm pretty sure my Aunt was wearing the same outfit when she was buried, and that was eight years ago! You haven't been digging, have you?" Sofia giggles, but abruptly stops when she sees my expression has quickly changed from confused to worried, and that really wasn't what she had intended with her little joke.

"Besides," she gently adds, "'technically' a mature student is defined as aged twenty five and over, remember, and what age are you supposed to be?"

"Twenty five, or so it says on my recently doctored and scanned birth certificate." I smile as I wave the documents I have to take for registration today. I can't think of a time when I thought I would be thankful to my sister. In fact, I can't think of her at all without grinding my teeth to the point of inducing a mind-numbing headache, which is why I don't think of her at all. I have not thought about her for years, not since the day she died. She didn't die, but she was dead to me. She'd wanted a clean slate; hers was dirty, I was sure of it, not just her reputation, her juvenile record for theft and drug dealing, but I always just got the sense she was hiding more. I gave up caring what that was when she stole all the money from the sale of our home and left me to pick up the tab for our mother's on-going health care. Our mum was diagnosed with Alzheimer's when I was fourteen, but she'd deteriorated rapidly,and when I was sixteen, Kit and I made the decision to sell the house. I had found a nice care facility, the sale would mostly pay for, and between us we could make up the rest. Kit had Power of Attorney and ultimately had access to the money. She'd talked about starting afresh, rewriting her life, and I didn't understand why that was important at the time. I never believed she meant a fresh start away from me. I was staying with Sofia for a couple of months while Kit stayed at her boyfriend Dick's flat. She said it would take a while to sort out her new life and find somewhere we could both live. She just disappeared one day, and shortly after that I got notification from the care-home that the next quarterly payment was due, which was when I knew, really knew, what she had done. Sofia's family helped me with a full time job and sorting a payment plan with the nursing home. I couldn't move my mum into state care after seeing that she was settled and happy. I could still do my A-levels at night school, it would just take a little longer. I wasn't giving up on my education. The promise I made may haunt me because of what I'd lost, but it keeps me focused. "Ok, I may have overdone the age thing."

"Ya think?" mumbles Sofia.

"Let me change, just wait a moment." I try to spin quickly, only managing to jerk and squeak on my flat, square, crepe-heeled shoes. Really, what was I thinking? I return moments later.

"Oooo, yes, that's much better." Sarcasm dripping from every slowly uttered word. "An amorphous blob is exactly the right way to go." She raises her perfectly shaped eyebrows and I sigh. Damn those judgmental eyebrows! I slump on the edge and fall into the one and only armchair. I am actually feeling a little lost, and Sofia seems to know this, as she quickly has me in her tight embrace, squeezing the very uncertainty out of me.

"Bets, you have always been 'mature', regardless of the clothes you wear, I'm afraid, 'an Old Soul'. Remember that's what Mama has always called you? So how about you forget this," she says, waving her arms erratically around the array of clothes I'm wearing and have dropped in a heap. "Just wear something you are going to be happy in, comfortable, more confident, and more you?"

The uncertainty I am feeling right now and the knots I have in my stomach aren't me. I know I don't reach the dizzying heights of super confident Sofia, but I have had to assert myself from time to time, and I'm not shy. I don't have hang-ups and insecurities, because frankly, I don't have the time to care. I don't want a relationship other than my friends, and everything I have gained in my life is down to my own abilities and hard work. I'd like to say I wouldn't want it any other way, but I'm not a masochist, and I'm not an idiot. But I am definitely floundering here. I am uncomfortable with the fact that I'm pretending to be an age I'm not in order to study for a degree I want. It has to be part-time because I can't afford to not work full time. I'm uncomfortable with living illegally above the restaurant, a commercial property with no permission for residential use. Sofia's family is so sweet to let me live here, but this is a risk for them. The benefit of additional security, which I afford, could easily be performed by a decent alarm system.

"Bethany Edith Thorne!" Sofia scolds, interrupting me from my inner flagellation. I hate it when she uses my middle name, it means she's losing her not-so-famous patience. I exhale despondently, and I bury my head in my hands.

"This just isn't you, Bets. I'm your best friend and I don't understand why you're trying to hide who you are. You're bright and confident, and you've got a cracking bod under all that shit! I mean killer curves. You know it's not just your sparkling personality that has the boys lining up, right?" She's sitting directly in front of me now, daring me to break eye contact. She knows I'm not happy with the direction this conversation is heading, but before I can challenge her, she interrupts. "Brothers, I know, they are all like brothers. This is me, sweetie. I know how you feel and I know why you feel like that. I understand, I do, and I can see you're shutting down, so I won't push, but you know I want to, right?" She nudges my leg, and I give a weak grin. "Just don't hide." She whispers.

I smile with a bit more life and give a sharp nod of determination. "All right. All right, then!" I leap from the chair, lifting the gloom that had descended, forcing Sofia to fall on her butt.

"Give me five minutes." I call over my shoulder as I leave the room once more.

"Your last chance, Miss, or I'll dress you myself. I've got hot pants, boob tube, and high heels with your name on them!" she half threatens.

Well, okay, so I shouldn't want to hide, just stay under the radar, maybe, blend in, and I'm thinking six inch heals clip-clop-ping across the cobbles of the Quad would not aid this objective. So third time lucky, I emerge.

I've settled on my soft and worn pale blue Levis rolled up with my favourite red lace-up pumps, a fitted plain white T and my dark green, short, leather jacket, and striped cotton scarf wrapped loosely several times around my neck. My wavy dark chestnut hair is scooped into a loosely manageable knot, and my make-up is barely there, with some mascara and a splash of nude lip gloss.

"Beautiful butterfly, beautiful butterfly." Sofia beams and I lightly punch her on the arm for taking the piss, but I know I'm good to go.

"I'll want all the deets later…so call me?" Sofia's hug is get-ting a little emotional and tight.

"Stop! You're making me nervous and I don't need to call. I'll see you later. I'm working the late shift."

"I thought you would take tonight off at least, you know, just in case you hook up?" She teases.

"Bye Sofs." I leave. She has a key, and she can lock up.

I tend to walk everywhere, but today I'm running late and don't want to spend the rest of the day sweaty from rushing. All the same, it's a shame to get the tube when London is in midst of Autumn, and there has been no wind severe enough to strip the trees bare. It's my favourite season, and the only time of year when you really notice the sheer number of trees around the city, which are now golden bronze and fiery copper.

The campus itself is spread over a few locations across the city, but the oldest and main part is the Quad, a cobbled courtyard surrounded on three sides by early nineteenth century buildings. They may no longer dominate the skyline as they once had but they are imposing nonetheless. I pass the Gate House and make my way through the crowds of students to the Student Information Center. My main objective today, aside from the actual registration, is to work out how I can fit my part-time degree into a full-time timetable without raising suspicion. I need to double up on the part-time units in whatever way my work timetable will accommodate. I really don't want this degree to take the typical eight years, when I know I can do it in three. As I see it, I just have to approach each subject tutor individually and get them to accept me taking their extra lessons in addition to the lessons I'm actually assigned and just hope they don't compare notes. Simple.

I move slowly down the corridors, which have notice boards brimming with information on either side. Course and lecture information, clubs and interests, jobs and welfare; every food group is represented. I quickly scan the boards. Not that I will be 'joining-in' anytime soon, since free time is a luxury I haven't had in a while. I'm naturally drawn to the jobs and opportunities board, and am surprised and intrigued by a simple small flyer pinned and fighting for space. Call center, flexible late night hours, excellent pay. Not a huge amount of information, but I tear off one of the strips with the contact number and slip it in my jacket pocket.

I head toward the library with all my course information and stacks of flyers, which have been pressed into my hands as I've wandered, trying to get a feel for where I am and where I need to be. I would always gravitate toward the library, regardless. I can't live without my Kindle, but really there is no comparison to finding yourself lost in a room with shelves stacked high, soft chairs scattered, and quiet secluded corners surrounded by tombs of literature. Especially seductive if the building is as old as this; it's like a warm blanket of knowledge waiting to unfurl around me. I find one of the silent areas and a comfy seat, sinking down I take my notebook and pencil from my bag and start to doodle as my mind drifts. The shapes my pencil makes are repeating patterns of tightly bunched ears of corn, and the image makes me smile.

It was late August, and I had agreed to open my exam results with John in the hayfield. I had waited for the postman, and when he arrived, I took the letter addressed to me, a blanket, some provisions, and a notepad, then made my way to the hayfield. I walked through the churchyard and into the field, which was full of dozing Friesians, and guide to the field recently harvested for wheat. The farmer had baled and stacked the straw into several large blocks, and I couldn't see from the ground which one John would be on. He wasn't going to make it easy by leaving any clues or answering me when I called. I know he was there; he was always there before me.

I walked around three of the stacks and couldn't even see any tell-tale flattened footprints or bent stubble, the only thing I could do was climb and look from the top. I called again.

"You know a gentleman wouldn't let me climb all the way up there, especially when I've brought food!" It was a semi-whine, but I knew questioning his manners would get a response.

"Low blow, Boo, you're no fun, you know?" He peeks his head over the edge of the stack I'm directly next to, and I smile at his pout. His dark hair is flopping into his warm chocolate eyes.

"Yeah, I know, but you'd feel bad making me haul my arse up the wrong stack, and you know it." I sling my bag over my shoulder, tie the blanket around my waist and start to climb the straw bales. Poking my fingers and toes in hard to get purchase, I manage to grip and climb while John has his hand dangling for me to take as soon as I can reach it.

We sit cross-legged, knee to knee on my blanket with our letters in our hands. We both rip the envelopes at the same time, and I stare at mine in shock.

"Well, I've got what I need, how did you do, Boo?" He takes the letter from me.

"Bloody hell, Boo!" He leaps forward and knocks me onto my back. "You're a freaking genius!" He laughs, but I'm still in shock, I got nine As and one C in PE. I hated PE. He rolls to his side and grabs my notebook. "Right, we need a plan, you know you can do anything with these, Bets, I mean it; you could be *anything you want to be."*

I smiled at him and he looked so happy for me. He didn't care about his results at all; they were enough, and that was that. But for me, he was, well, he just looked so proud. "Well, it gets me into college, but let's not go crazy. It's not like I won the lottery!" I nudge him but he pitches up on one elbow and looks stern.

"No. No, it's not. That's just money. Money you can lose, money can be taken away. This, this is yours; this gives you choices and no one can take that away from you." He holds my gaze, "I mean it, Bets. It's really important to give yourself choices in what you do with your life, you can be anything you want to be." He leant in and kissed my cheek. "You are already everything to me, but this," he takes the letter, "this is for you." He looks deep into my eyes. "You have to promise me, Bethany, you'll do this. Whatever it takes, you have to give yourself choices. Promise?" He looks so serious, and he's used my real name.

"I promise."

Confirming with a nod he looks relieved and flops back down beside me. "What did you bring me to eat, wench?"

I laugh at him, and when I look at the faces staring at me, I realize I have laughed out loud in the library, but I also notice the curious looks, and I can feel my wet face. I quickly wipe the tears with my sleeve. I am always shaken when I remember, but at the same time I don't want to forget. I get back to sorting through all the information in my overstuffed bag. I spend the next hour sorting through the timetables and think I can juggle a few seminars and double dip a few units to get the extra credits I'm going to need. It looks like there will only be a few gaps in the four days I have to attend, which will suit my working hours at the restaurant perfectly. I'm starting to feel a little more confident I can pull this off.

There is an informal gathering for the new mature students in one of the basement classrooms, an opportunity to meet with fellow students and current students to get an insight, that sort of thing. I thought I should pop my head in, so I pack my bag and make my way back to the Quad.

I lean my entire body against the reluctant fire door to the classroom and the sprinkling of people inside turn my way. God,,I hate these things. It's not that I find making friends particularly difficult, it's just that I find these forced situations excruciating. I take in those in the room as I make my way to the safety of the coffee table. I am not sure if they are all mature students, or if there are Lecturers here, too, but I am by far the youngest, feeling that my first choice of outfit wouldn't have been misplaced, after all. There are some dodgy double denim combinations, some corduroy, I'm thinking Lecturer, and a few leather jackets, which belong to much younger men. The women seem to fare a little better and are dressed in either pant suit and blouse outfits or thick woollen type matching skirt and jacket. Being slightly thankful that I really don't have time to socialize, I start to fix myself a drink with purpose and confidence I'm not really feeling. A double espresso would be welcome, but I'll settle for the crappy instant coffee from the dripping silver canteen style dispenser.

"Don't look so scared, Bethany, they are all in the same boat and just as eager to make friends, I'm sure." A kind gentleman's voice speaks directly behind me.

I turn with my coffee in hand to see Mr. Wilson, my course leader, smiling at me. His wrinkled face gives way to more wrinkles, if that was possible. Mr. Wilson is in his early sixties with wavy grey hair and dark grey eyes which are framed by square, black-rimmed glasses that perch on the indent in his nose indicating many years of use. He wears a worn dark green tweed three-piece suit, a bright shirt, and an even brighter bow tie. I understand he was a formidable businessman in his youth, having built and sold several companies. Now, however, he is firmly entrenched in academia.

I couldn't apply for the undergraduate through the normal channel. Although my actual grades were good enough, the dates and ages on the documents would conflict and might have been flagged up as suspicious. I am too young and they would insist I take the full-time degree route. Instead, I had to fill out a departmental application form, have a general entrance exam, interview, and a date of birth stating I was in fact twenty-five. Mr. Wilson was, at the time, quick to put me at my ease at my interview earlier in the year, and we have exchanged a number of emails since I accepted my placement. He is the least intimidating academic I have come across, and I am thankful he seems to have taken me under his wing.

"Oh I'm sure." I return his smile. "Actually, I'm really glad you are here. I was hoping I could confirm my timetable amendments and just make sure I'm getting the most from what's on offer?"

"Yes, yes, of course, my dear. I said at the interview we would accommodate as best we can, and you were quite explicit in your requirements. I promised at the time I would help, and I wouldn't have offered you a place if I felt you wouldn't take every opportunity on offer, or if we couldn't fulfill our promise." He gently squeezes my hand as if to reinforce his sentiment.

"That's very kind, later in the week, maybe?"

"You have my email, my dear, anytime." He leans past me and picks up a handful of biscuits, which he tries to balance on the saucer holding his tea.

He doesn't seem to have any compulsion to mix and as I have a full cup in my hand I am a little reluctant to navigate the room. So we remain standing together at the edge of the gathering, and he begins to munch noisily on his biscuits. The room has started to fill, and like many basement classrooms, it feels a little stuffy, but the noise level has risen from awkward silence to gentle hum. A number of Mr. Wilson's colleagues have come over and it is clear he is well liked and respected. He kindly introduces me as some will be my Lecturers, and I try to commit their faces and names to memory, but it's hopeless until they leave, and Mr. Wilson fills me in with some inappropriate piece of information that makes me laugh out loud and will definitely make it easier to remember them.

Ms. Stephens was a Karaoke queen, Mr. Philips nearly drove away with his newborn baby in his car seat on the roof of the car after several weeks of interrupted nights, and I was lucky not to spit my coffee all over him when he revealed Mr. Peters, from finance, nearly didn't get married last year, because there was a fight as to who would wear the wedding dress! I can feel my eyes start to water as he turns a wicked grin my way.

I look over toward the still closed door as I feel a cool wave of fresh air flow over me and a rush of goosebumps prickle my skin. Before me, Mr. Wilsons' eyes widen as he fixes his gaze directly above my head. I can't seem to move.

"Daniel! How simply wonderful of you to join us, I didn't expect you to accept my invitation to this little gathering, but I'm so pleased you could make the time," Mr. Wilson gushes.

Wow! I can't help but smile, this man is too sweet and obviously a little in awe of whomever is standing behind me.

"I didn't, and I don't." The deep voice growls his response.

"That's rude!" My hand immediately flies to my mouth as I realize I did in fact say that out loud. My shoulders tense, and I try to sink into myself as I notice the instant evaporation of Mr. Wilsons' smile. I would like to think that his change in demeanour is a result of the rude man behind me, but I can't help feel it is because of my inappropriate contribution.

I give a tight smile and try to apologise as I mouth, "I'm sorry," to Mr. Wilson. I straighten my back and turn sharply only to have my field of vision blocked by a wall of chest encased in a black, fitted suit jacket over a crisp white shirt. I lower my eyes taking in his smart well- fitted jeans, large thighs, and shiny black boots. I drag my eyes up. This feels like it's taking forever. I'm hoping it's only seconds, especially as my gaze lingers a little too long at his crotch.

Christ! Move your eyes, Bets! I do, up and up. .He is standing really close. My breath hitches when I take in the fierceness of the stare his eyes are giving mine. They are a 'divers dream' ocean colour blue, deep blue, with even deeper flecks. He narrows them slightly, and I see a tiny twitch in his jaw. He is intense. I can feel the anger radiating in waves. I am only guessing it's anger from the few words he has spoken.

"I need the keys to your office, Jack. You did say I would have access?" Curt and to the point, but his question has me confused, as he hasn't taken his eyes from mine.

"I'm sorry, Sir?" I'm generally confused.

"Accepted." He gives a flicker of a grin.

"Errr?"

"Yes, yes." Mr. Wilson interrupts. "Of course, Daniel, I have a set in my briefcase." He pauses to see if he is being acknowledged in any way. He isn't. Mr. Wilson continues, "Allow me to introduce..." He sounds flustered, but I interrupt.

"Mr. Wilson." I turn away from the unfathomable tension that's starting to build between this man and me. "Don't bother, really, I should try and meet some of the others here... Well, those who do want to be here, at least. You've been wonderful so far, but I better brave this myself and leave you to help this--" I can't help but pause, knowing it's rude, "--man sort the keys so he can get on his way." I go to move off and find I am again blocked by that large chest I can now smell it's so close. Fresh with spice and something exotic and a surge of heat returns like taking a direct hit in the chest.

"Jack, please continue... allow you to introduce?" I am again looking into his eyes as they briefly flick toward Mr. Wilson for encouragement only to return their fix to mine. I'm trying to swallow, and I am hoping the slight tremble I am experiencing now is not visible. With slightly less enthusiasm Mr. Wilson continues;

"Daniel, allow me to introduce one of our mature students starting with us part-time this semester...Bethany Thorne. Bethany, this is Daniel Stone. He is a respected and very successful businessman, and also a 'Friend of the University'. Daniel has kindly offered his valuable time to give a series of lectures for our entrepreneurs'...we are very lucky." Mr. Wilson seems genuinely thrilled and his smile is infectious.

"Mature?" Daniel raises an eyebrow, but his intense gaze doesn't break contact with mine.

"Friend?" I challenge. I'm trying to be brave and counter his question. It's not working. His obvious query removes the smile from my face, and I look nervously at my hands, which are now gripped together. I reach to tuck my hair behind my ear and tug gently at the nape, feeling the skin lift and pinch as I do.

"I'm twenty-five," I venture boldly, more bold than I'm feeling at any rate. "Yes, twenty-five. I'm twenty-five." Smooth, Bets, really smooth. I risk a glance up toward his face. His dark eyes crinkle as his grin transforms to a full on, breath-taking smile. He is possibly the most stunning man I have ever seen, and he can't be the most important man in the room, yet I feel the power and command like a force holding me rooted to the spot.

"Really?" He leans in further and I can feel his breath on my neck. I feel my face flush instantly. I must be seven shades of red right now, and I know my heart is pumping so hard, it might just succeed in escaping my chest via my ribcage. I try to swallow but manage only to make a whimper leave my dry throat. I lick my parched lips and notice his eyes fix on the slight movement. Christ, Bets! Get a grip. You'll be swishing your hair and swooning any minute now. He lifts my hair away from my neck, an impossibly intimate gesture, which does nothing to quell the raging heat building between my legs. I am only thankful that Mr. Wilson seems to be distracted from this very intense exchange.

"Interesting, Miss Thorne, now why are you lying?" His voice is rich and luxurious like velvet caressing my skin.

Shit! I don't say this out loud, but I'm screaming it to myself, and I make a sharp intake of breath, which has drawn Mr. Wilson's attention back to me. I try to take a step back and notice a number of eyes focused on our little exchange, just what I need. So much for staying under the radar, and it doesn't help that Mr. Stone has neatly mirrored my retreat keeping the intimate distance between us.

"I'm not, I mean, I don't know what you mean…" I fumble quietly hoping Mr. Wilson is catching none of this.

"Oh Miss Thorne, you most definitely are, but what puzzles me is why? But I do love a good puzzle." His tone is pure temptation.

"Well." I recover. "This has been delightful and as charming as you are…" I leave the statement unfinished as I turn my back, effectively blanking Mr. Stone and take hold of Mr. Wilson's hand. He looks a little confused, and I'm thinking, *join the club*!

"Thank you, Mr. Wilson, so much for this opportunity, I really am so grateful, Sir."

"Bethany, there is no need for 'Sir', please. I don't mind if you call me Jack."

"I'll be more comfortable with Mr. Wilson, Mr. Wilson." I smile.

"And I would be more comfortable with Sir." I freeze as his hands grasp my shoulders and his lips are again brushing my ear. I pray to God no one else can hear, because they can sure as shit see my face flame once more. "In fact… I insist." He gives a gentle laugh. I shift slightly to try and ease the pressure in my groin.

"I have to get to work. My shift starts soon!" I rush to announce it, as if this revelation will save me from this excruciating encounter. It's not a lie, but I could have stayed a little longer if I wanted; I don't. I step away and feel the sudden loss of heat. I have to lean awkwardly around an immovable Daniel Stone to place my coffee cup down. Only when I am safely on the other side do I release the breath I had been holding. I risk a look back into the room through the small window in the door. There are several groups of people now, but undoubtedly most eyes are fixed on the mountain of a man next to Mr. Wilson. His eyes are, however, undeniably fixed on me.

"So?" Sofia leaves a long dramatic pause. "How was your first day? Did you make any friends? Did the other children play nice?" She is carrying a bottle of white wine and two glasses from downstairs and flops into the armchair opposite me. I am curled up in a ball wrapped head to toe in a blankie.

"Pour first." I instruct, pointing at the empty glasses.

"It couldn't have been that bad; you didn't even have any lectures, did you?" She passes me a very full glass.

"Urghhh." I take a large gulp, this is not going to touch the sides. "I think I've been rumbled."

Sofia laughs then stops. "You're serious? How?"

"Some guy at the gathering, a 'Friend of the University' they've roped into giving some free lectures, flat out told me I was lying in front of my course leader."

"What? Oh my God, Bets. What did you do? What did Mr. What's-His-Name say?"

"Mr. Wilson, well, he didn't say anything, he didn't actually hear, this guy whispered it in my ear." I get a shiver as I say this, like I can still feel his breath skim my skin. I can feel my face heat, and I quickly down the rest of my glass.

"Oh my... Miss Thorne, I do believe you're blushing." She giggles.

"I know! What is that about? Some random hot guy whispers in my ear and I light up like a red light district. They all swear like sailors in the kitchen, and the topics they share, well, it's no holds barred most of the time and not a hint of colour!" I am just as shocked.

"Hot guy?" She hums with excitement.

"Oh yes." I swallow. "Did I not mention that he was off the charts, hot as hell? And he knows, I don't know what he knows, but he knows I'm lying." I'm frowning now and waving to get more wine. Sofia leans forward and tops up my glass. I take a smaller sip this time. "Oh God, I can't lose this place, Sofs." I drop my head in my one free hand.

"Random guy, you say, so he is not on the staff?" She muses.

"No." I like where she's going with her thinking.

"And you didn't confirm he was right?"

"No."

"And your Mr. What's-His-Name didn't hear?" Her lips begin to curl in a reassuring way.

"Mr. Wilson, and no." I mirror her pleasing smile.

"So then there is nothing to actually worry about, nothing material has changed here, so don't worry. Nothing will come of this, I promise, other than me laughing at you for actually blushing over some 'random hot guy'." She moves to sit next to me and nudges my arm, not quite spilling my drink. I think about what she's said.

"You are right, he's not staff and not a student. I probably won't even see him again." I take a satisfying sip to drain my glass.

Chapter Two

I WISH I HAD a bath. I stand under the less than powerful staff shower at the rear of the kitchens and attempt to dodge the range of temperatures, which fluctuate from skin flaying hot to freeze-your-nipples-clean-off cold. In fact, I think I would sell my soul for the luxury of a roll top bath with deep hot water and endless silken bubbles; throw in some candles and I wouldn't even put up a fight. I squeal as I'm blasted with a final spurt of ice water as I turn the tap off and step onto the slatted wooden tray, which in the winter prevents my feet from freezing directly onto the concrete floor. I wrap myself in my large fluffy towel, slowly open and peep around the door. The corridor is empty, and I'm pretty sure I am early enough to brave the mad dash upstairs without the other employees catching a flash of flesh. This fact alone is the reason I am always awake at five in the morning. A brutal and mortifying lesson learned the hard way, and even though I cringe at the recollection, I am ever thankful no phone camera was at hand at the time.

I have lived here for two years. My sister's disappearance kind of left me homeless, and my temporary month-long stay at Sofia's turned into two years until I was eighteen. Sofia's family took me in. They have a large town house in a fabulous part of London, and although they clearly have money, they are really down to earth; so friendly and welcoming. The house was always full. Full with friends and family, of wonderful aromas and of love. I dated Sofia's twin brother, Marco, for a short time, not my smartest move, but he was funny, smart and persistent. He didn't cover himself in glory when I found out he had been bragging about me to some friends. He was a little shocked when I didn't take the opportunity to shame him and deny it all when I had the chance. I had my reasons and laughed it off, even gave him a high score when pushed for details. Sofia was not so kind and tore into him in private. She was the only one I ever told about John and completely understood why I was the way I was, but she was protective of me all the same. This, in itself, could have made my move into the family home awkward, but I have a talent for turning fragile relationships into strong friendships. Next to Sofia, Marco is my best friend.

Marco works in the Knightsbridge restaurant with me while Sofia is studying a food and wine diploma at an exclusive private school in central London. She is happy to live at home, forgoing the student experience for the utter luxury her five star home offers. She also chose not to work in the family restaurants, opting instead to work at a private members club, learning the hospitality and event side of catering. As the only girl, she is spoiled and indulged, and could have so easily become a proper princess. She can spend money like there is no tomorrow, but she is generous, too, and she works really hard.

I knew I was welcome to stay as long as I needed, but the house was full and sharing a bed with the human starfish meant I never slept all that well. Even though Sofia's father kept on about not leaving me to "wander the streets," I started to look for a room as soon as I turned eighteen. Realistically, sleeping on the streets wasn't going to happen, I could afford a room, it just wouldn't be pretty, and it might be a little out toward the sticks. However, one Sunday I was wiping down at the end of my shift and getting ready to leave, when Sofia's father took me upstairs. He wanted to show me what his boys had been working on. The confusion on my face must have been a picture as he laughed and led the way. Above the restaurant were two small box rooms, which were too inconvenient to use for extra storage for the restaurant so had been relegated to a dumping ground for dying furniture and dead kitchen equipment.

I stood on the threshold and was completely overwhelmed; I couldn't take a step further when I saw what they had done for me. Sofia leapt from behind an armchair shouting, "Surprise!" That was the understatement of the year. I had no idea this was all happening above my head. The room had been cleared and painted a warm honey white. The threadbare patchy carpet had been removed and the wide wooden plank flooring had been stripped and polished. Two large chocolate and charcoal coloured rugs almost covered the entire floor, but you could still see the rich polished wood around the edge.

In the far corner below the window, a book lamp illuminated a small white desk with a high backed wooden chair tucked beneath it. In the centre of the room was a two-seater sofa with a huge, fluffy, cream-coloured throw, which was hiding a rather hideous seventies style geometric pattern. Next to that was a faded and battered leather armchair, which I recognised from Marco's bedroom. It was a much loved piece of furniture and very comfortable. The permanent indent in the seat cushion was a testament to that. Sofia had obviously been raiding my storage boxes and sixth form art portfolio case, as the walls now held two of my abstract landscapes. She'd had them mounted and framed. There was also a silver framed picture of my mum when she was my age on the coffee table and a cork notice board above the desk declaring, 'Welcome to Your New Home ☺' in the form of a colourful homemade poster.

Sofia came toward me and grabbed my hand, excited to show me all the improvements. There was a corner unit, which acted like a kitchenette with a single ring hob, kettle, and toaster. To be fair, there was a much larger kitchen downstairs if I was ever feeling more adventurous than tea and toast. Behind that was a separate toilet and sink; next to those, two smaller store cupboards had been knocked into one to provide a perfect sized bedroom. The queen sized futon bed dominated the tiny space and Sofia had hung white fairy lights all along the headboard. It looked magical. It was perfect. My new home was perfect! I was speechless and about to turn, when I noticed a tiny framed picture beside the bed. It is the follow on picture of the one I always keep in my purse. It is the photo of me and John, my soul mate and best friend since I was five years old. It was taken on my sixteenth birthday. It was my fault he never made it to seventeen. It was my fault he was murdered.

I couldn't stop the tears that had been building since I stood on the threshold. I let out a sob and was quickly muffled to silence by tight embraces from Sofia and her father. I had decided a long time ago that crying accomplished little other than huge, puffy, red eyes and a snotty nose. So I reigned in the breath-stealing sobs I could feel bubbling under the surface, which I knew I was capable of in private, and gave a light laugh to lift the mood. After all, I was genuinely over the moon with my new pad. I thanked them again and again. The grand tour took no more than five minutes and after seeing how truly happy they had made me, Sofia and her father left for the evening. I was able to wallow in the solitude of my new home, because although I am often lonely, I am rarely alone. It was bliss.

I work a split shift on Mondays, so having confirmed my timetable amendments with a quick email to Mr. Wilson, I head down to the kitchen. I am capable of turning my hand to most jobs in and around the restaurant, and Sofia's eldest brother Anthony, Jr., who runs this restaurant, is pretty flexible where I work. He prefers me front of house, and I don't flatter myself that I would ever be let loose cooking, but I can prepare vegetables and wash up like a pro. Besides, I am happiest in the kitchen. The pressure can be intense, and the language can be blue, but I like the banter and buzz that comes from working in a predominately dominant male environment. The guys never make any concessions for me being there, and they certainly don't censure their language or the topics up for discussion. Frankly, what I didn't learn in biology, I more than made up for in that kitchen. They would happily enlighten me, giving me tips and tricks, which would make a hardened professional blush but just made me laugh.

I prepped vegetables all morning; one of the specials today was zucchini fritters, which meant mountains of shredded courgettes. It's the only way to eat such a dull vegetable and the way Joe cooks them; they are light, crisp, and melt in your mouth. I had a taster as I finished work and headed upstairs to change. I planned to go to the library to make a start on my reading. I can't afford to buy all the course books, but reading them in the library is no hardship. As I put my jacket on, I dig in the pocket and pull out a crumpled piece of paper with the contact details I took from the job board, the one with the very vague but intriguing information. I decide to give the number a call, It was worth that to at least establish some details. I sit on the arm of my chair and punch the numbers.

The call is answered, "Late Night Calls…let me help you?" The voice is slow and sultry, and the question threw me. I couldn't speak.

"Come on sweetie, don't be shy," The voice encouraged. I'm pretty sure it was a female voice, but it was low, so I couldn't be hundred percent certain.

"Right, sorry." I stumbled, "I got your details form the jobs board at my University, you know about flexible hours, extra cash… um, could I speak to someone about that?" I definitely sounded like I have the wrong number and am just about to hang up.

"Oh, sure thing, sweetie, I'll just put you through to Mags, she'll sort you out. Bye!" Her bright voice is cut off abruptly, and my call is clicked over and put through before I could thank her. This gives me enough time to compose myself, maybe not sound like such a moron.

"Hello?" I ventured tentatively as the line goes silent.

"Hello, my darling, what can I do for you today?" Her voice

was equally low, and I wonder if that is a job requirement or maybe just something in the water.

"I was calling about the job, but to be honest I don't really know what the job is, where it is, or, well, any of the details, really, so that would be a good place to start?" I try to come across as professional as possible, my voice a little lower than normal.

"Don't you just have the sexiest voice?" Mags says, ignoring my actual question.

"Urgg?" She can't see my confusion, but my eloquent noise must make that clear.

"Well, not when you grunt like that, you don't." She laughs a deep throaty sound, which still sounds inviting but not mean.

"Oh!" I am shocked, and given I work in the kitchen below, that is saying something.

"Yes 'Oh'. Now *that* I can work with." She laughs lightly this time. "I am going to say right off, I will be able to offer you something, but I think we should meet, despite my type of business, I really prefer to do this sort of thing face to face. Can you come by at three this afternoon? We are quiet then, and we can go over everything and start your training." She is super friendly and can't hide her enthusiasm.

"Training?" Pretty sure my 'sexy' tone had been replaced with pure panic.

"I know I'm getting ahead of myself, but I know people, and I have a good feeling about you. What is your name darling?" she encourages.

"My real name?" I ask, and she laughs out.

"Yes, darling, your real name." She is still laughing but I can't take offense. She makes me smile.

"Bethany." I tell her.

"Take my details down, Bethany, and I'll see you at three." The light laughter is gone, and this is purely business. Her tone shifts, and she gives me everything I will need to meet her later.

After ending the call I am a little dazed. I now have a pretty good idea what "Late Night Calls" is, and yet I still agreed to meet with Mags. More interesting still is that I am actually a little excited about it.

The door to the Late Night Calls office was unnamed, and I almost missed it, nestled between the arches behind Waterloo station. I knew the pub to the left, The Hole in the Wall, but I had no idea there was office space too. I was half right; it wasn't really office space at all. I press the buzzer and the intercom lights up.

"Please come on up, Bethany." The same voice from earlier has lost a little of its sultriness with the accompanying crackle.

I climb the narrow stairs and tentatively open the only door on the landing. The room is more like a hotel lobby, luxurious and welcoming, a complete contrast to the slightly grimy exterior and not like any office I know.

"Hello, Bethany." The girl behind a small reception desk smiles. "I'm Susan, and Mags is just on the phone." She points to a closed door behind her. "She won't be long… they never are." She giggles.

"Please take a seat, and make yourself at home." She gestures to the seating area, which resembles an adult playpen without the bars. I could choose from a large corner sofa, which takes up most of the room, or alternately, I could perhaps romp on the oversized cushions piled high on a faux fur rug. As no one can get up from those things with a modicum of dignity intact, I decided not to risk the lure of their softness and opt for the safety of the sofa. I sit on the edge, which is apt because I am on edge. I smile at Susan, who has returned to flicking through, what looks from here, like a lads' magazine.

"No frowning, darling, you'll get wrinkles." Mags, I assume, enters the room with a dramatic swish emphasised by the flow of her chiffon three-quarter length bright pink jacket. She must be in her sixties and is immaculate. Her make-up is a little heavy around the eyes, and she has the brightest pink lipstick on. Her hair is cut in a sharp grey blonde bob, and her tailored suit and silk blouse perfectly fit her shapely curves. She's wearing six inch gold Louboutins, and I know this because they are Sofia's favourite, not because I am lucky enough to own a pair. After taking me in carefully, she sits beside me and sighs.

"Well, you are just as sexy as your voice. Pity we don't do video calls." She pauses. "Yet." Her smile is warm, and she gives a light laugh. I don't know why, but I find myself grinning back. She is warm and friendly, and I am about to be a huge waste of her time. I'm thinking it's going to take a maximum of five minutes for her to conclude I am wholly unsuited to provide the type of service Late Night Calls offers. She squeezes my knee, her eyes soften and she looks intently into mine. I think that might be a record for interviews, not even five minutes, and I can feel a 'Don't call us' heading my way. "Come on into my office; let's give you a test run!" This woman has managed to shock me twice in the same day. She grabs my hand and practically hauls me across the room into her office and closes the door before I can change my mind. "Darling, don't look so nervous. You know what we do, yes?" She raises her perfectly drawn on eyebrow at her query.

"Yes, Miss," I quietly reply. She raises both eyebrows in surprise and almost imperceptibly utters, "interesting," under her breath.

"Well, I will tell you the whys and wherefores, we will have a little trial and go from there." She is very encouraging, and her face is alight with misplaced enthusiasm.

"Yes, Miss." I hesitate and suck in a shallow breath. "I'll try".

"I run an exclusive service." Mags continues proudly. "Top service, top quality, and top price." She grins. "You work the hours you want, though I would like a minimum of one hour per day, I provide the phone and calls are directed through my switchboard. This protects you *and* the client. You can work wherever you like, you can come here if that suits, and you can earn up to a hundred pounds an hour if you can keep them on the phone that long." She chuckles and I'm starting to wish I was up to the task. She continues, "…or more if you provide one of the speciality services." As the obvious horror on my face must show, she quickly adds, "Oh, darling, I don't mean *that* sort of service. I'm no Madam, although I've been called worse." She laughs again. "I just mean we have dedicated lines, which cater to specific tastes." She pauses and eyes me carefully. "Any questions?"

I am actually speechless, another indication of my unsuitability for a job totally reliant on speech.

"All right, then, let me hear your audition piece?" She fixes me with her expectant kind eyes.

"Oh." I breathe. "Well, I'm not sure." I hesitate and can feel my face flush.

Sensing my extreme discomfort, Mags smiles and hands me her phone. "Use this as a prop if it helps. Imagine it's an actual call; all you have to do is imagine." She is sweet and encouraging, but I am so out of my depth. I look at the phone in my shaking hand, sigh, and hand it back to her. "Listen, why don't I let you listen to a few calls first, a few samples as it were, once the initial shock is over, I'm sure you'll get the idea…what do you think?" She places her hand over mine but doesn't take the phone back.

I am not given to running at the first sign of a challenge, even if I am so very far from my comfort zone and have no idea why she is being so kind, but I don't want to disappoint her.

"Yes, Miss, that's very kind. I'll do that." I am too embarrassed to raise my eyes to meet hers at this point, so she takes the phone, presses a few numbers and hands it back to me.

I am thankful she leaves the room as I put the phone to my ear and begin to listen to the sample calls. It turns out I wouldn't need that much imagination, as the calls give me vivid flashbacks to many a conversation in the kitchen. The descriptions are full on, and the details are explicit, extremely explicit. It isn't that I doubted my imagination or my ability to be detailed in my descriptions, but my actual lack of sexual experience is undoubtedly going to be a deal breaker here, and I know it. Still, as my face continues to flush, I continue to listen. The last call starts.

"*I've got your big hard cock in my hand--*" the breathy voice began "*--can you feel my tight fist? I'm gonna pump you hard. I'm gonna pump you into my hot wet mouth... mmmmm.*"

I can hear the caller's deep inhaling breath.

"*You're so hard against my tongue; it's hot and wet and I'm licking around the head and all the way down. I can feel your veins throbbing as I lap and lick it; it's like velvet over iron and tastes so good I can't get enough. Ahh, I can feel your rock hard cock twitching in my fist, I think I'm going to lick you all the way down to your balls. Mmmm, I'm cupping your balls with my other hand, and I'm fucking you with my fist, but I want more. Are you going to give me more?*" She pauses and breathes loudly. I'm shifting in my seat, more than a little uncomfortable, as she continues.

"*I am going to take your big hard cock and push it between my tight swollen lips, and take you deep, deep in my throat, and you're going to fuck my mouth, yes?*"

"*Mmmm... yeah, that's right.*" The deep rasping reply of the caller was the first real indication there was someone on the receiving end of this call.

"*Fuck my mouth, and make me swallow.*" She gives a long drawn out satisfied moan. The line goes dead.

"Wow!" I say as Mags returns. If I thought I was red before, I must look like I'm about to haemorrhage.

"The endings are always a little abrupt, but they are paying by the minute, so what do you expect, really?" I am hoping that's a rhetorical question because all powers of speech have deserted me. She hands me a glass of water, which I gratefully accept.

"I'd love to be that confident. I mean she seemed to really…" I'm struggling to articulate full sentences now, another stellar example of my ineptitude for this role. "And she was in control, assertive. I don't think I would be able to…you know…but-"

Interrupting, Mags states, "You're a virgin." She smiles warmly.

"Well, yes, to this sort of thing." I attempt to qualify her statement.

"No, darling, I mean you are a virgin; you've never had sex." It was no longer a question; it was a statement of fact. "It doesn't matter, you know," she continues.

"Umm, not to presume to tell you your business, but I would think that was kind of important, if not *the* most important part." I frown as she shakes her head at my incorrect conclusion.

"Don't get me wrong, it *is* unusual in this business, but you are not 'an innocent', or if you were, you would have run a mile as soon as you realised what we did, and you certainly wouldn't have been able to endure a whole sample call. So despite the adorable colour in your cheeks, you are still here. You have a great voice and a good imagination, I assume?" She raises a questioning eyebrow to which I nod my reply. "And you're a submissive!" My eyes widen. "Quite perfect." She adds.

I laugh out loud. Wow, that couldn't be further from the truth. I don't remember a time when I didn't make every decision myself. There is no one to tell me what to do, not that I would let them, and I kick arse at Krav Maga each week with Marco. Does that sound submissive? I know she has made a mistake, but I like her, and I find I can't be affronted by her misguided character assessment.

"Darling," she soothes, "I know people, I read people, and I can read you like an ABC or should I say D/s." She chuckles. "You are all, 'Yes, Miss. No, Miss', without a hint of irony." She seems so pleased with herself I almost hate to disillusion her.

"I was being polite." I point out.

"Yes, you were, but there's more, trust me, and what a wonderful way to explore this "worldview", through the safety of your telephone." She was being genuine and I can't take offense, even if she is way off the mark.

"Look, I have a proposal: take your time, think it over, and do some research, but remember to clear your browser history!" She laughs at her own joke. "I would like to take you on as a submissive for one of the premium lines. There will obviously be some artistic license, you won't be a to-the-letter submissive, after all, can't very well hold a conversation over the phone if you're gagged." Again she seems to find herself hilarious. I take another sip of water and give a very nervous laugh, trying to share her carefree attitude to the whole other world crashing into mine. "If you agree we will start you off one hour each night. From midnight onwards tends to be busiest. It's completely anonymous and completely safe, no one needs to know. You look like a girl who can keep a secret?" She looks directly at me. She is either the master of the understatement or she really can read people.

"I can, I do and I will... but are you sure?" I hold her gaze. Her lips twitch into a smooth smile, and she merely raises her brow, sweeping her knowledgeable gaze around her immaculate office and over her expensively clothed body, finally resting her eyes on her diamond laden fingers, the final piece of evidence of her good decisions.

"Here, take this phone, if you decide it's a no, then you can drop it back, but if we are good to go, it will save me a courier."

"Thank you. And thank you for your time Miss, sorry... Mags, just a few days?" I tell her.

"I'll be waiting." She was grinning as I left her office.

I have an email from Mr. Wilson waiting when I arrived home. It was an urgent message to come to his office after class tomorrow. Crap.

Chapter Three

MY FIRST WEEK at University, I could pinch myself about actually being here, given my recent meeting with Mr. Wilson, and I'm on cloud nine. I had initially thought Mr. Sinfully Sexy might have disclosed my lie, not that he was specific as to what he thought I was lying about, and I certainly wasn't going to volunteer the information. This line of thinking, however, would at best make me paranoid, and at worst mean I am suffering from an over inflated sense of self-importance, so I was relieved it was neither. Mr. Wilson informed me that the IT bursary I had applied for had been successful. Colour me shocked! I didn't really think I was eligible for any type of assistance as a part-time student, but I had applied all the same, because I also didn't have the luxury of not at least trying for some assistance, and an upgrade on my ancient laptop was decades overdue. That said I wasn't sure if what I felt was joy or just a huge sense of surprise, but I found myself inappropriately hugging Mr. Wilson at the news. Like I said, I was on cloud nine!

I am a little intimidated, sitting high in the Gods of this ultra-modern lecture theatre, and the blank page of my notepad isn't helping. I smile to myself, because now when I get the IT grant money, I can buy a decent laptop, like all the students around me are sporting. Mine takes around two days to warm up and weighs the same as a small car. In other respects, though, I look like a typical student. At twenty, I am perhaps two years older than most of the students and five years younger than is permitted on the part-time program, but most people wouldn't notice, and that might be why I was so taken back when Mr. Stone called it at our first meeting.

The theatre is starting to fill, and I am lucky that my choice in footwear resembles a mountain boot with crampons, as the angle of climb to my seat is perilously steep, and I am hugely respectful of the girls who attempt the climb in heels. Glancing around there does seem to be a disproportionate number of females and not dressed in what seems to be the standard asexual garb, but more like that of a catwalk or night out clubbing. Strange.

This series of lectures was a real coup for the University, leading high profile business people giving an 'up close and personal' guide to Entrepreneurship. The Lectures are mandatory for mature students in the Business faculty, but you would have to be an idiot not to take this opportunity. Each student had to give a biography and an outline detailing what they expected to gain from the program. I had never heard of that before, but perhaps it's not so strange, important people wanting to make sure they were not wasting their time. Still, given that this was all extra work for each student here, and it is an evening lecture, I am surprised to see the theatre almost full. An email reminder was sent earlier in the day to emphasize a seven p.m. start – PROMPT.

Although no one person is shouting, the general level of noise has risen to something akin to an airplane take-off. My course has a weighted nine to one ratio of males to females, and I find I am surrounded on all sides by the men from my course. I have introduced myself as the part-time mature student, which in itself seems to make me non-threatening and extremely approachable. As such I have easily made friends with anyone kind enough to sit next to me, and many have. I can't make out any specific conversation, and I don't want to add to the noise, so I continue to gaze at my page. It is no longer blank as my habit, which I find both relaxing and distracting, covers the edges of the page, from top right to bottom left. A large intricate doodle of interweaving petals, teardrops and crested waves flow together. My pencil hovers mid pattern as a loud click cuts through the noise, and I quickly look up to see… Oh God, my stomach clenches, and I feel an instant heat between my legs, crap and crap again. Daniel Stone slowly walks from the now locked theatre door to take center stage. It's seven p.m. on the dot.

All right, that would explain the full house. God, that man is stunning, even from up here. His presence commands the silence of the room. Why didn't this information click with me earlier? I even saw his name on the screen. Nothing. Oh, I know why, because I have been on cloud nine since my windfall. I feel the plummet from said cloud as my mouth drops open, and I gasp. That's embarrassing, no wait, it's not. I'm up in the Gods, hidden in a crowd of eager faces, too high to be heard. Mike, on my left and Pete, in front, however, both turn with questioning looks. I quickly smile, shake my head, and tap my throat, frowning a little to indicate I am experiencing a tracheal problem. Sam, on my left, is unaffected by my dramatics, as he has yet to remove his earphones. I nod my head to indicate all eyes to the front and hope it will help the gentle rise of heat in my cheeks.

"Don't worry, I will unlock the door so you can leave, but I am just not going to pretend to tolerate lateness." His voice is quiet, but holds the room's attention. I give a light laugh and quickly slap my hand to my mouth. I thought it was a joke. I mean, why did I think it would be a joke? He's just locked the door, for Christ sake! He is obviously serious, and, yes, I was the only one to laugh. His fierce glare fixes on mine, and I shrink in my seat, which has certainly helped the blushing. My throat feels dry, and I swear the whole room can hear me struggle to swallow. I can't look away. His eyes look black from here, dark and deadly, but I know they are intense pools of crystal blue. A flush prickles my skin, and the heat building at my core is fighting to match that on my face. I try not to squirm in my seat, only giving the slightest unavoidable movement and curling my toes tightly.

I know he can't see those from there. His face certainly shows no signs of recognition from our previous awkward encounter, which is definitely a good thing.

The door rattles, and Mr. Stone breaks his gaze to turn toward the noise. The two small square windows in the double doors frame the faces of a couple of striking girls, their bright blonde hair pulled back to expose severe make-up and huge smiles.

Mr. Stone smiles, but even from here I can see it doesn't reach his eyes. He strides toward the door and reaches up to unlock it, pausing, he then pulls the blind down over the windows and returns to the stage. If he didn't have the complete attention of the room before, he does now. Beside me, Sam very carefully removes his earphones and glances at me with wide eyes. I am sure my eyes are just as wide, and I give him a very quick and nervous smile as a response.

The harsh lighting on the stage does nothing to diminish the impact of this man. He is tall, probably around six two, with broad shoulders and a trim waist. He is immaculately dressed in a fitted dark navy suit, pale blue shirt and no tie. His inky black, glossy hair is rough styled; it spikes and flops, slightly long, brushing the collar of his shirt. He rakes his hand through it and gathers his notes. His face is striking, but up close it's breath-stealing, sharp angles and shadows emanating intensity and power. I imagine fixing on his eyes as I explore the tight feel of his abdomen, flat and hard; the muscles on his back flexing as my hands crawl their way up his body to his thick shaggy hair, only to grip and pull. Christ, get a grip, Bets! I shift in my seat, the warmth in my face moving decidedly southwards. Thinking about my conversation with Mags, if I decide to do Late Night Calls, maybe I wouldn't need imagination if I had a muse. My lips curl at the thought as I ponder the prospect of Mr. Stone as my private muse; either way having a sneaky personal picture of the delicious Mr. Stone is a must. I just have to get close, again.

His introduction is pretty standard information that anyone could and probably did Google. Something, I am thinking, I should most definitely have done, but in my defense, I didn't expect to see him again. Daniel Edward Stone is the CEO of Stone, International; a group of companies, which started as an IT intranet software provider and expanded into other IT specialties, then rapidly into other areas: Telecommunication, Specialist Security Providers, Media, Entertainment, property, even a chain of hotels and nightclubs. In the past, he has provided funding for research and start-up companies identified through this University, and more specifically the Entrepreneurial program. The parent company is global, and he is the sole shareholder; his not so many fingers are in a lot of pies. I understand it's highly unusual for a company that size not to have shareholders or a board of directors. Maybe he just doesn't like sharing or is just a massive control freak, but, on second thought, there is no reason why he can't be both.

His 'brief' description does go into a bit more detail than a Wiki page, and he is not afraid to sing his own praises. It's lucky he did lock the door. I don't think there is any more room now that his ego has landed. I can't help but roll my eyes, which wouldn't have been so bad had I not made a kind of involuntary humph noise just to highlight my action. I close my eyes momentarily, only to open them to the seriously hot scowl of Mr. Stone. To my credit, I hold his gaze, careful not to give in to my increasing urge to squirm. I don't even acknowledge the subtle shifting of my neighbours as they try and distance themselves from the troublemaker. My cheeks do flame though, and just when I am about to cave and drop my gaze, he turns away, the corners of his mouth giving way to a wolfish grin.

He stands at the lectern and picks up a folder filled with lose leaf sheets of paper, his fingers numbly pick through to pluck one from the rest.

"Miss Thorne... What are you doing here?" His deep voice is barely raised, but he could be using a bull horn for the shock I feel at the unexpected question. His tone is clipped, cold, almost angry. I don't know how to answer, like I am suddenly mute. I simply shake my head embarrassed and mortified with the sudden shift of focus in the room.

"Would you like me to repeat the question?" He raises his brow and stares deeply into my eyes, which I manage to hold, but I can feel my face flame. Why is he picking on me? We've barely started, and he has singled me out with his accusatory tone. The tension is palpable as the whole room waits for my answer. Mr. Stone, however, merely taps his fingers lightly on the lectern and looks amused at my discomfort.

"No, I don't want you to repeat the question. I just didn't think stating the obvious was necessary, but I see that it is. I'll speak slowly… I am here for the Entrepreneur Lectures, Mr. Stone." I know my face is radiating enough to heat a small family home right now, but I am pleased I have progressed from mute to indignant.

"Hmm, thank you Miss Thorne but let me be more specific. Why are *you* here? I have your biography and I am asking why are you here…specifically?" He holds my biography in his hand like it's contagious, and the distain on his face has made my brief but righteous indignation vanish. I hate him so much right now, but I can't find any words to answer his question, let alone tell him he is currently starring in my recurring school days' nightmare. I might as well be naked, too, just to complete my torture. "Allow me… Does this look like a reality show? Are there hidden cameras? No? Do you think a background story will endear you to me? Do you think writing a wish list is appropriate? Do I look like Santa?" He steps down from the stage and has started to walk up the aisle toward me. I hold my knees to stop them trembling, and my knuckles are white from the effort.

"No," I manage to speak. It's not loud, but it is audible, because the room is silent.

"No?" He repeats, but doesn't stop his ascension.

"I didn't realize it was supposed to be a referenced journal. It's just a biography." I tip my chin and hold his gaze. He has reached the end of my row and my heart is thumping so hard, I'm sure the whole room can feel it.

"It wasn't, but I expected more…Where's your drive, Miss Thorne? Your fire? Your passion?" He thumps his fist on the flimsy bench and makes the whole row of students jump from their seats. "Success in business isn't about wishing and hoping, it's about *doing*… until your fingers bleed, living and breathing every minute of every day, because if you don't, someone else will. It's not enough, this"--he waves my solitary sheet high for emphasis-- "is not enough. To succeed, what you have here… is not enough. So don't waste my time, Miss Thorne, with prose that is better suited to a Liberal Arts degree." He holds my paper and tears the sheet in two, then four, and continues until the sheet falls to the floor in a sprinkle of tiny white flakes. His dark eyes seem to hold for endless seconds, waiting for my response. Fine, I can respond.

"It's not fiction. It's not a wish list. It's just a list. It's fact, not a sob story; just the truth and the fact that you would showcase it, and in front of everyone as a flaw, well, Mr. Stone… no offense, but that kind of makes you an arsehole, and if being successful means I have to be more like you, I'm happy to remain flawed, and I am happy to fail." I swear the entire student population took a sharp intake of breath, but Mr. Stone simply holds my gaze as if we are the only two people in the room. His jaw is tight, but he doesn't look angry, more like he is trying to suppress his amusement. There is something else in his eyes, an intensity I can't fathom, but it's only a flash, and it's gone, and briefly replaced with the most breath-taking smile I have ever seen. I think my heart stopped.

"Interesting you would choose to caveat your insult." He places both his palms flat on the bench and leans a little closer. Not that he is anywhere near me, but the boy at the end of my row must be feeling his presence like a thundercloud in the room. "How very polite of you, Miss Thorne, but I couldn't possibly take offense when you have revealed that you do have passion after all--tempered as it is." The way he says the word passion, feels weighted and indulgent, and it makes the hairs on my neck tingle. I hope I won't have to speak again, because I am struggling to swallow the lump in my throat. He pushes back and stands to his full height. He breaks his gaze with an abrupt turn and begins to walk back to the stage. "Besides, I've been called worse." His smile is gone, but the whole exchange leaves me stunned and speechless. I let out a deep breath and glancing around, I wasn't the only one. He returns to the stage and picks up his notes continuing with his presentation as if he hadn't just bulldozed through my quiet little world. Mike leans in and whispers something about not envying me and wondering what his problem is. I give a tight smile, because I think that would be me. I appear to be his problem.

Thankfully, the remainder of the presentation proceeds without my unwelcome input, but equally there is no other interaction from Mr. Stone with any other student. I find myself filling my notebook with some very useful information. I have some business ideas of my own, safety products for 'off the beaten path' cyclists and runners, which could have multiple uses in healthcare, too, but have no idea what to do with them. So information on seed funding, grant applications, patents, access to research, access to markets, even exit strategy preparation are hugely helpful. I hardly have time for a single doodle in the entire hour. Despite this encouraging recovery from a disastrous start to the lecture, I don't think it's enough, especially if I have a target stamped to my forehead like I obviously have today. I'm starting to think that I won't bother coming to the other lectures. I can always pick up the handouts later, and there is no sign-in sheet as such, so no one will know.

Mr. Stone addresses the room once more. "I feel it is important to remind you that for some of you these lectures are not optional. I *never* miss a lecture and I demand the same courtesy. I very much look forward to the next time." At this closing statement, there is an enthusiastic round of applause as he turns his winning smile to the appreciative audience. It is my turn to scowl.

"Great, freaking great, he's a mind reader too!" I am grumbling to myself. There is a general scramble to leave en masse. I am trapped high in a row of students, who are moving at a glacial pace. Below me there is a huge rush of people trying to vie for the attention of the "wonderful" Mr. Stone, and the gathering of bodies is large enough to block the exit. The crowd around Mr. Stone is easily ten people deep, and as I try to push my way past, I can hear the sycophantic adoration. The saccharin praises alone, I swear, cause a little bit of vomit to make a surprise appearance in my mouth. However sore I am from his attention earlier, I can't deny he is still the hottest man I have ever seen up close, and now is the perfect opportunity to get my sneaky picture. I reach into my bag, grab my phones, and quickly determine which one I need. Not a difficult task, as my one is ancient, barely has the ability to make calls and is the size of a brick, and the one Mags gave me, which is sexy, sleek, and can do everything but make a cup of tea.

I select the camera bit and press myself into the crowd. I manage to slink my arm into a gap and fire off a few rapid snaps, hoping that I have captured something which does the subject justice. Dropping the phone into my bag, I turn after just hearing a particularly vomit-inducing summation of why Mr. Stone is the most amazing person ever to grace this theatre. The level of brown nosing is quite exceptional. "Urggg." I grunt as I continue to shoulder my way to the exit. Mission accomplished, as I reach for the door.

"Miss Thorne." The voice is familiar, but the volume of the boom is not, and I freeze, as do the remainder of the occupants in the room. I slowly turn with a slight smile and fake confidence.

"Mr. Stone." To my surprise, I manage to sound normal, because in my head I am definitely screaming, 'What the Fuck?'

"Any other issues or questions I will address next time…that will be all." He informs those waiting in a tone that brooks no discussion. The room quickly empties, and I'm left standing by the door like a naughty schoolgirl. As the last person is about to leave, Mr. Wilson enters, almost flattening me to the wall, and hurries over to Mr. Stone.

"Mr. Stone, thank you so much. As always, a great inspiration and treat for the students." Not sure I'm feeling the treat bit at the moment. I sigh, but really quietly, still Mr. Wilson turns to me, smiles, and lifts his chin in a fashion to encourage my dismissal. This is tricky, he doesn't know I have been, well, I'm not sure what I've been …yet, but my hesitation results in a click from his tongue and a deep frown. I start to step back, slowly, toe to heel, my heart is racing, and I'm holding my breath.

"I have asked Miss Thorne to remain. Is there something you need, Jack?" His tone is rude and dismissive.

"Um, well, no. But I thought you would need to get away. I mean, if there is a problem, do you need me to-" Mr. Wilson stutters and looks with confusion between Mr. Stone and me. I share his confusion.

"No," interrupts Mr. Stone, and I look over to see his heated eyes on me. "I need just a moment of Miss Thorne's time. I am quite capable of securing the room before I leave, so if you wouldn't mind?" As far as Daniel Stone is concerned, this conversation is finished. He certainly hasn't taken his eyes from mine, not even for a moment to acknowledge my poor department head.

"Yes, of course. I'm in a hurry myself." The room falls silent with the soft suction of the fire door closing at his departure.

"Your bag, Miss Thorne?" He strides toward me until I have to look up to maintain eye contact. I can feel a heat and energy that scares the shit out of me when he is this close, his strong frame, his deep voice, and, oh, God, his smell. I try unsuccessfully to step back. My feet won't move, and I definitely need a bit of distance. I try to clear my throat.

"Excuse me?" My confusion is evident in my croaky tone.

"Unlikely." He replies, then a little slower repeats himself. "I said, your bag, Miss Thorne." Although I don't feel like I understand what is happening, like on autopilot, my body responds to his command. My hand slips my bag from my shoulder and places it in his outstretched hand.

"Good girl." My core clenches at the softness of his voice. I'm thinking how I would like to hear that tone, those words, and feel that power over me. I shiver. He is a full on attack to my senses, blocking my field of vision with his firm, fit body. Rich exotic aromas of citrus and spice invade my nose, and he is so close, my fingers ache to touch him. I am losing all my good sense. This just doesn't happen to me; this can't happen. I shift and squeeze my thighs together to try and gain some relief from the distracting pressure and heat that's building. A small smile creases his lips as he notices this movement. He is doing this to me, and he knows it. I can't think straight. He's too damn close.

"Well, Miss Thorne, what have we here?" He sounds smug as he reaches into my bag.

"To be honest, you take your life in your own hands delving in there. You've been warned." I am trying to make light of this, no need to antagonize him further.

"Warning noted, your life is in my hands." His voice is hypnotic, but that wasn't what I had said. He starts to pull out my phones and I feel the blood drain from my face. He holds *my* phone and raises a brow.

"That's my brick." I smile. Silence ensues, so I add, "It's my phone, you know, in case of emergency I can call someone, or in case I'm attacked, I can throw it at them. Its heavy. Heavy is good, right?" Trying for light humour I get nothing, maybe a little tumbleweed rolling down the aisles, but not a peep from Mr. Stone. In fact his jaw clenched momentarily at the mention of being attacked, but just as quickly released.

"So then, this one," he says holding my sleek new phone. "Is the one you chose to steal my soul?" Is he serious? I made that mistake once already, so I'm going to assume yes. He begins to flick at the screen.

"What luck, Miss Thorne, no security, but then, how hard would it be to guess your PIN?" He muses but he is smiling now, and he quickly accesses the camera function and gallery. He casually holds up my phone to show me the perfect close-up of the quite stunning Mr. Stone. However I explain this, it is going to look bad. Two scenarios come to mind: I am a pathetic groupie, or worse, I'm a crazy stalker. Surprisingly, that is not the question he asks. "Why do you have two phones, Miss Thorne?"

"Well," I smile too sweetly. "I am pretty sure that is none of your business." So much for contrite. It appears I still have some residual anger, and it looks like I'm going for full on confrontation after all. I hold his gaze, willing my body not to tremble. His eyes narrow, and they definitely look more black than blue now.

"All right, why have you taken my picture?" My face flushes seven kinds of red, and I can see him holding back a smile. I am so glad my mortification is amusing him. He is having an unwelcome and uncontrollable effect on my body, and now he is playing games with me. I no longer care if I was rude. I am angry and need to get out of there. I return his narrow gaze. The door opens, and Mr. Stone scowls at Mr. Wilson. I really feel for the poor man. "Jack, I thought I made myself clear?" His voice is cold and stern.

"Quite, you did, Daniel, but I really need to speak to Miss Thorne, urgently." He looks really embarrassed, and I am confused why I'm causing such a problem. I would settle for the ground swallowing me in favour of my earlier under the radar request. I look toward Mr. Stone and smile tightly as I back away, but I stop and hold out my hand out for my phones and bag.

"You won't be a moment I'm sure, I'll just hold these until you return." I hesitate and he grins. "What do you think I'm going to do, Miss Thorne?" His grin transforms into a wide stunning smile, which I find myself returning.

"Nothing, I'm sorry." I don't know how I have gone from anger to contrition so quickly, but I continue to smile as I leave Mr. Stone with my worldly possessions and meet Mr. Wilson in the corridor.

"Mr. Wilson, have I done something wrong?" I ask tentatively.

"Not at all, Bethany. I just wanted to make sure you were okay. Daniel can be a bit overwhelming, and I wanted to make sure you were all right?" His smile is comforting.

"Oh, wow. That is so kind, and, yes, he can be a bit intense, but I think we just got off on the wrong foot. Maybe a little misunderstanding we are just sorting out. Nothing to worry about. It's not like he is my actual tutor or anything." I laugh lightly.

"No, I know, my dear, but he is heavily involved with this program, so you will probably come across him again outside of this lecture series. So it is best if you can iron out any crinkles now." He laughs this time and I smile kindly in return, but it feels strange on my face as I begin to process what he has just told me.

"Yes, of course. I don't want to cause any trouble. Speaking of which, I probably shouldn't keep him waiting." I nod toward the theatre door.

"No absolutely, in you go, I will see you around, Bethany." He cheerfully remarks as he heads up the stairs.

I walk back into the room, but my attempt to keep some personal distance either goes unnoticed, or is more likely just ignored, as Mr. Stone strides toward me again, closing the gap to a *very* personal distance.

His lips curl in a knowing smile. "Now where were we? Ah, yes, why have you taken my picture?"

I pause a moment as my mind races, but I decide on a mix of honesty and mind your own business. "Well, now, that may in fact be your business, but since I am not going to tell you, and I have no intention of attending the other lectures, we will just have to add this to the list of life's little mysteries." I go to retrieve my phone, and I think my answer has taken him by surprise as he lets me take them from his hand. Our hands touch briefly, and I actually make a physical jump at the intensity of feeling from this simple contact. Sudden. Shocking. I hesitate, then quickly turn and go to pull the door handle. In an instant the door is slammed shut with the weight of two large palms on either side of my head. His hard body presses into my back, holding me in place. He slowly sweeps his knuckles down the side of my cheek and slides his hand under my hair, taking it away from my neck. The cool air created only intensifies the heat that is raging through my body. My breath is rapid shallow gasps, and I drop my head to the side to give him better access. I feel wanton. His fingers gently trace the curve of my neck around to my collarbone. I bite my dry lips to suppress a moan that's desperate to escape. He pushes against me, his lips lightly brush just below my ear, and I think I can feel his erection brush against my arse through the thin material of his suit. I have never had such a blatant sexual encounter, and I guess I should feel shocked, but I'm trembling. My head is swimming and thick with too much rushing blood; it could be fear, but it feels a lot like white hot desire. I barely hear him whisper.

"You are right. It is my business, and unless I'm very much mistaken, your attendance is mandatory, and *that*, Miss Thorne, makes *you* my business. " He grips my hips as I make to move out of his hold, grinding gently. I find myself inexplicably pushing back against him, welcoming this slow erotic dance. I'm lost, my head drops to the door with a crack, and the shock of pain breaks through this thick fuzz.

"May I go now?" I can barely breathe.

"May I go what?" He still has his lips pressed to my ear, his breath is warm and my body responds with an involuntary wave of prickles to my skin.

"May I go… Sir?" I release the breath I hadn't realized I was holding. He stands to move away, and I sag slightly at this loss of connection.

"Good girl..... Yes, you may leave." His voice is low and commanding. "Oh, and Miss Thorne"--I turn to see the heat and desire in his eyes--"I take *my* business very seriously. Until next time." It wasn't a question. It was a statement.

"Yes, Sir." I pull on the door so hard, I nearly knock myself out in my rush to leave the room, the space, that man. The stale air in the corridor is stifling, and I run to the main doors and burst out into the Quad, gulping for fresh air before I faint. I have no idea what just happened in there, but I do know I can't let it happen again, and next time I'll tell him as much. I'll just keep my distance when I do.

Chapter Four

I HAVE HAD A number of lectures this week and none of them played out like the one with Mr. Stone. The Lecturers have been enthusiastic and insightful, at worst some may have been a little dull, but none had behaved like Mr. Stone. I become more and more irritated after each lesson, because I am unable to bring myself to participate. Even in Mr. Wilson's seminar, where he positively encouraged me to engage. I really wanted to. I had something to say, but every time I tried, I had this hideous flashback of hundreds of eyes silently staring at me, with pale faces of sympathy and relief. Relief it wasn't them under the spotlight. My mouth dried, and my throat felt like sandpaper. Mr. Wilson looked with kind eyes and patted my hand at my failed attempt and deftly moved to someone else.

By Thursday evening, I was ready to put an end to my misery. I was ready to fight. Mr. Stones' second lecture would be very different, for me at least. I had my speech prepared, something along the lines of, 'How dare he…Did he have any idea how insensitive…' and something about being a coward and a bully, but I would wait and see how the first part of my tirade played out before I resorted to more insults. It didn't go unnoticed that, although the theatre was full, I had empty spaces on either side of me this week. My leg bounced nervously as the clock on the wall blinked closer to seven o'clock, my stomach knotted uncomfortably, and my palms were clammy. It felt more like a high noon showdown. The door opened, and I held my breath, only to let it out instantly in disappointment as Mr. Wilson stepped through.

"Mr. Stone is unable to present this evenings' class, but I do have his notes, so I will take the lecture. I will do my best and hope you are not too disappointed." He grinned at the room, and there was a little ripple of laughter. I did feel disappointed. Strange that I didn't feel relief. After all, I don't do confrontation as a rule, so I should feel relieved, but no, I definitely feel disappointed. There wasn't going to be a confrontation. No fiery exchange, no burning tension, no heat at all. The next week was worse.

"So spill... you are so out of sorts, Bets, I'm ready to send out a search party for my missing best friend." Sofia climbs under the covers, wriggling to get comfortable next to me, whilst precariously balancing a steaming mug of hot chocolate in one hand.

"I think I should stop calling her...She just get so upset, and it breaks my heart that I can't comfort her, you know." Sofia had caught the tail end of my telephone call with my mum. I had such a terrible day, I just wanted to hear her voice. It was a long shot she'd know who she was speaking to, but sometimes I just need to hear her softly spoken words of nonsense. But it's selfish of me, and I always feel much worse after.

"I'm sure she appreciates your call. Even if she doesn't know who you are, it's still nice talking to someone different for a change, and it's not like you're trying to sell her a change of mobile provider." Sofia slips her arm around my shoulder and pulls me against her in a protective hug.

"I might as well be." I let out a deep heartfelt sigh. "It's actually better when she doesn't know who I am, and we can talk about nothing and everything. It's when she remembers bits or suddenly recognizes my voice, and I can almost hear her struggle to recall more. That's when she breaks, and I'm too far away to do anything about it. I know I'd make it better if I could cuddle her. We'd make us both better with a cuddle." I sniff back the building sadness and allow the comfort of Sofia's hug to work its own magic. It's a constant sadness and it's just bearable most of the time, but today it just got the better of me.

"But that was just one call, and it's not like you haven't had many just the same. So, what's new, and if you tell me you're just tired, I will just repeat, you've been tired before." She pulls back, and I catch her narrowed, but kind, scowl.

"I don't exist." I slowly breathe out my poor explanation.

"Is this a 'if a tree falls in the woods' existentialist thing that we mere catering students won't understand?"

I chuckle. "Not exactly. Today during the Lecture, Mr. Stone…it was like I didn't exist. No eye contact, no humiliating exchanges, no heated glares, and definitely no erotic embraces." I'd told Sofia the next day what had happened in my first lecture, and each day she called for an update. I knew he was around, because I had heard other students talk about him, spotting him with Mr. Wilson or just walking across the Quad, but I never saw him.

"You're upset because he didn't humiliate you this week? You are so strange." She barks out a short laugh. " Tell me…are you more upset that you didn't get to vent all your pent up irritation, or that you didn't get to release more of that pent up heat?"

"I'm not upset he didn't humiliate me, but I am more upset he didn't acknowledge me at all. Did I imagine it?"

"Did you imagine the hot male grinding against you? Hmm…I doubt it. It's his loss, honey, but I am happy he's at least sparked an interest, because, frankly, that's a first. We just have to tend to that little flame and make sure you don't stamp it back out." She plants an aggressive kiss on my head.

"Trust me, I'm happy to stamp it out," I snort.

"So you wouldn't want a repeat? You'd be happy if he just acknowledged you with a nod or a handshake?" Her tone is mocking, but I think seriously about her question. My body is too quick to respond to the idea of a repeat, but I shake my head and the accompanying visual away.

"It's for the best."

The next evening after Uni, I change into my work uniform, which is a simple black skirt, matching tight-fitted blouse, which I pair with my sneaky black timberland boots for comfort. Anthony, Jr. is a little more forgiving than his father, who insists his waitresses wear proper shoes with at least a small heel. I can barely walk after a night out in heels, let alone shift after shift. I skip downstairs and enter the kitchen, the rich aromas of tonight's specials hit me with the same intensity as the heat from the cookers. It smells wonderful, I think I've had a smoothie since breakfast, but that could easily have been yesterday. My tummy rumbles, and I realize I'm starving. Still my shift officially started ten minutes ago, and we will be fully booked tonight. Fridays are always hectic, so I doubt I will have the chance to grab anything to eat until we close.

"Mmmm… that smells so good, Joe." I grab my pad and tie my apron twice round my waist. "What's the special?"

Joe is Sofia's uncle and the head chef. He sets the menus for the restaurants and is the most amazing talent in the kitchen.

"Take a seat, Bets, and I'll set you up a plate." He winks at me and points to the stool at the end of the workstation.

"You trying to get me fired?" I turn to make my way into the restaurant and squeal as I am lifted clear of the door and plopped roughly on the stool.

"You will eat! Don't want you losing any of those curves, and I'll have Anthony's bollocks if he says a word." He grins and casually waves a very large shiny knife.

I laugh but try to get up again. "They're probably swamped already, save me some for later."

"It's no use," he growls angrily. "I'll force feed you if I have to, girl, and that'll hurt you more than it will me." He tilts his head and, with a pleading tone to his voice, he says. "Come on, Bets, you're hurting my feelings, I've never had to force anyone to eat my food. Don't make me start now!" He places a large warm bowl of fresh ravioli stuffed with ricotta and spinach in a simple sage butter in front of me. It's not the special, but it is my favourite and judging by the smug grin fixed to Joes' face, he knows he's got me. I cut the first piece and can't help an exaggerated moan escaping my lips.

"Heaven on a plate, Joe, as always." There is no way I can manage to finish this huge portion, but I tuck in as he explains the specials. There is a seafood: Frutti Di Mare Gratinati, which is baked shellfish, topped with seasoned breadcrumbs and baked until golden, served with fresh bread and lemon wedges. A Costoline Di Agnello Ripiene, which is lamb cutlets stuffed with Gruyere cheese, Parma ham, and sage, which are breaded, then fried, and served with a green bean salad. "Yum." I smile. "Not going to having any trouble selling those tonight." I push my plate away as Joe raises a brow.

"I'm not going to fight you on this, Joe. That was delicious, but I can't eat another bite." I blow him a kiss and dash for the safety of the restaurant. I was right, it's heaving, all the tables are full, and the bar is starting to fill with people waiting to be seated.

The main rush of the evening has ebbed and I am starting to do a final clear of the tables. My section has a few tables left to clear, and Lilly is the only other waitress who has a few tables tucked away in the booths, which edge the back and side wall. Customers linger, enjoying their after dinner drinks and who seem a little reluctant to leave. The front door opens, and I inwardly groan. It's late, but it's not unheard of that customers might still want to take a table at this time. I sag in relief when I see Sofia's face. She goes to grab my arm and lead me away.

"Hey, you might not be working but I have to finish here!" I reprimand her lightly.

"No, no, no, I got your message, but I want more than a text with a winky face. You must tell me *all* about Mr. Demanding; sorry Mr. Hot, Sexy and Demanding. I want more," she giggles.

"Oh, My God, Sofs, volume! I sent that text yesterday. We've already discussed Mr. Stone. I've got to finish, and I promised Lilly I'd finish her section, so she could shoot off for the babysitter." I continue to gather the salt and pepper mills to refill in the morning.

"Now, why would you do that, you don't have enough on? Oh while I think if it, you free next Friday? There's a private do the club is catering for and needs bodies, so I put you down." She helps clear the tables with me.

I'm grinning. "What was that about me not having enough on?"

"This is different, and you know it. It's way better pay, and Anthony doesn't mind, as long as he has notice. Besides, you'll be working with me!" She gives me a hug because she knows I won't refuse, can't refuse, and she's is not wrong about the money.

"Look I'm helping you finish, now spill, we talked …but nowhere near enough." She grabs a cloth, and I fill her in again, as we work together to clean my section before we move over to Lily's.

"So, I'm still not sure I see what the big deal is?" She has slowed considerably as she ponders my predicament.

"Really?" I shake my head. "I guess it isn't a big deal, it's just that I felt"--I shake my head because it feels muddled--"I don't know. He just seems to see right through me. He's intense, and he affects me." My words are more reflective, as my body appears to all too easily recall its response.

"Go on?" She steps closer.

"Look, I can't think straight when he is there, I mean, when he is *right* there, Sofs!" I place hand right to my nose to emphasize the lack of personal space. "He had his huge cock rammed tight against my arse, right in the lecture theatre! I've just never, you know, never…felt so hot. And then nothing, the next week a no show, which he never does, apparently, and then when he does turn up this week, nothing. Absolutely nothing, like it was all in my head." My face is heating, and Sofs takes pity on me and swallows me in her arms.

She laughs and presses a kind kiss into my hair. "Huge, eh?" She laughs again as I pull back. "Bets, you're just feeling horny, that's all. Get some perspective. Some rich, good looking guy – How old?" She cuts herself off with her own question.

"Late twenties, I think?"

"Ok, this sexy, young, successful business man wants to fuck you. I'm struggling to see the downside here, Bets." Her eyes crease with amusement and shamelessness.

"Christ, Sofs! I didn't say he wants to fuck me. He doesn't. Whatever, look it's not that, I have never had this reaction to a man, ever. I was worried he knew about the age thing, you know after that first meeting. So I guess it's good he's ignoring me now. I can't risk losing everything, no matter how hot he made me feel--" There is a loud crash from one of the booths, and I look to the floor and notice a vase with dried chillies has smashed, which have exploded onto the floor. Lily had balanced several vases on a ledge above the booths that was clearly too near the coats. I rush over onto my knees and start to gather the mess into my scooped up apron.

"I'm sorry, Sir, I'll clean this up. Did any of the glass catch you at all?" I look up into the dark blue intensity of Daniel Stones eyes.

"Sir?" I mouth, but with no volume.

"You know, Miss Thorne, I will never get tired of you calling me that." His rich voice is smooth and tempting. I feel a flash of prickles cover my skin and despite the instant heat in my core, my nipples peak hard and tight, and my breasts ache. Fuck! What is wrong with me? My heartbeat is hammering, not just the raw reaction he induces in me, but also the panic at realizing he has been here the whole time.

"Sir, Mr. Stone, what are you doing here?" I was trying for a calm tone, but manage to sound angry.

"Not sure that's very polite, Miss Thorne." His eyes are piercing me, and I'm thankful the ambient lighting is helping to hide the deep colour of my cheeks.

"Sorry, Sir, you're right, it's just creepy." Shit, I can't believe I said that out loud; now that *was* impolite. He grins and raises a brow. "Sorry, Sir, it is a surprise to see you here."

"Not really, I live close by, and I have been here from time to time." He maintains this intense stare and not knowing what to say and feeling an increasing awkwardness, I revert to default waitress mode.

"Of course, Sir, if you would excuse me, I'll just get this cleared away. Is there anything I can do for you--get you--is there anything else I can get you, or would you like the bill?" I know I'm flustered, because I sound like I'm rambling.

"You know there is." His lips quirk. "But the bill will work, for now." His deep tone resonates with smooth sensuality.

I flash a quick tight smile and rush to sweep the remainder of the debris on the floor into my apron. I manage to slice my thumb on a small shard of glass.

"Fuck!" I curse in a whisper and quickly stick my thumb in my mouth to stop the blood flow. I glance back up to Daniel when I hear him take a sharp breath, or it might have been a moan. I scrabble to my feet and practically sprint for the kitchen. I stick my hand under the cold running tap and wince at the delayed sting, which makes my thumb throb.

"I can seal that cut for you, Bets." Joe flashes the flame on the cooker.

"No, I'm good, Joe." Burning cuts sealed is not my idea of good first aid, even if it does work. Sofia is right beside me.

"You okay?" Her nose is wrinkled as she watches the water change from clear to dark red.

"You can add 'eavesdropper' to that description you've got for Daniel Stone. He's sitting in the booth at the end!" I nod toward the restaurant.

"No way!" She gasps, but also can't hold back a face-splitting grin.

"Yes, way! I can't go back out there. You're going to have to take his bill over." I plead.

"Not a problem. Can't wait to see who's got you so distracted, you're slicing body parts." She is practically hopping on the spot with excitement.

I'm about to head upstairs as my thumb won't stop bleeding. It's throbbing like it's been hit with a cartoon anvil, and I know I won't be much of a help finishing up, when Sofia returns.

"He wants to take you home. I said I was taking you, but he was *really* insistent." She has the grace to look uncomfortable.

"Oh absolutely." I bark out an incredulous laugh. "I am going to get into his car. I don't know anything about him, Sofs – What did you say?"

"I said I'd get you?" She mumbles and won't raise her eyes to meet my scowl.

"Where would I get him to take me, Sofs? I live here. I can't believe this!" Joe stands beside me as I peek a look through the kitchen door into the restaurant and see Daniel leaning at the bar. He is wearing low slung jeans, a fitted black shirt, which skims the defined muscles on his arms and sculpts his abdomen. He is carrying his black leather jacket in the crook of his arm. His hair flops over his eyes, hiding his intense brow, and he sips his drink as he carefully takes in the quiet of the restaurant. In a suit he is stunning, but dressed as casual bad boy he is lethal, and he looks like he has no intention of moving any time soon.

"That's Danny. You'll be all right with him, Bets." Joe smiles at me, and then he shrugs like I'm making a big old fuss over nothing.

"Well, I don't really have a choice now, do I?" I'm exasperated. "He seems to know enough about me already. He doesn't need to know where I actually live as well." I am not sure what he does know, exactly, but I need to find out, so a lift home might be an opportunity to get some information and do some damage control.

"Right. Is Marco at his place tonight?" I ask Sofia

"Yes, why?" She frowns at my change of topic, clearly not following this simple situation she has just made complex.

"Because I do actually have to go somewhere, and his place isn't far, so it won't take me too long to get back here." Sofia looks disappointed. "I would go to yours, Sofs, but I still have stuff to do tonight." I feel exhausted, my defenses are low, and it's not an ideal time to be putting myself in close confines with Daniel Stone.

"Mr. Stone." I'm going to try and steer clear of the 'Sir' thing that seems way too natural for me when talking with Mr. Stone and only contributes to this strange need I feel to comply with his demands, which for the life of me I can't understand. He raises a brow.

"Miss Thorne." He steps closer and smiles. His lips look soft, and I feel mine part with a small intake of breath. My throat is dry, and there is no way I'm going to survive a car ride feeling like this. "Shall we?" He places his hand in the small of my back; my body jolts and tingles. He gently drapes his jacket over my shoulders against the chill outside. His fingers lightly hold my shoulders, and I'm trembling once more at the slightest contact. We walk in silence, and as we reach his car, I stop as he opens the door.

"Why are you doing this?" My question surprises him, though it shouldn't. His smile borders on wicked, and I shiver, but not from the chill in the air.

"Well, Miss Thorne, I think you have some concerns I'd like to address. You have secrets I'd like to know, and you have drawn some incorrect conclusions about my intentions." The calm recitation of his list doesn't help to enlighten me one bit.

I slide into the car; it's an F-type Jaguar Coupe. I know this because Marco loves cars, I know nothing else other than it's pretty, dark green, sleek and shiny, with a pristine, soft cream leather interior. I look at my poorly bandaged thumb and see it's started to seep already. I wince as I grip it tightly to try and stop the flow. The pain will help me focus on the burn of the cut rather than the liquid pool of heat building between my legs.

"What's wrong?" His voice is filled with genuine concern.

"Nothing, just trying not to bleed all over your very clean and very *cream* interior." I smile waving my injured hand. "Number twelve Guard Gardens, it's about two miles from here and won't take five minutes in this thing."

"Thing? Thing," he repeats, clearly affronted. "This is an F-type R, five liter V8, 550 PS super charged engine with 680Nm of torque, nought to sixty in four seconds with a top speed of over one eighty."

"Very useful in a city with a top speed of thirty miles per hour." I snort. It's not very ladylike, but it can't be helped. "Sorry, it's a car, you know A to B."

"You don't drive?" He faces me for a moment, but even that short moment has my senses on high alert.

"I know how to, but I don't. I love to walk." The remaining journey is in silence. The tension is palpable. He pulls up outside Marco's flat.

"You didn't address any concerns?" I question the silence now that I start to undo my seatbelt.

"Your home?" He asks ignoring my question.

"Yep, that's right! Thank you, Mr. Stone." I go to open the door. He reaches across and holds my hand against the handle. My breath hitches.

"More lies, Miss Thorne?" He is leaning into the small space between us and his rich aroma is intoxicating. My fingers twitch to run through his hair, maybe touch his face. Unfortunately, his question is more like a statement and diminishes any rising temptation as I tense with renewed panic.

"I live here." I try to sound convincing.

"Mmmm, perhaps this will help." He is still leaning into me, still holding my hand on top of the handle of the car door, and, God, he still smells so fucking good. "Firstly, your concerns: I have no interest in your degree, I know who you are because I was introduced to you, and I am thorough in gathering information about people in my life, but you have secrets and as thorough as I am, I would like you to tell me yourself."

"You questioned my commitment to my course. No. You didn't question it, you attacked it, and picked on me in the process… but regardless, I would still attend your lecture program, I'd be an idiot not to." I drop my head and sigh. "Forgive me if I assumed you had an interest in my degree. I was clearly wrong." I mutter and added even more quietly "On every count." I push against the handle and he releases his hold. The door opens, and I get out.

"Yes, Miss Thorne, you were wrong. Your friend however, was spot on. I do want to fuck you." His voice is like silk, sensual, sinful silk. "To clarify, the comments I made, however forcefully, were said to make a point. You have a sound business proposition, but you won't secure the necessary investment to develop your idea further with your current 'hope to' attitude… and Miss Thorne…I didn't pick *on* you. I *picked* you." I can't bring myself to look into his eyes. A tiny moan escapes the back of my throat and is captured, silenced in my mouth. I open the door and walk away visibly shaking, then ring the bell on Marco's door and wait. I'm in shock.

A sleepy Marco comes to the door. and I push past his confused state.

"Sorry to wake you, Marco, but don't ask." I peek through the glass in the door frame. "I'll be five minutes, then I'm gone." Marco presses his nose against the glass beside me.

"What are we looking for, Bets?" His eyes are squinting, and his yawn is exaggerated.

"That." I point to Daniel's car as it pulls from the curb, and the red lights disappear down the road. I turn to give Marco a quick kiss on the cheek and leave him a little stunned as I close the door behind me and begin my walk home, to my real home. I set a brisk pace along the main road. It's not ideal walking late at night, but it's a pretty safe area. I'll grab a cab if I see one, but it won't take me long if I don't. I would normally be nervous at the speed the car was approaching, but my heart is racing for an entirely different reason as I recognize the growl of the heavy engine of a super-fast sports car. It stops abruptly just in front of me, and a very stern Daniel Stone exits, slams his door and storms up to me. His face is dark, scowling and fiercely handsome.

"Get in the car!" His voice is deadly quiet and I take a step back. He moves to match my retreat.

"I don't give a fuck about your secrets, Bethany, but you are not walking in the dark alone!" He tries for a more gentle tone. His face softens, and his anger is replaced with obvious concern. "Now, please get in the car." I pause, but only for a moment before I do as he says. I remain quiet as he starts the car and pulls away.

"Shall we try this again? Where to, Miss Thorne?" His tone is calm and commanding.

"The restaurant, I live above the restaurant." I reply quietly.

"There. That wasn't so hard,, was it?" I know he must feel it, but he doesn't have to sound so fucking smug.

"No." I mumble my reply with irritation and petulance.

"No?" His voice is deep, coaxing, and laden with promise, and I shiver when I suddenly understand his intent.

"No, Sir." He smiles.

Less than five minutes later, he is pulling up outside the rear of the restaurant. "I don't think it is very polite to lie. We are going to need to work on those secrets, aren't we, Miss Thorne?" He is tapping his steering wheel, I'm still in shock from his earlier declaration and he thinks I'm being rude.

"I didn't ask for a lift home. If I'm being rude, it's a result of your behaviour and not a reflection of mine."

"Well, my behaviour just saved you a three mile walk in the dark, and I don't think it would be too much to ask for some gratitude." He leans closer, and my senses are filled with his rich exotic smell.

"What?" I'm almost speechless. "I wouldn't, I didn't even need... you... you..." I can't construct a full sentence, because I am utterly astonished at his arrogance.

"Me? Yes, what about me?" He is holding my gaze with searing intensity, and his mouth curls in a deeply sensual smile. So despite his arrogance, I need to get out before I grab his face, claw my fingers tight into his hair, and consume those soft, full lips. I lick my lips at the very thought of their taste. The small movement is enough to draw his eyes to my mouth. His jaw twitches.

"Thank you for the lift... Sir!" I slam the car door and without looking back, make my way into the darkened restaurant, locking the bolts behind me. If I wasn't so exhausted, I think I would be taking one of those cold showers right about now.

Chapter Five

I HAVE DECIDED TO give Late Night Calls a go, and I informed a delighted Mags that I would take my first call on Monday. Although I am apprehensive, I like the flexibility, and the money is really good. You would have to be an alien to not be aware of the recent interest in erotic literature, but I was a little vague on the specific nature of submission and, given my chosen medium, I felt I was going to need specifics. So I spent a flushed and fevered Sunday researching all things D/s. My misunderstanding and subsequent offense at Mags' assessment of me was a result of my perception of weakness in relation to submission. As with many things, there's a spectrum, and although I'm not sure how I would handle a call with a guy set on demeaning, humiliating, or ordering me around like a pet, the notion of consensual 'total power exchange' I found, frankly, hot.

I had been offended when Mags first declared that I was a 'natural submissive', but it did go a long way in explaining my reaction to Daniel. He is definitely a Dominant, and I react strongly to him. On paper, it's simple; in real life, it's a different story. It's not that I am not surrounded by strong male characters all day, every day, but he just presses some seriously erotic buttons that have me trembling with pent-up desire.

So with a play on my name 'Bets' and gambling, all things Vegas and showgirls, I decide that, for one hour each night, I will become Lola; not hugely original, but it works. Mags is thrilled and extremely enthusiastic. I don't share her optimism. We discuss the obvious limitations and safety awareness, like I'd be giving anyone my personal details. But Mags was very clear that my identity would be entirely safe. Monday night I was set to take my first call. I found myself closing my eyes, and, all too quickly, Daniel's face fills my imagination. It is his face I see, his eyes on me as I mentally step into Lola's world.

"My hands are tied together, the thin soft black leather strip is bound and wound in an intricate bond. Looped between the silky soft skin of my wrists. You can see the blood pumping through the veins in my wrists, and the straps tighten as you pull my arms above my head and secure them high on a hook. My smooth skin is flushing." Everything I describe is slow and breathy, and I pause to moan. I take some encouragement from the caller's mirrored moan. "You are holding a black riding crop, which has a hard chrome handle and is woven with fibers in a crisscross pattern down its length to the end where there is an elongated loop of soft black leather. You hold the loop up to my cheek and gently trace a pattern along my jaw and over the swell of my bottom lip. My tongue reaches for a taste…Mmmm." I sigh and pause. "You are going to take the tip of that crop and trace it down the curve of my breast and pull back slightly to catch the tip against my tight peaked nipple, Arhh… I ache for some release, Sir." I draw in a deep, satisfying breath. "Taking the crop loop down, down, with long leisurely strokes across my stomach, catching the top of my panties." I'm in no hurry, the threat of punishment implicit. "You push the tip further into my panties and you can feel the rush of heat flash across my body and see the sheen of perspiration which covers my pale skin, you are going to have to slide your fingers between my legs to see if I am really as wet as you think I am, and I am desperate for that touch, Sir. I am desperate for the relief you can give me, Sir."

"Thank you." A hushed breathless voice breaks my flow, followed by a click, and the line goes dead.

I open my eyes and look at my phone only to be faced with the screen save of the picture I got caught taking a few weeks ago. I fall back into my bed and throw my hand over my eyes, trying to slow my own breathing. That was fun. I feel a little flustered, and, if I'm honest, wasn't expecting it to last that long, but I got a 'thank you!' That was my only call on the first night and I wasn't surprised. I think perhaps my lack of experience will make my calls a little tame. However, the following night was a full hour, much of the same, but with one guy who wanted a full description of my oral skills. Part of me did want to say that there's not going to be much of a description if your dick's in my throat, but I refrained. By Thursday, I have fallen into a comfortable routine, PJ's, warm milk, and some D/s before lights out.

Mr. Wilson had sent an email requesting I hand my work in directly to him as he wanted to check my progress personally, and, after my rocky start courtesy of Mr. Stone, I have welcomed his support and encouragement. I am back to my normal confident, if somewhat quiet, self. I knock and wait outside his office.

"Come in!" The identity of the voice is masked by the acoustics of the closed door.

"Oh!" I stop on the threshold, not who I was expecting. "Sorry, Sir, I have an appointment with Mr. Wilson. I'll just wait outside." The vision of a darkly intense Mr. Stone sitting behind Mr. Wilson's desk has me frozen to the spot.

"I don't think that's necessary." Mr. Stone grins at the flush to my face. I have got to stop wearing every reaction on my face. "Please come in, make yourself comfortable." He smoothly invites me in.

"Not sure that's even possible," I mutter under my breath.

"There are pigeon holes for that, you know?" He stands and moves silently around the desk continuing to step my way. I swallow loudly. Thinking he is some sort of mind reader, I glance down at my boldly titled course work pressed against my chest as a shield.

"Yes, I do, but Mr. Wilson wanted to see me." He is standing so close I have to tilt my head to look into his eyes, which are smouldering and his mouth is curved into a knowing grin.

"Mmmm. Well, I can't blame him for that." He hums. "Tell me, Miss Thorne, why are you trying to study a part-time degree in record time?" I take a sharp breath at this. He is leaning so the last words are whispered breaths against my ear. I am hoping the full body shiver I feel isn't visible.

"I, umm." I let out a short puff of air. "You are mistaken, my timetable is part-time... Plus your lectures, of course." I am a terrible liar and my hand reaches for the hairs on my neck to tug indicating as much, blatant as if my nose had started to grow.

"I thought we talked about lying. I know you are lying, but I want to know why?" He touches my chin with the tip of his finger, and I can feel the intensity of the heat from that tiny connection like a branding iron.

"How?" It's all I can manage and his lips curl in to a sinful grin.

"I know you, Miss Thorne. I know you better than you know yourself." He pushes my jacket open, and I gulp for the air that won't stay in my mouth. His strong hands hold my waist, his thumbs tracing circles over my hips, and his fingers hook over the waist band of my jeans and follow the band to the middle. "I know what you need." He slowly pops the buttons and I let out a small moan, his eyes darken from brilliant blue to almost black. I jump at the sound of the door handle. It's unlocked.

"Don't move." I barely hear his low growl as he takes one step to my side but remains flush against my body, his fingers gently stroking the top of my panties.

"Ah, Daniel." I recognise Mr. Wilson's cheerful voice.

"Jack, if you don't mind I just need a moment with Miss Thorne." His voice is soft but commanding, and with that he sinks his hand down the front of my panties and begins to leisurely move his index finger up and down my soft folds. I try to suppress a full on erotic cry at the intimate intrusion, and all that escapes is a strained squeak from the back of my throat. I begin to tremble. My legs are feeling weak, and my blood is rushing, deciding whether to flee to my head or my crotch.

"Yes, of course. Bethany, I hope you are well. You have my assignment completed, yes? Are you enjoying the course?" Oh, crap! I've got to answer. Daniel looks like he is asking for directions. I dread to think what my face looks like as perspiration forms a sheen across my skin, and I struggle to breathe.

"Yes, and yes, I am, thank you, Mr. Wilson." I manage to speak in a level but strained tone.

"How much?" Daniel says under his breath and sinks a finger further into me. I clench around him and squeeze my legs together. My hips want to grind, but I'm guessing the movement wouldn't go undetected.

"Oh, actually, Bethany, you've saved me an email." I whimper, as the pressure building is becoming more than a distraction. "We have a drinks reception, selected few, blah blah, but as a representative Mature student on my course, I would be grateful if you would come." His offer is kind but barely registering with me as Daniel continues his deep rhythmical movement, slowly in and out, in and out.

"She'll come, I'm sure of it." Daniel answers on my behalf but not for my benefit. I look at him with heated, pleading eyes. He grins but continues to look at Mr. Wilson, his glance the picture of calm whilst sinking a second finger deep inside me.

"Oh good, the details are on my desk, I'll just…" I hear him step further into the room. I freeze. Daniel interrupts him.

"I'll make sure she gets them, but if you wouldn't mind, I need to finish with Miss Thorne." He barely whispers the word *with,* but the deep timbre of the rest of his commanding dismissal weakens not just my resolve, but my knees, too. Mr. Wilson closes the door. My eyes are so wide and my body quakes as I am stepped forcefully back towards the door.

"I can't believe, -arhhhh" Daniel strokes a sweet spot inside me, and I feel my knees give way. He holds me up with his frame and continues to move his finger deep inside. His thumb puts light pressure in tiny circles on my clit. My hips move of their own volition, grinding against his hand, riding him, needing release.

"You're so wet, and I'm so fucking hard." He growls into my neck as he flicks the door locked. "No interruptions, I want you to come for me." Like I could stop. "Now!" He demands through gritted teeth.

"Oh God, Sir. What? Oh God!" The most amazing climax rips through me the instant he said that word, pulling wave after wave of intense pulsing heat through my body, contracting my innermost muscles around his fingers. The tightness and the slow rhythm of his fingers seem to keep this heightened state of arousal at its peak, forever. Minutes, maybe hours later, still trembling, I finally give in to my weakened knees and slide down the door sinking to the floor. He gives me a few minutes to regulate my breathing, and he gently lifts me from the floor and begins to carefully tuck my clothes back in neatly and does the button up on my jeans.

"You're so fucking responsive, Bethany." He slowly sucks on his fingers, and I can see the raw desire still in his eyes. That's maybe the most erotic thing I've ever seen and certainly the most erotic act I've ever experienced, but even so, I realize I am seriously out of my depth with this man. He returns to the desk, picks up the details of the drinks reception, and hands me the information. He is unaffected, and I'm a wreck.

"Until Friday, then?" His casual dismissal has me gawping like an idiot.

"It's Saturday; the reception, Mr. Wilson said Saturday." I can't even construct full sentences. I'm in so much trouble. I turn to leave.

"Yes…Saturday, too." I close the door, and I swear I can hear him laugh. Well, I am glad he has something to laugh about. I don't know whether to scream with frustration or sigh with satisfaction, but I definitely don't find it remotely funny.

That evening I manage to pick the saucepan from my single ring hob just before the milk boils over, and I stink the apartment out with the smell of burnt milk. I make myself a decaf milky coffee; I like the flavour, but I don't need the buzz from caffeine this late. I wriggle to get comfy, not an easy task on a futon, but it helps that I have a ridiculous number of throw pillows. I place Mags's phone next to my coffee, sit back and wait. It's literally a second after one a.m. when I get my first call. I pick it up instantly.

"You kept me waiting," A low stern voice informs me. The call has a slight echo, and I strain to hear through the muffled connection. This is new. I get a strange prickle over my body like an instant chill, but I'm toasty warm in my fluffy pj's. I reach down to pull the covers up to my neck.

"I'm sorry, Sir," I reply with a deep exhale of breath. "It won't happen again."

"No, it won't!" His curt reply makes my breath hitch and core clench. "Tell me what you are wearing." He practically growls.

"Yes, Sir." I pause as my mouth feels suddenly dry. Maybe this is just a follow-up reaction to events this afternoon. I'm probably just hypersensitive right now. "I'm wearing tiny black lace panties and I'm wearing my six inch black leather thigh high boots… and nothing else." My response is slow, not to extend the length of the call; I'm just having a little more trouble breathing tonight.

"You are lying," he replies, his voice is deep without inflection.

"I-" I try to speak but he interrupts.

"It doesn't require a response, you are lying, and I will allow it tonight, but next time there will be no lying, understand, Lola?" His stern command brooks no opposition.

"Yes, Sir." Why do I suddenly feel guilty for lying?

"Now, what are you doing?" He continues smoothly.

I shift a little. "Sir, I am kneeling with my head lowered, waiting for your instruction, Sir." My hand is tugging at my hair at the nape.

"Mmmm." He grumbles. "You are a dreadfully poor liar. Should I allow that, Lola?" I sigh, Christ, what am I supposed to do if he is just going to call me a liar every time I open my mouth?

"Sorry, am I boring you?" His tone is angrier now.

"No, Sir. Sorry, Sir, I didn't mean…" I am really struggling and feel flushed. Maybe I should hang up. I wonder if Mags gives refunds.

"Lola." His firm tone interrupts my panic.

"Yes, Sir." My response is quiet and utterly submissive.

"I want you to do exactly what I say, do you understand?"

"Yes, Sir." His tone is captivating.

"You've lied to me? " He waits for a response, the silence is excruciating.

"Yes, Sir." I am tentative and expectant. I can feel the heat building in my body.

"Do you think that is appropriate?"

"No, Sir," I respond immediately.

"Do you think it is acceptable?"

"No, Sir."

"Do you think you should be punished?" I'm sure he heard my intake of breath, and I push the covers back away from my body as a heat surges through me from my core.

"Yes, Sir." I suck in my bottom lip to prevent any involuntary sounds escaping.

"Good girl." A pool of molten liquid burns between my legs, and I start to wiggle to get some relief.

"Did I say you can move?" I freeze. "Good. Now, Lola, you don't know what I look like, but for this I think you might need some help. You have a picture, perhaps? Something that you can look at while I am instructing you?" His voice is seductive and encouraging, and I know exactly the picture I would like to use.

"Yes, Sir, I do."

"Good girl. Now, I want you to stand up and remove whatever it is you are wearing." My mind is racing. Does he expect me to actually do what he says? How will he know? He can't possibly know. I make a snap decision and stand.

"Good girl." His deep voice rumbles through me. "Put me on speaker so you can move freely."

"Yes, Sir." I start to remove my pj's when I stop. "Sir, would you like me to remove my clothes slowly?" I can't believe I am actually doing this, but I might as well go all out. He laughs

"Really, Lola, there is nothing seductive about peeling layers of pj's. I just want you naked so we can begin." I don't know whether to laugh or be creeped out at this point, so I remain silent, my heart pumping with the speed of a frightened rabbit. I finish stripping.

"I'm naked, Sir." I exhale, trying to push the mounting nerves out through my breath.

"Good girl. Isn't it better when you don't lie? When you do as you are told?" I am not going to analyse this now, but I do feel better. "Now, I want you to lie down." He waits as I crawl onto the bed. I am guessing he can hear the creak of the wooden slats, because when I am still, he continues. "I want you to tie your hands tight above your head and tie your legs wide apart so you are completely open for me… but as I am going to need your hands you are going to have to pretend for me. Can you do that, Lola?" I can hear the gruffness in his voice, and I wonder if this is having the same effect on him as it is on me.

I make to swallow and take a steadying breath. "Is that not like lying?" I venture.

"Lola." He rumbles his angry response.

"Sorry, Sir. Yes, of course, Sir." Jeeze, it's hard to gauge him, he should add 'frowny face' to his commands, so I can respond appropriately.

"Your hands are my hands, yes? Picture me, picture my hands." He instructs with such clarity, my hands no longer feel like my own.

"Mmmm," I am right with him now. "Yes, Sir."

"I am holding your face lightly, and I'm going to kiss you just below your ear. Can you feel that, Lola? My hand is tracing the edge of your jaw, down your throat along your collar bone." He croons, and I mirror his description with the tip of my finger. It sends shivers and racing heat all over my body. I want to press between my legs to relieve the ache that's building. If I'm honest, I'm seriously turned on and confused. Shouldn't I be the one talking?

"I'm kissing along your collarbone, my hot tongue rough and wet, my teeth nipping at your flesh. I move down your delicious body, your skin feels like silk, warm and fevered." He is right about that. "I squeeze your heavy breasts; they ache for my touch, your nipples hard and taut, begging for my mouth." He pauses. "My hands are your hands, Lola, yes?"

"Yes." I can't help but let out a heated moan as I squeeze my breasts. I go to pinch my hard, aching nipples.

"No! Don't pinch, I want to suck. I want to run my tongue all around that tight peak and place my hot wet mouth over it and suck, pull the hard nub into my mouth, and scrape the sensitive flesh with my teeth. I want to make you moan." His voice is so deep with desire, I think he could be reciting a grocery list and I would still melt to hear his voice, but the words he is saying have me on fire, wanton and helpless.

"Arghhh." I can feel his warm mouth around me, sucking, pulling, grazing my puckered nipple. My back arches from the bed and I squeeze and pinch to get some relief. I let out an agonizing moan.

"My hand is holding your hips steady, and I'm putting slight pressure on the indents above the bone. Do you feel that?"

I jump a little. "Yes, Sir." I manage to reply, frankly I'm surprised I can respond at all, I'm so hot. The throb between my legs is unbearable.

"Your legs are wide, you are open wide for me, you're so

responsive, you're so fucking wet." I hear him moan, but I jolt at this sharp reminder of this afternoon, the exact words Daniel used, but maybe I'm over-sensitive, pretty standard words in this type of situation I'm sure.

"Lola?" I'm back with him. "Take my fingers, run them down between your breasts, and I want you to take your index finger and sweep it down between your velvet folds. I want you to see how wet you are, how wet you are just for me." I hear him moan and his breathing is more laboured. It makes me smile, but then I gasp as my finger trails through my slick sex. Fuck, I'm going to come.

"Hold it, Lola! You don't get to come until I say you can come." His demanding tone leaves no room for discussion.

What? Really? Luckily my outrage at this new information was only in my head. I don't want to voice this, and I don't want him to stop.

"My fingers are stroking the depths of you, and I want you to sink two fingers inside yourself. Can you feel how tight you are? How you grip and squeeze? You're so greedy." An audible moan softly escapes my mouth.

I do what he asks, the build-up in me is intense, I start to tremble, and my breathing is rapid and shallow. I can't help but release a deep needful moan. I am panting, waiting for my next instruction, desperate to hear him tell me what to do to take me over the edge.

Nothing. My heartbeat is hammering. I have sweat gathered in droplets on my forehead. I crawl up from the sprawled position I had found myself in and grab the phone. I check to see if I still have a connection. Looking at the screen, I can see the seconds continue to tick, and the call that has lasted an excruciatingly delicious thirty minutes continues in silence.

"Sir?" I am more than a little breathless, but my imminent climax has retreated.

"Lola?" His steady reply is followed by silence. I am instantly cooled. "Did you come, Lola?"

"No, Sir." I can't hide the frustration in my voice.

"Good." He laughs lightly. "Be sure you don't. I want you to remain frustrated. Consider it your punishment".

"What the…" I snap my mouth shut before he interrupts.

"Something you want to say?" His voice is seductive again as he interrupts me from crying out what would've been something more than impolite.

I'm fuming, but petulantly reply, "No, Sir."

"Good girl. Until tomorrow night." The line goes dead.

I repeat, "What the Fuck!" to myself, safe in the knowledge that I won't be punished this time. I am hot, frustrated, and exhausted, but even so I can't bring myself to finish the deed. I am thankful for the small mercy that I receive no more calls for the remainder of my thirty minutes on duty. Once my time is up, I slump angrily into the plethora of pillows and settle down to a restless night.

Chapter Six

I HAD A DREADFUL night's sleep, and I woke up in a foul mood, but despite the lack of sleep, I was surging with energy and decided to go for a run. I don't tend to do this often, as walking keeps me fit, and Marco insists on taking me to a Krav Maga class at least once a week. I was a single girl in a big bad city. He signed me up to the toughest self-defense and martial arts class in the area. It does mean I will have to take a shower later in the morning when there is likely to be bodies around. Still that can't be helped this morning because I need to try and clear my head, as Sofs said, I need to "get some perspective". I make my way to Hyde Park Corner and cross into Green Park. This early there were only a handful of runners, and I set a brisk pace, picking a route that would take in St. James Park, too, before bringing me back to Hyde.

I can't get my head around the events of yesterday. The call last night was unreal, and I'm reeling with confusion. It was undeniably 'off the charts' hot, that the caller could make me feel the way I did, react the way I did and with such intensity. I felt real guilt at lying even when, realistically, how could he know? I was alarmed by the shocking surge of pleasure from obeying him, pleasing him. But seriously, why should I care? Not to mention the desperate burning need for him to make me come. His cessation and subsequent denial of my climax had been my punishment, and I took it, not entertaining for a moment the notion that I wouldn't continue to obey his demand. I am so confused that I'm okay with that. No, I'm not okay with it, I bloody loved it! Maybe that is the difference between being a submissive and being merely subservient, either way I feel I'm on one hell of a learning curve. As with learning anything new, there is always an element of confusion to begin with. I just have to accept this as a lesson or lessons in self-discovery, learning new aspects of 'my kinky self' with no harm done. My feet pound the path, and I can feel the sweat gather in droplets and trickle down my spine

Then there is Daniel Stone. I don't understand why he needs to know my secrets, why he needs to know *any* information about me, or why on earth he wants to fuck me. It's not that I'm a troll, but I have seen pictures of the women he dates, and I am not them. Glorious blondes with luscious manes of hair, legs up to their armpits and likely to scream at the sight of a bowl of pasta. Maybe I should just fuck him. The last thing I want is to be a challenge to a man like him, a man who thrives on challenges or puzzles to solve. He doesn't strike me as the sort of man who'd back down from a perceived challenge. He is obviously used to demanding and getting exactly what he demands. If fucking him will diffuse this before it escalates further, then maybe he will forget about my secrets, forget about me.

I am unlikely to rock his world in the bedroom department. I can just imagine a man of his considerable talents, if his fingers alone are any indication, is used to something close to professional perfection in the sack. Not an inexperienced virgin, who puddles in a useless liquid mess at his mere presence. Christ! I could probably come from his scorching gaze alone, and I seriously doubt I'll able to incite the reciprocal reaction. I am not the champion of low self-esteem, but I am a complete novice. It must take years of experience to hone those skills he wields like a well-handled weapon. This thought makes me uneasy, but why should it? Why does it matter how many years and how many partners it takes? Maybe he is just a perfectionist, and *that* thought makes my mouth water. I grab the railing to steady myself as I cool down and stretch. I walk back toward Knightsbridge glad that I am working with Sofia tonight. It's a private function at a private residence, so there will be plenty of time to discuss my sex life at length. I laugh out loud, my sex life! There's a first.

Joe is already unpacking the first delivery when I return. "You better hurry in that shower, girl, unless you want an audience." He gives a cheeky wink as I run upstairs and grab my work clothes.

Back down and outside the shower, I turn back to Joe. "I'll get changed in here, then there's no danger of frightening the staff!" I smile.

"It's not you frightening them that concerns me…it's them thinking about their hard-ons all day rather than their work!" He calls after me.

"Ewww, Joe! Gross!" I close the door to the sound of his laughter.

I finish my shift mid-afternoon. Sofia is picking me up at six, so I have all afternoon to do some course reading and relax before getting ready. I start up the stairs when Joe calls me back.

"I signed for a package for you, it came first thing this morning but I forgot, sorry, sweetheart." He hands me the box.

"Not a problem, thanks. If I don't see you later, see you Monday, and give my love to Christy!" I head back upstairs, shaking my large but intriguingly light box.

I open the box and pull the pink ribbons to remove a black and pink box. Agent Provocateur, I recognize the colours before I even see the name. Inside there is a card.

No more lies. –S.

Pulling at the tissue there is a beautiful black lace bra, the material is fine and delicate. It has straps that would lie in a cross tied pattern just under the cups. There are matching French knickers, suspender belt and silk stockings. This can't be good. My hands are shaking as I dial Late Night Calls.

"Late Night Calls… Let me help you." I recognize the breathy voice of Susan.

"Hi Susan, its Bets. Is Mags there? I've got a problem." I am trying to remain calm.

"Bethany, darling, what's wrong? Did you get the parcel?" She sounds excited.

"Um, yes." Now I'm confused. I didn't think there was a uniform. "You sent it?"

"Well, yes, I got the delivery this morning for Lola, and sent it straight to you, but with a different courier company, for safety, you know. Why? What is it?" She asks kindly.

I breathe out a relieved sigh. Okay, that's not so bad. "It's a set of really beautiful, sexy, and expensive lingerie, and it's from the caller from last night. Is that usual?"

"Oooo, how lovely. Well, it's not unheard of, but what is unusual is that that caller has pre-booked your calls for the next week." Her tone is pitched with excitement.

"Can he do that? Mags, I have to say I'm a little creeped out right now. Are you sure I can't be identified?" My heart is thumping but her overt calmness is having the desired effect on my nerves.

"Absolutely, darling, I couldn't sleep if it weren't so. Pre-booking the call, well, it's simple enough to do. We just keep your line free until his call comes in, even if he doesn't call, you still get paid for the hour. Why? Didn't the call go well? You were on for nearly half an hour, so you must've done something right?" She giggles lightly.

"Not sure if me doing something right was the purpose of the call, but it was different...intense." I don't know how to describe it without disclosing too much of *me*.

"Well, darling, it's your call. If you don't want to..." She pauses and I interrupt.

"No." I hesitate. "No, its fine, Mags, just different. Not that I have been doing this long enough to make a decent comparison really." I ramble with fresh nerves. "I'll just stick with it for the time being, but I can't work until Sunday now, I have some previous commitments, will that be a problem?"

"Not at all darling, I'm here if you need me, always!" She hangs up.

Sofia is loading boxes into my waiting arms as we unpack the van and start to bring the supplies for the evening up to the private residence on the corner of Hyde Park. We have to be quick, as the traffic wardens here are pure evil. This apartment is gorgeous, I mean out of this world, lottery-winning price tag luxurious. The kitchen is all sleekly polished granite. I am sure every gadget and machine available is here, but it is all cleverly hidden behind smooth shiny surfaces and seductive lighting. Exploration, however tempting, is extremely unprofessional, so we are confined to the hall, dining room and kitchen. Jean, the chef for the night is already unpacking ingredients when we bring up the last of the boxes.

"What's first, Jean? Would you like us to help prep here or shall we start setting the table?" Sofia asks.

"The table first, I'm fine here. It's only five courses tonight." He doesn't bother to look up, which is good, because he is slicing onions at lightning speed.

"Well, shout if you need us," Sofia calls as she grabs my hand and pulls me toward the dining room.

"I'm a chef, of course I'll shout!" He shouts after us.

The dining room is open at either end and has a walled mirror down one side creating a never-ending image of light and space. The reflection from the adjoining room shows just a glimpse of the floor to ceiling windows of the lounge and a view, which stretches across the city as the sun begins to set. It is stunning, and I am stunned. Sofia knocks my arm waking me from my dreamlike daze.

"So are you going to fuck him?" Her tone is as casual as if she had asked me to pass the salt.

"Crude much?" I gasp in mock shock at her shameless question.

"Bets, he's seriously hot. I'd tap that if I wasn't already with the love of my life." She smiles languorously. She is engaged to Paul, a really lovely guy, who adores her and, as such, I adore him. She continues to explain as we set the table. "He affects you like no one has. I mean you've messed around a bit, maybe given the odd blow job I don't know about, but you've never let anyone get *that* personal with you before. There is obviously something there, and he's obviously into you." I blush from root to tip at Sofia's summation of my abridged sexual history.

"Oh God, I shouldn't have said anything." I shake my head at my own stupidity for sharing too much.

"Are you shitting me? This is like a whole new Bets, and I love her. Grrrrrr." She curls her fingers into powerful paws but she's the lioness whereas I'm definitely Bagpuss, the old saggy cloth cat in the Children's show.

"He does affect me." I pause, pensive as I fold an intricate swan from the napkin. "I can't explain it, and I can't control it, and for me that's a huge worry. What if he keeps turning up? It can't go anywhere. I'd just be a quick fuck, and I'm not sure I'm okay with that, but when he's close? Oh, My God!" I'm fanning myself. I think I've shocked Sofia, as her mouth drops open and her eyes are wide. I get a cool shiver all over my body, and the hairs on my neck prickle to attention. I spin around to see what's shocked Sofia, sure that it wasn't me. It wasn't.

"Fuck!" I manage not to drop the glass I am now polishing, but at the expense of the language filter on my mouth.

"Miss Thorne, now that's not very polite, is it?" Daniel grins with amusement. He is the picture of calm, with dark grey tailored trousers and a crisp white shirt, with two open buttons at the top, just giving a glimpse of his tanned skin. His hair is messy, as if he has just run his fingers through it, and his eyes are the darkest clear blue, they crinkle at the side. He has the most amazing smile, which he is using at full strength to dazzle. I'm dazzled. Mortified, but dazzled.

"Sorry, no," I exhale my reply.

"No?" He raises a brow in query and his grin is now pure sin.

"No, Sir," I answer softly.

"Mmmm." His smile broadens. "Would you introduce me to your very insightful friend?" His reference to the conversation he overheard between Sofia and me at the restaurant doesn't go unnoticed. My shoulders tighten, and my face starts to flame. Great, I'm going to be flashing like a beacon all night. Perfect!

"Of course, Mr. Stone. This is my best friend, Sofia. Sofia's father owns the restaurant you were in the other night. Sofia, this is Mr. Stone." Sofia quickly steps to my side and holds her hand out.

"It's good to meet you, I've heard *so* much about you." Her shameless suggestive tone makes me want to kick her right now, and if I had my Timberlands on, I would, but with ballet pumps I'm likely to do more damage to myself.

"Really?" Daniel laughs. I try to swallow the lump in my throat while wishing the ground would swallow me whole. I am just thinking how unprofessional it would be to get roaring drunk tonight, because I don't think I am going to get through this evening without liquid courage. "Well, you look busy, so I shall leave you to it. No doubt we shall catch up later. And Miss Thorne?" He turns and is about to leave the room.

"Sir?" He holds my gaze with heat in his eyes.

"I shall, very much, look forward to being served by you this evening." I keep the breath I'm holding until I am sure he has left completely.

"Holy fuck, Bets! Smoking Hot!" Sofia squeals in my ear. I flinch.

"And you were *so* helpful." I'm trying to be pissed, but she is beaming, and technically she isn't wrong. "He can think again if I'm serving him all night. Wherever he sits I'm doing the other end, got it? You owe me!" I growl.

There are ten guests in total, all male and all business associates judging by the topic of conversations gleaned from serving the five-course meal. I only glanced at Daniel once during the night as I served at the other end of the table. He was smiling, looking directly at me with dark intense eyes and an enigmatic grin. I didn't dare hold his gaze for any length of time, as I felt the instant heat in my cheeks and a deep ache between my legs. Sofia and I have just served coffee and Jean left five minutes ago. Really it's just waiting to do the final clean, so I feel it's safe to grab a glass of wine. It's allowed, sort of.

"Did you hear what that drunk guy just said about Daniel?" Sofia leans in to whisper.

"What drunk guy? That doesn't narrow it down, since they are all drunk." I snort, the half glass of wine working its magic. Teach me to drink on an empty stomach.

"The one that seemed more than a business associate, like he's known Daniel for a long time?" She adds.

"I know the one, but, no, I didn't hear anything. I was helping Jean down to the van with the gear." I start to buff the already polished marble top. I like the way it shines with tiny metallic flecks.

"Oh, right. Well, he was saying something about Daniel never having had a relationship he didn't pay for. I wonder what he meant?" Her eyes are wide, and she wiggles her brows, intrigued.

"Well, he doesn't look all broken up, so I'm guessing it's not about paying emotionally, so if it's financial…I'm thinking, he maybe likes a professional." I giggle and add, "Oh, he sounds like a keeper!" We are giggling together when Daniel enters the kitchen.

"There is a man at the front desk asking for Sofia." Daniel sternly informs us as we snap to attention.

"Oh, Bets, I'm sorry! I forgot, Paul is picking me up. He is flying out early tomorrow, and I said to come get me here." She looks pleadingly in my eyes, and I could strangle her for putting me in this situation.

"Go. I'll finish." I assure her, and I don't want to make her feel bad, so I hold off the throttling for another time.

"Oh, Bets, you're the best! And don't forget, tomorrow night you're my wing girl." She kisses my cheek as Daniel interrupts.

"Bethany, you have a drinks reception at the University tomorrow?" His brow is furrowed like this is a problem for him in some way.

"Yes, but I'm bringing a change of clothes for her. I am meeting her there and then we will head out. It's a charity thing, fancy dress, retro eighties and Bets is a backing singer with me." Sofia smiles enthusiastically. I want to match her smile, but my jaw is just gaping at the amount of information she'd just dished out without fear or favour.

"Fancy Dress?" Daniel enquires.

"Yes, you know, all fluorescent pink, and 'Frankie Says Relax' t-shirts." I offer through a tight smile and a grimace aimed at Sofia.

"You sing?" His interest is piqued, I can tell, really not what I wanted.

"Oh, good God, no! Mime, and badly." I laugh at the very idea of holding a tune. "Go Sofs, I'll see you tomorrow." I push her toward the door before she can do any more damage.

"Be good and if you can't be good…" I slam the door before that sentence is finished and let out a heavy sigh.

Daniel has left the kitchen, and the men have moved from the dining room. With any luck, I can finish clearing and leave while they are still deciding on which strip club to go to. I load the final bits in the dishwasher and wipe the kitchen tops once more, when I hear the front door close. "I didn't think they were ever going to leave." Daniel's smooth low voice sends a flush of heat across my skin. "Would you like another glass of wine?" He makes it sound like ambrosia, and I find it all too easy to nod at the offer.

"Yes, thank you, I would. It's been a long day." I stretch my neck out one side then the next to ease the sore muscles.

"And a late night?" He smiles at my frown. Does he mean tonight or last night? "Why did you not serve me tonight?"

"Oh, no reason." My hand reaches for the hair on the nape of my neck. I twirl it between my fingers and lightly tug.

"Lies, Miss Thorne. I thought we had come to an agreement about lies." He walks toward me. No, he stalks towards me; I am definitely feeling like prey in this situation. I swallow, my lips part, and I try to maintain the simple function of sucking in oxygen. I just need to swish my hair and push my tits out to make my attraction to him just a bit more obvious. I push out a steadying breath through pursed lips. Get a grip, Bets!

"I don't mean to lie, Sir. It's just I don't think *this* is a good idea." My voice couldn't sound less certain. My heart is trying its hardest to escape my chest, my body is on fire, remembering the pleasure it was brought to by this man. His body brushes close to my back, and he places his heavy hands on my shoulders. His firm grip squeezes the tension from my shoulders. Oh, God, that feels like heaven.

"Arhhh, mmmm." My head drops to the side exposing my neck, and I close my eyes. His finger traces from my ear down my neck, resting on the indent in the center of my collarbone. He taps lightly.

"This *is* a good idea. We are a good idea, understand?" His voice is low and demanding.

"Yes, Sir," I exhale, tension and uncertainty evaporating with the air from my lungs.

"Feel what a good idea this is?" He grinds his huge erection into my bottom with a slow roll of his hips. A small moan escapes the back of my throat, and I can't think for the blood rushing in my head. Think, Bets! Think! This is so not a good idea! He holds my hips firmly and pulls my bottom into his rock hard length, releasing a groan of his own at the movement.

"You're so fucking beautiful, so responsive. You glow when you're aroused, when I arouse you. I've never been this fucking hard!" He feels hard, hard as iron. He pushes deeper, his desire undeniable, and I am so turned on that I've done this, or my body has done this, and I feel empowered by the thought. He made me come in Mr. Wilson's office, I'm going to make him come in his kitchen. I turn and drop to my knees, my heart racing ,and my mouth tingling with anticipation.

"Fuck!" He cries out and slams his hands on the counter behind me before he pushes one into my hair. He gently massages my scalp then his grip tightens. He is not going to stop this, and I'm not going to stop. I want this: to taste him, to make him tremble. I reach for his belt and quickly undo the buttons. I tug his trousers down and carefully pull his boxers over his fierce arousal. His cock lies heavy in my hand as I wrap my soft fingers around its thickness and grip, gently at first and tighter as I hear him moan. I move my hand rhythmically up and down to the base. My lips are close, and I can see the glistening drops of his excitement on the tip. I lick my lips and sigh a warm breath on the velvet crown. I take my tongue and flicker lightly over the head and around the sensitive edge, dragging it down the length of the pulsing veins and back up where I enclose it with my lips and push the tip slowly into my mouth.

"Holy Fuck! Bethany, Christ, yes! Suck it, suck it all the way down." His raspy command is punctuated by short deep breaths, as if he is struggling to control himself. I shift on my knees, the hard floor only a mild distraction. I begin a slow rhythm, my head bobbing with the gentle guidance from his fingers as they massage and lightly pull my hair. His cock is big, thick, and long. I don't have a huge frame of reference, but I'm thinking that it would hurt like fuck to, well, fuck. I want to take him deep, I want as much as I can take, and I want to taste his come. I hollow my cheeks and increase the suction, but this time I swallow as I take him to the back of my throat, and I continue to try and swallow, try to take more of him. "Jesus. Fuck, Bethany, what are you? Shit! Fuck I'm going to come. Fuck!" His grip tightens on my hair, and his hips jerk. Taking over, he fucks my mouth as I try to keep his pace, and he growls.

"Arhhhhh!" I feel the hot liquid swirl, filling my mouth, and I try to swallow. It takes two attempts, and I'm more than surprised I don't gag, given the force of his final thrust and the amount of liquid in my mouth. I lick my swollen lips and gently lick him dry. His hands are braced on the kitchen counter, and we both fight to regain some sort of normal breathing pattern.

He helps me stand, as my legs are stiff, and my knees are sore from the hard marble floor. He puts his strong arms around me and pulls me tight to his firm chest. He holds me, his head resting on mine. His breathing is deep, and his heart is beating like mine.

"Not what I had planned for this evening, Miss Thorne." He takes his finger and lifts my chin, making me look into heavy lidded eyes almost black and full of desire. I can feel the raw need for my own release like I need my next breath. "I'm going to fuck you so hard." The promised threat is absolute in his tone. It brings me back to planet Earth like a violent NASA touchdown. Even if it isn't just what any girl would dream of as her first time, 'demanding, angry man wanting to fuck you hard', I swoon. Besides, can he even do that so soon? Well, I'm not waiting to find out.

"The bathroom?" My voice is more shaky than I was hoping, and I clear my throat and repeat more confidently. "I would like to use the bathroom?"

"Of course." He cups my face with his large warm hands and kisses me firmly on my forehead. He continues to hold me. "I'll show you. It's just down the hall." He takes my hand, and I follow his lead, his fingers gently stroke my wrist, and this tender act feels strangely intimate. He stops to face me, his hands cup my face again, his eyes intense, and I know I won't be able to leave if he kisses me now. I want him to kiss me. His warm, mint breath and his full soft lips are just millimeters from my own parted lips. He hesitates, and a grin begins to form. He pulls back, and I collapse a little at the loss. "I am going to head to my shower, second room on the left, join me." It isn't a request. I swallow and nod, afraid if I say, Yes, Sir,' that is exactly what I'll be doing.

I head toward the bathroom but quietly slip past and out to the front door. I've left my coat, as it was in the cloakroom, but I manage to grab my bag. I hit the street and since it's Friday night, there are plenty of black cabs. I take the first one with its yellow light on and slump back once the door is closed. I pull my lips through my teeth, I can taste him, and my body is still trembling with desire. I did the right thing, I think. I am not under the illusion that my first time would be all hearts and flowers, but I didn't think it would be a quick hard fuck, either. Although I am not sure that's what it would be with Daniel, and that's what shakes me to my core. However, running like I did, now, that *was* impolite. I can't help but smile and I draw a deep breath. I'm thinking one of two outcomes could happen now: outcome one, I could be out of his system, brilliant; or outcome two, I have just sealed my punishment-laden future. I shiver a little at that thought. Either way I'll be the one choosing when I get fucked.

I knock on Marco's door. It's late, again. I decide not to go back to my place, as Daniel knows where I live, and if he has decided to go for outcome two, I think it's better he doesn't find me tonight.

"Bets?" Marco is still asleep as he opens the door. I should maybe get a key.

"Hey, buddy!" I smile, my tone way too cheery for this late hour. I give him a quick kiss on the cheek. "Sleep-over at yours tonight – don't ask?"

"As if…" he rubs his face and leads the way to his sofa bed.

Chapter Seven

I CATCH A RIDE with Marco to the restaurant in the morning. Having showered at his place, I just need a quick change of clothes before he drags me to class.

"Walk of Shame, Bets?" Joe laughs and is joined by a chorus of jeers from the kitchen.

"That's right, Joe, blame your niece, though, this time." I smile and nod my head toward Marco.

"Danny came round real early this morning asking for you. He looked pissed when I told him you weren't home. You owe him money or something, girl?" At this he barks out another loud laugh.

"Something like that. Did he say what he wanted?" I can feel my face flame as I fail to pretend that this is a normal occurrence in my socially barren life.

"No, but he must have met the courier on his way in at the same time, because he left the exact same box you got yesterday …I put it outside your door." He nods toward the stairwell.

"Okay, thanks." I can feel my face flush a deeper hue and turn before it's noticed.

Marco takes me to our Krav Maga class and I spend a good hour being pummeled into the mats. I bruise like a peach, so I'm going to look like I've been hit by a truck for the rest of the week. Back home, I start to strip, as the gym is very basic and with no showers, I am left to body wash in my sink before my next shift starts downstairs. My mind drifts, I bet there was a glorious bath--no, baths, plural--in Daniel's apartment. How sad is that? Instead of Paris in springtime and deserted islands, I fantasize about heated flooring and plumbing facilities. Before I head downstairs, I pull the unopened box onto my lap and peel the tape off. Inside, the distinctive pink and black colours of the packaging mean I know exactly what I've been sent. I lift the tissue paper and see an exquisite lace corset with matching thong in a deep purple with black lace trim. There is also a pair of black silk hold up stockings. I think I will have to make space in a separate drawer if this continues. There will be mutiny if these saucy little numbers are forced to share space with my plain white cotton combinations and thick fluffy socks.

Sofia has assured me that she has my outfit for tonight and will meet me in the Quad at eight tonight. I can then change in the ladies, and we can grab a taxi and head to the party. I pick a conservative light grey shift dress and black boots with a three quarter length charcoal cashmere cardigan, courtesy of Sofia. My wardrobe is a little light on elegance and a drink reception suggests elegance; well, it does to me. I check my cardigan into the cloakroom and enter the Gallery room where there is a large gathering of Heads of Departments and I am guessing, because I am here, some students, too. I take a glass of white wine and look to see if I can see any familiar faces.

A tall gentleman approaches in an immaculate grey suit and pale pink shirt with a silver tie, his hair a dirty blonde and short. He has two days' worth of stubble, which gives him a slightly rough demeanour, and his eyes are a light brown. He smiles, all white teeth and charm.

"Please don't tell me you are a student?" He seems friendly enough even if I don't understand his question.

"Sorry?" I didn't bring the email invitation but I know I was invited; Mr. Wilson invited me. I will die on the spot if I have to be escorted from the building for gate-crashing. Seeing the obvious look of worry flash across my face, he quickly adds, "It's just that as a member of staff, there are rules." His lips curl in a knowing smirk. "And I'm afraid looking at you, I would be sorely tempted to break those rules." Oh, he's smooth. I was right about the charm, but then again, I'm sure he is right about the rules.

"Ha, that's funny." I smile and laugh. "Yes, I'm one of Mr. Wilson's mature students, Bethany Thorne." I offer my hand.

"Christopher Taylor, finance and accounting. Call me Chris, and it's lucky-" I don't get to learn what is lucky exactly.

"Lucky for me, that I am *not* a member of staff. Good evening, Miss Thorne." Daniel interrupts, as he steps to my side, his arm and thigh brushing mine, and I can feel an instant heat where we touch. He whispers, but loud enough for Christopher to hear, "Not that the rules would concern me." His warm breath heats my neck, and the sudden, and now familiar, prickles spread across my skin. I take a sharp breath and I feel my face glow. I take a step away and toward Christopher, my heart is thumping wildly. I expected him to show up at some point, he mentioned he would, but I didn't expect this degree of invasion of my personal space and in such a public arena.

"Mr. Stone, it's nice to see you again." I straighten my back and lift my chin, conveying a calm and strength I do not feel. He grins, and his dark blue eyes dissolve into inky pools of desire. His lids are heavy, and he steps once more to close the distance.

"Nice? You hurt my feelings, I believe our recent meetings have been more than nice?" I glance a quick and panicked look at Christopher, who is frowning at this last comment. I can't believe he is going to do this here. I'm fuming, obviously flustered and off the charts aroused with him so damn close, but mostly fuming.

"Nice, yes! The lecture you gave was extremely useful, and it was nice to meet you." I hope that has clarified my meaning, but I add just in case, "When Mr. Wilson introduced us at the 'meet and greet' the other week." I look again to Christopher as I add a context to the meeting, "It was....*nice* to meet you then." My throat is dry, and I take a large sip of my wine.

"What about Mr. Wilson's office, was that *nice*?" He chuckles. He is such an arse.

I ignore his last comment. "It was *really* lovely to meet you, Christopher. Maybe we could check out those rules another time?" His face flashes with shock, followed by a huge smile. I can't believe I just said that. Since when did I start flirting? I don't flirt, but looking at Daniel as he scowls and grinds his jaw, I think I know exactly why I chose this time to start. "I have just seen Mr. Wilson. If you would excuse me gentlemen, Daniel." I add pointedly and hope he picks up on the deliberate differentiation as I turn and walk away. I don't quite make it to Mr. Wilson, and thankfully he doesn't see me, as Daniel grabs my elbow and guides me through a nearby door into a vacant vestibule.

"What the fuck do you think you are doing?" He growls low, his face close to mine, his breath fresh, and his scent warm and intoxicating. Luckily I'm still fuming.

"What the fuck do you think *you* are doing?" I return his heated glaze. He laughs lightly.

"Not very polite, Miss Thorne." He draws in a deliberate, steadying breath. "You know you react to me. Your body glows, the hairs on your neck spike when I'm near, your skin prickles, you tremble under my fingers and your smell." He takes another tortuously slow, deep, and sensual breath. "Oh, Miss Thorne, you intoxicate me." Interesting choice of words, I believe I had the same thought not a second before. "Why do you deny this? Why do you run from us?" He pushes his strong, hard frame into mine, his hand on the small of my back exerting enough pressure to bend my body into his body, enough to make me soft and pliant.

"It's not rocket science. Of course I'm affected by you, look at you!" I push against his immovable chest, my fingers just touching the ripped definition of the muscle beneath his shirt. "Oh, Christ," I let out an exasperated breath. "Look, this," I wave my hands between us and around indicating our surroundings. "This isn't a game for me, I can't afford to lose this. I won't risk this." I pause, gathering another steadying breath. "So I will 'deny this'." I pull on his narrow hips and hold myself tight against him, just to emphasize I know exactly what I'm denying. A deep groan escapes the back of his throat, and I shake my head softly. I push against him this time, and he actually steps back.

"Self-preservation, Mr. Stone, you need to find someone else to play with." I easily match the intensity and desire of his gaze before I turn away. I hate the feeling of sickness in my stomach, of losing this intense heat between us, and I abhor the heavy ache in my chest the further away I walk. I am starting to understand this is exactly the reason I have to walk away. I would never survive Daniel Stone.

I can't bring myself to mingle now, but manners dictate I at least thank Mr. Wilson for the invitation. I finish my wine and grab another glass as I approach a small group of people, which includes Mr. Wilson.

"Ah, Bethany, so glad you could join us." He smiles and leans in to kiss my cheeks. I guess this is more a social gathering than a formal occasion.

"It was very kind of you to invite me." I smile as he introduces me to his colleagues. Three other department heads, two fellow students, and Christopher Taylor.

"We met earlier, only too briefly, though." He remains effortlessly charming. "Perhaps you've come to make amends now, and let's hope you won't get frightened off this time." He continues to hold my hand in a slow handshake despite having already met.

"Funny again, Mr. Taylor." I laugh lightly, but he has a cheeky grin this time.

"I don't think Bethany would scare too easily, maybe on a Ghost Train, eh?" Mr. Wilson chuckles and comes to my defense, bless him.

"Never go near them, I find life is scary enough." I add quietly. "Actually, I have to leave, but I did want to thank you again for the invite."

"Oh, not me, my dear." He looks a little embarrassed. "Mr. Stone selected you, did you see him yet? You must thank him." He looks around trying to spot my sponsor. Oh, I can't catch a break. I get the strength to push him away, and, *wham,* I have to go over and thank him, with an audience this time.

"There he is!" Mr. Wilson waves to Daniel, who causes the sea of people to part before him as he strides toward us.

"Cold, Miss Thorne?" His mouth curls to one side trying to contain his grin. I look down to the offending articles; my nipples puckered to hard tips pointing directly at him. Ground, swallow me now! My face flames, and before I can stutter a response, he continues.

"You have goose bumps all up your arms, so I just wondered if you were cold?" I can see his fingers twitch. I think, maybe, he is trying to control his urge to stroke the bumps along my arm, and I am definitely trying not to imagine his touch.

"I'm fine; a little warm actually." I cough to clear my throat. "Mr. Wilson just informed me I should thank you for tonight's invitation?" I look back to Mr. Wilson for confirmation. He nods.

"A random selection, I assure you." He is quick to confirm, "But I will happily take the credit." He takes my offered hand, his palm soft against my skin, his grip firm and secure.

"Well, I'm grateful, nonetheless, so thank you." I attempt to pull my hand free, and he holds firm for a moment more, before allowing me to move away. I quickly wish everyone a good evening and start to leave.

"It's not necessary, but I'll show you out." Christopher steps in front of Daniel and places his hand on my waist, escorting me to the cloakroom. I have to physically fight the urge to glance back at Daniel. Is he looking my way? Does he notice where Christopher's hand is resting? Does he care, and, more importantly, why do I care? I see Sofia's head peek around a column down the corridor, and I couldn't be happier to see her.

"Hope to see you again, Bethany." Christopher smiles. "I'm going to be checking those rules, you know."

"Funny again, you're on a roll tonight!" I laugh and start jogging toward Sofia.

I'm scrabbling in the bag Sofia handed to me trying to find the 'Relax' T-shirt or even the "Wake Me Up, Before You Go-Go" T-shirt. "You've got to be shitting me, Sofs!" I pull out what can only be described as a dress, which would fit Barbie, it's *that* small, but Barbie is obviously in mourning. "Do you want to explain this to me?" I dangle the offending article in front of her mischievous face.

"Marco had a change of plan, he's doing Robert Palmer's "Addicted to Love", instead of Wham's "Wake Me Up Before You Go-Go", and we are the super-hot honeys at the back. I've got plastic guitars and everything." She is doing excited little bunny hops.

"Sofs, this is so short you can see what I have for breakfast!" I cry. It's my own fault. I should've run when I noticed her suspicious grin and her trench coat hiding her own indecent outfit.

"You've got the legs, and I brought the heels. You'll probably have to go commando though unless you've got a thong on?"

I'm going to hyperventilate. "Yes, that is just what I was thinking, because what I'm really worried about now is this look being ruined by VPL!" I am hoping she can hear the real panic in my voice.

"Relax, Bets, it's for charity." I can hear her holding back a fit of giggles, "And besides two broken nights' sleep? Marco said you owe him. That, and I didn't bring an alternate costume. Put it on, then come out here, so I can fix your hair and make-up." Her tone is no nonsense and resolute. I resign myself to an evening of pure hell.

I wrap my cardigan tightly around what there is of the long sleeved, scoop-necked, short, short lycra dress. I declined the stockings and took the heels. Sofia scraped my hair slick and painted my face with dark smouldering eyes and fire engine red glossed lips. I don't recognise myself in the mirror and I am hoping no one else does either. We leave the ladies and make our way out across the Quad avoiding the cobbles.

"I'm not walking. We're getting a taxi from here. I don't care how long it takes. or how much *you* have to pay for it." I grouchily inform my friend, but we wait for ten minutes and still no luck. A very sleek Bentley limousine pulls up slowly and stops in front of us. "You know whoever is in there thinks we're hookers, right?" I accuse Sofia.

"Yes, but we're expensive-looking hookers." She laughs and squeezes my arm. The driver has come around to our side and opens the door. I feel him before I see him, but drop my eyes, praying for an invisibility cloak in place of my cardigan. Daniel goes to get into the car. He looks up and stops.

"Bethany?" His wide eyes and sharp voiced question reinforce his utter surprise.

Oh, crap! "Daniel." I flash a tight smile but manage to hold my chin high and meet his astonished gaze.

"You look…" He bites his bottom lip. "Ah, yes, fancy dress." He smiles as he remembers the details from last night.

"Well, I'm not working late if that's what you think!" I laugh nervously. He raises his brow but smiles.

"Well, ladies, allow me to take you to your destination. After all, it's the least I can do, I believe you said it was for charity?" He moves to the side to allow us to get in. I hesitate, but it's too late, Sofia already has her head in the vehicle. I sigh and follow with a weak smile.

"Nice ride you have here, Mr. Stone." Sofia seductively strokes the soft leather. She's incorrigible.

"It gets me from A to B, and, please, call me Daniel." I smile as he repeats my sentiment about cars. We head out toward the Kings Road after giving Daniel's driver the address. Sofia chats, and Daniel politely fields her questions, but his eyes burn through me, igniting a fire in my core that I am struggling to contain. Each time, a little more of my resistance falls away, and I forget one more reason why I shouldn't embrace this scorching need I know he can fulfill. We reach our destination, and just as I go to thank Daniel, Sofia speaks first.

"Daniel, why don't you come in for a bit, check out my Bets' talent onstage?" She nudges me as my head whips round with pure shock and outrage. "You could come as the diet coke man?" She starts to giggle as I try and manhandle her out of the car.

"She didn't mean it, sorry. Thank you for the lift." Daniel is standing on the pavement towering above me.

"Didn't mean I could come or didn't mean I could come as the diet coke man?" His lips curl with barely contained amusement.

"Oh I'm pretty sure there's no contest between you and the diet coke man." I note, but not giving him the opportunity to follow, I turn and add. "Thank you again for the lift." Grabbing Sofia, who is still giggling, I lead her into the club.

"You're fired!" I turn to face her "Officially NOT my best friend anymore!" I huff indignantly and turn to take in the bar. It is colourful and crowded, loud and luminous. Someone has gone all out on the décor; fluorescent lighting, film posters from the decade and even some impressive sculptures of iconic 80's memorabilia. There is a large suspended Rubics' cube hanging beside the mirrored disco ball and a three-foot free standing 3-D Arctic Roll dessert complete with packaging, which is doubling as a table in the center of the room. The 'acts' for the evening have already started and two identical Michael Jackson's perform a polished routine to "Billy Jean" on stage. This is beginning to feel a lot like a competition. We make our way to the bar and some familiar faces. Sofia gets the first round, handing me two shot glasses. I raise my brow.

"You need this, trust me." She nods toward the door.

"I know he's there I can feel him." I close my eyes for a second and just absorb the sensations that have become so familiar so quickly, and that my body now seems to crave.

"Bets, can you not tell how fucking sexy that is! Stop fighting the fun, listen to your body for once. Look, if you enjoy what he does to your body, and, no, don't interrupt, if you enjoy it and you obviously do, just let it happen. What's the worst that can happen?" She shakes my shoulders and maybe some debatable sense into me.

"Famous last words, Sofs." I down the first shot and wince as the burn rips down my throat. "Look I'm going to try one last thing to end this, then... well, then I've got nothing left, no more resistance." I give a little shrug and tip the second tequila back. I give an exaggerated shiver. Marco makes his way over with a sheepish grin, I can't be angry at him, especially with the warm, slightly dizzy feeling I'm getting from the shots.

"Hey, Bets, looking good!" He winks, he's being brave, and I narrow my eyes.

"Your sister's fired and you may well be next, mister!" I poke him in the chest. He is looking nothing like Robert Palmer, but his hair is slick and his suit is sharp so he'll pass. I feel the wave of heat at my back and I know I have company. I lean into Marco,

"You'll be off the hook if you play along." I whisper and turn, just catching the confusion on his face.

"Daniel, you decided to join us, that's nice." I pause to take in his dark eyes, and I lift my chin. "Let me introduce my boyfriend, Marco." I look toward Marco's face and hear Sofia choke on her drink--thanks for having my back guys! "Marco, this is Daniel Stone. He is a guest lecturer at my University."

"Boyfriend, Miss Thorne?" He shakes Marco's hand, but doesn't take his eyes from me. "Your recent behaviour would lead me to think you might be lying." I can see the glint in his eyes that he knows I am, but the muscle at his jaw is ticking with tension from something.

"Today, we became official today. All very star crossed, very sudden, very passionate." I purr and awkwardly lean into Marco, who is transfixed at my performance.

"Really?" His response is deep and slow. "Are you insulting

my intelligence, Miss Thorne, because I would consider *that* to be extremely impolite?" He narrows his eyes, and I take it as a challenge. I turn, thrust my hands into Marcos hair and fix my mouth to his in what has to be the least passionate kiss in history. I hear Daniel growl, and I break the kiss, turning to see his fierce eyes and clenched jaw. He takes my hand and pulls me away from Marco. "Enough, Bethany!" His voice is firm, and it makes me stop. "There is no way Marco is your boyfriend. He is a friend, yes, but he looks like he has just been French kissed by his sister!" His tone is quietly serious. "I would challenge you, Bethany, that it isn't *nice* to use your friends in such a way." I blush and feel completely reprimanded. He is right. "Not that I think he minds, but the girl he was dry humping when you first arrived certainly seems to." I look over to where Daniel indicates with his eyes and see the death stare from a petite blonde dressed as SuperGirl. I'm mortified.

"Marco, I'm so sorry, you know I didn't mean-" He hugs me tight pulling me away from Daniel.

"Don't think about it, really don't, I'll always have your back." Marco interrupts my apology with the best of hugs, the kind that warm the soul. "Hey, Man." He addresses Daniel. "She has her reasons. You should respect that and back off." He smiles at me and starts to walk away. "You need me, I'm there, Bets." Only he is not looking at me when he speaks. This display of Alpha maleness makes me tremble, and I think I am going to be sick, but I won't let that play out. I turn to diffuse the tension.

"Daniel, I am sorry, really it's just that ..." I'm lost for words

"Bethany." He leans in, and I am engulfed in his smell and the sparks that fire between us. "Tell me, what is it about me that makes you think I am not a man, who gets exactly what he wants, when he wants it?" The rawness in his voice has me panting. He steps into me, and I can feel his erection press hard against me. I lick my lips remembering the taste of him. His lids are heavy, and I think he is thinking the same thing.

"We are going to leave, I need you to come with me now."

He tightly grips my hips, growling his demand. I clench, my core on fire.

"Bets, we're on in five, you better have a few more of these." I let out a huge breath as Sofia places two more shot glasses in front of me. Daniel takes them from her, and for a moment I think he is going to tell her we're leaving, and I'm pretty sure I wouldn't stop him, but the corners of his mouth turn up.

"If you are going to do tequila shots, Bethany, there is only one way to do them." His voice is hypnotic. He takes a piece of lime and holds it up to my mouth.

"Open." I obey, and I swear I hear him moan. I gently grab the fruit between my teeth. With that, he cups my chin and tilts my head, exposing my neck. He leans closer and drags his warm tongue along the vein that must be pumping madly, if my heart rate is anything to go by. I shiver at the contact, and my breath hitches. He sprinkles a small pinch of salt on the damp area he created and picks up the shot glass.

"Cheers!" He has the widest grin. He firmly licks the salt from my neck, downs the shot, and presses his lips hard against my mouth and sucks the juice from the lime. "Mmmm, your turn?" He raises a brow.

"Holy Hell!" Sofia gushes in my ear. I gape at him, I'm a tingling ball of desire but manage to shake my head, laughing as a deep breath rushes from my body.

"Wow!" I silently gasp, utterly speechless and dripping wet.

Daniel's eyes burn through me. "Looks like you're on, ladies?" he informs us coolly, nodding toward the stage. I reach behind him to grab the other shot.

"I'm still going to need this." After I swallow, I blow out a cooling breath to calm the effect of Daniel, not the liquor.

The heat from the lights is fierce on the stage, but it also has the effect of making the audience invisible, which is fantastic. I put the guitar strap around my neck and tug ineffectively at the hem of my dress.

"Bets, sultry and sexy. No smiling." Sofia winks at me, the

picture of confidence.

"Too scared to smile, Sofs." I snort. The loud bass and drum kicks in of our chosen track, "Addicted to Love" and I watch as Marco dramatically grabs for the microphone stand, casually winking at me over his shoulder. I laugh again, then quickly remember no smiling, so I pout instead. The song belts out from the wall of speakers behind us, and with the effect of the shots making their way through my body, I start to sway, synchronising my movements with Sofia's at my side. It's easy, fun, and the audience is cheering and, better still, I can't see any of them. Sofia shouts at me to stop smiling, but I can't help it, I'm having too much fun. I love dancing, although this is really just a gentle roll of my hips. Sofia is right, it does feel good to do what my body wants for a change. Marco is giving his all for his big finale and the stage lights go out. There are shouts for another track, and before I can leave the stage, I hear the first bars to "Bad Case'" I look to where Daniel is standing and can't help my own grin, because with the lights out momentarily, I can see clearly and I catch a glimpse as he sets about adjusting his trousers.

The lights go back on on the stage, and Sofia comes up behind me to spoon, grinding gently against my butt, taking our routine up a notch in the sexy scale. She has ditched her guitar, and I do the same; she has her hands on my hips. This song is a little faster and it's more fun to jump around a little. Facing each other as Marco dominates the front of the stage, Sofia starts licking her lips suggestively, I laugh and mirror this, and it doesn't feel like exhibitionism because I can't see anyone else. The edge of the stage starts to fill with some of the audience and I feel strange hands rest on my hips, only to be snapped away. I turn to see a man stumble away from me and Daniel's furious dark eyes, and all too quickly the seat of his pants, as I am swept up and over his shoulder. He tugs roughly on the hem of my dress preventing full exposure and I can't help giggle at his attempt to protect my modesty.

"I don't share!" He growls as way of an explanation and

strides off the stage. My head inches from his backside. I giggle again. It's the alcohol. I'm thinking I could just sink my teeth into that tight arse; definitely the drink talking! He strides through the crowd until he is outside, and I can hear him speaking to his driver. He carefully slides me down the front of his toned firm body and places me on the pavement. He looks angry.

"This is normal for you?" His face is dark, and there is fury in his eyes, effectively killing my playful buzz.

"Yes, Daniel, absolutely fucking normal, between working full-time, a full-time part-time degree, and visiting my…" I stop myself, and he raises a questioning brow. "Between all that," I continue with just as much anger as he is radiating. "I do this *every* night!" I point toward the club and return his scowl.

He shakes his head and runs his hand through his hair a few times before he speaks again. His voice is softer. "Sorry Bethany, it's just, you look so sexy, so natural, so confident. Did you hear the crowd?"

Oh, the irony. "Well, Daniel, that's called drink. It gives me courage and makes men horny, and that has very little to do with me!"

"Why do you do that?" His dark brow furrows, but I can't get my head round why he is angry. Why he is even here? Why me?

"Do what, Daniel? What do you want from me?" He is standing so close we are touching, He takes his hand and sweeps it up the back of my neck, fisting my hair and pulling my face to his.

"This is going to go two ways. Firstly, you have been extremely impolite, and your behaviour has been disappointing, for which you will be punished. Secondly, I believe we have some urgent unfinished business, and because of this, your punishment will have to wait. Because now, right now, I am going to fuck you until morning… Miss Thorne, I am going to make you come until you beg me to stop." His breath is hot against my mouth, "And I know I'm going to love to hear you beg, do you understand, Miss Thorne? Is this acceptable to you?" He looks deep into my eyes.

"Yes, Sir." My head no longer has a say, because my body has chosen.

Chapter Eight

DANIEL FIRMLY HOLDS my hand as he waits for the doorman to open the side door, opting to avoid either of the rotating doors. He walks briskly across the checkered marble foyer of The Savoy, I actually do a 'Pretty Woman' style stumble as I take in the grandeur. The vaulted ceilings are cream moulded plaster with pale green inset squares. The polished dark wood paneling and hanging glass light fittings are in keeping with the art deco period of the furniture placed at either end of the vast reception area. If I wasn't so nervous, I would be extremely intimidated. I have been to The Savoy before, but only to do my silver service training, and I am wondering why Daniel has brought me here and not to his apartment. As if he senses my unease, he squeezes my hand lifting it to gently graze his lips across my knuckles.

We walk in silence along the narrow corridor, the thick carpet bounces under my aching feet. He glides the key card with precision and steps aside the open door to let me through. Inside the suite he drops my hand and walks toward the built in bar, while I tentatively walk toward the window. The floor to ceiling glass allows for the most spectacular view of the Thames; directly across the river, the London Eye is lit in ever changing colours, and the lights on the boats along the river sparkle. The view is stunning, romantic, really, with a million city lights shining the length of the river bank. I can hear him pour some drink, and I tremble as he walks over to me.

"Drink?" He hands me a crystal glass with two fingers of golden liquid. I take it, I don't much care what it is, and I sip. My face wrinkles.

"That good?" Daniel's laugh is warm. I drink the remainder in a large gulp. He laughs again.

"Someone's in a hurry." He takes my glass and together with his, places them back on the bar.

He stands close behind me, his arms slide around my waist and he pulls me tight against his body. His mouth is hot against my neck, and I tilt my head back against his chest. He whispers in a low voice, "I am going to take my time with you, Miss Thorne, and I would very much like you to do exactly as I ask." He runs his nose down my neck, inhaling, sending a shiver the length of my body. "Do you think you will be able to accommodate me? Do you think you can obey?" I have no choice but to listen to my body. All my sense of self-preservation I left, along with my head, back at the party just before I stepped into his car. My heart is racing, and my breath is rapid The heat at my core is forcing a pressure between my legs like I've never felt, and the urge to grind back to get some release is unbearable. I sigh and sink a little, but his strong frame holds me in place. I so don't want to embarrass myself and come across as the novice I am. It's not a big deal, because it's not like I was intentionally saving myself. It's just that life got in the way before now, and now I really do want to obey him.

"Yes, Sir." He steps away and I am instantly cool. He brings the chair from the table over and places it in front of me. He removes his jacket and tie and eases back into the chair. He stares at me with heavy lidded eyes and slowly pops the first two buttons on his shirt.

"Good girl. Now I would like you to take off your dress." His voice is smooth and rough at the same time. I am nervous, but this warm fire inside burns and fills me with courage I was unable to glean from the alcohol I just drank. The material of my dress is very stretchy and I am able to pull and slip it off my shoulders, a slightly better option than hauling it over my head. I peel it down my body and allow it to slip to the floor, stepping out of the material I return my gaze to Daniel. He raises a curious brow.

"Something wrong?" My voice catches. I panic at his expression and drop to my knees to pick up my dress, I can't do this. I am so far from being a temptress. He surprises me and instantly joins me on his knees. He holds my shaking hands, the concern etched on his face.

"Bethany." His voice is so soft, so calm, and he has the sweetest smile. "You are breathtaking. I was just surprised by the 'Plain-Jane' underwear. Because if you're trying to detract from how fucking beautiful you are, you are shit out of luck." He grins and gathers me in his arms, lifting me as if I weigh nothing. He sits me on the edge of the bed and my bottom sinks into the thick soft covers.

"Now, shall we start again? " He tilts his head and flashes this killer, heart-stopping smile.

"Yes." I sigh, my skin prickles. "Sorry…yes, Sir."

"Good girl. I want you to lie back and hold your hands above your head and keep them there. You will want to move them, but I want you to keep them right there. Do you understand?" His commanding tone makes me shiver even though I feel able to burn marks into the sheets with my body heat. I nod.

"I need to hear an answer, Miss Thorne?" His sterner tone makes me jump.

"Yes…Sir." I manage to speak past the lump in my throat.

He stands beside the bed and pushes between my legs. He runs his strong hands, exerting a light pressure from my knees to the tops of my thighs in long sweeping strokes. "Your skin is so soft," he rests his warm hand on my hips before tracing his fingers lightly up my side across my stomach and down to the edge of my panties. "Cold again, Miss Thorne?" He chuckles as my hard nipples strain against my plain white cotton bra. I struggle to contain a moan and I feel my back lift a little from the bed.

"Did I say you could move? I don't think I did?" He removes his hands and I whimper at the loss of his touch. I instantly still. "Good girl." I can hear the smile in his voice and it makes me smile too. He hooks his fingers into the edge of my panties and gradually pulls them down. My breath hitches, and I pinch my eyes shut. "Eyes, Miss Thorne. Oh I want to see your beautiful eyes when I make you come; keep them open." It's an effort, but I open my eyes, my stare fixed on some innocuous patch on the ceiling. I feel a slight dip in the bed, and then his arms cage my thighs as he holds my hips and draws circles with his thumbs. I want to wriggle and squirm, but I don't want him to stop. The scorching heat from his breath is just above my sex, and I'm trembling in anticipation. He can feel it, he chuckles. "You're so responsive. I bet you're dripping right now, before I even touch you." I'm thinking he's probably right.

"Arhh!" I yell as he drags his finger through my soaking folds.

"Fuck, Bethany, that's so fucking hot!" He continues to stroke in a tortuously slow rhythm. I need to move to release this pressure or I'm going to…

"Arhhh!" My body arches from the bed as he sinks a finger deep inside and curls to stroke the most sensitive of spots. Fuck! An uncontrollable full-body shudder engulfs me, and I can't catch my breath. Sparks of light dart across my tightly squeezed eyes, and my core clenches and continues to contract around his fingers, trying to make the pleasure last. He massages me lightly bringing me down from the *second* most amazing orgasm he has drawn from me--two for two, Mr. Stone. I sag deeper into the covers.

"Did you close your eyes?" His voice is raw, his eyes intense.

"Oh, sorry. Yes, I did, I couldn't help it." I lift my head and smile, surely that's a compliment. I can't read his expression, I can see the desire, but I can't read the mood.

"Well, let's try that again, then, shall we?" He is grinning.

"Again? You're serious? I don't think I can, no offense," I

quip.

"None taken," he replies playfully. Oh, good, he is in good mood.

"Fuck!" I scream as he takes a long sweep of his tongue up the sensitive folds and circles my clit. He is in a good but serious mood.

"Eyes!" He growls. I force my eyes wide and breathe deeply to try and steady my racing heart. He clamps one arm across my hips to hold me in place as I feel the need to evade this onslaught of pleasure. His tongue is relentless and despite my misgivings I can feel the familiar build of pressure as he takes long steady sweeps, from the top of my clit down to my entrance where he dips the tip of his tongue further into my body.

"Oh God, Daniel, I…" I'm panting, breathless and gasping.

"Don't you dare close your eyes, I want to see you come, I want you to come." He looks up through his long lashes as his tongue is replaced with expert fingers as he pushes me once again over the edge.

"Fuck." I manage to grind out through gritted teeth and I manage to keep my eyes open. A warm sheen covers my body and I am equally on fire as I am chilled with uncontrollable shivers. Before I can come down fully from my second high of the evening, Daniel once again places his mouth over my clit and sucks in a deep swirling motion, gently grazing the nub with his teeth. I feel the rush of an instant orgasm on me, and I scream. I hope he can't see my eyes now, because there is no way I can keep them open. My hips buck wildly against the extra pressure Daniel has placed on me to prevent that very movement. My back arches as I release an agonising moan. I don't know where that orgasm came from, but it has shaken me to my core, and I am left in a quivering heap, unable to move. Daniel continues to lightly lap at me with his tongue carefully avoiding the over-sensitive tissue.

He crawls up my body, and he sits, his strong thighs pinning me to the bed. My eyes may be open, but I can still see large black blobs floating across my field of vision. His fingers trace up my tummy and push behind my back. He unclips my bra and gently pulls it from my arms. "You have perfect tits." This makes me smile. This whole situation feels kind of out of this world, so to hear such a normal, somewhat crude, turn of phrase, makes it a little more real. His hands are hot, and he squeezes then runs his thumb and fingers across my tightened nipples, rolling and pinching. The sensation is sending sparks directly to my clit. I can again feel a slow throb between my legs. Jeeze, this can't be normal?

"Mmmm, now I'm pretty sure you could come again if I continue to do this, but really, I am so fucking hard, I can't think of anything else right now other than being buried deep inside you." I smile, and my breath hitches. He is right about coming again. I'm insatiable. I like the feel of his weight on me. I like that his frame covers mine, and he looks so happy. "I want you on top." He demands, my smile fades. He repeats in a reassuring tone. "I would like you on top, Bethany, because you are very tight and I am…" He pauses to look down.

"Fucking enormous!" I add my contribution with a grin.

"Well, anyway, you can control how deep and how far much better if you are on top." I hear him swallow deeply at his own explanation, but that sort of makes sense. I nod tentatively.

"I need to hear an answer, Miss Thorne." He holds my gaze, his eyes pools of liquid lust.

"Yes, Sir," I say with a mix of false confidence and true nerves.

"Good girl." He stands and removes his trousers and boxers in one smooth move, taking his socks and shoes too. He pulls his shirt over his head and my mouth waters. His chest is carved muscle, tanned and defined. He has a sprinkling of hair that gathers at his happy trail and he has that curve of muscle at his hip that seems to point to all the goodness. He is way, way better than the diet coke man, because he is real, and he is in front of me. My mouth is dry, and as I think about his taste on my tongue, I lick my lips to try and generate some moisture.

"Hold that thought, Miss Thorne, I need to bury myself inside you first." He tears the foil wrapper in his hand and expertly sheaths himself. I push the unwelcome thought of why he is so proficient at the task from my own lust-addled brain. He then crawls, again like a panther up my body, devouring me with a predators' gaze. He slides his strong arms round my back, and he holds me tight. I can feel the hard steel of his erection against my stomach, and I clench at the thought. He flips me over so I am on top, my face pressed against his hard pectoral as he runs his fingertips up my spine, leaving a tiny trail of sparks. He takes one hand up into my hair and pulls it into his tight fist. I am forced to meet his gaze. The look we share is pure desire.

"I want this; I want this so fucking much it hurts! Tell me you want this, Bethany." His voice is ragged. I try to nod, but he tightens his grip holding my hair and raises his brow.

"Yes, Sir," I exhale my reply.

"No, Bethany, I need to hear *you* say you want this." His tone is serious, and I look again and see a flash of uncertainty in his eyes, but then it's gone.

"I want this, Daniel." I do, I have never felt desire like this, didn't know you could feel like this. It's a paradox; I am scared shitless and horny as hell.

He holds my waist and pushes me from his body, he then takes my hips and lifts me above his proud erection. I take my weight on my knees and hover. He reaches between us and positions the head of his cock at my entrance, sliding it back and forth through my wet folds. I drop my head, and he lets out a small groan. "Relax, baby, you're in charge." This sweet endearment makes my chest clench. I swallow and take a long breath out as I push down onto his waiting cock. I instantly clench at the pain and shut my eyes. When Daniel growls softly from the back of his throat, I open them and am rewarded with such intensity and desire, I will myself to relax or at least not grimace quite so much. I continue to push down, taking inch after excruciating inch. I focus on my breathing in an attempt to relax and take more of him. "Jesus, Bethany, you're so fucking tight." He is gripping my hips, but not pushing me down. I can see the concentration in his face, as he tries to control himself. I shift slightly and sink a little further.

"Fuck! " He presses his head back into the pillow. "Take it all, baby. You have to take it all." He moans. I feel a burn inside me spur me on and I push myself hard and finally sink low enough to take his cock whole. I am throbbing, I'm on fire and I am full, stretched to a point of pain. I let out the breath I'd been holding and draw in some smaller pants as my body begins to accommodate the intrusion of a lifetime. My head drops to my chest. I take a few steadying breaths and start to move my hips. Not sure what to do with my hands I place one on my thigh and one on his, I can feel the muscle in his leg flex and relax with every roll of my hips. "Oh, fuck." Daniel's voice sounds shaky and raw. He continues to hold my hips, ,but now that he is buried deep in me, he seems happy to assist with the rhythm. He pulls me up and down in a controlled motion, and I rock my hips feeling him move deep inside. There is no sharp pain now just an intense feeling of pleasure from the friction and a deep stirring within.

"I want you to come with me Bethany, can you do that?" His voice is strained, concentration evident on his handsome face.

"I … I" I stutter, my concentration is all over the place. There is no way I can control this.

"Listen to me." He takes a deep breath and continues to grind a movement against me that is insanely good. My head falls back. "Bethany!" I snap back to him, my eyes wide. "You are going to come with me, and you are going to keep your eyes open, I need to see you?" His stern tone has me instantly nodding my compliance.

"Yes, Sir." I slide a little further up and fall back firmly. I'm feeling a little bold.

"Fuck!" He growls. He grabs my hips more firmly and begins to control my movements. I am under no illusion who is in control now, as if I ever was. I am rolling my hips with him and he is moving and changing angle all the time to touch my sensitive spots. I feel the build start within me right away, and I am hoping he can feel it too, because I am nowhere near proficient enough to control the 'when' of my climax. "I can feel you're close, Bethany, you need to look at me." I fix on his dark pools, the intensity sears right through me.

"Oh, fuck." I gasp, my body starting to convulse, and my core beginning to clench around him. "Daniel, please," I beg. "Please, I can't."

"I know baby, it's all right. Let go, Bethany, I've got you. I want you to come for me." His soothing tone and sensual words send me right over the edge, again. "Come with me." He continues to thrust into me and continues to maneuver my hips to make sure I take every bit of his release. I'm suspended in a daze of ultimate pleasure. Every muscle in my body contracting, pulsating, and from the muted sound in my ears all I can hear is the beat, beat, beat of my heart. I fall flat against his heaving chest and have no intention of moving, ever.

He does, though, a moment later, he sits up taking me with him, and we are nose to nose, panting breath to panting breath. "Eyes, Miss Thorne?" I open mine to see his dazzling smile, but we are back to Miss Thorne again, and I think I prefer baby, or at least, Bethany. He thrusts, and I can't believe he's still hard; I grip my lips together to stifle a yelp. He chuckles and the vibrations ripple through my body. "I believe I said I would take my time with you, Miss Thorne. I also believe I said I was going to fuck you all night, and you will come to appreciate I am a man of my word." He leans to plant small kisses below my ear and whisper, "And there is so much more to explore, Miss Thorne." With this promise, he resumes his languid thrusts as he holds my shoulders pulling down with some pressure and holding me firm. The guttural growl from the back of his throat fires up my senses and I can feel my core begin to respond. I am running on adrenaline and lust, because I barely have the energy to lift my eyelids. "Eyes!" He warns. "You have the most amazing fucking eyes. I need to see them, do you understand?" I keep them open and look deep into his.

"Daniel." My voice is breaking. I'm very distracted by each heavenly thrust. Building the pleasure, pushing me but not enough to gain the release I know I am going to need, the release that I'm going to be begging for if he continues this pace. "Please, please Daniel, I don't think, I mean I know you can but I'm not so sure I can…" I falter and he interrupts.

"Sorry, Miss Thorne, did I tell you to speak? I must apologize if I gave you that impression. The only words I will accept will be if you scream my name when you come, although you seem to favour 'God' so that will be acceptable too." How can he sound so calm when I am struggling to construct a full sentence? He lifts me slightly and maneuvers smoothly so he is above me, and I feel his delicious weight press down, his thighs angled to keep my legs spread wide. He hooks one of his arms under my knee, lifts my leg onto his shoulder and thrusts. I can't help the cry that escapes me. Fuck, that's deep. Oh, it's so good, though, every nerve and muscle contract wildly against the deepest point of penetration, the euphoric part where pain morphs into sublime pleasure. God, I like it deep but his slow rhythm is driving me mad. I release a frustrated groan, as noises are allowed, I think, and he looks down with a knowing grin.

"In a hurry, Miss Thorne?" He grins as I whimper, but he takes pity on me and begins to increase his speed. I can see his jaw tick and his eyebrows are wrinkled, like he is trying to think of the answer to a really difficult equation. My breath quickens with the speed of his thrusts. He holds himself above me, and his eyes express the same raw need I feel in my core. He takes his hand and slides it between our bodies, and just above our union he uses his thumb to draw circles over my clit. Our bodies move together, slick with a sheen of pure desire, his rougher skin scouring mine, setting mine ablaze. His leg entwines around mine, and his hot sweet breath is like a flame against my neck. Again the familiar tingle and heat begins to build. Just before I am about to explode, he stops and pulls back, sitting on his ankles. I let out a breath and raise myself on my elbows with what little strength I have. I hope I look as confused as I feel.

"God, you're amazing!" He fixes his eyes on mine. He leans forward, and with one hand he squeezes my breast. with his mouth he covers the hard nub of the other. Swirling his tongue and sucking, he switches breast and repeats the same move, each flick of his hot tongue making my core spark. Sitting back up, he runs his hand down the center of my body before he places his hands on my hips and flips me over. My heart has leapt to my mouth. He reaches over and grabs one of the overstuffed ultra-soft pillows. Tapping my bottom, I lift to accommodate the pillow beneath my hips. I swallow hard, wondering what I've gotten myself into. I bury my face into my pillow and let out a smothered moan.

"Miss Thorne, it seems you like it hard, and you *really* like me deep. Well, I promise this will be deep, but we will take it slow. You need to relax." He says this as he must have noticed every muscle in my back and bottom tense. "Bethany, do you trust me?"

"Yes," I reply without hesitation.

"And I think it's safe to say you have more than enjoyed yourself so far, yes?" I nod into the pillow. "Then you have to trust me that you will enjoy this, too." He leans to plant a soft kiss below my ear, and I immediately relax. "Good girl." He sits back, and with one hand he rubs the cheeks of my bottom, creating a scorching heat, and with the other he runs his fingers into my wetness, drawing it back up to my other entrance. His finger rubs in the moisture, applying small amounts of pressure. I moan and take a deep breath. This is extremely sensitive, the slightest touch creating an extreme reaction within my body. His lips are again at my ear. "Relax, that's right, push back against my finger." I do and the tip enters my body, he begins to move his finger in and out, and the feeling of fullness is good, enjoyable even, and I push back a little more. He ventures a little deeper and I get the sensation of a million prickles emanating from my core, spreading wildly across my body, but that is just his finger, his cock is so much bigger. The thought makes me tremble, and I can't stop. My whole body begins to shudder. "Shhhh," he whispers. "It's all right, baby, maybe not tonight?" I must visibly relax because he gives a light laugh. "But this feels good, doesn't it?" I turn my head around to try and see his face. He has a wicked grin, and I smile.

"Yes, yes, it does." My face instantly flames, and I quickly plant it back into to pillow.

He slowly removes his finger and positions his heavy cock again between my sodden, sensitive folds. He pushes slightly against the entrance, and I sigh and push back. In truth I'm a little sore, but I am also hot and needy. "This is going to be deep and hard, and because I've been playing with your arse for the last ten minutes, it's not going to last too long, either. Just thought I should warn you." With that he plunges deep, sinking his entire length into me with a groan. I cry out into the pillow. Oh, my God, he wasn't lying! That is so fucking deep! He pushes harder and faster, hitting the end of my womb again and again. He wraps his hand around the front and strokes my clit in time with each thrust sending me higher. My core instantly clenches around him, gripping, and I push back to meet each thrust. He reaches to grab my hair, fisting it in his grip, pulling my head, and arching my back to accommodate this dominant move. He releases pure guttural sounds, which vibrate from the back of his throat, the urgency of each demanding thrust and the desperate hold he has on my hips combining to ignite the inevitable explosion within me. This level of ecstasy literally causes my eyes to water, and I am thankful that my face is now pressed against the pillow. I know I don't have a huge frame of reference, but I'm thinking crying during sex is not a good thing.

He falls half onto me, half onto the bed. His heavy arm drapes across my back, and I love the feeling of being trapped by him. Certain there are no stray tears, I turn my face to his. He regards me carefully, like I've confused him. He is so handsome, so flawless. His eyes are again brilliant dark blue, and he has the beginnings of stubble, which adds a roughness that would not look out of place on a billboard. His skin sparkles with the sheen of sweat, which lightly covers his body. His full lips give way to a wide smile, which I return.

"Shower?" He doesn't wait for a response but scoops me up in his arms, walks into the bathroom, and carefully places me on the marble top next to the sinks.

"Fuck! Fuck! Fuck!" I bounce and try to put my hands underneath my bottom. The surface is freezing.

"You kiss your mother with that mouth?" He quips.

"Yes, but since she doesn't know who I am most of the time, she doesn't mind." Too late I snap my mouth shut. Shit! Where did that come from? Way to unload.

"What?" He widens then narrows his eyes, as I inwardly curse my big fat mouth.

My laugh sounds faked, but I try deflecting all the same. "Nothing, just a really cold surface." I'm still hopping from one butt cheek to the other, trying to distract him from my comment. "Can I have a bath?" I look longingly at the bathtub. I can't help being seduced; it is a large oval free-standing white bath with overhanging chrome fittings, and it's deep. A bath with Daniel wrapped around me, well, that has to be heaven.

"Sure, but no bubbles. I'll see if there are any salts. It will help with the soreness." He can't be saying sweet things like that or calling me baby. It's confusing as hell and makes my chest tighten. He starts to run the water and the room quickly fills with steam. He comes to stand between my legs and cups my face. I suddenly feel exposed, and my face flushes. "You're so beautiful when you blush." He strokes my newly reddened cheeks.

"You are beautiful all the time." It was his turn to look uncomfortable. I quickly smile, give a slight shrug, and slip off the unit. I slide carefully into the searing hot bath. "Arhhhh. Oh. My. God." I sink back and let out a dramatic sigh. Daniel climbs in behind me, wrapping his long legs around and over mine.

"Well, I'm jealous of the bath now. I want to be the only one able to make you make that noise." He sounds disgruntled, and it makes me giggle.

"You are, it's just I don't have a bath, haven't had a bath since I moved out of Sofia's nearly two years ago. So this is pretty special, but not going to lie, you're the icing!" I sink into his chest, and he wraps his arms around me and holds my breasts.

"Well, if taking a bath was always like this, I would definitely forgo the shower in favour of these." He playfully squeezes my nipples, which in turn happily respond, peaking into taut nubs, despite the heat of the bath. I giggle and wriggle my bottom, instantly feeling his erection harden against my back. "You lived with Sofia? What about your family?" I release a deep sigh and close my eyes, as his heavenly hands caress my neck. His strong thumbs press and roll with varying pressure around each vertebra up into my hair.

"I lived with her family for a while. I have some family but you know the saying, you can choose your friends, but you can't choose …" I can feel him nod. "Well, it's my mantra. Do you mind if we don't do the twenty questions thing? This is kind of perfect, and I don't want to ruin it."

"Not a problem, it doesn't matter, anyway." He lets out a deep sigh and stretches. I frown. I am not sure what he means by that, but I am pleased he doesn't pursue his questioning. He tilts my head back and begins to scoop warm water from the slowly running tap and wets my hair. His fingernails gently scrape my scalp causing an involuntary tremble, and he begins to massage the shampoo into my hair. He again begins to scoop the clean water to wash out the shampoo, taking extra care that no water runs onto my face. Once he is satisfied I am thoroughly rinsed, he kisses my head, then the spot below my ear, and on to my neck. I slip around to face him. He takes my breath away. His perfect features and his soft sensual mouth looks too tempting. I lean in to kiss his lips, but he shifts, and I find I am placing my feather kisses along his set jaw. I sigh, his skin is warm and slippery. His body glistens with a film of water. I kiss his chest, and I lick the water from his nipple and instantly feel his cock twitch beneath me.

"This is not going to happen, baby." He half chuckles. "You will be too sore. Besides, it's already morning, so your night's up!" I must look confused. "I said I would fuck you all night, so consider yourself fucked." He slaps my bottom and lifts me from the bath. I am engulfed by the enormous towel he wraps around me, and he methodically dries every inch of my body. Picking me up again, he carries me to the bed and crawls in beside me, pulling me back into his arms. His warm naked body aligned perfectly with mine, a perfect fit. I sigh as he kisses my hair.

"Daniel." I whisper not sure if he is asleep already.

"Yes." His voice is soft, and it sounds like it is only a matter of minutes before he is.

"Thank you." I want to say more, but at the least I want him to hear this.

"Goodnight, Miss Thorne." I can't prevent the silent tear, which escapes my eye at the disappointing return of my moniker.

Chapter Nine

I ACHE IN MUSCLES I didn't know existed as I embrace the first stretch of the morning. The cotton sheets feel like silk and the bed is deep and luxurious, it takes only a moment to remember where I am. Not that I could confuse this bed with my own. I am, however, alone in the bed. The chill I feel is a stark contrast to the warm covers. I look at the indent of the pillow next to me. I think we barely moved at all last night, but Daniel has definitely moved now. The bathroom door is open, and I can hear no movement, no running water, no sounds at all. I sit up and see that the clothes that were strewn across the floor are no longer there, well, mine are. I sink back into the pillow. My hand rubs my temples to try and ease the pressure I know is about to build. Daniel has left. I take a deep breath and tell myself, '*It is what it is, Bethany*'. I did know that, and I did it, anyway, pretty sure I begged on a few occasions. It was a quick fuck, and it was good. Hell, it was amazing. Sofia had said to listen to my body, and I did, and it was fun. End-of! So that *was* the worst that came from letting go for once. Move on, Bets.

I swing my legs round and sit up, but I flinch at the soreness and aches, I am tender everywhere. Then, too quickly, the world falls away and my stomach rushes to my mouth. I run to the bathroom and quickly and noisily deposit the contents of my stomach. There isn't much, and I am left dry heaving, exhausting my already spent and tired muscles. I collapse on the floor and press my fevered head to the cool tiled floor. Oh, God, this can't be happening. I stand on shaking legs and return to the bedroom, slowly walking over to the sight that made me sick, makes me sick. There, on the nightstand, on top of my purse is cash, lots of cash. The tears, which were waiting until I had finished throwing up, fall freely and silently. Of course, *this* is the worst that could happen. I have honestly never cared what anyone said about me, never, really, and certainly not since John died, but to think that Daniel has paid me for last night rips my heart right out.

God, I am such a fucking idiot. He took me to a hotel and not his apartment. I mean, we actually had to drive past his place. He fucked me all night but never kissed me once on the lips, and of course he didn't want to know about my family, why would he? He had me for the night, he paid, and he left. I look at the clock, its six thirty, but London will be quiet this early on a Sunday, and I need to be home; I need to *not* be here. I grab my dress and shoes; my panties and bra are under the bed. I dress quickly, tie my hair back, and grab my bag. I look at the money. I don't know how much is there, and I can't bear to think how much I was worth, because at this moment I think a penny would be too much. He still has to check out, so if I leave the money, he will think something is wrong, understatement of the year, but the last thing I want is to keep a door open for him now, and leaving the money would do that for sure. He believes I would take money for sex, let him. I take the money, transaction complete--clean, simple, brutal. I grab the cash and leave the room.

I make my way to the stairwell, I am less likely to run into other guests that way. I also make my way to the staff entrance and slip out of the cargo doors, which are open for deliveries. I cross the road and step on to the Embankment pathway. I feel like I am going to be sick again, and I put my head to my knees and take some deep breaths. I start to walk toward the tube station. I notice sitting on the steps of one of the many monuments that dot the Thames, a homeless woman wrapped in a torn sleeping bag.

Curled up next to the bags, which probably contain everything she owns, is a dog, some sort of terrier by the scruff of its coat. I sit next to her as she sleeps; her dog gets over-excited and jumps onto my lap and starts licking profusely at my fingers. She starts to wake and slowly sits up, she frowns and then smiles, picking up her dog and placing it back in her arms.

"Sorry, he's a little over-friendly." She has a rough cough when she speaks.

"He's kind of sweet, very friendly... my name's Bethany--Bets to my friends." I would smile, but I can't make those muscles work for me right now.

"I'm Ruth, and this is Buddy. It's a little early to be dressed like that, honey." She laughs, but it's a friendly laugh, and I'm hardly in any position to take offense. I take my hand from my bag, it's still gripping Daniel's cash. "I'd like you to have this. I don't know how much is here, but if it's more than you need." I sniff out a sad laugh at the irony of what I have just said, and a shameful smile briefly flashes across my face. "I'm sorry, it's just, you know, if you want to share. Look, anyway, it's yours." I press the money into her hand and walk away. I don't look back, but ahead I notice the bright yellow light on top of a taxi. I honestly don't remember how I got home, I don't remember getting in the shower, and I don't remember getting undressed. Which is why I am sobbing, fully clothed on the floor of the staff shower. The sound of the water drowns the noise of the bone-shaking sobs, which wrack my body. I search my mind for a time when my heart didn't ache, a time when I wasn't so lonely.

The sun is streaming through my bedroom curtains, and I would wake instantly, throwing my covers to the wall. It was the first day of the school summer holidays, and I know he's going to be waiting for me. I would grab whatever clothes I could find, cut up jean shorts, t-shirt, and plimsolls, and run down the stairs. If my mum was working, she would be gone by this time, if not,

she'd still be in bed. I would pour a glass of milk and search the cupboards for food I could stuff in my pockets and some extra for John. He never ate breakfast. I would open the back door quietly and leave it on the latch so I could get back in later when everyone was out. I would race around the side of the house. He would be sitting on my front doorstep, waiting, picking at the flaking paint on the door frame. Hearing me, he would look up and tap his arm where a watch should be. It was just after dawn.

At fourteen, he had just started to get a little taller than me. He had dark chocolate brown hair and darker eyes. The first day of primary school, when my sister refused to hold my hand and take me in to the playground, John had walked up to me and said the he would 'take care of me'. He was six years old. Every summer had been the same for as long as I could remember. Some days we would just wander the lanes, sometimes we would venture into the playground, but really we preferred our own company. He had a bike, and when it didn't have a puncture, I would sit on the back, and he would pedal. That way we could go further afield, and I loved that sense of freedom. I remember one hot summer the long grass in the playing fields at the end of my road had been cut, and we spent all morning gathering it up. We piled it as high as a mountain underneath a willow tree which had split and bent in half from old age. One of the thick branches curved high over a stream and into the field. We spent the afternoon in the blistering heat climbing high and flinging our little bodies with fear and delight into the freshly cut grass, only tiring when dusk gave way to the night time. My mother had shouted at John that night as I came home covered in grass cuts and nettle rash. The next day I was bed ridden with sun stroke. I'd had the best day.

John had been distant the day after, and when I pushed him to find out why, he had just said he shouldn't have let me get hurt. it was his responsibility to take care of me. I thought he was mad.

On the rare occasions I would call for him, I was always nervous. I would knock on his door and run to the end of the path, but one day I heard shouting coming from his back yard. I was sixteen at the time. I could hear Vince, John's older brother taking the piss about him for being a virgin, having a little bitch of a girlfriend, but never getting to fuck her. I could see the fury in John's face even from my distance, and my heart started racing. Vince called him, "Chicken shit," and said he only had to ask me. Hell, you didn't even have to ask my sister, he said, she'd fuck you for a fiver. He laughed and went on to say your little bitch will be exactly the same. John flew at him and knocked him to the ground.

I screamed and ran, throwing myself on top of the pile of fighting bodies. I pulled and pulled to break their fighting arms and managed to get between them. John instantly stepped back. I knew he would, he wouldn't risk hurting me. I grabbed his hand and led him away. I could hear Vince's caustic laughter, but I didn't look back. I took John's bike, which was leaning against the garden wall, and told him to take a seat. I rode awhile, heading to the edge of the village, under the motorway bridge. My legs burned with the weight of two teenagers, but I wanted to take him somewhere peaceful. I wanted to go to our lagoon.

When we first started to roam further afield we found this tranquil place that didn't look like it belonged in this world. It was a small shallow lake surrounded with overhanging trees, which hid it from the road and kept it completely in the shade. The banks of the water were soft sand, and if you lay on the shore and looked to the canopy, a million shards of sunlight broke through the foliage. It looked like a fairies' glen, magical. That was when we were little. Now it was just somewhere quiet to take John so he could calm down. John had taken a beating from his brother before, so I knew he wasn't hurt, but I had never seen him look so angry. I tried to laugh a little, attempting to lighten the mood. I said it didn't matter what people said. He could tell Vince and everyone that he fucked me, it didn't matter, it was nothing. He turned his head and his eyes looked so beautiful, but I could see the tears he was holding back. He held my face and told me

*I wasn't my sister, could never be like her, and it **did** matter. If **it** was nothing,, then that made me nothing, and that wasn't true. I wasn't nothing, I was everything.*

I had started college, and John was doing an IT apprenticeship, which meant he spent one day each week at my college. He would meet me on the bus, and we'd walk home together. It was the end of the Christmas term, and I had stayed after class to have a Christmas drink and only just missed my bus. The one I did manage to get was only twenty minutes later, but it turned out that it was twenty minutes too long. I started to walk up the dark footpath, which cut across the back of the fields to the small group of houses where I lived. The street lamp was ineffective, and the darkness meant I didn't see him straight away. It looked like a drunk had settled against the fencing, slumped over, and had fallen asleep, but as I got close, I saw his trainers and recognised his dark green jacket. I dropped my bag and ran the last few meters, kneeling at his side and holding his head in my hands.

John had his eyes closed, and as I pulled one hand away from his hair, my fingers were sticky, slippery, and warm. My hands are covered in dark red liquid, and I look up to see the five-inch rusty, crooked nail poking from the splintered fence post. The nail was glossy and slowly dripped the same liquid onto the damp ground. I cried his name, and he opened his eyes, the rich dark brown now a dull black in the poor light. I couldn't focus for the tears streaming from my eyes, trying to get him to speak. I didn't know what to do. I asked him what to do? His face was swollen with dirt ground into his cheek, and his jacket was ripped. His fists were clenched, and there was blood on his knuckles, but it was the blood gushing down his neck that caused the heart-wrenching sob to escape my lips; there was so much blood. It had started to rain, and I remember his warm eyes as he recognised me. Tiny droplets of rain were suspended on his thick lashes as he closed his lids. He smiled, and he told me again what he told me that day at the lagoon, that I wasn't like her, that I wasn't nothing, I was everything. He kept repeating: I wasn't nothing. He'd fought for me again, but this time I wasn't there to stop him. I couldn't hold him tight enough. I shouted for help, I screamed. I didn't have a phone to call for help, and I couldn't leave him. The world fell silent; it was silent for so long, and I was so cold when I finally heard the footsteps.

The nearness of the footsteps wakes me, my body is still heaving with unshed sobs, and I am so cold, my bones ache. My sore eyes open through the water, which continues to stream over my head and down my back. I look up to where the noise is coming from. There is a loud banging on the door, followed by the sound of splintering wood and a crash as the door to the staff shower flies open, and Daniel fills the doorway.

"Jesus Christ!" He calls over his shoulder, "I've found her." He takes one step toward me and reaches to turn the tap off, which stops the incessant flow of ice cold water over my huddled body. He puts his arms under my trembling knees and lifts me tight to his chest. I feel utterly exhausted, and I can get no relief from my body, which won't stop shaking. His shirt transforms from pale to dark as my wetness is rapidly absorbed by the material, and I can hear the sloshing on the floor as he carries me out into the corridor.

"I'm wet." My teeth chatter as I quietly state the obvious.

He laughs. "Yes, yes, you are, and not in a good way." This makes me jolt, and I stiffen and push myself from his chest, slip to the ground, and stumble on the wet floor. "Shit, what are you doing?" He reaches to steady my fall, and I shrug out from his grip and turn my narrow eyes on him. I must look a state, my hair slicked long to my face, my clothes hanging shapelessly with the weight of the water and the remnants of my make-up dripping down my face. I must resemble Samara from The Ring.

"You don't get to touch me!" I am quiet but my tone is serious. He is shocked, but his face flashes with a look I don't recognize.

"What's going on, Bets?" I turn to see Marco. He too looks shocked.

"What are you doing here?" I ask Marco, but my voice starts to break, and I struggle not to cry again. I really don't need an audience for my meltdown.

"You disappeared." Daniel answers. "You wouldn't answer your phone. I was worried. I came here, but there was no answer, so I went to Marco's flat and followed him here. Like I said, you left, and I was worried." He growls the last few words, like he is trying to control his temper. I don't need to match his temper, I just need him to leave. I speak very slowly and clearly, so there is no misinterpreting what I am about to say.

"I didn't disappear, I left. You paid me. You left. I took the money. I left. Now, I would like you to leave. Again." Each word is softly spoken, clipped and perfectly clear.

"What? Seriously, what do you mean, I paid you? For what?" His tone is incredulous, and his face darkens with a scowl.

"What did you pay her for?" Marco steps closer to me and rests his hand on my shoulder. Daniel narrows his eyes and clenches his jaw at this.

"I didn't pay her for shit! I emptied my trouser pockets and put the contents on the night stand!" He barks out his explanation through gritted teeth.

"Bets, did you take his money? Bets, what were you thinking?" Marco has turned me to face him, but I'm really confused.

"I did, I thought…" Marco picks up my bag, which I had dropped by the door this morning, and starts to search inside.

"Bets, there's no money in here? Bets?" He is looking from my empty bag to my bewildered face.

"No, there wouldn't be. I gave it away to a lady with her dog. She looked cold, and she was sleeping on the monument steps and…" I am rambling now, my head is spinning, and I am trying to understand what is unfolding before me.

"You gave five thousand pounds to a homeless woman?" Daniel asks, the calmness of his tone focuses my attention only on his words

"No, Christ no! I gave her the money on the side. The money

you left for me on my purse!" The pitch in my voice raises, as does my anxiety.

"Yes," Daniel says slowly, "that would be five thousand pound." He pauses and bites his lip with amused understanding. "You think I paid you five thousand pounds?" My worth is irrelevant, but I feel a sting at the reference, and I shake my head to dispel the unpleasant thought.

"What? Didn't I earn it?" I snarl my reply, push past Marco and run upstairs. My door is open, Marco had been looking for me. It was his footsteps above that had filtered into my dream. I don't bother to shut it, as I am quickly followed by both men. Daniel pushes past Marco, but Marco grabs his shoulder. I tense and can feel an overwhelming surge of panic well inside. I am still raw from my recent trip down memory lane. I see the fury in Daniels eyes, his fist is clenched, and he is about to swing round when I scream, "Stop!" I run between them and turn my face to Marco. Out of the two, I know him. I know he will do what I ask and what I do know of Daniel is, he will do exactly what he wants to do. But I can't have them fighting, ever.

"Hey, Marco, it's all right. Look, thank you. Thank you for coming to find me." I hold his face to make sure he is looking at me, not scowling over my shoulder. "You need to leave so I can sort this, okay?" He looks at me now, and I see nothing but concern.

"Boo, are you sure?" I smile when he uses my oldest nickname, brought out at special occasions and tender times. I know he is worried about me.

"He won't hurt me, Marco." I assure him.

He leans in to whisper, "No more than he has, promise?"

"No more, I promise." He glares once more at Daniel and leaves. I shut the door and walk toward my bedroom. I am still shivering and need to get out of these clothes.

"Why did you emphasise the *no more*? What did that mean?" Daniel goes to follow me.

"It's my thing. It means people will always hurt you, but

how much depends on me, so 'no more' means exactly that." I close my bedroom door and start to peel my sodden dress off my goose-pimpled body. The door opens, and Daniel strides in, the tiny space is filled with his immense presence. I stop mid peel.

"What are you doing?" My jaw drops.

"That's fucked up, you know?" He goes to unbutton his shirt. "Besides, I didn't hurt you, Bethany, *you* had a misunderstanding."

"What the fuck are you doing?" I can't believe what I'm seeing. "Stop that! Stop doing what you're doing. Stop it now!" I shout.

"What? I'm soaked! It's a little late to play shy now, don't you think?" He wiggles his brow and continues to strip. I pick up my jeans and a sloppy jumper, underwear, shoes, and storm back out and into my toilet where I lock the door. Christ! I can hear him chuckle through the thin walls. I enter my living room to find him sitting on my sofa in his boxers. His clothes are draped over the back of my arm chair. He flashes the most amazing smile. His skin is golden, his stomach muscles ripple, and his long arm rests on the back of the sofa as an invitation to join him. His black boxer shorts are fitted, and I can see the outline of his cock, semi-firm and growing firmer as I continue to look. My face is instantly hot, and I suck my lips together.

"Bethany." He smiles and beckons me with his fingers, "Don't you think we should talk first?" He is so confident this is going to happen, he can't even pretend to keep a straight face. I straighten my back and meet his heated stare.

"Yes, Daniel, *that* is exactly what we are going to do, talk!" I cross my arms tightly in front as myself, my first line of defense.

"Please sit with me. I would very much like to close this unnecessary distance. I would very much like to feel you close again." His voice is soft and tempting, but I made my promise.

"Not likely." I scoff.

"Really, why? Is it because of the money? Don't think about it. It's already forgotten." He seems genuinely confused by the shock on my face, so I enlighten him.

"You may well be able to do that, but I've spent the last few hours thinking that *you* think I'm a whore! So excuse me if I don't come over, all gushing and eager to resume where we left off! But now that I know you don't think I'm a whore, it's a relief, because, well... that just makes me a thief, now, doesn't it?" My temper is a perfect mask to hide the raw vulnerability I feel.

"The money doesn't matter." His fixed impassive expression heightens his stern tone.

"Doesn't matter? It was five thousand pounds, Daniel! Who does that? Who keeps five thousand pounds in their trouser pocket?" I'm yelling now, but I am so cross. All the anger and hurt from this morning and the pain from my nightmare are all combining to make me more than a little unstable right now, and I have no intention of falling apart in front of Daniel again.

"Well, not to state the bloody obvious, Bethany, but I do." He goes to stand, but I know if he gets close I'll crumble. I grab my bag and head for the door. He can't follow, I hope. He's in is boxers.

"Lock the door when you leave." I run down the stairs and onto the street. I jog to the end, when I hear him shout my name. He did follow me, but just to the door. He looks really mad. I'm not going back there today, maybe not ever.

Chapter Ten

THE TRAIN TO the South Coast town nearest to my mum's care home takes just over an hour, and if you are lucky, there might be a drinks service. The coffee is disgusting, but the tea is bearable, even if it is served at a nuclear temperature. I take a tea and a couple of raisin flapjacks, as I realise I haven't eaten much since lunch yesterday, and my tummy grumbles loudly in acknowledgement of this self-deprivation. I try and spend every other Sunday visiting. This is not one of my weeks, but if I have to be out all day, it's a perfect use of my time. Besides, right now I could really use my mum. I dig in my bag and find my iPod. I put my earphones in and select Snow Patrol *Eyes Open* album to listen to on a loop as I watch field after field speed past. I catch myself in the window as we pass under a tunnel, and even in the faded reflection, I can see my eyes are red and swollen. I rest my head back and close my tired lids hoping to sleep before the haunting lyrics of "Set the Fire" bring more tears.

I wake just as we near the hills of the South Downs. The sheer expanse of green is a stark contrast to my normal urban terrain. It is beautiful, and when she was able, I would take my mum to walk up one of the beacons for the breath-taking views. It was such an effort, it would take most of the day, but she can no longer make that climb. Most visits we sit in the conservatory or walk around the gardens. The buses don't run on Sunday and it's a five-mile walk, which at a good pace I can do in an hour. The gravel drive sweeps up to the main Georgian house. More modern accommodations have been added to the side, but the main house holds most of the facilities: games room, lounge, conservatory, and dining room. I sign in and am told my mum is in the craft room.

I open the door and swallow a lump back as she turns to face me. She is bathed in sunlight from the large window and, with her pale clothes and grey hair, she is encased in a warm glow and looks like an angel. She smiles at me, and I hope in my heart it's a good day. On a good day she remembers my name, remembers who I am, and she talks for hours about our life, about the holidays we had, the meals she likes to cook, and how I was never there, always off gallivanting. I take a seat next to her and put my bag at my feet. She takes my hand and squeezes, hers are soft as silk and warm to my cold.

"Hello, my dear. Have you come to help me with these flowers?" She points to a spread of wild flowers, which have been carefully pressed, losing only a little of their vibrant colour. She laughs a little and looks into my eyes. I can see the extra wrinkles form in her brow as she fights to remember. "I think I am going to need all the help I can get. I'm getting in a pickle. What's your name, my dear?" She smiles at me, and I feel the tingle of tears behind my eyes, but I don't let them fall.

"My name is Bethany, and I would love to help, if you don't mind." My chest pinches, but I manage to smile.

"Not at all, not at all. My daughter usually helps me, but she isn't coming this week." She pats the table to make a start.

"No, that's right." I murmur, happy that she remembers this is not my week. We spend the day making pictures with the flowers and a book mark for me. We read and have afternoon tea on the patio. I would normally head home after tea, but I stay a little longer. I know I'm hoping she remembers me before I leave, and I also know it's not going to happen. We settle in her room and

I put on one of her favourite films, *Gone with the Wind.* I know this was before her time, but I think it was my Gran's favourite, too, so it may well be a shared memory. I will have to slip out before it finishes. It's over three hours long and the last train back is at nine. *Tara* is burning, and I choose this time to leave. She is asleep in her chair, so I kiss her on the head. I wouldn't do this if she was awake, only if she knows who I am.

I look outside the front door. Wow, my luck just keeps getting better. The heavens have opened up. I didn't grab my coat in my hurry to leave, and I don't have enough money for a taxi. I hunch my shoulders and walk out into the rain. Twice in one day, soaked to the skin in seconds, a new record for me. It's dark, and the paths are poorly lit with sporadic street lighting. The cold rain is trickling down my neck, its seeps through my jumper to my bra, and through my jeans to my panties. My soft canvas pumps squelch with every step and are unlikely to survive the night. I am cold in my bones, and my body tries to compensate with violent shudders. I hear a car draw up slowly behind me, and I pick up my pace. In my peripheral vision I can see it gaining on me, and I start to jog looking for a road to turn down or a house with lights on to walk up to. The car pulls in front and stops, my heart stops. I hear the door open, but turn before I see who gets out. I run flat out when I hear the loud commanding voice. "Will you stop fucking running away from me!" I skid to a halt and turn, my eyes squinting against the driving rain. It's him. Daniel is standing against his opened door. He gets in and reverses next to me, screeching to a halt. He leans over to open the passenger door.

"Get in the car." He demands curtly. I hesitate. "Get in the fucking car, Bethany!"

"No, I mean I would, but I'm soaked and your car, your leather will get ruined." I bend and add a small smile.

"Get in the car, if I have to ask again I will put you in myself, and believe me, you do not want that." He looks fierce. I grab the door and slide in, hovering above the seat in a poor attempt to keep the leather dry. "Just sit down, Bethany. Put your belt on and sit down." His voice is softer, and his eyes crinkle in a gentle smile. I sit and pull my seatbelt across. He starts up the car when I have an idea. I unclip the seatbelt and the car instantly starts to 'ping' at my disobedience. "Bethany, I swear," he grumbles.

"-No, look I'll only be a minute, I really don't want to ruin your leather." With that, I pull my sweater over my head and put it in the foot-well behind my seat. Daniel coughs, and I can see his eyes widen. I undo my jeans and peel them down my wet legs, taking my dripping socks with them. I put them on top of the sweater and reach back to clip the seatbelt in place. "There, damage limited to a minimum, but some extra heat might be good." I grin and vigorously rub my naked arms.

"You honestly think I'm going to be able to concentrate on driving with you sitting there half naked, wet and pert? I'd rather risk the leather than crash the whole bloody car!" His voice is deep, throaty, and he sounds deadly serious.

"Oh, sorry, I didn't…" I go to reach for my clothes but his hands stops me.

"It's fine. In fact, from where I'm sitting it's more than fine." He flashes a playful grin that borders on wicked. "Not so shy now, Miss Thorne?"

"Well, you've had your finger in my arse, just how shy can I be around you?" I raise my own brow at my rhetorical question.

"Fair point, Miss Thorne." He presses some buttons, and I feel a warm glow radiate across my back and on my bottom. He also points a stream of warm air directly at my body. I shiver slightly, but I am starting to warm through. It is silent in the car, and I look out into the darkness. We hit the motorway, and neither of us has spoken.

"How did you find me, Daniel?" I break the silence first.

"You never answer your phone. Why don't you ever answer your phone?" I can hear the frustration in his tone.

"That's another of my things, the phone, I mean. My phone is for my convenience. I use it when I need it, not to be at everyone's' beck and call. It's for emergencies only."

"This was an emergency!" I jump at his volume. He lets out a long breath, his voice a little softer when he speaks again. "I found Sofia's number in your flat, and she told me, after my twelfth unanswered call to you, that you were probably visiting your mother, but she didn't know the name of the home, just the name of the town. Do you know how many residential care homes there are in this town?" He still sounds irritated.

"No."

"Lots!" The car goes silent again.

"Bethany?" His deep voice breaks the silence but not the tension.

"Mmmm?"

"Why didn't you tell me you were a virgin?" His voice is soft and soothing. It needs to be, as I am instantly on edge.

"How did you…who told you?" I suck in a sharp breath.

He sighs softly. "No one told me. No one needed to tell me, and before you start berating yourself that you were a lousy lay," he pauses and almost whispers, "you were amazing."

"Does it matter?" I ask softly.

"Yes and no." I look at his face all hard lines and strong features, but his smile is sweet and kind. He reaches over and holds my thigh gently tracing circles with his thumb. I feel the electricity with each stroke. "No, I still would have wanted you, but yes, I would have taken more care with you, if I had known, if you had been honest with me." He grumbles the last part.

I laugh at this. "Really? And how would that conversation have gone exactly? Would I have told you before you told me you were going to punish me, before you told me I was going to scream your name when you make me come, or after you told me you were going to fuck me hard all night? At which point was I going to disclose that nugget of information and not see you running for the hills?"

"I don't run, Bethany." He calmly replies. "And we will never know how that conversation would have gone, will we?" He is quiet for a while before he asks. "So are you telling me that you didn't want me running for the hills?" He looks at me with a raised brow but not an ounce of doubt in his expression.

"No, Daniel, I didn't want that. I wanted last night. But this morning--after this morning I don't want..." I drop my head, unable to finish this line of thought.

"Bethany, what did I do to make you think what you thought?" He voice is laced with genuine concern.

I pause for endless seconds before I answer. "It was the money that made me think it, the other things just made sense after the money."

"What other things?" He catches my eye and he looks genuinely shocked.

"You took me to a hotel, Daniel. A hotel we had to drive past your apartment to get to. You said it didn't matter about the information about my family, and your friends the other night said that you've never had a relationship that you didn't pay for."

"You heard that?" he interrupts.

"I'm staff, Daniel, we hear everything." I am quiet, and I barely voice the words, "You never kissed me." My body jerks as he swerves the car on to the hard shoulder and punches the hazard lights. In an instant, he has released my seatbelt and has pulled me on to his lap, his hands gripping my face as he covers my mouth with his. I go to gasp, and he takes this opportunity to dart his hot moist tongue in to find mine. His lips are full and soft, his kiss is heated, demanding, breath-stealing, everything I wanted last night and so much more. His hands move to my hair, and he grips, causing a moan deep in my throat. He moves his mouth, hungry for mine, his tongue dipping in and around, tasting and swirling with mine. My pulse is racing, and a fire in my core makes me shift on his lap, fully aware of the massive erection straining in his jeans. He moans and presses harder against my mouth. My hands move to his hair, tentative at first, then hungry too. The glossy strands slip between my fingers, and I grip and pull, securing his head as I return each of his heated moves with my mouth. He pulls my hair back, breaking our contact. My eyes are glazed, but his are feral. He rests his forehead to mine and takes a deep calming breath. I'm still panting.

He picks me up and carefully places me back on my seat. He leans his strong arm across to grab the seat belt and places a warm soft kiss lightly on my lips before returning to his seat.

"Have I addressed *that* concern for you, Bethany?" His tone is calm yet commanding.

"Yes, Daniel." I smile and drag my lips through my teeth, tasting the tingle he left behind.

"Good, now for your other concerns, allow me: I took you to the hotel because I wanted to have breakfast in bed with you, and my housekeeper is away, and I have no food at my place, as you will know from Friday. I thought it would be special and would give us some more time in bed." He turns a sinful grin my way. "The other night my *friend* was referring to the fact that I do not have relationships. My relationships are business relationships, and as such, I do pay for them. I make a great deal of money from them, but I do pay in some fashion, either with my time or financially."

I pull my legs to my chest and turn in my seat to face him. I don't know if he is telling me the truth, or whether I just want to believe what he is telling me, and that is a worry.

"You weren't there." I hate that I sound so needy; that he makes me needy.

"I know, and for that I am truly sorry. I woke up and went to find the night manager about opening up the boutique downstairs. I wanted to get you something to wear for when we left. I didn't think you would be comfortable leaving the hotel in the same clothes. I thought I would be back before you woke up." He has a slight frown. I can't help thinking if he hadn't been so thoughtful, none of this would have happened.

"That's unbelievably sweet. I can't believe you would do that and I can't believe what a complete shit that makes me." I let my head drop, feeling the rightful rush of shame.

"No, don't. You're not, not at all. When you explain it all like you have, I can understand why you felt the way you did, and why you reacted the way you did." He is quiet for a while, and I ask something that's been swirling around my head since I met him.

"Daniel, what do you want from me?" He flashes me a wicked smile, and I tingle with heat and anticipation.

"What I want, what I would very much like, is to start over, now that you *know* I don't think you are a whore." I lightly snort, I am not sure I'm quite ready to joke about this yet, but a 'do-over' sounds good.

"Ok." I return his grin.

"Good girl." His tone is sensual, and he waits a few agonizing minutes in silence before he continues. "Now, what I want you to do is turn and face the front and put your feet on the dash."

"Oh," I let out a heavy breath.

"Oh," He exhales slowly. I put my feet on the dash and wiggle down. He presses a button to fully recline my seat. "Now Miss Thorne, I want you to do exactly as I say." I can see his grip on the steering wheel tighten and his knuckles whiten. "I want you to run your fingertips slowly from your knees all the way down your thighs up your stomach right up to your perfect tits. Skate the edges of your bra and then back down your sides, to your thighs and back to your knees." My fingers twitch and start to follow his instruction. My light touch almost tickles, and I wiggle and flinch as my contact touches my side at my waist. "Hold still, or I will pull over and use that seatbelt to restrain you." I feel his hand grab the inside of my thigh, the heat scorches my skin, and I breathe in sharply. I continue to stroke my body, my skin hypersensitive to my touch, and I feel an increasingly desperate need to move. I moan and grit my teeth. I hear him chuckle as he drops his hand to the apex of my thighs and draws his finger back and forth along the top of my panties. "I want you to hold your tits and pinch your nipples, but I want you to picture it is me holding your firm soft tits, and it's me pinching and tugging at your hard aching nipples". Oh fuck, he has the sexiest voice. I reach for my breasts and moan as my back begins to arch. "Miss Thorne." He sternly brings me back to attention. I let out a frustrated breath. "We can stop if you would prefer? If you are too frustrated?"

"No. No!" I slowly release a breath. "No, Sir." Trying my hardest not to reveal my continued frustration, I do not want him to stop.

"Good girl. Now you are going to want to move, but it's really important that you keep still. I can't have you flailing about while I am trying to keep this car on the road. Do you understand?"

"Yes, yes, Sir, I understand." My throat is dry, and I swear you can see my heart thumping against my chest.

He resumes his leisurely trail of his finger along the edge of my panties, and I release some of the building ache from my breast with a gentle squeeze. "If that is me who is supposed to be doing that, don't you think I would be a little firmer, pinch a little harder?" I follow his instruction and am rewarded by a guttural noise from his throat. He slips his finger beneath my panties and into my wet soft folds. He draws a sharp breath, and I bite my lip at the ecstasy of this movement. "Fuck, Bethany, you're so wet." He shifts in his seat but keeps his finger deep in my folds, curling up and around. I swallow and fight to remain still. I can see his jaw clench, and I know he struggles, as I do, to keep control. He slows his movement. "I think we need to finish this later." We are nearing the outskirts of the city and there is more light in the car now. My face is flush, and I am struggling to catch a decent breath.

"No, no, Daniel, please, please, don't stop." I am wound so tight, I'm not above begging right now. He laughs.

"All right, Miss Thorne." With that he plunges as deep as the angle of his arm will allow and curls his fingers enough to put pressure on a sweet sensitive spot inside while simultaneously using the heal of his hand to rub my clit. He has me trembling instantly. I can't breathe, and I push my head hard into the seat to stop any involuntary movement from my body as it spasms and contracts in wave after rippling wave of intense orgasm. I can't help my legs clamping together, trapping his hand, and extracting the last bit of pleasure from the slow and tortuous movement of his finger. I shudder, and my skin is sprinkled with a million goose bumps. "Should I turn the heaters up?"

"God, no! I'm on fire!" I gasp, trying to regain a normal breath. I release my grip on his arm, and he slowly removes his fingers, squeezing my thigh with his hand briefly before he brings his fingers to his mouth and sensuously sucks them clean. He takes them from his mouth with a popping sound.

"Yes, you are, but given that we are likely to be stopping in traffic when we hit town, there is a blanket behind my seat. I would like you to use it to cover yourself." He looks to me and adds. "My eyes only, Miss Thorne. I told you before, I don't share." His tone and expression are extremely serious. I lean my arm back and grab the softest blanket. It feels like cashmere. I sit up and wrap it around my shoulders and fold it tight across my body. It's large and covers me completely.

"Better?" I ask.

"Not in the least, but I'd rather have you covered than take the risk of someone else seeing what's mine." The timbre in his deep voice is filled with authority.

"Daniel, I'm not yours. I don't belong to anyone, but I'm definitely not yours." I admonish.

"Really?" He sounds playful, but I'm not sure he wants to play this game with me.

"Really, Daniel. This"--I slip my arm from the blanket and wave between us--"is fun, amazing, really, hot and mind-blowing. Not that I think your ego needs a boost but I'm being honest when I say I couldn't have fantasized a better first time. But it's nothing more than that, it won't ever be anything more than that. So you need to be fine with that or this"--I wave again--"ends tonight."

"Oh, I liked that little speech, Miss Thorne, especially the bit about mind-blowing." I laugh, I knew he would. "Would you like to tell me why, or is this just another of 'your things'?"

"One of my 'things', and no, I'm not going to elaborate." I happen to think he has learned enough about me already without my help, and this isn't a full disclosure type of arrangement.

"Well, Bethany." He reaches under the blanket to gently hold my leg, squeezing and stroking with his thumb. "I would like you to know that you are quite wrong, but like you, I choose not to elaborate." He smiles a hugely confident smile, which makes me laugh, but I just shake my head and mumble under my breath.

"Whatever." I look out of my window and see we are nearly at my place.

"I'm not taking you home. You're coming to my apartment." He states.

"What! No! I can't, I have to go home, I have work to do." I panic, it's late, and I still have a Late Night call to deal with.

"Work? This late?" He looks across and grins. He thinks I'm making excuses.

"Daniel, yes, I still have work to do. I should've been working on my reading all day, so I'm behind. I have other stuff to deal with, and I'm a little tired, so I would really like to go home-- to my home." I plead. His eyes soften, but he is not giving up.

"What stuff?" He presses for details.

"Ok, specifically, I have some clothes soaking on my toilet floor that will be ruined if I don't sort them out. They aren't mine, and I kind of rely on the wardrobe share deal I have with Sofia. I have my other laundry to deal with. I have to sort out how I'm going to catch up on my reading, and I have to body wash. Oh, and I probably have to call Sofia, who will be really pissed I haven't called her. Is that detailed enough for you, Sir?" I add with a bit of unnecessary attitude.

"You know when you call me Sir, I'm instantly hard and much less likely to drop you home?" He murmurs. "What do you mean by body wash? I'm extremely interested in what that is." He deepens his timbre.

"Well, as sexy as you make that sound, since you broke the

shower door I now have to wash myself in my sink." I look over to him. "My reality is not quite so sexy now, eh?" I know I'm putting a downer on the mood, but my life is so far removed from his, and I'm too tired to pretend that it's not.

"I'm sorry. Why don't you come back with me, have a bath, relax, and I'll drop you back in the morning?" Oh, God, he couldn't be sweeter, and now he's found my Achilles heel.

"You honestly have no idea how good that sounds, but I can't do the walk of shame three mornings in a row." I cringe at the very thought.

"Three?" He is shocked.

"Yes. Friday night I panicked, thought you might show up all angry so I stayed at Marcos' and he dropped me back in the morning. Having to walk past a kitchen full of men in last night's clothes wasn't my finest hour." I smile weakly, but he is frowning, and his jaw twitches.

"You stayed at Marcos'?" I sense the agitation in his tone.

"Wow, that's what you took from that? Yes, I stayed with my best friend. You know what I said about me choosing my friends, not family? Well, Marco is my best friend and my *brother*." His shoulders relax a little, and I reach over and grab his thigh. Its hard and has very little give as I try to squeeze some reassurance. "Any other time and I'm there, really. Me and a luxury bath; separated at birth! But tonight I need to be home." I squeeze again, still no give, but I notice he turns off the main road toward the back of the restaurant. He parks on the pavement beside my door, gets out, walks around to my side, opens my door, and asks for my keys.

"Stay there, don't move!" He looks grumpy as he opens my door and returns to me. He lifts me and holds me tight to his chest and carries me up to my apartment, then places me like I'm made of china on my sofa. He runs back down to the car and I think he's gone when I hear the door slam. Less than a minute later he re-enters my apartment with my wet clothes and my bag. Placing them on the floor, he comes to sit next to me and pulls me into his lap, his big arms holding me, warm and tight. I feel my body relax into his, and I am dangerously close to falling asleep. I shift to move, and he tightens his hold.

"Did I say you could move, Miss Thorne?" His rough tone makes me tingle and giggle at the same time.

"You know I would love to play the 'Sir' game with you right now, but that isn't going to help my plans for tonight." I wriggle again, and he releases his hold with a grunt. "Thank you for the ride." It's my turn for a cheeky grin, "…and thank you for coming to get me. Oh, and thank you for carrying me in, very gallant, Sir." I smile and give a mock curtsey. A rumble sound comes from deep in his throat.

"Oh, and you expect me to leave when you come over all subservient?" He stalks toward me.

"Oh, shit!" I jump out of his reach. "No! No! Oh God! I really don't have time. Please, please, Daniel, you have to leave." I'm begging, and the submissive remark has just made my plea more urgent as I have a booked call in fifteen minutes.

"Oh, and now you're begging? There is no way I can leave now." His grin is dangerously wicked, my heart is beating rapidly, and just the thought of succumbing makes my mouth water. I lick my dry lips.

"Daniel," I try to warn as he approaches.

"Miss Thorne." His voice is deep and throaty.

"What do I have to do to get you to leave right now?" I plead. I'm desperate.

"Mmmm, well, it would have to be pretty spectacular given what I want to do to you right now." I try to swallow, and my face flushes bright red. "Dinner tomorrow, and you stay at mine, so I have you all night. No walk of shame, you can bring a change of clothes."

"I'm working tomorrow." I plead.

"Don't!" He snaps with irritation, real life interfering with his plans again.

"It's not that simple; I have commitments" I try to argue.

"Make me your commitment.'" He goes to sit down.

"Okay, I'll swap my shift. Dinner, but I can't stay over, I have to be back by one." I huff with exasperation.

"Why? Do you turn into a pumpkin?" He grins, and I laugh out loud, but he goes to lower himself on to the sofa.

"I'm definitely the pumpkin in that fairy tale," I mutter. "No, I do have some bits I can't do in the day, and I do better at night." His grin widens, so I add, "Without interruption. Dinner would be lovely. An evening with you would be more so, but, please, I need to be home by one." My final plea has him hovering above his seat before he stands up.

"You know, Miss Thorne, I am going to put that begging to much better use." He reaches me, and I tilt my head to maintain eye contact as he towers above me. His eyes are dark and deep; he reaches his hands to my face, leaning in, his warm mouth covers mine. A small moan escapes, and I feel my knees weaken. His strong arms encase my small frame, and he holds me against his tight body. The heat and desire I feel build from my toes and course through my veins. My heart starts racing as his tongue swirls and laps at mine, devouring every bit of me with sweet tender adoration. His lips are soft, and he captures mine lightly between his teeth and draws my bottom lip as he moves away. I am chilled by the loss of his heat and hot from the intensity of his kiss. I sag and whimper as he turns to leave. "Until tomorrow. And Bethany?"

"Yes?" I can barely hear my own words.

"Answer your fucking phone!" His demand is clear, and as I hear the door slam and click locked, I answer.

"Not an option tonight!" I softly reply, glad he doesn't hear.

I'm naked in bed with my phone in front of me. It's twelve fifty-nine. My phone starts to ring, and I answer exactly on one.

"Sir."

"Good evening, Lola." His voice sounds deeper than the other night, but the background echo remains.

I was unaware of my nerves until his smooth voice calms me. "Good evening, Sir."

"I have missed talking to you this weekend. Have you been a good girl?"

"I don't believe I have, Sir."

"Really? Interesting." He draws in a slow breath before he continues. "Would you like to tell me what you are wearing for me tonight?"

"Sir, I am naked and lying in my bed"--I pause--"waiting for your call." I smile because I am happy that I am not telling a lie.

"I like that, but tell me, did the items I sent you not fit?"

"Oh, I don't know, I haven't tried them on." I feel a flush of embarrassment at this rudeness.

"Is that how you show your gratitude for gifts?"

"No, Sir." I don't think it's appropriate to give excuses, given the nature of this type of conversation.

"No, I agree. I would like you to put the first set I sent you on, now. Please put your phone on speaker, and I want you to tell me everything you are doing."

"Yes, Sir." I press the speaker button and place the phone on my pillow. I retrieve the box from the corner of my room and remove the bra and panties. "It's quite beautiful, Sir. The black lace is very delicate. I am slipping the panties up my legs and over my hips. The material is soft and sits high on the arch of my hip. It's very flattering; it makes my legs look longer. The bra is a little tricky, and I am having to slip it over my head because of the multiple straps. The lace lifts my breasts and holds them firmly. They look more prominent."

"Are your nipples hard, Lola?" His voice is like gravel.

"Yes Sir, they are. They ache a little. The delicate lace moves over the sensitive ends and I can feel tingles shoot through me." I feel warm inside because again it feels good to tell the truth. "The straps that cross my body make me feel like I'm being restrained."

"And how does that feel, Lola?" He pauses before he says my name, like he is having trouble with it for some reason.

"I like the way it makes me feel, excited with anticipation." My breathing is becoming a little deeper.

"Good. Now, Lola, I want you to lie back down on your bed." He pauses until he hears no more movement. "You will know by now that I have pre-booked all your calls and I will continue to do so. I don't like to share." I get a shiver at this sentiment. Daniel has expressed the same with the same determined tone, but my caller sounds nothing like Daniel. His voice is low and deep, and Daniel's is raw, like pure undiluted sex. He continues. "Sometimes I may not call but I will know you are waiting for me. That makes me hard and you will spend the time thinking about that, do you understand?" My breath hitches, and I swallow to clear my throat.

"Yes, Sir." I am thinking about that now, but it's Daniel in my head, it's his perfect body I crave, and his hard cock I want inside me.

"I want you to tell me about what you want, Lola, what you like, and how that makes you feel. Remember, I will know if you are lying, and I won't be happy."

"I'm sorry, Sir, I don't think I understand." I think it's better to be upfront rather than start saying something wrong and get into trouble. I want to do what he asks. I want to please him.

"All right, Lola, I'll help you a little. Do you like it when I tell you what to do? Do you like your hair held in a tight fist when you are kissed? Do you-"

"-Sir, I can take it from here," I interrupt with a slight moan. "I like it when you give me instructions. It makes me happy to please you. I want to please you. I like to be pushed with the weight of your body against a wall or on to the bed. I love it that you force my legs apart with your legs and push your body against mine. It makes me hot that I can feel how much you want to fuck me, it makes me wet." I swallow. God, this is liberating. "I love that you hold my hands tight above my head and tease me with your delicious mouth, kissing from my ear and along my neck. I love it when you can't control the growl that comes from deep in your throat, and I love it when you bite down on my neck like you want to devour me. When you hold your hot mouth just out of my reach, it drives me insane, and I beg for your kiss. I love that you make me so desperate that I have to beg. It makes me need you so much, and I hate that it makes me need you." Shit, I can't believe I said that. Can I take it back? Maybe he didn't catch it, it was a long list. I continue. "I like when you dominate me, when you make demands. I like when you restrain me, tie my hands and my legs wide so I am open for you, exposed and vulnerable. It makes me tremble that you have such control over my body, over my pleasure." I draw in a deep breath as my heart pounds fiercely behind its cage.

"Lola? Have you ever been punished?" His voice is wickedly seductive.

"No, Sir."

"How do you think you would feel about that?"

"Honestly, I don't know. The thought excites me, the pain and pleasure excite me. Pleasing you excites me. But I don't want to lie to you, Sir, so I can't say for sure."

"Good girl. You have given me a great deal to think about. Goodnight, Lola."

"Have I pleased you, Sir?" I need to know.

"Yes, Lola, very much. Sleep well." The line goes dead, and I let out a relieved sigh. I honestly don't know what is going on with me. Why I need his approval, why I feel genuinely happy when I have pleased him, and why I feel so hot at the thought of the things I listed that I would love him--well ,would love Daniel--to do to me.

Chapter Eleven

I GRAB MY LIGHT grey yoga pants and Ramones T-shirt, scrape my hair high on my head, and skip downstairs. I overslept, not a huge surprise given my weekend, and luckily I'm due to help in the kitchen this morning, so my appearance is not a priority. I slink into the store cupboard and emerge with an armful of vegetables, hoping no one will notice I'm late.

"It's no good trying that trick, girl. You'd have to get up a whole heap earlier to pull that one over on me, and"--Joe looks at his watch--"that didn't happen this morning, did it, Bets?" His kind eyes betray his reprimanding tone.

"I'll work extra hard Joe, promise." I smile my biggest smile, hoping to charm him a little. I still have to ask for a shift change.

"You always work hard, girl." He grins, then barks, "Get to work!" By ten thirty I've prepped the vegetables and salads, and I'm just about to grab a coffee, when the doorbell to the back entrance rings. I open the door to a group of workmen who proceed to stream past me and into the corridor. Anthony, Jr., comes out of his office and starts to direct the men to the shower room and up the stairs.

"Oh, morning, sweetheart. How are you feeling today?" I cringe a little at this since I know it's a direct result of my meltdown on Sunday, and I am not sure how much Marco has disclosed to his older brother; knowing Marco, it's probably just enough.

"Anthony, I'm fine, thanks. Good, actually." I certainly sound chipper. "What's with all the workmen?"

"Oh, that. It's nothing. Fixing the shower door and some extra security." He starts to back up into his office. "It's been a long time coming." Just as he shuts his door, I jump in front of it to prevent him from closing it.

"Anthony, this has nothing to do with me, does it? You're not going to all this expense for me?" I am just about to die of embarrassment if that's the case.

"Not at all sweetheart. You can check with Dad. We had this planned for a long time, just had to shuffle which of the restaurants we were going to trial it in, and, lucky you, you get to be guinea pig!" He ruffles my hair, and I'm instantly at ease. I would hate to think Sofia's dad was having to pay because I went a little 'postal'.

"Oh, okay." I am a little relieved.

"Bets, I need you to do me a favour, though?" He flicks through his phone like he is looking for some information.

"Anything." I reply but he still doesn't look at me.

"Can you work through? I was landed with Marco's Ski crowd group booking at lunch. The little shit gives me no notice, and even gets Mama to call it in, so I can't refuse. You can have tonight off in exchange. I'll fix it with Joe." He lifts his head with a grin, but I have already agreed.

"Sure, not a problem. Well, other than the relentless come-ons with that lot, harmless but exhausting." I smile and roll my eyes.

"Just tell Joe if they give you any trouble, sweetheart. He has some very big knives." He winks and returns to his office. I return to the kitchen and mentally high five myself, because this is a good result for me. Just before one I change into my work clothes and set up the big table for Marco's crowd. Throughout the morning, I have had a steady stream of texts from Daniel. His playfulness makes me smile. His texts range from questions regarding what type of food I like, what drink apart from tequila, to deeply detailed descriptions of how he intends to make me scream tonight, and how often. Seriously I'm at work, surrounded by possibly the most flirtatious men on the planet, and I'm blushing like a nun in Amsterdam. I slip my phone in my apron for the hundredth time.

"Hey, Marco, when are you going to convince Bets that I'm the man of her dreams if she would just give me a chance? Look, she's blushing already. You know that's a good sign, right? It means your body wants me." I stand at the end of the table as Marco snakes a protective arm around my hip and glowers at his best friend.

"Stef, don't flatter yourself, man. That colour is not for you, and if it was, I'd lock her in a tower and throw away the key. She is too good for you. I've yet to meet a man good enough, but it certainly ain't a player like you." Marco laughs at his best friend, who tries to look offended.

"Takes one to know one, Marco." He tips his beer bottle and clinks it with Marco, and the whole table erupt in boisterous laughter.

"Men are pigs." I lean forward and kiss Marco on the head, just so he knows I don't mean him. I finish serving the last coffee and retrieve my phone once again. Every question Daniel has asked, however silly or obscure, has made it really hard not to ask my own. I feel myself wanting to know about him, his family, his life, and I actually have to physically curl my fingers into tight fists to prevent that line of enquiry. It's not that I am not interested--I really am. It's just that knowing more will make this less like the *fun* it is supposed to be. I have to keep this fun; fun is temporary, and temporary I understand.

His last text reminds me his driver will pick me up at six. He also suggests for the third time I get some rest. I can't believe in the space of a weekend I've gone from virgin to nymphomaniac. I feel like the sexual equivalent of his supercar, nought to insatiable in three point zero days. I head upstairs to rest, read, and I really need to catch up with Sofia. I notice the small flashing green then red lights in the corner of each room straight away. I don't have a television, so anything electrical would stand out like a sore thumb. I run back downstairs and knock on Anthony, Jr.'s, office door.

"Hey, sweetheart. How was lunch?" He grins widely.

"Are you fishing for compliments or information?" I narrow my eyes. He holds his hands up in mock surrender. "Lunch was fine. Marco kept the wolves at bay... I just wanted to check something. The flashing lights in my apartment, they're just motion detectors right, no cameras? I don't want to find out my super exciting life has gone viral?" Anthony laughs and slaps me on the shoulder.

"That would have to be the dullest YouTube ever, sweetheart." I can see full-on hysterics bubbling beneath his laugh, but he holds off to add, "No cameras, just sensors." I must look relieved when he adds. "Just a safety thing, okay?"

"Okay, thanks." I head back up to my new 'super safe' apartment.

Having smoothed things over with Sofia, I'm a bad friend for leaving her to worry, but she was placated when I told her all the details of my weekend with Daniel. She has a penchant for the dramatic and is a complete romantic, so she has read way too much into the 'rescue in the rain' incident. Her world view is a little rose-tinted, and it's wonderful for her to have found her perfect match in Paul, but I am much more likely to think horse when I hear hooves, while Sofia hears unicorns. I have washed as best I can, and I am thankful that Sofia takes me for regular waxing treatments, because I would easily sever an artery trying to shave my legs, balancing with one leg high in the sink. I am now in a panic. What underwear? I know what's on the agenda tonight, and I would love to wear something sexy and alluring, or even pretty would be good. I can't wear any of the lingerie I have been sent. Another box came today, cream silk lace bra and panties; that set would be perfect. But it would feel wrong to wear underwear bought by one man to fuck another. It feels like cheating, and I know how he feels about lying. What if he asked? Okay, that's ridiculous, but it would still feel wrong; plain Jane it is, then.

I wish I had asked a few more questions about tonight, because now I'm getting nervous. He said dinner. Did he mean dinner at his apartment? Is he going to cook, or is he taking me out? Where would he take me? What should I wear? I look in my wardrobe and eighty percent of what is hanging there belongs to Sofia. She comes over, hauling armfuls of clothes that she is bored with, some of it still with tags, and she switches my wardrobe around so it is a constantly changing entity and full of surprises. I find a thin jersey wrap around dress in black, a cropped leather jacket and my knee-high boots. The evenings are chilly now, so I take a scarf, too. I have straightened my hair and put a little lip gloss on, but I don't want Daniel's driver ringing the bell, so I go to wait outside by the back door just before six. I see the sleek Bentley pull around the corner and not that this is a rare sight in Knightsbridge, but the fact that my tummy starts to churn means I know this is Daniel's car. The car pulls to a gradual stop and with impeccable timing; it is then that the kitchen porters decide to take their cigarette break.

"Whoa, Bets. Is that sweet ride for you?" Ricky, one of the youngest porters can't hide the awe in his voice. "Hey Joe!" He yells inside gaining the attention of the remaining chefs and waiting staff, all of whom scramble outside. I close my eyes and curse myself. Why didn't I just walk? "Looks like Bets, has bagged herself a rich dude!" He laughs, and Joe slaps the back of his head. My shoulders slump, and I return a tight smile.

"No, Ricky, I'm not interested in his money… It's his fucking enormous cock I'm interested in. Not that you'd know much about that. Now, if you don't mind my ride is waiting?" I wink at Joe and throw myself arse first in to the back of the car, snapping my knees together as I do to make sure I don't flash the audience, which is now standing with mouths slightly open.

"Good to know." Daniel's deep voice makes me jump; I didn't see him in the darkened interior.

"Oh God, I'm sorry about that. It's just the guys, well, it's what anyone would think anyway, so I thought I'd put them straight. Really I wasn't thinking. I should've just walked to your place. It's not like it's far." I start to mumble, and I can feel my face heat.

"But I wanted to collect you." He is quiet for a little while before he adds, "So the only reason you would be with me is because of my money?"

"What? No!" I laugh, but he looks deadly serious. "No, Daniel, you can't possibly think that. You do have mirrors, don't you? It's just we are not exactly on a level playing field, are we? You're well…" I try to swallow the dryness from my throat. "Daniel, you're gorgeous. I mean seriously hot as hell, and I wasn't joking about your cock." I can't help bite my lips together. "But you're seriously wealthy, too, and although I don't care, no one in their right mind is going to believe me. Just like anyone would think that your interest in me is either as a charity case or purely about sex. Personally, I think it's about the charity, but then I don't know anything about you, and that is how it should be. This"--I wiggle my finger between the two of us again--"is off the charts sexy and intense, but it's just a bit of fun." I nudge him playfully, with a wide grin spread across my face.

"Bethany." He reaches for my hand. The familiar spark of heat ignites inside. "I think we need to qualify what constitutes *fun,* because I think our definitions are poles apart." I shrug and whisper as I turn to the window.

"Whatever." I feel the seat dip as he leans over and pulls me on to his lap, one arm curled around my waist, and the other hand holding my chin millimeters from his face. His breath is warm, his eyes dark and serious.

"So I'm a philanthropist, is that right? That is why I want you?" He tucks my hairs behind my ear.

"I have no idea why you want me, and I don't care; it's just fun, Daniel." I'm getting aggravated, and so is he. He grinds his teeth.

"Bethany, you are-" I interrupt, and by the look on his face, I am not sure this happens to him much.

"-Daniel." I narrow my eyes and repeat slowly, "I. Don't. Care. It's. Just. Fun!"

"Dammit, Bethany! You think this is fun, feeling like this is normal?" His voice is a loud rumble and his jaw ticks.

"I have no idea what normal is, and, yes, it is fun." My voice wobbles, "It has to be." I blink back the tears I can feel rising, but I have to close my eyes tight to hold them back. I try to move from his lap, but he strengthens his hold, waiting for me to open my eyes again. I don't understand why he is pushing this, but he has the same intensity in his eyes when I open mine. "Look, Daniel." I don't know how to explain this; I've never had to ex-plain this. "It's one of 'my things'. Another one of 'my things', which you can also deduce, is my way of surviving." I push with more strength and manage to sit back on the car seat. I have trou-ble thinking when his body generates such turmoil in mine. "Al-though, this one actually takes care of two of 'my things'. First, everyone leaves. Second, everything is temporary. So *it's* never going to be anything else, and if that doesn't work for you, that's fine, too! We can stop the car and end it here." I lift my chin to punctuate my determination at this point.

"God, you're infuriating!" His tone filled with fury. "How can you deny this? How can you pretend to be so indifferent? I fuck-ing know you're not indifferent. I can feel you, Bethany, every pulse, every increase in your heartbeat. I feel you respond to me, react to me, need me." He has closed the distance again, and the heat between us is stifling. I can't think, "Why don't you trust this? Why don't you trust me? Why can't you be honest with yourself?"

"Daniel," I say softly. "I do trust you, I just don't trust myself. And honestly? For the first time in my life, I don't know what to do, and I'm scared shitless." I let out a nervous laugh, which actually lightens this intense mood. He covers my mouth with his soft full lips, sucking in my bottom lips and grazing it over his teeth. He presses into me and dips his tongue, inviting mine to join his sensual dance. He tastes divine, sweet mint and erotica. I grab at the lapels of his jacket, tightly fisting the material. I need to feel his weight on me. I need the release I know he can give me. He builds this desire so easily, so quickly, it makes my head spin. I groan my response as he pulls back. His eyes are warm pools of desire and lust, matching my thoughts precisely.

"You know that's fucked up, right? You're an intelligent woman, and you have to know that's fucked up?" He laughs, and I stiffen a little as he dismisses my insecurities with his cocky smile. "Don't get all defensive, I understand. Well, I mostly understand, but we can work with that. I have a plan." His wicked smile is infectious and he screws a firm kiss into my hair and exits the car, which has been parked a while.

Chapter Twelve

D ANIEL HAS PLACED me on a stool in the kitchen next to the large marble island, while he grabs two wine glasses.

"Wine?" He tips the empty glasses toward me.

"Definitely." I grimace at my over enthusiasm for liquid courage.

"You wound me. Do you really need to be drunk to spend an evening with me?" He slaps his free hand playfully against his firm chest and supposedly injured heart.

"Ha, that's funny! The drink is for my nerves. You have me on edge in more than one way. So, yes, I can definitely use a drink to help me survive an evening with you, Mr. Stone."

"Red or white?" He smiles softly.

"What are we eating?" I inhale deeply.

"Sea Bass." His confident reply has me surprised.

"You are cooking?" I raise a teasing brow. I know he's not. There is not a cooking smell to be sniffed, as yet.

"No, Miss Thorne, I'm ordering in. My housekeeper in on holiday for two weeks, and if you were staying, I would have taken you out to eat. You have insisted on this ridiculous curfew, so I have a very limited time with which to enjoy you. So we are eating here, and I am ordering Sea Bass, Thai Sea Bass." He is so sure of himself, it is easy to be seduced by his confidence and even more impossible to resist his demands.

"Yum, white wine then, please." He pours a large glass of Pinot Gris, and I take two substantial fortifying sips. It's crisp and fresh and goes down far too easily. "Would you like me to set the table, put my talents to use?" I offer mostly for something to distract my nerves.

"No. Those aren't the talents I want to exploit, Miss Thorne." He holds my gaze with implicit intent. "There are two things we need to address first." He stands in front of me, takes my glass and places it on the island. He lifts me from my stool, as if I am no weight at all, and strides out of the kitchen. "First, I am going to make love to you like I would have *if* you had been honest with me on Saturday." I gasp, and he grins, then whispers wickedly in my ear, "and second we are going the have a luxurious bath together, where we will explore the nature of all this *fun* we are going to have." We've entered the largest bedroom suite I have ever seen. The floor to ceiling glass wall along two sides gives an unobstructed endless view over London, which is now aglow with evening lights. He carries me over to the corner where the two windows meet and stands me in front of a sumptuous looking chaise. "And then I'll feed you," he states as a matter of fact.

The lights in the room are low, soft and warm, but I shiver all the same. He stands close to my back but doesn't touch me, and I quiver with anticipation. He leans so I can feel his warm breath against my neck, and I know his lips are suspended just above my skin. My skin flushes with a heat and instant rush of prickles. He has yet to touch me, and I'm burning up. I tilt my neck, a blatant show of submission, as I open my vulnerable neck to him. He groans approval but still doesn't touch me.

"You know." My attempt at a casual tone has failed with the high-pitched squeak mid-sentence. "My first time was pretty amazing, you really don't need a do-over." I press my thighs together to quell the burgeoning ache and get some release. This may well have been extra amazing if it was the first time, but since I now know exactly how high the heights of ecstasy are that this man can take me to, this tortuously slow pace is insufferable.

"Only pretty amazing? Had you said 'mind-blowing' or 'out of this world' even, I might forgo the 'do-over', but since neither expression passed those beautiful lips, I'm afraid I am going to have to go all out, Miss Thorne. I'm nothing if I'm not a perfectionist!" I can feel his wicked smile as his lips curl closer to my neck. "Bethany, I am going to drive you insane, I am going to make you come so many ways, so many times, and you're going to scream my name so fucking loud, you won't be able to speak after. Which will be a shame, because you're going to be begging me to stop, and, baby, I won't be able to hear you." He plants the softest kiss on my neck and is rewarded with an uncontrollable full body shudder.

He wraps his strong arms around my waist and unties the bow which holds my dress together, and it falls open. He puts his large hot hands flat against my stomach and presses my body back against his. There is no mistaking that he is as turned on as I am; the thought makes me moan, and I grind a little into his hardness. He slides his hands up and cups my aching breasts over my bra, pinching and rolling the hard nubs between his thumbs and forefingers just to the point of pain. Instant sparks shoot straight to my core, and I start to draw rapid breaths, trying to keep up with my pounding heart.

"You're so fucking perfect, Bethany, and you have no fucking idea what you do to me." He mumbles into my neck as he drags his teeth along my skin, leaving a searing mark in its wake. He moves his hand to slip my dress from my shoulders and lets it fall to the floor. He again scoops me up in his arms and strides toward the bed and carefully lays me down. He frowns, and it looks like he has changed his mind.

"I know you take instruction very well, but I think this *first time* I want to worship your body vanilla style." His smile is stunning, he has a strong jaw and defined cheekbones. His crystal eyes sparkle with lust and desire. He could keep me as a sex slave for all the kink he could dream of at this moment in time, but the decadent way he suggests vanilla is pure sin. I decide to keep my first thought to myself. He kneels on the bed and takes my feet in his lap. He starts to massage and stroke. He varies the pressure as he makes his way up my legs, using his thumb to draw out long strokes easing tension from my muscles. I close my eyes and release a heavenly sigh. He gives a light laugh, but continues his ministration up my legs. He has to kneel up and his muscled thighs flex as they encase mine, trapping me, not that I would want to be anywhere but right here.

He lightly traces his fingers along the outline of my panties but moves on to my tummy. He slides his hands and grips my waist as he bends over and kisses a path from my belly button to the top of my panties where he releases a burst of warm breath. He then kisses a trail all the way up to my throat, avoiding my aching, heavy breasts. My fingers twitch, and I start to raise my hand. He looks up to my eyes, which are now open. "I said I wasn't going to give you instruction, but that doesn't mean I don't want this *my* way." His calm tone leaves no chance of misunderstanding his meaning, and I lay my hand back flat against the bed. Is it too early to start screaming his name? He swoops back to my neck and sucks hard, pulling my tender skin into his mouth, marking me, releasing a scorching heat deep inside, and I buck a little, but I manage to still myself before he stops again. He hovers above me, holding his weight from my body.

"Can you turn over, Bethany? I'd like to work on your back, but I can't promise I'll be quite so restrained when I reach that glorious arse of yours." I wiggle and flip onto my front, sad that I can't kiss his lips from here. He unclips my bra and shuffles down, then starts to pull my panties down. "What the fuck is this?" He sounds really angry, and I jump and try to crane my neck around to see why. "Who did this to you?" It usually takes a few days for the bruising to show, especially on my butt, and I sag back into the soft covers and laugh. "It's not fucking funny, Bethany. Who hurt you?" His harsh tone is filled with misplaced concern.

"I did. Well, me, Marco and the mat; it's from my Krav Maga class. It can be brutal, and I bruise like a peach. It's nothing, always looks worse than it is." I wiggle my bottom to indicate just how fine I am.

"Marco is responsible?" He sits back on his ankles and crosses his tanned arms. This highlights the defined muscle of his biceps, and I get distracted by the tempting sight. "Bethany!" He barks, his is *so* not happy about this. Talk about a mood changer!

"Yes, Marco is responsible for dragging me to self-defense classes every week, so that if I were ever to be attacked, I could fight them off with more than just my bad language." I lift myself onto my elbows to half twist around so I can challenge his angry stare. "Do you have a problem with that?"

"Yes… no, not the classes, no. Just you getting hurt, and I would very much like it if you didn't talk about getting attacked." His deep frown mars his perfect face. It's kind of sweet, though.

"Not another word." I smile and make to lock my lips and throw away the key, but before I do, I add with an arched brow, "You were definitely in the middle of something more interesting than this conversation." I throw the invisible key and flop back down, slightly arching my hips to lift my bottom. He growls, but his hands begin to slowly caress my bottom in smooth circles. I know he is tracing the bruises, because I can hear his teeth grind, and he is being extremely tentative. He begins again, starting at my feet, repeating the moves he made on my front. By the time he reaches my neck, my whole body is thrumming with desire. My teeth are clenched, he must be able to feel the tension as I fight my body's desire to writhe with pleasure and come. I just need to come. I think if he so much as put the tiniest pressure on my clit right now, I would explode.

"Something you need, baby?" He whispers in my ear and traces his tongue around the shell, nibbling on my lobe. I tremble and whimper into the pillow. His deep rumble vibrates his chest and sends waves of shivers across my body. I feel his hand on my bottom, his fingers slide between the cheeks, over my tight entrance, which twitches at his light touch, and his finger slides into my wetness. He plunges two fingers deep inside. My hips buck instantly, and my core contracts greedily, grabbing at his fingers, which he pumps into me, riding my climax and pushing me on and on. He reaches and presses my clit, rubbing with a light circling motion with the pad of his finger. Before my body has stopped pulsing, he continues to pump and rub, building the pressure once more. This time I scream. I scream with shock and wonder, loudly into the pillow, which I have grabbed tight against my face. It muffles the sound but also prevents me from taking in any oxygen, and I turn my head and gasp. I'm seeing spots before my eyes as he takes my hips and flips me over. I must look a little dazed.

"You need to breathe, Bethany." He has an undeniable cocky grin fixed on his face but refrains from laughing. "Don't pass out! You know I'm not finished." He sinks his teeth into my neck again, drawing an agonizing moan of pleasure from me, and I wrap my arms around his back and feel his strong muscles move and flex. He covers my mouth with his and swipes his tongue, forcing my lips apart, tasting and taking everything I return. He breaks the contact and hovers above me. I clench my tummy to raise myself to meet him, to reach his soft mouth. He smiles, and I lunge again, but his reflex is too quick, and I am left wanting, needing to feel his delicious kiss again. "Na ah, now, what's got you so greedy?" I try and pull him down, but he is solid muscle and I don't stand a chance of taking him with me, unless he wants to give. I blow out a frustrated sigh. "Oh, poor baby. Want me to kiss it better?" Oh. My. God. Yes! No, I said that in my head, and he needs to know this.

"Please. Oh, God, yes, please, please, I want that." I pant shamelessly. He widens his smile. He is so gorgeous.

"Oh, I do love it when you beg." He drops his scorching kisses along my collarbone and skims down to my breast. He palms one and suckles my nipple on the other. He swirls his tongue, flicking the sensitive end before he repeats this with my other breast. He then nibbles and sucks his way down. My breath hitches, the anticipation unbearable. He sits back and with his strong hand forces my legs wide. I am completely open for him and his gaze is on fire. "You're so beautiful, Bethany. I have to taste you." He swipes his tongue the full length of my core and laps my clit. I instantly tense with the familiar feelings of an imminent climax.

"Oh, Fuck, Daniel.... Ahhhh!" Christ, that was quick, intense, and not over as he continues to swirl and suck. He dips his tongue inside, and I grab his hair. My hips are shaking, and I am desperate to get more air. I'm panting. With that he fixes his mouth over my clit and sucks. "Ahhh, God!" I scream again, and my thighs grip his head, trying to stop the overload of pleasure his talented mouth is bombarding me with. I fall limp, still trembling. He sits up, and it's only then I realize he is still fully clothed, and I am naked, sated, and limp. He reaches into his pocket and pulls out a foil packet. He holds my heated stare as he tears the packet with his teeth. He unbuckles his belt and pushes his trousers down to his thighs. His erection hard against his stomach, I bite my lip. I know how good he tastes, and I can't take my eyes off him as he sheaths himself.

"Nice thought, but tonight is all about you, baby." He covers my body with his weight, God, I love the feeling of being dominated in this way. It just feels so primal. He positions his wide crown against my slick folds and rubs, spreading my wetness along his shaft. "Baby, I've tried to make this easy, making you come like that, but I can't wait any more so this might still hurt a little. We'll take it slow." His voice sounds ragged, and I can see the tiny droplets of sweat bead at his temples. The softness in his eyes and the concern in his voice has me fighting a lump in my throat. Not quite able to speak, I simply nod. "Okay, baby?" He fixes his eyes on mine as he pushes slowly into me. My body contracts at the intrusion, but it's not so bad. He pushes further, and the feeling of fullness and stretching is wonderful. He groans and starts to change the angle and rolls his hips. Oh, good God, that feels amazing--again in my head.

"Oh, God, Daniel, that feels amazing," I cry out. His slow steady thrusts drive into me and I can feel his reticence, his hesitation, his tender intentions. It's Heaven, and I want more. "Do you think you could go faster? Deeper?" I want every bit of him. He laughs.

"Yes, Bethany, I can definitely do that." He groans as he plunges deep.

"Ahh, fuck!" I yell, and he freezes. "No, ahh, Fuck, in a good way Daniel. Don't stop, please, please, don't stop." He pulls back and plunges again; deep, hard, and it's fantastic. The friction and burn set a fire racing inside me. He thrusts and pumps into me, shaking my body, filling me, riding me. His eyes are heated with lust and the guttural sounds escaping him are a wild addition to the sounds of our bodies moving together. I wrap my legs around his waist, and he grabs my arse cheeks and pulls me tighter against him, closer against each thrust. The exquisite deep sensation I feel, as his cock rubs and touches sensitive tissue deep inside, takes my breath away. My body takes over and starts the steady climb to ecstasy. I feel Daniel shift, and he starts to pump faster into me, chasing his own release.

"Bethany, come with me?" The urgency in his voice has my body spiralling.

"Yes, yes, Daniel. Ahhhh!" I scream.

"Fuck!!" He pumps and grinds deep, filling me and taking every bit for his own release. His hot heavy body covers mine and we lay, two sweaty bodies, entwined and exhausted. Well, I know I am. Not sure where he gets his stamina from, but Daniel has already rolled from the bed, left the room, and returns with a bathrobe. I am still a quivering mess.

"Here. I don't want you getting dressed again." He hands me a robe which is enormous, so at least I know it's his and not his girlfriend's. Wait! This is just a bit of *fun,* right? But I frown to myself at this unwelcome thought.

"What's wrong?" His obvious concern does nothing to quell the troubled feelings swirling inside, causing an unsettling tightness in my chest.

"Nothing. Nothing at all, so stop worrying. You didn't even hurt my bottom." I smirk.

"Yet." He calls over his shoulder as he disappears again. I get goose bumps at the veiled threat. I wrap his robe around me and head off to find him. He is in the kitchen pouring more wine.

"Change of plan. Food first, you for dessert." He grins. "Then bath. Sound good?"

"Sounds time consuming?" I hate that I have to bring my reality into this fairy-tale.

"I'll have you back by one, Cinderella." He grumbles but kisses me on the head, and holding my hand, he sits me back on a stool while he orders the food. He then sets a bowl with hot water on a warming plate and places a small pouring jug and a fancy looking jar of chocolate praline in the water. He has a smirk that makes him look both devilish and young. He walks back to me and places his large palms on my cheeks and smothers my mouth with his hungry lips. "For dessert." He adds but doesn't explain further.

There is a buzzing, which announces our food. The exotic aromas of ginger and lemongrass follow him back to the kitchen, and we sit at the island and eat with chopsticks out of the boxes. The sea bass is juicy and melts in the mouth; the food is light, fresh and utterly delicious. More so because most of my meal is fed to me and he keeps having to adjust himself in his loose fitted lounge pants, every time I lick my lips in appreciation as I suck the food from his chopsticks.

"Are you always hard?" My unfiltered curious mind is getting the better of my manners. He shifts again.

"Always around you, yes, which is lucky for me, because I always want to fuck you." He playfully picks up a large chunk of fish and drops it in his hungry mouth.

"And lucky for me, because it seems I always want to be fucked." That sounds wrong now that I have said it aloud, and his frown confirms this. "Always want to be fucked by *you*. Yeah, definitely meant to say it like that." I put my chopsticks down and climb onto his lap, my legs wrapping around his waist and my naked sex resting directly above his straining erection. "You said something about a luxury bath?" I roll my hips enjoying the friction from the thin material over his hard length.

"No, I said something about dessert, then bath." His hands hold my hips still but keep the pressure securing me fixed against him.

"I don't think I could eat another thing." The food was heavenly, but I am stuffed.

"You may not, but I'm still hungry." His eyes are liquid heat. He stands with my legs wrapped around his waist, and he carries me over to the large leather sofas in the corner of the room. He slips his robe from me and lays it flat on the sofa before he sits me down on top with my feet on the floor. "Don't move." Wouldn't dream of it. He returns carrying the small pouring jug and a clear bowl with milky white cubes which he places on the coffee table. He kneels on the floor and spreads my legs. He runs a finger up my core. I jolt, my body instantly responding. "Mmmm." He sucks the same finger slowly. "Now, you taste fucking amazing, and there is nothing that could improve what I've got before me, but you did mention something about *fun*?" I nod, because I am now breathless with excitement. "So in the spirit of *fun,* I'm going to add a few ingredients to this beautiful dessert." He sweeps his hot palm across my tummy and squeezes my breast. "God, your tits are perfect". He leans towards the table and picks up one of the cubes.

His eyes scorch my body and fix on mine. "Now, hold very still, or this will get very messy very quickly." He takes a white cube and draws tiny circles around my tight puckered nipple, and I instantly arch at the sting of the freezing cube. I can feel droplets as the cube melts against my flushed skin, and he dives to suck up the droplets before they run from my breast. The heat of his mouth and roughness of his tongue has my skin ablaze. "Hold still, remember?" He admonishes me with a warning scowl. I swallow the dryness in my throat. This is going to be impossible. He repeats the circling motion of the cube, moving from one nipple to the other. The initial shock of the cold has subsided, and I am able to remain still, despite the building pressure and need between my legs. The cube has melted, and my body is streaked with rivulets of white liquid. He then leans to retrieve the white jug and pours a single drop on my tummy. It's warm liquid chocolate. He trails a line of chocolate droplets up between my breasts to my collar bone where the liquid pools in the indentation in the center. He continues to pour single drops on my breasts trying to hit the sensitive peaks, and each time sparks of desire shoot straight to my clit.

He puts the jug down and admires his Jackson Pollack attempt at food art before leaning down and tortuously and slowly licking every drop from my body. I'm trembling on the edge, and although I know he poured no liquid there, I am molten hot between my legs. He eases his way down my body and carefully brings me to a mind-blowing climax with his gifted tongue. He holds me until my body stops convulsing, and my breathing becomes a little more normal.

"Oh! Oh, wow!" I throw my arm over my face, still drawing in deep breaths. "I have got to try that. My turn." I lift my head to meet his darkly heated glare and relaxed smile.

He laughs. "No time, your timescale, baby, not mine." He reminds me and laughs at my instant frown.

"But?" I pout. He has already removed himself and the ingredients. "What are the white cubes?" I grab the robe, which is now a little sticky.

"Frozen cream." He places all the remaining ingredients on the island top.

I take one of the cubes, dip it through the chocolate and pop it in my mouth. "Mmmm, that's good."

"Chocolate, cream and you, nothing better." He grins and wickedly licks his lips.

I lower myself into the corner bath, which is the size of a small swimming pool. It's so deep, I am floating and have to steady myself holding the edges. My smile is so wide right now, it's too easy to believe this is real. Daniel strides in gloriously naked, and I know this isn't real. No one really looks like that, with toned strong muscles, narrow waist, broad shoulders, and his thick long cock hard against his stomach.

"It's rude to stare." He walks over and steps in behind me, sliding all that manliness around my slick wet body.

"It would be ruder not to." I sigh and lean back into his chest. He starts to cup water into my hair and washes me. I am relaxed and sated, soft and pliant. He could ask me anything and I couldn't think of a good reason not to tell him or deny any request; but then I think, that is exactly the point when he begins to talk.

"Now Bethany, this." He waves his wet hand mockingly between us. "This is not just *fun,* and you know it. That's not even debatable. But if it helps us to move forward by calling it that, if it helps you, we will call it *fun*. So, now, I would like to have as much *fun* with you as possible, as much as I can get." I can't help but giggle at this, abundantly aware that his heavy cock twitches against my back each time he says the word fun. "That means I want your schedule, so we can synchronize, and I want you to cut your work hours. I also want you to stay here with me." He sounds like a petulant child, which just makes me laugh again.

"Wow, Daniel, that's some list." I laugh and twist my neck round to see his own face fixed and frowning.

"Before you respond, think carefully if you think I have got where I am today by not being single minded and determined at getting what I want." His stern tone might be intimidating if he wasn't all naked and wet, with his massive hard-on pressed against my backside.

"And it's very impressive, brilliant and inspiring, but getting what you want in this instance, well, it's not that simple. I have commitments." I pause before elaborating, "You can have my schedule, but it's kind of full. I can't cut my hours, as I need the money to pay for mum's care. I guess I can stay here, sometimes, but I have to make arrangements first." I roll my neck as I feel some tension start to build, I hate confrontations, and this feels a lot like one. His hands are on my neck in an instant squeezing and pressing the knots with his thumbs.

"Cut some of your hours, and spend some of that time with me? It would make me very happy." His soft voice is pleading, and I get the feeling that doesn't happen very often, and I'm touched. I don't understand, why me? And I don't understand why I want to please him so much, but I do.

"Daniel." I exhale and lean my head to the side to look up to his face. I need to see his eyes; they are intense, sincere, and beautiful. "I'll try, okay? But this *fun* has my flight instinct on high alert. You may be single minded and determined, but I'm all about self-preservation." I nudge him with my elbow and receive instant hard fingers digging in my ribs making me squirm. "Bruise like a peach, remember?" I plead, and he stops, then squeezes me tight instead, holding me like that until the water starts to cool. He pats my body dry with the fluffiest towel and then proceeds to slather my skin in a ginger soufflé body cream. His hard erection brushing and poking my body throughout the process is driving me mad, but every time I try and make a play for him, he steps away with an arched brow and taps the watch he is wearing. I am being punished for my ridiculous curfew. But I can hardly cut my Late Night commitment if he wants me to reduce my hours at the restaurant.

I'm dressed but with no panties and sitting on the corner sofa in the lounge with my legs tucked beneath me, holding a glass of golden liquid, Cointreau over ice. It burns and warms.

"This *fun* has some rules, Bethany." His serious tone piques my interest.

"Go on." I swirl the golden liquid, my lips curling with

amusement.

"I believe I mentioned I don't share, and you can expect a reciprocal arrangement, although you wouldn't ask because that might give away your feigned indifference?" He cocks a brow, but I respond by taking another sip of my drink. "No lies. I don't expect full disclosure, but if I ask you something, I don't want you to lie. There will be no boundaries in the bedroom." My eyes widen at the implications of that statement "But you trust me, and it is only ever about pleasure with us,so that won't be an issue, and I want you to take some birth-control, because I don't want to wear a condom with you. I fucking hate condoms." His recited list sounds more like points of action at a board meeting.

"Please?" I say seriously but have to bite my lips to keep up the façade.

"Excuse me?" His face shows utter astonishment. It's funny.

"I want you to take some birth control…please?" I slowly emphasize the 'please'.

"Bethany." He rumbles, his jaw tense. "I would like you to take some birth control," He leans in to my ear and whispers, "please." Shivers ripple over my body, and I lean into his warmth. He stands and takes my hand. It's time to leave.

He drives me home and escorts me to my door where he folds me in his arms, his head resting on mine.

"I've had a wonderful evening, Daniel; mind blowing." I add and he laughs.

"I can't promise not to fall in love with you, Miss Thorne, but if you can promise not to fall in love with me, we will be safe having *fun*. By your definition, then it can only be *you* that does the leaving. And, Bethany,"--he looks deep into my eyes--"I am never going to let that happen." He kisses me with such passion, I want to crawl up his body and take him again. I can't believe he just said those things and kisses me like that then casually walks back to his car. "Email me your schedule, first thing!" He demands and gets in his car. He is waiting until I am inside, but I don't think my legs will move. I finally move at the sound of his horn, and hurriedly turn, then go inside. Once in my apartment, I realize I don't have his email address. Thinking I'll text him in the morning, I notice another box just inside my door, but I had already had one delivery. I pull at the tape and remove a folded Harvey Nichols bag; it's light, and a card falls to the floor. It is handwritten:

> In my absence the only thing next to your exquisite skin should be silk and lace
> Xd
> d.s@si.com

Seven sets of individually wrapped beautiful lace lingerie in white and pastel shades lay in my lap. I am again speechless.

My life feels very much like a fantasy at the moment. I am sitting in my *other* lingerie, the deep purple silk and black lace set, waiting for my call. If I'm honest, I would rather not take this call tonight. I've had so much sensory thrill with Daniel tonight, I don't want to have that memory replaced, just yet. I would like to savour the evening a little more. I close my eyes and my mind wanders: each touch of his hand, each heated kiss, each graze of his teeth, each thrust from his cock. I moan and arch, wriggle and writhe. I am loving the detail of this recollection. My heart is beating fast, and it's all too vivid, and I find I have a desperate need demanding attention between my legs when the phone rings. I'm dazed, and I jump for the phone, taking a little longer in this state. It is nearer to two in the morning, this call is very late.

"Sir." I answer on the second ring.

"Lola." His deep voice vibrates through me. "I trust you have a good excuse for your delay in answering my call?"

"Yes, Sir. I was thinking and got a little carried away." It's the truth, at least.

"Something good, I hope?" His voice is both calming and seductive.

"Yes, Sir, something very good." I am glad he didn't ask if I was thinking of him, because as it is I haven't lied.

"Would you like to tell me about it?" I don't ; I don't want to share this and I hesitate.

"No?"

Interesting... I think the purple suits you. You look good enough to eat, dessert, perhaps?" I sit up shocked at this remark. "I assume you chose to wear the second set of lingerie I sent you? It's the logical choice, and the lace reminds me of icing, sweet like a dessert." I hear the words, but I'm still a little freaked by the reference to dessert.

"The lace is very beautiful, Sir." I barely manage to reply.

"Yes, very." He pauses "Good night, Lola." The line goes dead.

That was strange, mercifully brief, but very strange.

Now, I sit wide-awake, a little bit freaked and a little bit horny. I slip out of my underwear, back into my soft oversized T-shirt and pull my ancient laptop onto my lap, groaning at its weight. It sounds like a tractor starting up and I probably have time to make another bedtime drink before it's open but I wait patiently. I decide to send Daniel my schedule:

To:d.s@s.i.com
Subject:Schedule
Mr. Stone,
Schedule as promised. Also a woman of my word. Work your magic!

Regards,
Miss Thorne

TIME	MON	TUE	WED	THUR	FRI	SAT	SUN
8-1	UNI	WK	WK	WK	UNI	GYM	LIB
1-6	UNI	WK	UNI	UNI	WK	WK	MUM/FREE
6-12	LIB	WK	WK	WK	UNI	WK	LIB

I am about to power down when I get a return email:

To: B.Thorne@gmail.com

Subject: Ridiculous schedule

Miss Thorne,

Your revised schedule as approved. I accept that some library time is necessary for your studies, but at the expense of work, not time with me. Any free time is also to be assumed to be mine. Ensure your work schedule is amended accordingly this week. Note that this revision allows for you staying over on Sun, Wed, Fri and Sat evening. So make necessary arrangements for your other commitments, which currently prevent this. Your class on Saturday will now be with my personal trainer and you also have a doctors' appointment Monday at 1:30 p.m. I'll send a car. This is an unprecedented level of compromise on my part.

You're mine, Miss Thorne.

Daniel Stone

CEO

TIME	MON	TUE	WED	THUR	FRI	SAT	SUN
8-1	UNI	WK	~~WK~~ds	WK	UNI	~~GYM~~ds	~~LIB~~ ds
1-6	UNI	WK	UNI	~~UNI~~LIB	~~WK~~ds	WK	MUM/FREE ds
6-12	~~LIB~~ds	~~WK~~ds	~~WK~~ds	~~WK~~ds	UNI	~~WK~~ds	~~LIB~~ds

I decide to call him rather than play email tennis, as it is too difficult to gauge tone that way.

"Miss Thorne?" His voice is low and soft. Oh, God, he sounds like sex.

"Mr. Stone, don't you sleep?" I quip.

"Not very much, no, although I probably would if you were beside me. Would you like me to come and get you? Are you worried if I'm getting enough sleep?" The thought of him coming to get me heats my cheeks and has me off topic. Ignoring his questions, I continue.

"Mr. Stone, don't you think your amendments are a tad unreasonable?" I try to argue lightly.

"Not in the least." His answer, abrupt and decisive, and I sigh.

"Even if I could cut my hours I can't just leave Anthony short staffed like that, it wouldn't be fair."

"So letting Anthony down is your only objection?" I can sense he is fishing for obstacles he can obliterate.

"No, it's not. You work long hours, I'm sure; although there's not much evidence of that lately." I scoff. "What am I supposed to do if you're working and I'm not? I think I mentioned my aversion to being at someone's beck and call?"

"Bethany, all I ask is that you cut your hours slightly and spend that time with me. More than likely we'll be working alongside each other, but I would just rather have you there with your head in a book than in a library with your head in a book." He makes me sound so unreasonable and I can't deny I like the idea of spending more time with him, perhaps a little too much.

"But I have a life too--well not much of a life--but I am not going to cut my family from that. I will still be attending classes with Marco and I will still be going out with Sofia, like I am on Friday." I thought I should put that in while we appear to be negotiating. The truth is I really like spending time with him, outside of the sex, which is awesome; I really enjoy his company. He makes me feel safe, and no one has done that in a long time. That in itself is why I know I am fighting this losing battle. What Daniel represents and what he is offering are wholly seductive and scary as hell.

He ignores my Friday comment but grumbles in frustration. "You have no idea how frustrating this is. I don't capitulate, I rarely negotiate, and I always get what I want, and you have me compromising left and right! Impossible!" He exhales dramatically. "All right, you get the gym but you also come with me to my personal trainer. You get your Uni-time--although one of those lectures is mine--and you also get one day working a daytime shift, which I am happy to sort with Anthony if you would prefer? The rest is mine!" It is a closing statement.

"Wait!" I call out before he hangs up, "I'll speak to Anthony, please don't." I plead because I have not had someone intercede on my behalf for I don't know how long.

"All right, but tomorrow, Miss Thorne. Do it tomorrow. Now if you don't mind, I'm feeling sleepy now, someone wore me out today." I can hear his smile.

"Ha! You're so funny! Says the one with Red Bull running through his veins. Goodnight, Daniel." I smile and sink into my covers trying to recreate the warmth he incites, a pointless exercise.

"Goodnight, Bethany." The phone goes silent in my hand.

Chapter Thirteen

MAGS HAD SENT me a statement with my income for the week, which looks all wrong, but she assured me that was the fee less her commission and extra courier costs. It did look like I could cut my hours at the restaurant on the strength of that alone, and I could really use the time, not just for study, but to explore my other business ideas. I like the idea of spending more time with Daniel, more than I should. I am trying to be cautious but he is so damn tempting.

I spoke to Anthony at the start of my shift. I knew he would be supportive and accommodating, which is why I wanted to talk to him and not have Daniel flatten him with his demands for my time, like a big old steamroller. I agreed to work Tuesday all day and help out at the weekends when they need. I'll probably be twiddling my thumbs with this much time to myself.

I leave the restaurant at one. It's a twenty minute walk to my doctor's, and I don't need Daniel's driver to take me, but I don't want the confrontation either, so I just leave a little early. I get to the corner of the street when I see his car draw alongside me, and the window in the back begins to lower.

"Going somewhere, Miss Thorne?" Smiling like he is, it's difficult to be irritated at this borderline obsessive behaviour; difficult, not impossible.

"I don't answer obvious questions, Mr. Stone." I continue to walk and the car continues to crawl much to the irritation of the cars following.

"You're causing a traffic jam, Miss Thorne. Would you kindly get in the car?" he calmly demands.

"You're causing the jam!" I'm exasperated, but since the horns have started blaring, I open the door and get in his damn car.

"Good afternoon, Miss Thorne. Did you sleep well?" His voice is cool and reserved, ignoring my temper as I slam his car door. His dark suit is impeccable, his blue tie matches the intense blue of his eyes, and his hair is just tousled. I want to run my fingers through it.

"I slept very well, eventually." I turn with a somewhat angry scowl. "How did you know who my doctor is?"

"I have access to the University records. I know a great deal about you, Miss Thorne." He actually smiles at my dropped jaw.

"Do they know you freely rifle through private records?" I'm incredulous at his brazenness and disregard for privacy.

"Just yours," he calmly states, as if *that* makes it okay because it is just my records. "Do they know you're really twenty?" My mouth snaps shut.

"I hope not." I softly reply and nervously pick a strand of hair at my neck. He takes my hand and gently kisses my fingertips.

"Why do they think you're twenty-five, then?" His eyes hold mine, but his query has me on edge.

"What are you, the University police?" I pull my hand away, but he grabs it back and holds it more firmly.

"No, Bethany, I would just like to know. And you are a terrible liar, so let's not go down that road." He pulls me onto his lap and kisses my hair, below my ear and onto my neck.

"Mmmm, ahhh." I drop my neck to the side, and he swipes his hot tongue, then clamps his lips in the crook of my neck and sucks. "Oh, God, Daniel." A sudden rush of tingles spread wildly from his kiss throughout my body and I quiver from head to toe.

"You were saying, Miss Thorne?" He lifts his head and fixes

his dark eyes on me.

"Easy for you to say," I mumble on an exhaled breath. "I can't afford to study full-time. I need my job for my mum's care. But I also don't want to take eight years to get my degree. As a mature student, aged twenty-five, I qualify to do the part-time program. It's all about unit credits; if I can double up on credits, like a full-time course I can try and complete the degree quicker. Maybe not the three years, but working hard, I might be able to do it in four." I don't know if I have just sealed my own expulsion from the course, but I do know if I hadn't told him, he would just keep investigating, and that in itself would probably result in the same.

"Why is a degree important? I didn't finish at Oxford, and I didn't turn out too bad." He looks more like a rogue rather than a successful businessman with his sly grin.

"No, you didn't, but I just always felt that my education was something that was mine, something no one could take away. I like the idea of having choices, and…" I add quietly, "I made a promise. Besides," I lighten my tone, but he holds me tighter. "I have some new product ideas, and no idea what to do next. They have this lecture program with this super successful, smoking-hot business type,, who gives all this great advice. It's a win-win for me. If I don't get kicked out." I shrug trying to make light of this. It's not light, it's my life, but he doesn't need to know that.

"Smoking-hot you say? Should I be jealous?" He dips his head to dig his nose into my hair, causing a shiver of cool tingles up my spine.

"Definitely, I can't get enough of this guy." He shifts around in a swift move, which has me pinned to the seat with him above me and a scorching glare.

"So I take it you have amended your schedule to meet my requirements'?" He rasps.

"For now." I whisper.

"For now, that would be because everything is temporary?" His eyes search mine. They are intense and questioning.

"Yes," I confirm, and he makes a loud frustrated noise in the back of his throat before his mouth slides over mine. His soft full lips are sweet, and his tongue flicks and searches, entwining with mine. He plunges deep, demanding and devouring. I match his desire, and as he pulls away, I bite his bottom lip between my teeth and suck hard. We arrive at my doctor's.

"You're not coming in!" I cry out in horror. There is no way that could be misinterpreted, but I push his solid chest back to be sure as he doesn't try to follow me out of the car.

"Why?" He seems genuinely confused.

"Seriously? I haven't had a chaperone since I was ten, not going to start now. I'll be fifteen minutes. You can wait here, or I'll see you later, your choice." His mouth forms a thin line.

"I'm not a chaperone, and this is about us." Oh, that is kind of sweet, but no! I raise my brow, waiting for his choice.

"Fine!" he barks. "But I'm waiting because you're coming back with me."

"Your apartment?"

"No, work. I'd like to show you what I do." He says with pride.

"When you're not fucking me?" I grin.

"When I'm not fucking you, but since you're coming to my work, I can't guarantee that won't happen there, too." He flashes his amazing, sexy smile, and now I can't wait to go to his office.

Fifteen minutes later I am back in Daniel's car, where he hands me a printout with his name on it. A brief look at the information and I glean that Daniel is fit and healthy. Not instantly picking up on the relevance I hand it back and smile. "I guess you have to have that done regularly for insurance purposes or something. I'm glad you're fighting fit."

"Did you read it?"

"Yes, it says you're fit and healthy… good for you." He hands me back the paper and points at the information indicating sexual health status.

175

"Oh," I say softly, not really comprehending what this has to do with me.

"Oh! And no, I don't have this type of check-up regularly. I always wear a condom--always." I don't know why he is grumpy, it's not like I called him a manwhore. He is the CEO of a global corporation. I thought his health would be important for the company, since he is the company. I know nothing about his sexual history, other than he doesn't have relationships, but I can't imagine him having long periods of abstinence, not with his sex drive and not looking like that. I find this thought unpleasant, and I sink back into my seat and look out the window. We have passed Trafalgar and are heading along The Strand. He takes my hand and starts to nip and suck my fingers, sending a ripple of sparks across my skin.

"Ask the question, Bethany." His tone is quiet but demanding and he looks stern.

"It's none of my business, Daniel." I turn my head again, his eyes burning right through me, but he reaches over and holds my chin firm, his steely gaze fixed on me.

"Ask the fucking question," He demands.

"Argh! It's none of my fucking business!" I don't move my head, and I return his glare. His jaw is twitching, and I think he is going to lose it, when he captures my mouth in a violent, demanding kiss, thrusting his tongue aggressively between my lips like he is trying to drag the question from my mouth. Stiff at first at the intrusion, I quickly soften as my lust for him takes over. My hands fist his shirt as he holds my face, then slides his hands into my hair. He pulls, tilting my head to allow better access before he pulls my head right back to break our heated exchange. I gasp to regain my stolen breaths.

"I don't want to feel this way, Daniel," I sigh, and his eyes crinkle with concern.

"What way?"

"I don't want to feel upset that you've been with other women--of course you've been with other women, hundreds probably, to be as good as you are--and it doesn't matter. But it shouldn't make me feel, I don't know, I don't know what this feels like, but I don't like it." I fold my arms defensively around my body. How can he make me feel safe and vulnerable at the same time?

"Now I wish I hadn't asked," He pulls my arms away from my body and scoops me into his lap.

"I know, I know. You don't need some crazy, needy, cling-on, which is what this feels like at the moment." I try to wriggle away.

"Will you stop! Stop wriggling, you're making me hard." He shifts his hardening erection to make me fully aware of this fact. "That is not why I wish I hadn't asked. In fact, I love that you're a crazy, needy, cling-on. It's the nicest thing you've said about 'this'." He waves his hand between us. "But you seem to think I'm a manwhore, and for that I wish I hadn't asked."

"Not a man whore, just a sexy as sin guy with mad skills in the bedroom, stamina of a long distance runner, and the sex drive of a teenage boy," I mutter, but he laughs aloud.

"I work a lot, I work out a lot, and the women I have fucked in the past have been *very* casual acquaintances, and there haven't been hundreds. There have been a lot, though." He narrows his eyes, expecting a reaction, but this is not news to me. As unpleasant as the feeling in my stomach is, I never imagined he was celibate. "Because I rarely fuck the same woman twice. I don't want them to believe that it is more than what it is, physical exercise."

"Physical exercise?" I must look shocked.

"Yes." He is unapologetic, "And I would like to clarify my sex drive mirrors yours, Miss Thorne, and it has never been like 'this'"--again with the waving hands--"with anyone before. You make me like this." He nestles in to the crook of my neck and inhales. "You drive me fucking crazy."

"Oh." Although I am not sure I entirely believe him.

"Oh, indeed." He draws a deep breath and runs his large hands up and down my spine.

"I like your type of physical exercise, beats getting pummelled into a mat any day." I shift and slide my legs on either side of his waist, and he grips my bottom, needing and pulling me hard against his crotch.

"I'm not averse to pummelling you into the mat, too, you know." He smiles wickedly, "Anything to keep you in line." He slaps my cheeks. "But, this"--he grinds up with a thrust of his hips--"is not just fucking, and it's not just physical exercise. You need to understand that, Miss Thorne." He kisses the soft spot below my ear, and I melt, but I don't respond to his declaration. I open the door and scramble out as we've reached our destination. I look back in the car as Daniel is busy pulling at his trousers, and I smirk.

"Problem, Mr. Stone?" He releases a guttural noise that makes my sex clench. So to help the situation I bend down and whisper, "If it helps, my birth control is effective immediately, so we're good to go bareback any time you're ready." I wink, slowly licking my dry lips and smiling sweetly.

"Fuck!" He growls. "There is no way I'll be getting out of the damn car now. You had better get back in here." He lunges for me, but I skip back just out of reach. "You really don't want to do this, Miss Thorne." His tone is menacing but his eyes are on fire with lust and mischief.

"You're probably right, but I'm not sure I want to get back in there, either, you look feral." I laugh nervously but keep my distance.

"You have no idea." His voice is low and controlled; his only tell being a slight twitch in his jaw. His lips are in a thin line and his eyes are more black than blue. My tummy is dancing with butterflies, and I make a snap decision to turn and head into the building. I hear the car door slam. I am a mixture of lust and panic, and my heart is racing. He can't be really angry, but now that I think about it, it was mean to leave him with a raging hard-on. Then again, by his own admission, he is always hard. Besides we are at his place of work, so I can't imagine I will get the full force of his retribution surrounded by his employees. I think I'm pretty safe and I take a seat in the sparse but plush reception area.

I may need to think again. Daniel strides purposefully towards me with a dark scowl and a smile that doesn't touch his eyes. Shit! He stands before me all menacing and male, blocking out my field of vision. He radiates power in a wave that washes over me, and I quiver as I look up through my lashes.

"Miss Thorne, allow me to show you around." His voice is calm; this might not be so bad. "Before we address the serious issues you have raised." I stand, and he places his hand on the small of my back, then moves me toward the security desk. I burn at his heated touch and tremble at the thought of what 'addressing the issues' entails.

"Eddie," Daniel addresses the man behind the desk.

"Mr. Stone, good afternoon, Sir." Eddie straightens his shoulders a little in Daniel's presence.

"Is Mrs. Jones feeling better, and did she get the flowers?" Daniel inquires.

"Yes, Mr. Stone. It was very kind of you, and she's definitely on the mend now, moaning about my cooking, which must mean she is getting better." He chuckles.

"Good to hear, not about the cooking, but I'm glad she's better. Eddie, this is Miss Thorne, I would like you to swipe her print and give her code five clearance." Daniel's request causes a sharp look of shock on Eddies face and a quick glance my way.

"Code five?" His query is obvious in his tone.

"Would you like me to repeat my request?" Daniel switches from warm to ice in an instant. It's unnerving.

"No, Sir. Miss Thorne, would you mind placing your finger on this pad?" I look to Daniel and he gives me a curt nod. I am not going to defy him again—well, not today anyway. "There, all done. Here is your ID card for general access and you just need your print for everything else. It was a pleasure to meet you, Miss Thorne."

"You too, Mr. Jones." He returns my smile, telling me to call him Eddie. I am again moved along by Daniel's large hand on my back. We enter the last lift in the row, and the doors close. The tension is palpable, but he makes no other move to touch me, just his hand on the small of my back. "What does code five mean?" I ask tentatively.

"It means you have the same access as I do, to the building, the private lift, my offices, and my apartment."

"Well, no wonder he queried your request." I shake my head at this, my eyes wide with disbelief.

"No, he shouldn't have done that. My requests are not queried. Ever." His clipped tone highlights his extreme irritation.

"Why have you given me code five access? It's crazy, Daniel."

His stern expression softens for a brief moment. "Because I want you everywhere I am, and I don't want the slightest possibility that my security might prevent that." His sentiment is touching and sends an instant warm glow through my chest, but the rapid return of his fierce glare disperses the warmth just as quickly as it came.

His secretary is a smart young man named Colin, who unfortunately wears a little too much product on his hair. He is handsome in a skinny, waif, model kind of way. His smile is genuine and he seems really friendly, although I don't get to shake his hand as my outstretched arm is intercepted, and I am drawn into Daniel's office. He does seem to have a thing for panoramic views, and this one is no exception. The view takes in the docks, over toward Greenwich, and beyond on a clear day. His desk is a vast expanse of glass and chrome, and he has a wall of ever-changing screens behind his chair. There is a soft seating area and a smaller desk directly opposite his. It seems odd that he would share an office, given that his company takes up the top four floors, and he owns the building.

Daniel walks over to his desk and I walk to the window, which is not for the faint-hearted or sufferers of vertigo. It is breathtaking. "Colin, move my three o'clock meeting to now, and I want my schedule cleared from three on today, is that understood?"

He cuts the call. "Now, Miss Thorne, that desk"--pointing to the smaller one--"is yours. The laptop is yours, and if you need anything else--supplies, books, whatever--ask Colin, and he'll source it for you." I go to object, but the serious look he fires at me has my mouth snapping shut. "Good girl. Now, I have a meeting that can't be avoided." He stalks slowly toward me. He is all predator, and by the rate of my heart, I am definitely hunted prey. I stand my ground, willing my legs not to quake. He is so close, my body thrums with desire for him, and he hasn't even touched me. "You can work from your desk, but I also want you to take this time to think *how* I should punish you." I suck in a sharp breath and pinch my thighs together at the instant tingle. "I don't think your behaviour was very polite, do you?" He runs his nose up the side of my neck, his voice, warm and breathy, whispering against my skin.

"No, Sir," I softly reply.

"What should I do?" His kisses along my collar bone, searing a scorching trail across my sensitive skin. "Mmmm, Miss Thorne, what do you want me to do?" A muffled moan escapes my throat and I can feel my body tremble. I know the words he wants to hear and I know I'm wet, because I want to say them, but mostly I tremble because he *knows* I want to say them.

"I want you to punish me, Sir." He drops his eyes to meet mine, and I have never seen such pure undiluted desire. He steps back, and I am wishing I had a fraction of the cool reserve he displays. My body slumps, and I press my hand against the window for support.

"And I will, Miss Thorne." His slow smile is filled with wicked promise. He presses a button on his desk. "Send the Projects team in, would you, Colin?" I'm startled as the door to the office opens, and I can only imagine what I look like, all flushed and panting, wide eyed, looking like a deer in the headlights. Three suited men enter and shake hands with Daniel. I turn to take 'my' seat behind 'my' desk in an attempt to hide. Daniel proceeds with his meeting, and I try to focus on some coursework, which is impossible, because all I can think about is my impending punishment. I spend the next hour shifting from one butt cheek to the next in a futile attempt to detract the building pressure in my core. I get practically no reading done, as I am fascinated by the meeting before me. Daniel commands the room with power and authority; his demands are stern and never debated. He barks a few orders, which make me jump, and he is not afraid to use colourful language. But it's when he is quiet that he is his most menacing. His low tone is followed by an absolute refusal to accept any excuses for the slightest deviation from his objective. It makes me shiver, and it makes me wet.

The sound of the door locking brings my attention back to the room, which is now empty. I had eventually managed to start some course work and hadn't noticed his team leave. It is just me and a smouldering mountain of lust and desire advancing toward me. I can see the obvious strain in his trousers, and I'm pleased he is as turned on as I am. I feel like I've had an hour of foreplay, and I am just about ready to explode. "You weren't joking about not negotiating, you just demand. It's very intimidating. Do you have a high success rate with that approach?" I gaze up through my lashes.

"In all things, Miss Thorne, one hundred percent until I met you." His voice is sensual like velvet, and my mouth is instantly dry.

"Oh, I don't know," I laugh nervously, "are you telling me you haven't got everything you wanted from me; that you are not a hundred percent satisfied with our *fun*?" I challenge.

He laughs loudly. "Oh Miss Thorne, you have no idea. I am more than satisfied. It is just that I have had to make adjustments for you and your commitments, which is something I never do. I am not in the least satisfied with that; you distract me, and again, that is not something I am used to." He stands in front of me, and I open my legs for him to stand between. He groans in appreciation. "Like now, you have distracted me." His heated gaze fixes on mine, but I am not at all distracted. I know exactly what

I want, and I frantically fumble for his buckle and zip. He places his hand to stop me, and I look up, incredulous. "Is that a punishment for you, Miss Thorne?" And I grin, he knows it isn't, and I panic a little that he might deny me.

"No, no, it's not, but I really want to taste you, really want you deep in my throat." My own breathy request makes his breath catch and his blue eyes darken. He is trying to keep control.

"That's not how punishment works, Miss Thorne." He runs his hand through my hair and gently cups my chin. I pout. "Have you ever been punished before?"

"No, Sir." I shake my head.

"Never been spanked?"

"No, Sir." My heart is beating a deafening tattoo in my chest.

"Well, aren't I the lucky one?" His mouth curls, his pleasure at this information blatant in his eyes, and his voice is sinfully smooth. He takes my hand and leads me over to his desk, where he sits and pulls me in between his legs. He rakes his finger nails up my legs, lightly scoring my skin and setting it on fire. He grabs my panties and pulls them down.

"Really, Bethany, I don't know why you bother wearing these, when I am always going to take them from you." He screws them up and puts them in his pocket. He stands, our bodies touching, the heat immense, and he can feel me tremble with want and anticipation. He turns me and pushes so I'm bent over his desk. My heart is pounding and as he gathers my skirt and hitches it over my bottom, I sigh softly and drop my head to the desk with a dull thud. His breathing is deep and controlled, mine is shallow and ragged. He nudges my legs apart and groans at my easy compliance.

"Now, Miss Thorne, I am going to spank you for ten strokes with my hand, as it's your first time, and I'd like you to count. Do you understand?" I nod. "Miss Thorne?" His strict tone reprimanding.

"Yes, Sir, I understand." I'm so consumed by the rush of emotions inside, I doubt I could count to three.

"Good girl." He stands to the side and presses his thigh against my leg. His hand is hot on my backside, gently caressing, smoothing over both cheeks. "God, you look amazing, open for me, waiting for me, I am so fucking hard it hurts. I can't do more than ten strikes because I need to be inside you." My core clenches at the thought, and the pressure is sweet agony with my legs spread wide. The first strike catches me by surprise with its timing and sting, and I cry out.

"You need to count for me, Bethany, or I will have to start again, and that will make me cross because like I said, I need to be inside you." His gruff direction is followed by a moan.

"One." I exhale. My cheeks clench in anticipation. The second strike is just as hard and just as shocking. "Fuck, that hurts!" I say with gritted teeth but add, "Two," because I don't want to start again, and I don't want him cross.

"It's supposed to." He pauses, "But feel." He swipes his finger the length of my folds; I'm dripping wet. "You're so wet, baby." Three, four, and five are in quick succession and I pant each number. I begin to relax, and I can feel the fierce heat radiating from my cheeks and spreading like liquid, warming my entire body, making it tingle with need and desire. I am dazed when he pulls me upright and turns me to face him, slightly dizzy, I didn't realize we had finished.

"Please." I'm not sure what I'm begging for, but I need him. It's all I needed to say, and he lifts and holds me braced on one arm. I wrap my arms around his neck and my legs around his waist. He strides to the wall of windows and slams me against it. Pulling at his zipper, he frees his erection with a grunt, and I can feel the hot velvet tip move against my wet folds, sliding toward my opening. I try to sink down to take the tip inside, I need him inside, and I can feel myself quiver and clench trying to tempt him further, harder, deeper. He looks deep in my eyes, and I can't look away if my life depended on it. He slams into me with an animal wildness that winds me, and again he draws back and plunges deep, fucking me hard, relentless, feral. He is so deep this way, and he fills me, hitting the wall of my womb, but I am clawing at his back needing him closer. He grinds his hips into mine, steps into me forcing his cock deeper still, forcing a silent scream from me.

"You need to take all of me, baby." His voice is demanding, and I thought I had. "You're holding back, let me in." He's pushing hard into me, relentlessly, and I tilt my hips and feel the very last of him sink inside, and he holds his position, buried to the hilt, deep and throbbing at just the point of pain. His gaze is raw, intimate, and fixed on me. I see him, and he is looking at me, looking into my soul. There is only us, and I am rocked to my core with this revelation. The force of my orgasm takes me by surprise, and my whole body convulses, riding the pleasure and grabbing greedily at his cock. He lifts me away from the glass and walks back to his desk still impaled deep inside. Holding me tight until my climax ebbs and ripples away, I sink breathlessly into his sweat-dampened shirt.

"I could stay inside you forever. You feel so good, so perfect." He kisses me with barely contained passion, and I can feel myself start to build again I can't get enough of him, but he stops and withdraws from me. He is rock hard, and with a sexy smile he kisses the tip of my nose. I must look confused as to why he has stopped when he so clearly isn't finished.

"You took your punishment very well. I'm pleased, and I think a different kind of pleasure would be an apt reward." His eyes darken, and his smile is deeply sensual.

"Different?" I have barely regained my senses from my first spanking, and he wants to try something different.

"More intense." He once again turns me around and bends me over his desk. I can't stop the trembling in my legs. "I believe I said every part of you belongs to me. Let's explore that, shall we. Do you trust me, Bethany?"

"Yes." I have answered this question before, but I am glad he asked again, particularly now. I do trust him.

"Good, you're going to love this, but we'll take it slow." His timbre is guttural and raw.

"Okay." I'm sure I don't sound convinced.

His fingers slide down between my cheeks and I instantly clench. "Relax, baby, nice and slow." He leans over me, and I feel his weight and his warmth; I feel safe, and I relax. Not sure how long it will last, but at that moment I am relaxed, relaxed and needy. He runs his finger the length of my folds, circling with a small amount of pressure on my clit, making me jump. He glides over my opening and takes his now very slick fingers and rubs the wetness around my puckered entrance. He uses the pad of his thumb to begin to rub a circle with increasing and varying degrees of pressure. It's really sensitive and causes a throbbing sensation deep inside; I can't help the urge to push back. "That's it, baby, push back and relax." He slowly and gently inserts his thumb, working in a rhythm, which is sending prickles all over my skin. He shifts, and I can feel him position his cock where his thumb has just been removed, and I clench again.

"Fuck, sorry, involuntary response, Daniel. I'm nervous. It's going to hurt, isn't it?" He softly kisses my neck and below my ear.

"Shh, baby, it will to start with, but then it will feel amazing, intense and amazing, I promise. Now, try and relax again and push back onto me." I take a deep breath and exhale and push back. Ah, fuck! He is way too big. A thousand prickles and an extreme feeling of fullness cause an intense flush of searing heat through my body. My teeth clench as I try and relax again, as I feel Daniel rock slowly into me. Slowly, gradually, deeper and fuller. I take shallow breaths and feel lightheaded. "Almost there, baby, you feel so good. God, you feel so good." My body starts to welcome the invasion rather than fight it, and I get a deep and sensual stirring inside, touching my very core. I am hyper-sensitive as wave after wave of exquisite pleasure rolls from the fullness I feel throughout my body. I can feel my orgasm start to build, but it's different. It is like a deep rumbling, a steady enormous climb rather than a violent peak, and I begin to shake uncontrollably. I cry out, and Daniel slips his hand around my waist and, with the pads of his fingers, gently rubs my clit, and I collapse, body shaking, hips convulsing, and I think that might be me screaming, but the sound is muffled. Daniel holds the nape of my neck and my hip firm, and pumps slowly, deeply, thrusting only a few more times before releasing his own climax, breathless but controlled. He slips from me and pulls me into his lap, holding me tight and kissing my hair.

I don't know how long he holds me, but I am awakened by the sound of typing. He has me cradled in one arm on his lap, and he is typing with one hand.

"You can multitask, too? Are there no end to your talents, Mr. Stone?" My voice is heavy with sleep.

"Welcome back. You went out like a light." He squeezes me. "But you feel so good, I wanted to keep you here. Would you like a shower?"

"Oh, a shower sounds good. Where?" He lifts me in his arms and carries me to a concealed panel. In his bathroom he undresses me and washes me, reverently with gentle hands. He kisses every inch of my body as he dries my skin, and I feel adored. I fight to swallow the building emotions in my throat. His touch makes me feel alive, and I tremble. I am terrified.

Chapter Fourteen

DESPITE MY AMENDED schedule, I still managed to stay at Daniel's apartment every night this week. I really need to develop my negotiating skills if I'm to stand a chance at ever getting my own way. We have eaten take out, I have brought food from the restaurant, and I cooked on Wednesday. Joe had taught me how to make fresh pasta when I was sixteen, and I made my other favourite pasta dish, ravioli with a wild mushroom stuffing and an herb butter. I even made a lemon panna cotta dessert. We fucked, we made love, and we talked.

We spend the evening lying on his sumptuous sofa. I am wrapped in a silk robe, and my legs are draped across Daniel's lap. He is massaging my feet, while I am trying my best not to squeal. I am extremely ticklish there and don't want him to know this weakness. It's okay if the pressure is firm, but the minute it becomes feather light, I will be scrabbling for the ceiling. I manage to contain myself, and he starts to ask me questions about growing up and my family. I think I keep my answers detailed enough to be interesting and factual, but vague enough to not actually give too much away. The late night conversation, I believe, is the reason why Daniel woke me as I started sobbing in my sleep and now has lifted me into his arms and is crushing the breath from my chest. I am dripping with sweat and trembling. I wake up fully when he carries me into the bathroom and sits me on a warmed towel on the marble vanity unit. His large warm hands sweep my soaked hair from my face and tucks it behind my ears.

"Okay, that was new." His smile is wary, his eyes are kind and warm. "Care to share?" He starts to strip the wet silk slip I sleep in, which is now translucent. He has the shower steaming and carries my trembling body into the welcome heat. Within minutes I am again dressed in one of his T-shirts, which swamps me, but is warm and dry. He carries me into one of the guest rooms. I raise my eyebrow at the change of location.

"Did you see the sheets?" He laughs lightly. "I never knew the human body could hold so much fluid." He pulls back the covers and helps me in.

"Are you staying?" I whisper. "It's okay if you don't..." But I don't get to finish that sentence as he climbs in on my side and pulls me half onto his body.

"Now, if you've stopped being ridiculous, would you like to talk to me?" He plants a soft kiss in my damp hair.

"No." I can feel his glare. "No, I mean I really don't want to, but unfortunately I have to. It's the only way I will ever get back to sleep." I let out a defeated breath.

"You have these a lot?" His obvious concern is touching.

"Used to, not so much now." I nestle into his chest. It feels good, and I sigh. "Okay, the usual is just to spill the details of the dream, well, nightmare, but actually I think you woke me before it really started. How did you do that?" I crane my neck to see his answer.

"Hey." He kisses my forehead. "I just felt you. Anyway, who do you usually spill to?"

"Sofs or Marco the other week." I feel him tense. "He wasn't quite as quick as you though. He had to come from his bedroom, and that's after I had made enough noise to wake him." I flinch as I flashback to that nightmare. "Anyway, I don't remember what this one was, so that's good." I squeeze my eyes shut and take a

189

deep breath smelling his intoxicating aroma.

"You sure you don't remember, you're not just saying that?" He sounds doubtful, but I snort.

"Believe me, if I could keep this shit to myself, I would, but then I'd never sleep again, so yes, I'm sure. There, aren't you glad I sleep over now?" I nudge him, and he just holds me tighter.

"More so now." He grumbles. "I definitely don't want Marco coming to your rescue or anyone else for that matter."

"Well, that just makes you crazy." I yawn and relax into his strong comforting hold.

"You make me crazy." He kisses my hair and strokes his fingers up and down my body until I fall asleep.

It's Friday, and I am working in Daniel's office, which is more distracting than the library, but better than Daniel accompanying me to the library, which he threatened to do. Since my first visit, where Daniel informed me that my screams were nowhere near as muffled as I imagined, every time he wants me, he sends Colin on an errand around the building. It's like Pavlov's dogs - Daniel tells Colin to hold all calls and to visit some department, and I'm dripping wet by the time he puts the phone down.

Today he was distant at lunch, and his mood has deteriorated as the afternoon progresses. I feel for anyone who has a meeting with him today, and I feel for our lecture group later if this continues. He is giving one of his lectures at my University this evening. I start to pack my bag.

"Where the fuck do you think you're going?" My head snaps to look at him, his eyes glaring and his jaw clenched.

"Who the fuck do you think you're talking to?" I snarl back at him. He instantly softens and walks toward me, picks me up, placing me on my desk, and wedges himself between my legs. "I should go." He tightens his grip before I get the chance to move.

"No, you shouldn't." He declares firmly.

"Daniel, it's your fault." I push against his hard chest, which doesn't give an inch, and he smells so good this close. "You insist on all this time together, but it's too much, and now you're pissed, so let me leave. It's fine, I understand, and it's all right." My chest constricts painfully at this, and my hand reaches for my hair but quickly moves to his. He doesn't need to know I'm lying.

"And you could just shut down like that. It's that simple?" He is barely containing his temper.

"Yes, Daniel, that is exactly what I could do, After all, I am a fucking robot!" I can't do this, I can't let him know I'm in over my head with him, in over my heart, not if he is ending it. I feel needy and pathetic, but he doesn't need to see that, so I set my chin and meet his dark eyes.

"Wow, you are really stubborn. Kiss me." He demands, and I frown, not what I was expecting, and I hesitate. "Now!" He growls, soft but stern, and I reach up to gently kiss the corner of his mouth. His lips are sweet and seductive. I need more, and he obliges, slanting his lips over mine, taking control of the kiss. His tongue pushes between my lips, and he tangles with mine, tasting and searching. He stops too soon, and I let out a sad sigh louder than I had intended, and his mouth curves to one side. "I am angry, but assuming it's because I don't want you says more about you than it does about my behaviour, Bethany. Have I given you any reason to doubt how I feel about you?" I swallow hard at the openness of this conversation. He tells me he wants me all the time, shows me with his body, with his time, but I haven't thought about what that really means--I can't. He wisely decides not to push this. "I am angry because I have an obligation that I have to fulfill, and it will mean that I am unable to spend Saturday and Sunday with you, and it fucking pisses me off!" He shouts the last bit, and I jump at the volume.

"And tonight?" I add quietly. He has a look of panic, and God, it makes my heart swell. I'm so fucked. "I have a drinks thing with Sofia. I did tell you, I'm sorry." I stroke his jaw, which is ticking something fierce. He has the start of afternoon stubble.

"No, you tried to hide the request, and I ignored it. Shit, this is fucking great! I'm not going to see you at all then?" His irritation is bordering on downright fury.

"Well, you can join us for a few drinks if you'd like, but then I'm staying at Sofia's for some girl time. I'll work Saturday and can come over to you after work and after your thing. I'm at my Mum's on Sunday, anyway, and then back to *normal* on Monday." I like our normal and I flash him my warmest smile "That's not so bad?"

"Fuck." He is still not happy. "I'm not happy about this, Bethany."

"No shit, Sherlock. I'd hate to see you really angry." I placate him with more kisses but I have to leave.

His lecture is at seven, prompt, and I don't want to be late. Although I do get an excited twinge in my core at the thought of what he might do if I was. My phone buzzes with a text.

MISS THORNE, NO PANTIES, FRONT ROW, ALONE--NO NEIGHBOURS. UNDERSTAND?

I did try and sit at the front, but Sam and Mike called me to sit with them and it just felt rude to refuse with no good reason; I text back.

ONE OUT OF THREE'S NOT BAD? ;)

The theatre is full except the front row, which has reserved notices along it. The main door clicks shut, and the room falls instantly silent. Daniel dominates the room with his power and presence, and I shiver at my intimate knowledge of that dominance. He narrows his eyes, sweeping the auditorium until he spots me. He flashes a wicked smile. I blush and immediately worry what he might do in front of all these people. He pulls a piece of paper from the inside pocket of his suit jacket and clears his throat.

"Is there a, Miss"--he pauses to look at the paper, and my whole body tenses--"Thorne?" No. No, he is not going to do this.

"Crap." I mutter.

"What have you done now?" Sam elbows my ribs, mocking me with his 'you're naughty' expression.

"Sir." I raise my arm.

"You're assignment was not completed. Whether you were too distracted or too far away to understand the instructions carefully, I would suggest you take a seat in the front row to prevent this happening again." His eyes bore into mine, which must be the size of saucers. Oh. My. God. He cannot be serious?

"The front row is reserved, Sir." I am so red right now, I clash with my dark green woollen skirt and sweater.

"I know." He smirks and raises a brow. I have to move, as I don't know how far he will take this. "Do you think it is polite not to follow simple instructions, Miss Thorne?" Crap! All right, now I know exactly how far he will go. I pack my bag and have to squeeze awkwardly across the row of students to the aisle, where I begin my descent of shame. I am so fucking angry right now. I have a good mind to storm out, but the wicked look in his eyes tells me he knows exactly what I'm thinking and is challenging me to 'try him'. I sit and loudly throw my bag to the floor. I then rummage until I find my pencil and pad before I return to look at him with my angriest glare. He is delighted with himself, and I sit and stew. I also write pages of notes; he is really rather brilliant when he is not infuriating.

It suddenly occurs to me that I am alone in the front row, and the tiered rows with their desks shield me from the view of those above me, as does the one I'm writing on. I can only be seen from the waist up by everyone else but only someone on the stage would have a view below my waist, too. My turn to smirk. I give a light cough, and his eyes flick to mine, his cool expression gives nothing away. He doesn't even pause in his presentation. I quietly uncross my legs and spread my knees wide. His face is turned to the screen but on looking back, his eyes widen as he recognizes my change in position. His eyes continue to address the room, but my heated stare is fixed on him, and I catch every furtive glance my way. I pull the woollen material from my dress, bunching it at my waist just enough to prevent any material falling between my legs and obstructing the clear view. I sigh as I become very aware of the change in temperature. Now that my legs are open, it is cooler, but I'm heated by desire, and I wiggle a little in my seat. I see his throat swallow, and I lick my lips to mimic the dryness he is trying to moisten.

His jaw is clenched, but other than that, he looks the picture of calm. He does however, move to stand behind the podium, and that makes me grin. I think one last bold move and we're even. I slowly take my finger, wet the tip between my lips and in a movement so slow it would go unnoticed by the unobservant. I trace this finger down my body and start to slide it under the waistband of my skirt.

"The material from this lecture is available on-line, but unfortunately I will have to finish this lecture here, and I am unable to field questions tonight. Until next time." His abrupt finish halts my move immediately. He switches the presentation off, but remains on the stage. As he has dismissed the room, there is a surge of activity and deafening noise. I hear him call, "Miss Thorne," but I use the general level of disturbance as cover and hurry out the door. I know there was at least another ten minutes of the lecture, and he is a perfectionist. There is no way he didn't have the exact and appropriate amount of material for the time allowed. I can see as I leave that he is again surrounded by gushing students. Perhaps it wasn't the smartest of ideas to provoke him when I know he is angry. because of the weekend. anyway, but he wasn't the only one who is angry. Fuck it, I'm not going to dwell. I'm going to meet my best friend, get roaring drunk, and deal with Daniel's 'man-struation' later.

"I bought us a bottle, as I didn't fancy bar hopping tonight. Is that okay with you?" Sofia calls to me above the noise of the bar.

"Absolutely." She hands me a glass and starts to pour. We've managed to secure an alcove seat in a very busy wine bar. It's lively and intimate, but perfect for catching up.

"Are you going to get that? It hasn't stopped ringing." She nods to my vibrating bag.

I know who it is, and he's really pissed. "My phone, my convenience." We clink glasses and drink. I ask Sofia about her wedding plans, and she tells me at length the stress she is under. The only daughter with a huge extended family, trying to please everybody, and Paul just wanting to please her. I can tell she's really excited about it all, though, and she secretly adores all the attention.

"So?" She raises her brows and addresses the elephant in the room. "How's it going with Mr. Hot and Horny, still 'fun'?" She uses air quotes to mock me, but her expression is serious. I haven't dated since her brother two years ago, and before that it was only ever John.

"Oh, definitely *fun.*" I follow this understatement with an uncontrollable surge of heat to my cheeks and a large gulp of wine.

"You're not getting away with that Bets, spill! You've stayed at his place how many nights this week?" She tops up my glass, hoping for the "lots of liquor equals loose lips" scenario.

"A few, he's very insistent when he wants something." I try to bite back the giggle, but it's useless.

"And he wants you…lucky you." She giggles and nudges me.

"For now." I smile lightly, the sobering sentiment quelling the giggles. I may not like the feeling I get when I acknowledge this fact, but, when I am not in the thrall of Daniel Stone, I do see this for what it is and where it will end.

"Oh, I have missed your 'glass half full' world view. Look, he'd be nuts to let you go, Bets." She softens her voice. "How do you feel about him?" My shoulders stiffen, and she thinks it's in response to her question. It isn't. I'd happily tell her if I knew myself. No, my shoulders stiffen and my skin tingles because I can feel him. How does he do that?

"Holy shit!" Sofia's eyes widen, and she beams a huge smile. I don't turn but take a large gulp of my wine, empty the glass, and pour myself another. He stands behind me brushing his hands across my shoulders. He moves his hand and sweeps my hair from my neck, scorching my skin where his fingers lightly touch. He leans in and softly kisses my cheek.

"Bethany." His voice is low and husky. He offers his hand to Sofia, and they shake hands. "Sofia, lovely to see you again. Bethany invited me to join you for drinks. I must apologize for being late. I wasn't entirely sure I had the right address." I tense instantly under his fingertips at this comment. "Can I get you another drink? Some water to go with the wine, perhaps?" He is charming with a touch of menace.

"We're fine with the wine, thank you." I look at his gorgeous face, and he is all smouldering, sexy as hell with a dazzling smile.

"Very well, I won't be a moment." He disappears toward the bar.

"Late?" Sofia queries.

"I'm surprised he's only late. I didn't tell him where we were meeting. I have no idea how he found me." I whisper even though the noise of the bar easily drowns my words. Nothing would surprise me. He is like a super spy or something equally sinister.

"So you didn't invite him?" She smiles unaware of my growing unease.

"Well, yes, I did. He was really grumpy earlier about not seeing me all weekend, and I said he could join us. I told him that I was staying over at yours afterwards, so it was a compromise. But then he was a complete arse in the Lecture this evening. I may have provoked him and then done a runner. Really didn't think he'd show up. That's why I wasn't answering my phone, if I spoke to him I would've caved and told him where we were. He's really persuasive."

"I'll bet, looking like that, why would you say no? Still he looks cool about it now. So, we'll have a few drinks, I'll text Paul. We're still doing the girlie sleepover though?"

"Hell, yes!" although I don't quite agree with her summation of Daniel's demeanour.

Daniel returns with a large bottle of water and proceeds to pour me a glass. He has a beer for himself. I tell Sofia about Daniel's lecture, skipping the tense bits that have me on edge, or maybe it's the way Daniel is drawing patterns on the skin of my neck and along my collarbone with his thumb. He whispers while Sofia is checking her phone.

"I want to speak to you alone." I know he can feel me tremble, and he hums into my neck, inhaling the scent from my hair.

"I know you do, but I can't leave Sofia alone, she's a man magnet." I smile tightly.

"She's not the only one, or haven't you noticed?" Actually, no, the only thing I have noticed is the filthy looks I have been getting from every female who happens to clock Daniel. "But you're right, you're safe, for now." He nips my ear lobe with his teeth sending a current straight to my core. He is too calm, too controlled. This underlying tension has me on edge. Sofia's squeal makes me jump, and I turn to see Paul making his way through the crowd. I twist to give him a hug and a kiss on the cheek.

"Daniel, this is Paul Simmons, Sofia's fiancé. He works near your offices, in one of the finance houses, and Paul, this is Daniel Stone." Paul interrupts.

"-Yes I know who you are. It's really good to meet you." Paul shakes Daniel's hand vigorously.

"Right." I carry on. "Well …Paul, this is Daniel…" Daniel interrupts this time.

"-I'm Bethany's boyfriend." The shock on my face would be the same if he'd slapped me, but it was Sofia who gasped.

"What?" I gasp too.

"Well, I thought partner sounded like a business relationship, and although lover is technically correct, I feel that even though it is an intimate description, it also sounds temporary. I thought you would prefer boyfriend, for now." My mouth is open, and I am actually speechless. Paul steps in.

"Well, that makes you a very lucky man." He slides in next to

Sofia and winks at me.

"I'll drink to that," beams Sofia, and I can't help but love my cheering section, even if I am hugely embarrassed.

"Yes, it does." Daniel agrees softly, and he covers my mouth with a heated passionate kiss as if there wasn't a room full of people. "I need to speak to Bethany, I won't keep her long." I just manage to put my glass down before I am whisked off the seat and led away through the busy room toward the back of the bar. We walk through an entrance, which is clearly marked staff, and then a second door, which leads to a small intimate private dining room. My heart is racing as he turns to face me. He fixes me with heavy lidded eyes filled with lust. My lips are dry, and I moan a little with pent up need as I suck my lips into my mouth.

"I like your thinking, Miss Thorne." His words are pushed through deep desire filled breaths. "You know by rights you should be properly punished for your behaviour today. If we had time, I would make it so that you couldn't sit down for a week, but I am going to have to improvise. I am going to fuck your mouth, and you are going to swallow all I give you. It is going to be hard and fast and for me. Understand, Miss Thorne?" Oh, God, I'm so wet right now, I squeeze my legs together. "Oh, no, Miss Thorne, I don't think so. For me, remember?" I pout but nod at his raised brow.

"Yes, Sir." My breath hitches, and I don't know how I am going to stop my own building pleasure.

"Good girl." He steps close and pushes my shoulder with one hand as he releases his buckle with the other. This really doesn't feel like a punishment as I kneel in front of him. I undo his zip, and his trousers fall to the floor. I carefully release his rock hard erection and fist my hand around the root. Applying some pressure, I move the silk-soft skin over his long, thick shaft. The wide crown is soft against my tongue, and I lick around the tip before I sheath my teeth and suck him into my mouth. He lets out a guttural moan and fists his hands in my hair, pulling me into him as he pushes deep into my throat. I can feel his veins pulsing against my lips as I swallow and hollow my cheeks, taking as much of him as I can, skilfully using my tight fist to squeeze and pump him to his root. I cup his heavy balls with my other hand and feel him tighten. His thrusts are faster, harder, and I feel him hit the back of my throat. I have to focus on my breathing to stop the gag reflex because I want all of him. I feel him flex and tense, then suddenly his cock gets bigger and his hips jerks and stop as he holds my head firm, and I pump my hand, milking the last drop. He comes deep down the back of my throat with an agonizing moan.

That was hard and really fast. My lips are swollen from the rough thrusting, but even so it really didn't feel like a punishment. I don't even feel too frustrated at not having had an orgasm myself. It felt amazing to just please him, for it to be all about him. I smile a satisfied smile as he directs me through the crowd with his arm around my waist. We reach our table, and I slip back into my seat.

"Another round?" Daniel asks casually, and he and Paul disappear to the bar. Sofia is quick to notice my swollen lips.

"Maybe some mouthwash?" Sofia giggles after them. Luckily it's too noisy, and they're too far to hear.

"Sofs!" I cringe.

"Hey, don't shoot the messenger!" She laughs, and I join her. "You did say he's kind of hard to say no to." She is still laughing. This is such rich material for her and so out of character for me, she's loving it.

"Yes, something like that." I hang my head at my own wantonness.

The men return with fresh drinks and the conversation remains normal. But as we begin to discuss the weekend, I feel him tense beside me, and I hate that. I want to know what's making him react like this. I turn to speak just to him.

"Look, you don't have to tell me, and I don't want to know, but you get tense at the mention of the weekend, and all I want to know is if there is anything I can do to make it better?" I hold his strong chin and look with all seriousness in his eyes.

"You already do, baby." He kisses me so softly it, makes my chest ache. But he doesn't tell me any more, so I leave it. "Look, ladies, Paul, I will leave you to the rest of your evening. I have work to get back to. Do you need my driver to take you home?"

"Paul can drop us or we'll get a taxi." I lean up to kiss him but he frowns.,

"No, Paul will take you or my driver will take you." He demands clearly.

"Right, Paul will take us." This time I manage to kiss the corner of his lips.

"You are working at the restaurant all night tomorrow?" He questions.

"Yes."

"And then you're at your mother's all day Sunday, is that right?" He looks agitated.

"Yes, Daniel, and I'll see you after work and after my visit." I hold his gaze, but his eyes flash with uncertainty. It was only fleeting, but it was there. I hate uncertainty.

After Daniel leaves, Sofia grabs my hands.

"Oh, Bets." She sighs, and I know she's hearing unicorns. "You two are scorching hot together. Do you even notice there is anyone else around, because I know he doesn't." I smile, but now I feel unsettled. "He can't take his eyes off you, he's so intense. It's seriously panty-wetting material."

Paul coughs."Hey! I'm right here, babe." He points to his somewhat wounded face, which she instantly captures and kisses profusely. "That's better." He smiles as she finishes adoring him enough to restore his pride.

"He is intense." It's all I can say, my mind and heart elsewhere, somewhere much more precarious.

"I know you're probably shitting yourself right now." Sofia is hugging me goodnight. Paul decided to stay over, too, and I'm

in her guest room because I have a call booked. "But he is really serious about you."

"Well, I'm such a catch," I joke, but she looks stern.

"Don't! I know you think I'm all rose tinted and see romance everywhere, but I know love when I see it." She stands looking as fierce as anyone can in fluffy, pink pyjamas.

"Fuck, Sofs! He can't love me, he doesn't know me." I sigh at her sad face. "Look, there is definitely passion and lust, off the charts chemistry. I'll give you that, but anything else is you projecting, I'm afraid." My turn to look stern, or she will have me engaged by the end of the week.

"But what he said about 'boyfriend for now'?" She pleads her case.

"Goodnight, Sofs!" I go to shut the door on her pouting face.

"Do you trust him, Bets?" Her voice soft.

"Yes, I do."

"Then it's okay to let him in." She kisses my forehead and lets me close the door.

I hear my phone vibrate, pick it up right away, and answer quietly.

"Sir?"

"Good Evening, Lola. Why are you speaking so quietly?" His deep voice sends a familiar chill across my skin.

"Sir, I am staying at a friend's house, and I don't want to disturb her."

"Very well. Are you wearing something I sent you?" He continues, regardless of my location.

"No, Sir. It wouldn't feel right." I'm being honest.

"Interesting. Well, tell me, are you at least naked?" I did quickly remove my T-shirt before the call.

"Yes, Sir."

"And have you been a good girl today?"

"No, Sir." I can think of at least one occasion, and I feel a little rush of heat at the recollection and the consequence.

"Really? And were you punished?" His voice deepens with a

gravel rough quality.

"Yes, Sir."

"So you have been punished since we last spoke. Did you enjoy it? Did it make you wet?" I can hear him draw in a slow breath.

I take in my own deep breath as a raw need starts to build in my core, and I run my hand over the skin of my bottom remembering the heat from my spanking. "Yes, Sir." I pause. "It hurt at first, but it did make me wet; very wet." My face is flushed and bright red.

"So you have received administrative punishment since we last spoke. That makes me hard, Lola... and jealous. And you said you were naughty today. Were you naughty because you wanted to be punished?"

"No, Sir." I don't think so.

"Really? Are you sure? Did you believe your actions would go unpunished?"

I think about this carefully, "No, Sir. I knew I would be punished."

"You knew you would be punished for your behaviour, and yet you did it, whatever it was, regardless. Does that not strike you as the actions of someone wanting to be punished?" He is coaxing my confession.

"Yes, Sir, it does."

"Tell me?"

"Yes, Sir, I wanted to be punished." I sigh softly, and I tingle all over. My body is hyper-alert from my encounter with Daniel earlier. I feel hot and frustrated.

"Good girl. Now I don't want you to touch yourself. I know you want to, but that is my punishment for you."

"Why am I being punished by you?" I sound a little desperate and a lot frustrated.

"Because you want me to." I let out a slight moan. I know I won't touch myself now. Considering his knowing laugh, he knows it too. "Goodnight, Lola." The line goes dead.

Chapter Fifteen

MY PHONE BUZZES in my pocket as I'm heading downstairs for my shift.

MY CAR WILL BE WAITING FOR YOU AFTER YOUR SHIFT TONIGHT. D

I have heard nothing from him all day, and I've been unsettled since our conversation at the bar. I can feel my defenses going up, and I kick myself that I had started to let them down, that he made me feel safe. I make myself safe.

AND HELLO TO YOU TOO b

Nothing.

I am just wrapping my apron when Sofia rushes through the door in a panic.

"Oh, God, Bets, you have to help me! My manager has called in sick, I'm not supposed to be working tonight, but they have a Charity Drinks and Canapé reception at the club, and now I have to be hostess. I need another me!" She has her hands pressed together in prayer, but it really isn't me she needs to pray to, and I tilt my head toward Joe to indicate as such.

"Uncle Joe." She wraps him in a big hug, "I'm taking Bets. I'll make it up to you, I promise!" She finishes her request with a hard kiss on his cheek, and he laughs.

"Oh, yeah, how you gonna do that, Princess?" He holds her until she actually has something to offer in exchange.

"Oh, oh… I know, babysitting, I'll babysit your brats!" She barters.

"I'd pay to see that, Princess." He can't contain his laughter now. "You go, but I'll call in that favour one day, Princess, I don't care who your daddy is!" He calls after her, but she has my hand and is dragging me out the door into the waiting taxi.

I have changed at Sofia's club into a smarter server's uniform, fitted white shirt, mid-length black skirt, and black leather pumps. Sofia is flapping about with last minute adjustments to the room, and I am calmly pouring the pink champagne. "Sofs, calm down. You've done this a million times before." My tone is soothing, trying to calm my hyper- anxious best friend.

"I know, I know, but this is for the boss's wife. It's her charity thing, and there are lots of really important people here tonight. It's a who's who of corporate entertainment. I would've been more prepared if it was my show, and I hate being dropped in it last minute. It just feels like a huge test or something." She sucks in a sharp breath. "Now, I want you to start with handing the champagne out and then walk through with the canapés and then…"

I place my hand on her flapping arm. "Sofia, breathe. I know what to do, I can manage a tray of drinks and food. You just go and be a hostess. I'll sort the others, and we will be fine. Go." I gently usher her to the entrance and carry on filling the champagne glasses. The private dining room at Sofia's club is set up tonight for a standing reception for about fifty. The room is nearly full of beautiful people, beautifully dressed, elegant gowns and black ties. Most people have drinks, but I collect a tray of fresh champagne to make another walk through, I only take two steps into the room, when I freeze. I don't know how I still manage to hold the tray, but I can't help my hands from shaking and the glasses from singing their disapproval.

"Good lord, how difficult is it to hold a tray steady?" A woman exclaims, laughing loudly. She doesn't turn, but her comment is enough to draw attention to me. I really don't see anyone else. He is looking directly at me, and although I can see his hand on the small of her back, which he retracts, it's not him I'm looking at. It's her. It's my sister, Kit.

I don't know where my strength came from, but I hold the tray firmly, like my life depends on it, with white knuckles and sweaty fingers. I hold it steady and hold my eyes steady too. I fix a brilliant smile and feel my mask fall into place. Once my tray is empty, I slip out of the room, my steps falling faster the further I move away toward the staff room. I feel his tight grip on my elbow, and he spins me to face him. His face is cold, and his eyes are dark. I hope my mask holds up as I meet his look.

"Daniel, you're looking very dashing, quite the gentleman." I smile too brightly. This is really hard.

"Bethany this is…" He looks angry, whether he is angry at me or angry at being caught, now is as good a time as any to break my own heart.

"-None of my business," I interrupt, "but bringing more canapés is. I'm seeing you later, right? We'll talk about it then?" I hope this will end this now, if he thinks we'll sort it later. He releases my arm with a frown.

"It's not what it looks like." He steps toward me and I back away. I can't be close, I can't hold this together when he's close. "Bethany?" He reaches for me, and I back away some more. He looks devastated, but it doesn't come close to my pain right now.

"Daniel, it's fine. We'll talk later?" This awful empty swell churns in my stomach, gathering momentum, and threatening my fragile act.

"Damn it, it's not fine! " He grabs me by my arms, and I start to shake. I feel his heat rush through me, and I can feel my eyes start to water. I can't breathe.

"Right, okay, it's not, but we'll talk about it later, or maybe we should both go back in there and you can introduce me as your girlfriend?" I snatch my arms back and glare. I'm speaking through gritted teeth to keep the volume down. Conscious that this is Sofia's debut as hostess, I'm not going to let Daniel or me fuck that up.

"No." He quietly confirms and my heart plummets.

"No. Quite, so how about you let me do my job, and we'll talk about it later?" He lets me turn, just as I hear Kit's voice calling him. I think I'm going to vomit. I manage, I don't know how, to sweep the room once more with a tray of canapés. I can feel his eyes on me, feel the tension, but I don't risk making eye contact. Sofia waves me over.

"Take a break, Bets, I'll be there in two minutes." I couldn't be more relieved to sit in a sweaty cramped staff locker room.

"What a complete arse-wipe! Bets, I'm so sorry. God I'm so sorry." She opens her arms and steps toward me.

"Don't you dare cuddle me, Miss!" I hold up my hand to stop her advance. "Not if you want me to go back out there, because I am not going out there with red swollen eyes." I try and smile, but it catches and doesn't quite make it. "You know it isn't that." I let out a shaky sigh. "I'm really not surprised--more surprised he wanted me to start with. Kind of let that go to my head. No it's just...did you see who he was with?" Sofia's sympathetic face is not helping.

"Yes, some blonde bimbo with false tits, fake tan, dripping in diamonds, shoe horned into a Harvey Leger bandage dress. Gross!" Her lips curl with distaste.

I snicker. "True, but did you see her face?"

"Botox, probably." She sneers this time.

"I'm sure, have a look next time you go in there." I'm wringing my fingers as I try and sort through the mess in my head. Sofia doesn't really do shaken, but she does look furious when she returns.

"What the fuck is she doing here? I didn't recognise her at first, I mean she's blonde now, and those boobs, and what happened to all the tattoos?" I'm shaking my head, because I have no idea how to answer. I honestly haven't seen her in four years.

"Did she see you?"

"I don't know." I shake my head lightly.

"Does she live around here? I've never seen her at the club before. Not that I can be sure, if you hadn't told me to look again I wouldn't have known." She frowns trying to make sense of this but I'm clueless. "What's she doing here with Daniel?"

"I don't know." I whisper.

"God! You don't think?" My eyes flash to hers and she stops before she finishes that horrendous thought.

"Sofs, do you need me to finish up here?" She must see the cracks in my mask because she already has my coat in her hand. "I need to stay somewhere tonight, somewhere he can't find me?"

"Go to Paul's. I'll text him. His building has shit hot security; no one gets in without a rectal exam and a DNA test!" She snorts and already has her phone in her hand.

"Or if they're approved, I hope?" I give her a hug and a kiss, take my bag, and slip away down the stairs.

Paul looks like he is walking on eggshells, Sofia must have told him to 'handle me with caution'. I have had a steaming hot shower, and he's lent me some sweats and a t-shirt, which swamp me but are better than what I was wearing. I am snuggled on his sofa with a warm brandy and sugar. I have had to argue to sleep on the sofa. Paul's apartment is flash, but it is a one bedroom, and it was only when I said I would take my chances on the street that he got me a pillow and blanket.

My phone has been buzzing with unanswered messages since midnight, and I am just about to switch it off when I get one from Sofia.

HE'S JUST LEFT HERE, I DIDN'T TELL HIM WHERE YOU WERE BUT HE ANSWERED HIS PHONE AND SAID THAT HE'D FOUND YOU- JUST THOUGHT I SHOULD WARN YOU XXSX

CRAP! THANKS, JUST HOPE YOU WERE RIGHT ABOUT SECURITY XXBX

Thirty minutes later, Paul's entry phone starts to buzz. Paul was already woken by Sofia and goes to answer it. I pull my legs up and wrap the blanket tightly around myself. I feel suddenly very cold.

"No, he isn't approved, and I don't care who he is. If he insists, please feel free to call the police and have him arrested for trespassing." Paul slams the phone down and comes over to me. I feel awful for putting him in the middle of this.

"Hey, honey." He wraps his big arms around me. "He can't throw his weight around here. You'll see him when you want to, and *if* you want to." He plants a kiss on my head and returns to his bed.

My phone buzzes.

I KNOW YOU'RE THERE PICK UP THE PHONE BETHANY! YOU SAID WE'D TALK. IT'S THE ONLY REASON I LET YOU GO; YOU SAID WE'D TALK, YOU LIED.

I don't have the energy to retort, 'So did you', 'You're an arse-wipe' or 'Why?' God I want to know why. Why her? How long have they been together? I heard her talking about the evening they had planned and tomorrow being such fun. They were even staying at the Savoy. I notice my hands are wet when I touch my cheeks, and I feel the layers of tears that have coated my face. I wipe roughly, Fuck! It doesn't matter. It doesn't matter why he wanted me, it doesn't matter that he wants her, all that matters is the net result, which is always the fucking same; everybody leaves. The pain in my chest hurts like a bitch as I try to fall asleep, but I am not going to cry anymore.

I wake early and find some of Sofia's clothes to wear. I can't go back to my place yet. She has some jeans and a sweater, and I thank heavens we're the same shoe size. I buzz down to security to check if I can get out. They can let me out but the car from last night is still parked out front. If I come down the stairs and wait in the security guard's office for a delivery, I can use that to get out, unseen. I leave a note for Paul and make my way down to wait in the office.

I spend the day with my mum. She is looking pale and has no recollection of who I am or that I visited last week. I feel numb. I switched my phone off, since it kept buzzing. I might just change my number. I spoke to the manager of the home and have arranged to sleep on one of the day-beds tonight. I just don't want to go home yet. I decide to take a walk along the beach before lock-down. It's dark and cold, and the large pebbles are damp against my jeans. There is something really eerie about the sound of crashing waves when visibility is so low and I shiver, but not just with the cold. I switch my phone back on to call Sofia to let her know I'm not back tonight.

"Hey, sister, I'm staying at my mum's tonight, and I'll go straight to Uni in the morning, so will see you tomorrow evening, if that's okay? Oh, and thank Paul for being a super hero last night."

"Oh he loves it! Bets, are you okay? Can you even stay at your mum's?" She sounds so worried.

"Yes, and yes. It's not a normal thing, but they can accommodate, sometimes. Besides I can be quite persuasive myself."

"He came over today, Bets. He looked like shit. I think maybe you should hear him out." Her words may be softly spoken, but they feel too harsh to hear.

"Traitor!" I say without conviction. "Look, I will at some point, but not now. It really isn't going to change anything, I promised Marco a 'no-more' and I'm definitely there with Daniel. Love you, sister." My teeth are chattering as I sign off.

"Bets, where are you? You sound strange?" Her voice is tinged with concern.

"On the beach, just heading back." The noise of the pebbles breaks the silence as I shift to leave.

"Christ, Bets, it's got to be minus five out there with the wind. Get your arse back inside!" She orders.

"On my way." I have no energy to argue, I have no anything.

I am awakened by the night porter trying to placate an irate man at the main gate, when realization hits me that I recognize the irate man at the gate.

"I'm sorry, sir, there is no one here by that name." The porter insists calmly.

"I know there is no one by that name as a resident. I am telling you that you have Bethany Thorne staying there tonight, and I have come to collect her." His anger is barely contained to a level of moderate civility.

"Well, that would be highly unlikely, Sir, but even if that was the case, I couldn't let you in until the morning. We have a number of vulnerable patients here, and I can't risk upsetting them. I am very sorry, Sir, but those are the rules." His voice is firm but fair.

"I won't be upsetting anyone. I will just pick her up and take her home. Surely you are not insured for non-residents to stay on the premises?" Daniel obviously trying an alternative route, I look with panic at the porter, an old man with kind eyes.

"Hmm." He laughs "No, I'm sure we aren't. Why don't you raise that with the manager in the morning when I let you in? Good evening, Sir." He disconnects and winks at me, and I mouth a big thank you. I walk back to the day room where they had put up a camp bed for me when my phone rings, my other phone. I sigh. I couldn't be less in the mood for this.

"Sir."

"Lola." he sounds agitated but I wait for him to speak to try and gauge how this conversation is to go. "How have you been?"

"Good, Sir, thank you for asking."

"Really? I thought we had resolved the lying issue early on in our relationship, Lola. Why do you decide to lie now?"

"Sir, I…" I hesitate and sigh. If he really wants to know, what could it hurt? He'll soon tell me to stop talking, if it's not what he wants to hear. "I haven't been so good, Sir, but I didn't think it was right to tell you."

"If I ask you something, Lola, I want to know the truth, that's all, no lies. So tell me, have you been bad?"

"No Sir, not bad, just stupid."

"Stupid how?"

"Well, stupid or naïve, either fits… I mistook lust for something else."

"You are stupid for thinking that someone loves you when it is just lust, is that what you are saying?"

"No." I laugh. "I know its lust on his part, but I was stupid." Christ, my voice is breaking. "I was stupid because I fell in love with him when I should've known it was just lust; it was only ever going to be lust."

"Did you tell him you loved him?"

"No, Sir, no, I didn't, and I am really glad I didn't. But it doesn't stop me from feeling. It just means my humiliation is contained."

"-And you can't tell this person this?"

"Oh, yes, that would be perfect! I could perhaps cut my heart out as an offering, a side dish if you will."

"Sarcasm is not very polite, is it, Lola?" His stern reprimand stops my inappropriate tirade.

"No, Sir. I'm sorry, Sir." I feel bad for dumping on this stranger. "To answer your question, no, I won't be telling this person, ever. It's about self-preservation now, Sir."

"That is very sad, Lola."

"No, Sir… it's not sad. It's heartbreaking." I disconnect the call. I've never done that before, and I am glad he didn't call back. He'll probably cancel his booking now. There is no way he was expecting that when he selected the specialist line.

I wake at four in the morning to cut across the garden and leave the property without using the main gate. I need to get to the station at five to get the milk train back to London. I have back-to-back lectures today, the second of which is in one of the large lecture theatres. Some core units are shared over different courses, and my second lecture is one of those: Finance. The room is stuffy, and I feel slightly hot, sticky, and a sheen of perspiration is coating my body. My hands are shaking, and I realize I haven't had anything to eat today as my tummy rumbles in disapproval. I am rummaging in my bag for something edible when the Lecturer begins by explaining that today's topic of 'Small Business Financing' is going to be taken by a guest speaker. I get a watery taste in the back of my mouth, and I breathe through my nose; I think I'm going to vomit. I swallow a dry heave, thankful now that I haven't eaten anything.

Daniel walks in, he doesn't look at the audience, and I sink into my seat. I am too far from the door to escape, and I just hope he doesn't call me out to the front like last time. He doesn't. It's worse. He loads his presentation and begins.

"The best way to get an understanding of small business finance," His voice is smooth and deep, and I can't help the effect his being there has on me as my heartbeat races and a flush of prickles kiss my skin. "is to work through a case study of a small business. So in light of this, I have made up a company, and we will go through each key stage step by step." He pauses and turns to face the audience, but his dark hard eyes are on me. He clicks the laptop in front of him and the case study fills the ten foot high screen behind him: "Lola's Call Center." The corners of his mouth crease, but his smile doesn't reach his eyes. I feel the blood drain from my face, but it's also rushing in my ears. Large black spots float across my eyes, and I know I'm going to faint and/or have a panic attack. He knows, of course he knows. He's my caller, but why tell me... why tell me now? I start to blow breaths through my pursed lips in a controlled manner as I pack my bag. I start to shuffle my way across the aisle, but when I get to the floor of the theatre Daniel addresses me.

"Did I say you could leave, Miss Thorne?" His voice cold and angry.

"No, Sir, you didn't." I walk to the door and leave, just making it to the corridor when I hear a muffled sound in my ears, and I see dizzying lights above me as I hit the deck. I am being jostled and jiggled. My eyes are still closed, I can smell citrus and exotic spice. My face is pressed against soft cotton, and I'm being held tightly. I push my face against the firm chest and nestle, inhaling deeply and feeling a warm rush of familiarity. That familiarity also makes me jump, but I'm held tighter with a growl.

"Don't you dare fucking move, I've got you now. There is no fucking way you're going anywhere. I've got you." I relax into his stride and his warmth.

"I want to go home," I whisper.

"All right, I'll take you home, but then we talk." He changes his mind then, "After I've fed you, then we'll talk." He grumbles.

I'm sitting on my sofa with a large bowl of spinach and ricotta ravioli that Daniel has brought upstairs, along with some fresh bread and some milk. My tummy continues to rumble even after I have eaten half of the bowl.

"When did you last eat, Bethany?" His voice is low, quiet and I have to think. "The fact that you are having to think about the answer pisses me off. Look at you. You need to take better care of yourself. What if you'd fainted in the street? What if-"

"-Saturday." I interrupt. "I ate on Saturday, and to be fair this isn't my 'normal' type of weekend. So I think I can be cut a little slack in the caring for myself department." I snarl back at him. "Daniel, I'm grateful that you brought me home, but let's not get all 'overprotective' when it's…" I stop because I want to add 'your fault I'm like this in the first place', and I don't want to do that. It's not fair to make him feel bad when I am going to end this tonight.

"You didn't let me explain." His eyes hold a wealth of concern, and his voice is so quiet.

"No, because it really doesn't matter." I soften and touch his leg, his muscles flex, so do mine. "But it's important to you, so

I'll listen, but you have to listen to me, too."

"I did listen to you." His eyes are molten heat, and I sit a little further back, but he just closes this distance and holds my stare. "The obligation I had was for my mother's friend's chosen charity. I was bid on at the 'Bachelor's Auction'. I had to attend the drinks reception with the winning bidder and spend Sunday sight-seeing in London. I couldn't get out of it and I couldn't embarrass Kassandra by introducing you at the reception, which"--he takes my hand, sending sparks to my core--"I desperately wanted to do. You were so calm, but I knew you weren't okay with it, but I thought you were okay enough to wait and talk later. If I had known for a second that was not the case, I would not have left your side. You have no idea what fucking hell it's been, knowing where you are, but not being able to get to you." He grabs my face with both hands, his eyes intense with desire. "Don't you ever fucking do that again." He captures my mouth with his soft but firm lips, and I gasp, my parted lips an invitation he accepts willingly, plunging his hot tongue in, searching and tasting. I desperately engage with this demanding dance, my breathing laboured my heart racing. I push his hard chest, my fingers brush the curve of his muscles, his breathing heavy, too. He moves back.

"I love you, Bethany." He moves to capture me again but I stand up in shock.

"Fuck, no!" I yell and try and back away. He stands too, towering over me. "I can't let you, Daniel. There's no way, I said no-more." I have my hands pressed flat against his hard stomach, trying to hold him back, "I won't survive you, Daniel." I'm trembling and my voice is cracking. I try and regain some composure with some steadying breaths, "I won't survive you." I look up into his eyes, I'm pleading, and he forges on and scoops me in to his arms and strides to my bedroom.

"I won't survive you either, Bethany. I love you, and I know you think this is lust. Unfortunately, it's been three days since I've been inside you, so now it feels a lot like lust, but after we've made love, and I can think straight, I will tell you again, that I love you and you will tell me that you will never leave me. Oh, and that you love me, too." He flashes the most amazing smile before he roughly takes possession of my mouth and my body. He moves with purpose and a hungry intensity that has me breathless. He peels my clothes from my body, slowly covering the newly exposed nakedness with adoring kisses. His hands constantly caressing and stroking, my skin burns from his touch and rages inside. His body covers mine, pinning me to the bed, securing my wrists by my head, he pulls back to meet my eyes, lust and hunger, and something more. He pushes my legs wide with his weight, his hard erection pushing, nudging, keen to gain access. His mouth covers mine, and he moans into my mouth as he pushes deep inside. My sex greedily contracts around his cock, pulling him in deeper with a tilt of my hips. He moves slowly, rotating his hips trying to gain more access, to get deeper. I gasp out loud as he hits the end of my womb with such sweet agony, he swallows my pain, his eyes scorch through me, and I start to tremble.

"Sshhh, baby, I've got you." He holds himself deep inside me, not moving, his deep breathing vibrating through me. This is raw. Need and desire make my chest heave with the depth of emotion I feel for him. My eyes fight to hold on to my tears. "Bethany, you are everything." It's enough, and it's too much. He moves just a fraction deeper, and it sends me falling, fighting to breathe, flooded with immense waves of pleasure, spasms of uncontrollable bliss. I hang on to his broad shoulders, gripping tight with my nails and my head buried in his neck, tears finally falling. I'm such a mess. He holds me for the longest time, not moving, still rock hard. My body stops shaking, and as I refocus on the most beautiful eyes staring down at me, I am rewarded with the sexiest smile and most sensual kiss. I start to move my hips, thinking he must need some relief, if my climax was anything to go by. "Don't move, baby, I want to come, just like this, buried deep with you tight around me; my perfect fit." I gasp as he nudges deeper.

"Not sure you fit as well as you think." I explain with a cautious tone.

"Maybe not, but it's still perfect." He kisses me. He is hungry, devouring everything I return, swirling and plunging, fucking my mouth with his tongue, all the movement he is denying himself inside me. He holds me tight against him, and I moan at the passion of his kiss. I am full and stretched and I can feel him pulse deep inside, the smallest movement is enough to start another orgasm to build. "Look at me, I want to see your eyes when we come together. Do you feel that?"

"God, yes, you're so... so deep, ahh!" I'm panting because I don't want to move and break this amazing tension, balanced on an edge of unbelievable pleasure. I look into his eyes, and I feel him, all of him, and I love him. "I love you."

"Fuck!" He never breaks his scorching eye contact when he comes; when I come.

He wraps me in my duvet and holds me tight into his chest, kissing and stroking my hair. Some time passes when Daniel whispers. "It doesn't count, you know."

"What doesn't count?" I am tracing my fingers along the cut of his abdominal muscles, the ones that make my mouth water.

"Saying 'I love you' just as you're about to have a mind-blowing orgasm." I can feel his smile as he kisses my hair.

"Who says it was mind-blowing?" I poke his ridged muscles playfully.

"Oh, you're right. We should rematch and go for mind-blowing." He flips me so he is again on top, pinning me to the bed.

"It was mind-blowing!" I softly laugh, and he kisses the tip of my nose.

"I'd like you to say it when you're not in the throes of passion."

"I know." I say quietly, but I am still feeling raw and exposed. Maybe later, and he seems to understand. He smiles and falls back to snuggle with me against his chest and in the crook of his arm. "But I told you when I wasn't in the throes of passion, too."

"Yes…yes, you did." He kisses my hair, and I can feel his lips curl in a smile.

"Why didn't you tell me? You knew I was Lola. Why tell me now?" I tilt my head to meet his gaze.

"I liked your honesty. You are very open when you are Lola." His eyes soften. "And I needed your attention. That's why I told you now, but if I'm honest, I would have preferred to have kept Lola's secret."

"I can understand why, but having that level of access to my inner thoughts makes me extremely vulnerable."

"I like you vulnerable." I tense, and he pulls me tighter. "I want you to feel you can be vulnerable with me. I would treasure that level of trust. I want you to be that open with me, but I understand it will take time. All I'm saying is that now you know that I know. I will miss Lola's honesty."

"I liked that level of honesty, too. It was liberating and hot. It was safe."

"And you don't feel safe with me." It's not a question. "But you will…I promise."

I am quiet for a while, and although I have taken in everything he has said, there is one stupid question I can't ignore.

"How did you disguise your voice? I mean, you said things that certainly sounded like you, and sometimes I did get a chill, but I never recognized your voice."

He chuckles. "That's your only issue with this situation? Good. It was a simple filter, which changed the octave and pitch a little and gave a little echo, but enough to alter the sound."

"Oh…and it's not my only issue, but the other stuff we can sort out together." I stretch my body up his, and he leans down to cover my mouth with a soft kiss.

"Sounds good to me." He lets out a contented breath and then groans. "This is a fucking uncomfortable bed. How do you even sleep?" He wriggles beneath me in a futile attempt to get comfortable.

"It's better than the streets."

He sits up shocked. "Is that really an option?" His brow is heavy with instant fury.

"Not if Sofia's parents had anything to do with it. No, if I couldn't live here I'd just live further in the sticks."

"No family home?" He gently probes.

"No family home."

"No brothers, sisters, uncles…" He pushes.

"No Daniel, no family. I told you Sofia's family is my family, well, and my mum." I need to know what Kit told him, but it's just going to come across as jealousy. "So who was the lucky lady?" I try for mild interest.

"There's no need to be jealous, Bethany." His voice is deadly serious, no teasing with this potentially volatile subject.

"Just so as you know, I don't actually get jealous. You either want to be with me, or you should have enough backbone to say you don't. It's not about jealousy or cheating, it's about trust, and it was never about not trusting you, Daniel." He looks a little confused, and I can't explain further without exposing Kit.

"She's a widow, sad, really. She had amnesia when she was twenty-two. Can't remember a thing. She's had to build her whole life by herself. She was married to some rich financier but he died earlier this year in a car accident. They weren't married long apparently. Anyway, she met my mother at some function, and my mother adores her; thought the auction would be fun."

"Amnesia?" I try not to choke on my disbelief.

"Yes, she's has a rather nasty scar."

"On her neck?" This seems to make a little more sense.

"Yes." He draws his brows together. "How did you know?"

"Saw it, saw the back of her." It would've been where her tattoo was removed, not the right image having 'Dick's', her then boyfriend's brand, for all to see. Only works when you're a horny teenager, I guess. "What's her name?"

"Kassandra, Kassandra Shaw."

"Did you like her?" I don't know why I insist on knowing

this; it hurts to just know she's spent time with him.

"Fake gold digger? Oh yes, I loved her. We've got a date next week." I know he's trying to joke, and he has no idea the baggage I carry for that woman. So rather than him think that I really don't have a sense of humour, I lean over and pinch his nipple, really hard.

"Fuck! It was a joke!" He pouts, rubbing his poor injured body part.

"So was that!" I smirk and roll out of bed. "Hot drink? Ovaltine, Coco, Bailey's...Me?" He lunges to grab my leg growling.

"Definitely you." I slip through his fingers, giggling. I put some milk on to heat and go to fetch the cups, when I hear loud footsteps up to my door. The door swings open and Sofia's standing with tears in her eyes. I drop the cups and run to her. "Sofs, what's up? Is it Marco? Is Paul all right? Sofs, why are you crying?" The pitch of my voice is rising with every question.

"Bets, they tried to call you. Then they called me, and I came straight over." She swallows, "Bets, it's your mum, she's had a heart attack. She's stable, but they said you should hurry." For the second time today, I see dark spots and hear muffled voices only this time, I am swept up into warm strong arms before I hit the floor.

Chapter Sixteen

I PUT THE PHONE down gently after finishing my call with the nurse in the intensive care unit at the home. They had taken the decision not to move her to the general hospital, as there was really nothing they could do that they weren't doing in the unit. Daniel is holding my hand, and Sofia is making some warm milk.

"They said it was too late to go down tonight, and that I should wait until morning." I start to cry, and Sofia is at my side as Daniel stands and walks to my bedroom. My arms are wrapped tightly around my waist. I can't stop shivering.

"It's probably for the best, Bets. There's nothing you can do tonight. Maybe try and get some sleep?" She squeezes my leg, and I feel Daniel sit next to me. He is dressed and is carrying my clothes.

"Hey, baby, let's put these on." He takes my arms and carefully slips on a soft T-shirt and warm sweater with leggings and some sheepskin boots. He scoops me into his arms. "My driver is outside. I'm taking her to see her mum." Sofia nods, and I take enormous comfort from the strong chest my head is resting on, glad I am not making these decisions.

Daniel's fast car makes light work of the nighttime motorway traffic. We pull up the gravel drive just before two in the morning, and the night porter from the other night kindly lets us in.

"I'm so sorry, my dear." He holds my hand, and I wonder if I will be able to handle this, if this is the norm in these situations. What do I even say, 'It's okay' when it clearly isn't? 'Yes she is or was'? Did they even know her? I literally don't know what to say.

"Thank you, that's very kind." Daniel moves forward to shake the porter's hand. Yes, that's what I need to say, thank you, I'll remember that. I feel strangely detached and on autopilot at the same time. I walk toward the intensive care rooms where she has been moved. The nurse greets me.

"I'm so sorry, Bethany. She's comfortable now, and she is talking a little, but I'm afraid there's nothing more we can do. She's such a lovely lady. We're going to miss her." She presses my hand in hers.

"Thank you." I say quietly. "You're very kind." I let her hand slip from mine and go to find my mum. Her door is closed, and I open it quietly. She's sleeping, and I take a seat by her side. I hold her delicate hand, her skin fragile and soft like silk, translucent and very thin. Daniel takes a seat in the corner of the room, squeezing his large frame into a tall backed chair. I sit beside her bed until the morning light starts to break through the curtains. The day shift has just taken over, and for the first time since I sat down, my mum moves a little. "Hey, mum, I hear you're causing trouble? They brought me back specially to sort you out." I swallow back the rising lump. She looks so pale, not like her at all. Her glow is no longer around her, but she still looks like an angel, with her light grey fluffy hair spread around the pillow like a halo. She opens her eyes, and her gaze is glassy, but she looks straight at me, a spark of recognition and a faint smile.

"Hey, baby, Boo." She squeezes my hand and instant tears pool my eyes. She hasn't called me by my nickname for years. Even when she did recognize me, it was always Bethany.

"Hey, Mum." My voice is breaking, and I don't want to cry. I don't want to upset her. I want her to talk, and I want her to remember.

"I'm so sorry, Boo, I try so hard to remember. I try so hard for you, my baby." Her eyes glisten.

"It's all right, mum. You know it's fine, you mustn't worry." I want to reassure her.

"You have to know, you have to know." She looks so sad and holds my hand a little tighter. "They didn't leave you, they left, but they didn't leave *you*. Your Father, he never knew about you, I wrote to him one time, when you were sixteen. I thought I'd made a mistake by not telling him. I thought he would come, but when he didn't, I knew I was right that I kept it from you. That you never knew who he was. But you should know, he didn't leave you, he left me, and I tried so hard not to leave you, baby. I tried to remember, I tried not to leave you." She closes her eyes, and I use that time to take some deep tear-fighting breaths, if this is the last thing she remembers, I don't want it to be regret and sadness.

"Mum, I love my life with you, and I wouldn't change a thing. No one left that we wanted to stay. I miss you, mum, but you've always loved me, and I've always felt loved. You are the best mum, the best." I lift her small hand and press my kiss, holding it. Fuck, I'm going to cry. Don't bloody cry, Bets.

"She shouldn't have left you alone, you were still a baby, I won't forgive her. You didn't deserve that. I'm so sorry I wasn't there." Even in this frail state her anger is fierce.

"Mum. Mum, listen. Please listen. I wasn't a baby; I was your baby, but I wasn't a baby. You are a wonderful mum, and I'm so lucky you are my mother." I desperately need her to believe me.

"Promise me." She smiles, and her eyes sparkle.

"You name it? You want me to take you to the top of the Beacon again?" I want her to think about good things, remember good memories.

"Don't be afraid, don't let our past and your past, your past with John--" I suck in a sob "--don't let that make you too scared to live. For me, promise me that, Boo, and I'll promise to remember all the good things." I can feel my tears rolling down my cheeks. I know I won't be able to speak without releasing a sob, so I swallow and sniff back the tears. They need to stop.

"Mum." I squeeze her hand, and she opens her eyes. "I promise."

She smiles and closes her eyes again. "Good girl. You always were a good girl, when you weren't off gallivanting." I laugh aloud, a booming laugh combined with a heartbreaking sob. God, I've missed her so much. I hold her hand up and kiss the back of her hand again and rub the soft bony knuckles against my wet face.

"I promise, mum." I lean up and kiss her hollow cheek.

"Promise what, dear?" She doesn't open her eyes again, her grip on my hand loosens, and her breathing fades. My head is pressed into the bed, and I let out some bone-shaking sobs, muffled by the thickness of the mattress.

"Hey, baby, time to go." I have been sitting in the day room, the sun bright and the sky clear, a perfect day to see the spectacular views of the South Coast. I have signed papers and have been given a box with Mum's personal belongings to take. It seems everything was packed in readiness. I could think that cold, but I don't think anything at the moment. Daniel has dealt with the management and has taken all the details to sort through with me later. I go to stand, and he scoops me into his arms. I laugh, it's ridiculous. "I can walk."

"I know, I just want you close-- closer." I rest my head on his chest. I want that too.

The drive back is quiet; there's not much to say. I think the funeral will be in a few days.

"I know this is a stupid question." Daniel interrupts my thoughts.

"But you're going to ask anyway?" I smile.

He nods. "How are you doing?"

"Not a stupid question. I'm… well… I'm ok. I lost my mum a

long time ago. I visited because I always hoped she'd remember, but for the last eighteen months I've been visiting this lovely old lady who didn't have a clue who I was but knew I was really good at crafts." I laugh a little. "I've missed her for so long, and she was back today, and it was like a punch to the chest. I feel winded and bruised, but it was the best feeling to have her, even for a short time. I'll be fine." I put my hand on his thigh and squeezed his tight muscle.

"I fucking hate it when you say that." He mutters not wanting to be angry with me. I smile at him.

"I am enormously sad," I sigh heavily, "but I will be okay with this. I've had a long time to let go, so, no, I'm not fine, but I will be. Is that better?"

"Yes." He reaches for my hand. "What did she mean by not knowing who your father was? I thought you knew who he was?"

"I did... I do... he just left when I was born. I think maybe she was a little confused. I think maybe she wanted me to understand that it wasn't *me* they left" I laugh sadly.

"Mmm, maybe. And she was right, they didn't leave you." He pulls my fingers to his lips and softly kisses them.

"That's semantics, Daniel. I do believe the *net* result is the same, the *net* result is my life, and I am left *alone*." I turn my face to the now grey sky, unable to stop the falling tears. He doesn't allow me much time to wallow when he pulls me into his lap and folds his strong arms around me, encasing me in his warm embrace, stroking my hair and gently kissing my cheeks for the rest of the journey.

"Daniel?" I tilt my head to meet his somber face.

"Yes?" His tender smile warms me.

"Thank you." I can't think about all he's done and why, or I will fall apart, but he just continues to smile his amazing smile right back at me.

Daniel insisted I stay with him, and he's not left my side, although he does always have a phone attached to his ear trying to work. He has smoothed things over with the University and even had lecture notes couriered over, so I don't miss anything crucial. Sofia's family has been wonderful and have arranged the funeral and a small gathering in the day room after the ceremony. I have written a few things I want to say. I don't know yet whether I will, but that is my plan.

We travel down in two cars, I'm with Daniel, and Sofia is with Paul, her parents, and Marco. Other than a few residents and caretakers, the room at the crematorium is sparse and soulless. We file slowly into the room where a brief service will be given. I am grateful for the warmth I feel from both Daniel and Marco's hands, which hold mine, but it is painfully insufficient when I'm chilled to the bone at the image in the front row. Iron straight bright blond hair falls down from a ridiculously ostentatious hat, given the surroundings. Immaculate, in a black Prada dress and jacket, she turns dry eyed with a pseudo-sad face, and I stand transfixed. Daniel places his other hand on my arm to urge me forward, thinking I am overwhelmed by the proceedings.

"What the fuck is she doing here?" Sofia hisses in my ear, but I'm too shocked to answer. I have no idea. How did she even know?

Daniel seems equally surprised by the tone of his voice. "What is Kassandra doing here? Do you know her, Bethany?" His confusion was evident on his crinkled brow. "Why would she come?"

"I have no idea why she's here, but I do know her." Daniel waits for me to continue, but my head is spinning. What could she possibly want? Why now? I feel sick that she would make today about her.

"Bethany?" He is trying to get me to answer, but even the term identifying her relationship to me is alien.

"That's her sister." Sofia enlightens him with borrowed venom. I look at my best friend, who's ready to do battle on my behalf, but I shake my head slightly. This isn't going to happen today, and I walk to take my seat on the row opposite, surrounded by the best people in the world. I am numb to the words the priest is saying. He does his job well, I'm sure, but my mum never went to church, and he wouldn't have known her. So the sad words of comfort are just sad words. When the service is over, I choose to head back to the car. I don't need to see the flower arrangements, which will never be enjoyed by my mum, beautiful flowers that will fade more quickly because of their presence today. We are all heading back to the home for tea, and I just want to be alone in Daniels car.

"Bethany, is that really you?" I hear her voice, sweet and sad, with a slight wobble in the pronunciation of my name, practiced and perfect.

"Kit." I reply, my cold response glaringly obvious. She narrows her eyes. I think she must be taking a risk exposing herself today, and she is hesitant. I wonder how much she is willing to risk exactly.

"I'm sorry, Kit? That was my name Kit?" She looks puzzled, then a saccharine smile spreads her bright red lips wide. "Oh!" She laughs a little at the revelation. I am definitely going to be sick. Daniel comes to my side and puts his strong arms tight around my shoulder.

"Yes, your name *was* Kithara Thorne. Mum said it was the musical instrument Apollo played; it's Greek." I have no idea what I'm saying, it's not like she doesn't know this already. "I had trouble saying my 'th's so you were Kit to me, then everyone else."

"Oh, how darling, my name was changed because *you* couldn't say it." Her words are light, but I sense the bitter tone.

"Isn't this wonderful, Bethany? I know it's a terribly sad day, but I can't believe this. Look, you still have family, you're not alone after all." He cups my face, and tears spring to my eyes. I am so alone if *she* is the only family I have left. "I can't believe it." He looks to Kit and her eyes sparkle, and she looks back through her thickly painted lashes. "Kassandra, would you like to ride with us? I can't imagine how much you two have to catch up on. This is just amazing!" He seems genuinely happy for me, and I'm just going to come across as a huge bitch for not giving my 'amnesia-challenged sister' a chance to build bridges. There is also the fact that I don't know what she wants. It's obviously not me. She doesn't need to pretend to be Kassandra to have me in her life.

"Oh, Daniel, darling, that's so sweet, but I have my driver." She looks over to a Range Rover with a hulk of an ape standing by the front door, hair cropped so short he looks bald, no neck to speak of, and scary huge muscles fighting to escape his pale, ill-fitted grey suit. She walks over with an exaggerated sway in her hips and grabs Daniel's arms, squeezing them in a slow massage of his muscle. "I am just so happy to remember." A small tear trickles down her cheek for effect. She turns to me, my teeth are so clenched I think the enamel may crack. "Bethany…Boo." I swallow my cry as she infects my nickname with her vile voice. "I forgive you; I forgive you for giving up ever finding me." My fists curl, and my nails bite my skin. She leans in but must notice my eyes, because she hovers mid-air for a cheek kiss. She leans closer and with more success and kisses Daniel's cheek before she turns to leave. Daniel opens my door, and I slide in. I'm looking down on myself, because that was definitely an out-of-body experience. I don't know how to react because I don't know what she wants, but as I look at my reflection in the windscreen and then across at the handsome, kind and brilliant man beside me, I start to laugh. Not so much that I need sedating but enough to cause a look of concern on his beautiful face.

"Hey, baby." He squeezes my leg and sends a rush of shivers over my skin. "Why didn't you speak at the ceremony? I thought you wanted to say a few words?" His deep voice is laced with worry.

"I did, but then it didn't feel right sharing. I think what I wanted to say I had already said." I don't want him to think I will have regrets about today. I am sure I will have regrets about today, but I am yet to know what they will be.

"You have a sister, then? When did she go missing?" He

sounds hesitant, and I know it's because he is waiting for me to share.

"When I was seventeen." I don't want to share, not until I know what she wants.

"Was it easier to pretend you didn't have a sister than accept what might've happened? I just don't understand why you would say you didn't have one, why you would stop looking for her." He can't hide how disturbed he is. How did I know I would end up being the bad guy in this scenario? I can't bear the thought of him looking at me like I would be capable of walking away like that, and I can't bear the look of pity he would have if I told him the truth. I sniff and shudder a little, I can feel her effects working on me and the distance in the car, which hadn't been there on the journey here. "I'm sorry, baby. You know what, it doesn't matter. Nothing in the past matters. All that matters is, she's found you, and you're not alone. I won't like sharing you, but it's important to have family."

"I have a family." I whisper to myself, sadness overwhelming me once more.

"She didn't ask for your number. How is she going to contact you?" He muses, but I know why.

"She has yours, I take it?" His face is impassive at my query.

"Yes, and I will give her yours," he reassures me with a sweet smile.

I leave it at that. I have a library full of snide comments, which will do nothing other than paint me as a bitter bitch and further widen this unstoppable distance.

The day room is bright, I have been hugged and squeezed by the people I love, and I am thankful Kit didn't follow us here. Sofia takes me to one side. "What the fuck does she want now? A little late to be claiming the dutiful sister and doting daughter role. God, I'm so mad. I wanted to punch the Botox right out of her wrinkles." I can't quite manage to snicker. "Dad was really mad too. You know I had to hold him back. I told him you'd be devastated if he caused a scene." I can feel her rage because it almost mirrors mine, almost.

"Thank you, honey, I would've been mortified. I am pissed she's made today about her. Her and her *happy* reunion." I put my fingers to my temples and try to massage the pressure away.

"Do you know what she wants?" Her brow furrows, but I quickly ease her contemplation.

"I wish I didn't." I look across the room to the most amazing man on the planet, smile at the reaction he incites in my body with his presence. "But I've got a pretty good idea." I raise my eyebrows in Daniels direction. "She won him in the Bachelor Charity Auction. I saw her that night. He was her date. She must have seen me then or more importantly seen me with Daniel."

"But she can't have him, he's with you!" Sofia is righteously indignant.

"Not his type, either, but that won't stop her. Besides, Daniel thinks she's tragically sad, that I'm a bitch for giving up looking for her and pretending she didn't exist." I raise my own brow at the irony.

"He did not just say that!" She gasps in shock.

"Not in so many words, but it was there in his eyes. I'm not going to humiliate myself by clinging to a sinking ship, Sofs. But I need to know what she has to support her story before I can say anything. The only person who could verify my life just died. I know what she wants, but I need to know what she is prepared to do to get it. I am still dealing with the 'Krazy-Kit' I know, not the sad widow Kassandra, who has Daniel in her well-manicured claws."

I sink back into the deep jasmine-scented bubble bath, the hot water engulfing me to my neck. I hold my breath and sink below the surface, allowing my body to float and bob. I slowly release my breath in tiny flowing bubbles, which escape from the tiniest gap in my lips, trying to remain under the surface as long as my lungs will allow. It's strangely relaxing, hovering on the brink of desperation for air. I start to feel the burn, and I try to find my footing on the slippery bath bed when I am yanked with brutal force, lifting me clear of the water and against Daniel's hard chest.

"What the fuck are you doing?" He shouts as I squeeze the bath water from my eyes and take in some deeper breaths. His clothes are drenched by me, and he is still holding me naked in his arms. My covering of soapy bubbles is sliding gracefully down my slippery, wet body.

"Having a bath?" He has a look of utter relief, and I have no idea why. "Sorry, I didn't realize I needed permission. Wait! What did you think I was doing?" He places me on my feet and sweeps my wet hair from my face. His lips cover mine with a desperate hunger, his tongue frantic to taste me. He moans into my open mouth as I willingly accept his demanding possession of my mouth. He pulls back and sighs heavily. I shiver from my rapid removal from my lovely bath, and he holds me again, but his clothes are soaked and cold, so my body continues to shake. "Can I get back in? I'm shivering, if you hadn't noticed?"

"I thought it was me that made you tremble." His voice is soft.

"Oh, you do, Mr. Stone." I reach up on my tiptoes and slowly lick the tip of my tongue along his lips. "You make me tremble, you make me moan, and you make me scream, but best of all, you make me come." My voice is breathy with desire, but I pull back. "And in this instance, you make me shiver." I turn to step back in the bath, and he slaps my butt, the sound and sting louder because my skin is wet. "Ow! Planning on joining me, or are you just going to taunt me with that all night?" I am staring unashamedly at the large bulge in his now damp trousers, my smile a wicked invitation.

"I thought we should talk." He begins to remove his wet clothes, and my grin widens. God, I hope he means talk after. His skin shimmers from the moisture soaked through his clothes, and it only enhances the definition of the curves of his muscled arms. The flex of his chest as he strips each garment from his body and his lean frame, show he ia every inch a perfect male. He may want to talk, but his cock is most definitely on my side, hard, bobbing under its own weight, thick and heavy. He cups himself, and I whimper as he narrows his gaze, looking at me as I'm looking at his tight grip. "Dammit!" He steps forward and abruptly pushes behind me, sending the suddenly rising water spilling over the edge and flooding the floor. I push back into him and arch my back as he roughly grabs my breasts, pumping and rolling my hard nipples between his wet finger and thumbs, pulling and pinching. He sinks his teeth into my exposed neck and sucks wildly, biting and bruising the soft tissue. He wraps his arm around my waist and slides his fingers through my slick hot folds, and I instantly shiver from toe to tip. My breath rapid and my core on fire, he sinks two fingers inside and curls around, rubbing and stroking my sweet sensitive spots. My body responds, contracting and twitching, and I gasp for more air.

"Fuck, baby, I can't say no to you. I want you all the time. You're mine, understand?" His rhetorical question is more a guttural plea.

"Yes." I'm panting, and I'll say anything, but like being drunk, I'm still aware I'm saying the words I mean. I just have no reservations about saying them when I'm seconds from a screaming orgasm.

"Mine, you aren't going anywhere, understand? You are mine, say it, Bethany!" He growls in my ear and pushes deeper, and I fall. My hips are jerking, my head falls against his chest, my skin flushed with prickles. He stills before he slides his fingers out of me and brings them to his lips and sucks and hums his pleasure. I slip around to lie flat on his front, his hard erection sandwiched between our warm wet bodies. I push myself up onto my knees and hover as I take his thick smooth shaft in my tight fist and rub the wide head along my cleft, sinking slightly as he reaches my entrance, and I hover again. I need to see his eyes, see his need, see his desire.

"Fuck, Bethany, you're killing me!" He grabs my hips and

applies enough pressure to move me further onto him. "Ahh, yes, baby, it's been too long. I can't wait any longer." He tilts his hips and thrusts while pushing hard on my shoulders, and I sink further, deeper. "You're so tight baby, I don't want to hurt you." He eases the pressure on my shoulders, and it drives me insane. I want him, all of him, pain and all, and I lift and sink hard, tilting my hips to take all of his massive length. I stifle a scream. "Fuck! Fuck!" He sits up and wraps his arms around me, securing his hands on my shoulders to prevent me from making the same move again. I look into his eyes, deep with desire and love, and I can't fight the tears that escape the corners of my eyes. He is buried so deep, his cock twitche,s and I contract in appreciation, our breathing is synchronized.

"I love you, Daniel." I am not in the throes of passion. I'm in the arms of the man I love. "Don't hold back on me, I want all of you." I breathe these words out slowly, because I feel the incredible sweet pain of the tip of him against the end of me.

"Wrap your legs around me, baby. I'm going to need a hard surface to give you what you need." His eyes are alight with lust. He lifts both our bodies from the bath, and I grip, impaled and tight, against him. He swings me against the cold tiled wall, and I let out a cry as he surges forward, deeper. "Deep enough?" He grinds into me and takes my breath away.

"Deeper, all of you, Daniel, ahh!" I cry out and struggle to give him the words between my ragged breaths. He hooks my leg over the crook of his arms and lifts it pressing my thigh closer to the wall, stepping into each thrust, plunging into my core. My orgasm started as he lifted my leg, and I scream at the first wave of body-wracking convulsions, which start in my core and spread, tingling and pulsing, through every nerve like I'm on fire from within. He lunges as I tilt and scream then sink my teeth hard into his pectoral at the pain, as he comes, deep and hard, with long plunging strokes of his delicious cock. I am trembling uncontrollably, flushed and quaking.

"Fuck!" His hot breath gushes out into my hair, and he kisses the top of my head, all the while still slowly pumping the very last of him into me. He holds my face, and his tender smile is tinged with a sadness I don't understand, but I get a flash chill that has nothing to do with our recent intimate exchange. "I love you, but I won't tell you when we're fucking, just in case you think I don't mean it, understand?"

"Yes." I am curious why he keeps needing me to confirm I understand, maybe it's just that we are both new to relationships, and he doesn't want any misunderstandings, but it feels a lot like being treated like a child. "So what did you want to talk about?"

"Put your robe on, we've got company." He withdraws from me and I feel more than the physical loss.

"What? Fuck, Daniel, now I'm really embarrassed. There is no way whoever it is doesn't know exactly what we've been doing!" My hands slap my blushing cheeks in horror.

"So?"

"God! Arghhhh!" I wrap the silk robe tightly around my waist and walk out to the living room. I plan on getting changed, but I should at least say hello first. I skid in my bare feet because Kit is sitting in the lounge with a glass of champagne in her hand. Her smile is tight when she spots me. Her face changes, and I guess that is the result of the footsteps behind me. Daniel squeezes my shoulder and tenderly kisses my neck.

"It's all right baby, come on." He takes my hand, walks toward the sofa, and pulls me onto his lap, an extremely intimate position given my state of undress, but he is entirely comfortable and my discomfort has nothing to do with what I'm wearing. "You know, it's been over a week since the funeral, baby, and I thought, I'd hoped you would have contacted your sister. You know I'm worried about you. We're worried about you." I stiffen at this. "Kassandra came to me and asked for my help."

"It takes two to communicate, Daniel." I don't point out that she could contact me any fucking time she wanted to.

"Baby, she's hurt. She doesn't understand why you stopped looking for her. I don't understand but that's not important. She's frightened you're going to reject her."

"Sorry, sorry," I stutter "Kit, Kassandra, you're afraid of me?"

"Bethany, I forgive you, but I just feel so lost. In the space of a week, I've lost my mother and found a sister, who didn't *want* to find me. I'm feeling a little vulnerable, and I know you don't handle grief well. I just didn't want to let you slip through my fingers now that I've found you." She sobs into her pristine handkerchief. Wow! She is outstanding.

"We're not going to let that happen." Daniel's soft kiss on my cheek makes me start.

"What do you mean, I don't handle grief well? How would you know if you don't remember?" My voice is tetchy, and the volume is steadily rising, not helping my position if I want to maintain control of this wildly spiralling reality.

"Daniel and I had lunch today at The Ivy." I feel Daniel shift a little. "And I told him some things I remember now. When you were younger, you were in a very dark place one time, and we were worried that you might, well…" She leaves the sentence hanging, its understanding implicit. My head is spinning. "It was the time your little friend had his accident." I stand and scowl pure hatred. I hope my feelings aren't left 'hanging', subject to interpretation.

"You don't get to speak about him." I lean in with a menace I've have never felt before surging through my veins. "Ever!" I pull back and swing at Daniel, who looks like he is about to stand, maybe to intervene. "Is that why you pulled me from the bath? You thought I'd top myself? Ha!" I spin back around to face Kit. "Well, don't flatter yourself." I hug my robe a little tighter. "Was it everything you hoped it would be, *sister,* our little reunion?" I sneer, and I can see the look of mock horror on her face. My heart breaks, however, at Daniel's face, because I can't make out if it's disappointment or disgust. I leave the room to the sound of her light pretty sobs telling Daniel that she had to tell him. She couldn't live with herself if anything happened to me. After all, I'm all she's got.

He is sitting on the bed when I leave the en-suite. My chest hurts at the slump of his shoulders. I can't bear to see this, to see us erode before my eyes, but if she is hell-bent on playing the saintly injured party, I can't see how this is going to go any way but hers.

"Can you tell me about him?"

Well, my reaction was crazy enough to spark some questions. Maybe if I can shed some light, I might not look so unhinged. "Yes, yes, I can." I take my seat opposite from him. He is leaning against the headboard in his jeans and nothing else; even his bare feet look edible. "John." Oh my, I feel a surge of sadness, a lump like a rock hits my throat, instant tears prick my eyes, and I fight a sob breaking to free itself from my chest. He is on me in an instant, pulling me into his lap curling his warm strong body around mine, protecting me from my pain, but my pain is inside, and he asked. He wants to know, he wants to see, he wants me to bleed. "Okay." I try to laugh "This might not be pretty."

"I've got you, baby." His soothing deep voice helps me tell him stories I'd not told a soul. I told him of a pure love and a friendship. I spoke to him of our adventures. It wasn't enough to tell him the facts. Facts are cold, and although true, they never reveal the truth, and I wanted Daniel to know the truth. I needed him to see the truth. "He told me the day he fought his brother that it *did* matter what people said about me, that I shouldn't let them lie like I was nothing." My cheeks are so wet I can't feel the tears anymore. "He told me I was everything, and he died defending me. He died in my arms, telling me the same thing." I close my sore eyes, and Daniel waits until my breathing is calm.

"You didn't have a reputation. I don't understand." His soft words are filled with confusion.

"No, *I* didn't have a reputation, and he still died defending me. I know his last fight was defending me." When I'm not sad about this complete waste, I'm incredibly angry.

"Well, no wonder." He sighs and kisses my hair, but I stiffen, and the hairs on my neck prickle.

"No wonder what?" I calmly ask. I don't want him backtracking. I want to know how deep Kit's infection is after everything I've just told him.

"Well, no wonder baby, you were in such a state. No wonder you were in a dark place. It's understandable, completely understandable." He is rushing his words. He must feel my tension, but I'm not fighting this, my instinct here is flight.

"That's what you took from that? You know, I've never told anyone what I've just told you. But why would you believe me? I'm just an unstable sister-hating bitch, who should be on suicide watch. Didn't stop you from fucking the life out of me though, did it?" He flinches at my harsh words, and I know it was a low blow, but he needs to be hurt enough to let me go. His face is again a mixture of shock and disgust, two for two. I'm on fire, and I'm going to burn for him. I hope I burn for the look of loss and pain his face is showing. This look now mirrors mine as I crawl from his lap, put my clothes on, and leave.

Chapter Seventeen

S OFIA'S PRETTY FACE peeks around my bedroom door, closely followed by a bottle of white wine and two glasses. "Hey, Bets, how you doing?"

"Oh, much better for the gifts you bring, my dear. Come, don't be shy." I pat my bed, and she jumps and winces at the less than comfortable bounce afforded by the wooden slats underneath my mattress.

"How do you sleep on this thing?" She rubs her injured hip.

I laugh. "That's exactly what Daniel said," but I quietly stop my laughing. "Pour the wine, wench!"

"So have you heard from Queen Bitch?" She pours and hands me my liquid lifeline.

"Oh, yes. She's going all out, I don't stand a chance!" I dramatically confess.

"Really? You're going let her take everything from you? Leave you with nothing… again?"

"No, not with nothing. I've got you, I've got Marco and your family. God, I so love your family, you're so lucky, sweetie."

"Oh, yes, I have so many people interfering in my life, I pretty much live a collective existence." She sighs. "Yes, I'm very lucky… but you love him?"

My eyes flood with unshed tears. "Oh, fuck, Sofs, I'm sorry." I rub my eyes embarrassed that I can't hold this inside.

"Don't, Bets, not with me." She places her arm around my shoulders.

"Yes, I love him. I've never loved anyone like I love him. He sees me, and he knows me. But now, now, I see this distance I can't stop from growing between us, and it's killing me. She's poison, Sofs." I suck in my sob, but the tears keep falling.

"Don't let her ruin this, Bets. She can't make him love her when he clearly loves you. Don't give up, and don't run away." Her soft brown eyes are fixed with love and concern.

"That's definitely my gut reaction." I sip my wine. "I know he loves me, and you're right, she can't make him love her, but she *can* make him not love me. How could you love someone who is so quick to give up on family? Not give someone asking, a chance at reconciliation? Not to mention crazy unstable. He really hasn't known me long enough to give him the tools to challenge these questions." I release a breath I didn't realize I'd been holding. "Sofs, I told him everything about John, and all he heard was her. You didn't see his face when I flipped. He looked so disappointed. No, he looked disgusted." I shake my head in utter despair.

"Bets, he loves you." She repeats like *that* is really all I need.

"He did," I add softly, "maybe." I can't believe I doubt what I know in my heart, so quickly. "But he *will* let me go. She'll make sure of that. Now, my dear," I try for false levity. "I'm calling a 'no-more'. So let's pour some more wine." I tip my empty glass for a refill.

Sofia leaves mine around eleven-thirty, and I'm just about to get ready for bed. I've cancelled my contract with Mags after my 'uncovering' with Daniel, and it's just me now, so funding healthcare is no longer an issue. My phone starts to vibrate almost instantly and I get a twinge of excitement that it might be Daniel. The caller ID says Kassandra, and my heart sinks that Daniel must have programmed her number in my phone.

"It's me, dear sister." Her icy voice fills me with dread, but she wants to tell me something. She wants something, and I want her out of my life. I let out a controlled breath as she obviously waits to see if I'll hang up. "There, that's so much better, I do abhor rude manners." I don't know why she's talking like a fucking Jane Austen novel; it's just me and her.

"What do you want, Kit?" I am exhausted and see no need to play nice.

"Kassandra." She corrects. "Oh, good. We're going to get straight to it." Her excitement evident in her tone, she is enjoying her position. She is cold and heartless and loving every minute of this. "I want Daniel."

"I'm shocked," I respond flatly. "Well, my guess is he'll be yours soon enough." I sigh dejectedly, I'm so tired.

"Maybe, but I don't live my life by 'maybe'. I make sure I get what I want." She sneers.

"You always have." I quip.

"Yes, yes. Look, I was happy to let this pass when I saw you at the drinks reception at your friends' club. After all, you're a waitress, and they never marry staff!" She cackles. "But I believe he likes fucking you too much to discard you right away." I wince at this. "Oh, come on, Boo." She spits my name with malice. "You can't possibly think he actually cares for you?" She muses, carefully aligning her weapons. "Has he even taken you out in public? Introduced you to his friends or to meet his family, maybe? No?" Her voice is cruel, her aim perfect.

"We have been out." I offer quietly. "And he introduced himself as my boyfriend," adding mostly to reassure myself. I told Daniel the truth when I said I don't get jealous, but I didn't mention that I really never had the opportunity before, or that I have enough crippling insecurities, that jealousy didn't need to feature in my repertoire of vices.

"Really, where?" She is not surprised with my answer at all. "Somewhere local? To meet your friends, perhaps?" She has a sickening girlish laugh. "Don't beat yourself up. He does have a weakness for the wounded, and my darling, you are the very definition of the 'walking wounded'. Pathetic." She mutters. "The charity he and his mother attended was for disadvantaged children, did you know? Well, no. Anyway, I didn't realize he was so 'hands on' with his charity work." I have a clawing, empty feeling that's in the pit of my stomach and it's strange that I can feel pain, when I am numb with this new information. I hate her, but she's right. I had joked, a little, about his interest in me as an act of benevolence, but he has yet to take me out on an actual date, even our lunches were in his office.

"So I'm going to need your help," She interrupts my rocketing self-doubt.

"And why would I help you?" My laugh is a little uncontrolled. I am really curious why she would think I would actively break my own heart.

"Well, I happen to know you won't, willingly." She clarifies. "But you do seem to care about your friends." I sit up at this comment, not sure where she's going. "I didn't introduce you to my driver; he is ex-military. You might remember him from the old days? No? It doesn't matter, anyway, he is very handy to have, very good at solving problems. Well… I digress. You know what it's like to lose someone you love." The pain is acute in my chest when I think of Daniel, that she'd hurt him. "Sofia is a lovely girl, I met her the other night. I don't believe she recognized me then, but I knew her." She pauses as if she is weighing up her options, like she hasn't already made up her mind to ruin my life. "She's engaged, is that right?" She doesn't say anything else, her implicit threat crystal clear. Whether she hurt Sofia or Paul, the devastation would be the same. For Sofia, losing the love of her life or for Sofia's family to lose their only daughter, it's horrific, unimaginable, it's insane.

"I can break up with him." My voice starts to break at this. "But I can't make him stay away, I've tried before." I stifle my tears I can't imagine the desolation. Sofia would never be the same if anything happened to Paul. He is her light.

"Oh, I know, but I have something that may help with that. You need to do it soon, because I have plans." She says in a bright sing-song voice. "Tomorrow, tomorrow evening, I'll pop round, you know as a shoulder."

"Why, Kit?" I can't help my morbid curiosity.

"The money runs out, darling sister, and I want a man, simple. But I can't tell you how much better it is, now I know that it's *your* man." Her girlish laugh is hollow. She is pure evil.

"Will you make him happy? Do you even care?" I can't bear the thought of Daniel's pain.,

"Ha! Darling, like that even matters." She dismisses me with a shrill, biting cry. The line goes dead. I fall to the floor and cry. I cry until my eyes are dry.

My phone rings again, and I take it into my bedroom and crawl into bed. "Hey, sister, it's late. Is everything all right?"

"Calling to ask you the same. I tried to call you earlier, but the line was busy. Just wanted to check if you're okay?"

I snort a loud laugh. "Is it too late to have another glass of wine?"

"You go, sister. I'll join you. Paul's dead to the world." I get a chill at this quip. "So what does she want?"

"Oh I was right, she wants him, told me he's just fucking me. I'm his charity case, and that's why he's never taken me out. Out as in to meet his family and friends." I sniff back more tears, which threaten.

"That's bullshit, Bets, and you know it! Fuck, she's a total bitch!" Sofia's volume is such, I have to hold the phone away from my ear.

"She is…" I hesitate. "But she's also right." My voice is sad, but I have no more tears, so my shoulders just move with little dry sobs.

"Ah babe, it's bullshit. She's just going for the jugular; hitting your insecurities with a freight train. She's seen you two together right?" I mumble my agreement. "Well, then." She doesn't elaborate as if that was evidence enough. "She's desperate, low, and evil. Did I mention she's a huge bitch?"

"You might've said something along those lines." She's made

me giggle.

"You can't walk away from this, Bets. You have to play her game long enough for Daniel to see her for what she is. She can't sustain that level of duplicity indefinitely."

"I'm not so sure. She's had lots of practice, and she presses my buttons. She's this total ice queen, and I'm a raging bag of crazy by comparison. I'd stay clear of me, and I know me!"

"He loves you, Bets, simple, and it's worth fighting for."

"She threatened me, well, not me directly, but people I care about, and I can't… you know I can't, Sofs. I won't!" I am adamant.

"Oh, she didn't!" She laughs. "See? She is desperate! She knows I'm Italian, right? I know people!" Her bravado is almost visible. I imagine she's tipping her chin high and flipping her fingers up in an aggressive sweep.

"You know people in catering! So, steady on, Ms. Soprano. Daniel *is* worth fighting for but not at any cost." I let out a very sad breath. "She's a disease, and I'm going to treat her like an addict would their disease, one day at a time"

"It's a start. Better than that flight shit you're so good at." She blows a loud kiss. "'Night, sister."

"'Night." I blow one right back and put the phone down. I still may fly.

Oh I love these dreams. I moan seductively and move languidly, entwined on soft sheets, which float against my skin, which is warm and feels like silk, the warmth of his strong legs, the rough hairs scratching as he folds his leg over mine. Pushing back between mine, opening me with his weight, pressing his hard cock in the crack of my bottom and sliding slowly, tempting me to wake up with this erotic movement. His hot breath on my neck, my eyes are heavy, and I am aroused in my sleep. My breasts ache, and I reach to squeeze and release the rising pressure, my lips part, and I hear his deep moan in my dream. He feels so real,

I don't want to wake.

"I don't want to let you go." I whisper.

"Then don't." His voice is urgent, a demand. I wake when I feel his real weight on me. His legs forcing mine wide, his eyes wild and filled with lust.

"Daniel!" I gasp. He captures my mouth, forcing my lips wider, his tongue plunges into me stealing my breath. He sucks my tongue and bites my lower lip as he pulls back. He is trying to consume me.

"You're mine. You don't get to make that choice." His eyes are dark and dangerous. He is going to take me. I can feel his need to possess as he feels my need to be possessed. He pulls my wrists above my head and growls. "Don't move them, hold onto the boards if that helps." I obey. He fixes his mouth on my neck, biting and sucking, sending an intense rush of heat and need to my core, and I twist with overwhelming pent-up passion. "Don't move." His voice is deep and husky, commanding. I still, but this inability to evade this building pleasure causes my whole body to tremble with anticipation, and I'm rewarded with a satisfying grumble, which resonates deep in his chest.

He moves roughly down my body latching on to my hard, aching nipple and swirling his molten hot tongue around, then pulling the sensitive tip between his teeth, holding me on the edge, feeling my breath hitch, but not release. He looks through heavy-lidded eyes directly at me with a sinful grin and undiluted animal lust in his blue-black eyes. He releases me tortuously slowly, firing my pain sensors with the rough graze of his teeth. My back starts to twitch, and the muscles contract, forcing the slightest curve of my spine. He sinks his full weight, pinning me immobile, and I pant with frustration, my body a sheen of perspiration and alive with a flush of prickles sweeping across my skin. He moves down my body, as one hand remains holding and massaging my breast, his other traces down my torso. His nails lightly catch my hypersensitive skin, which flames at his touch. He uses his shoulder to spread my legs wide then he sits up and holds my inner thighs with his big strong hands, pushing them wider apart. I am so open, so vulnerable, so turned on.

My thighs start to tremble with the strain of his extra weight on the muscle, and he uses his strong thumbs to smooth the quivering flesh. My heart is racing, pumping blood loudly in my ears, and I can feel my swollen clit throb with the desperate need for some pressure, some friction, any attention at all, and I know I'll be howling like a banshee. He meets my eyes, which must be pleading and flashes me a wickedly sexy smile. "Something you want to say, baby?" He says darkly.

"Please." My voice barely a whisper. It's all I can say. "Please, please, Daniel" If I could move, I would be on my knees begging.

"Oh, baby, I love it when you beg." His mouth tips up on one side, and he slowly sucks the large pad of his thumb between his soft full lips. Raising a brow, he lowers his hand, and with the lightest pressure, presses my aching clit in small full circles.

"Fuck!" I scream, my hips jerk clean off the bed and he quickly secures me with the force of his other arm across my waist. My sex clenches, spasm after spasm ripple through my core and tiny white dots float across my tightly-squeezed eyelids. I catch my breath, my whole body shaking from the speed and intensity of the orgasm he held at his fingertips. "Fuck." My breathing slows, and I feel my inner contractions ebb, "Fuck." He kisses me hard and laughs roughly.

"I love it when you talk dirty. I've missed you talking dirty." My eyes widen, is he serious about our Late Night Calls? I don't have time to ponder, as he dives between my still spread legs and sweeps his hot tongue deep along my soaking wet folds. He moans, and the vibrations from the sound send a ripple of pleasure deep inside me. He licks and laps, his tongue dipping inside and swirling around the sensitive nub of nerve endings, all the more sensitive from my recent explosive climax. I instantly feel the uncontrollable pulse of an impending orgasm start to build, and he must feel it, too, because his tongue becomes more forceful, tasting and moving rapidly from tip to entrance. This and my immobility are driving me insane, and I cry and whimper at his incessant ministrations.

"Ah, ah, Daniel. Oh, God, please, please." I press my head hard against my pillow, wanting to thrash it wildly from side to side. My knuckles are pure white as I grip the boards above my head, hoping the cheap wood will not splinter in my grip. He shifts and purses his lips tight over my clit and sucks in the most deliciously intense and erotically painful manner. I crash and plummet from a bliss he so brutally demands. My thighs start to spasm, my body trembles, even my fingers shake, and I try to suck in some desperately needed oxygen. He continues to lick me intimately, reverently, softening my fall until I am limp and sated.

He rears up from between my legs, gloriously naked, his taut tanned body glistens with sweat, his scent is raw and his eyes are predatory. "Mine." He roughly forces the word through his tight jaw, and I shiver all over again. He is slowly fisting his hard angry cock, the tip dewy with pre-cum, and I lick my lips and swallow. He holds my stare and it's possibly the most erotically charged moment in my life. This perfect male is hard for me, possessive of me; feral for me. He kneels closer and presses the velvet head of his thick wide cock against my lips, smearing his juices along my lips. I flick my tongue to taste, and the desire I feel escapes as a small moan from the back of my throat. "Don't move, just take what I give you." His voice is deeply calm, but the inflection tells of the control he is fighting to maintain, and the thought makes me smile. My smile dissolves quickly as he pushes deep into my mouth, my tongue swirling his tip, lightly licking the slit and tasting him. I use my tongue and lips to bring him in deep, and he holds my head, giving me the support I need to take him deeper still. His hips start to move, and he throws his head back with a loud moan.

His cock lengthens, and he is fighting his desire to fuck me hard; he is holding back. I can feel him thicken, and his veins pulse. I hollow my cheeks and try to swallow him into the back of my throat, but he controls the depth. Frustrated, I shift up slightly, taking my hand I grab his fine muscular arse, feeling the flex as he continues to pump his hips. My nails dig into his flesh, and he releases a guttural sound from deep in his throat. "I said to keep your hands.... Ahh! Fuck." I push myself forward and swallow him to the back of my throat, and with his thrust he hits me hard. The muscles in my throat flex in defense at this intrusion, closing tightly around him. My grip on his arse tightens and my tongue frantically laps him as he withdraws slightly, but understanding my need to have him, all of him, he slams his palm against the wall, fisting my hair tight with the other, as he starts to fuck my mouth without reservation. He pumps hard and fast, moaning in agonizing pleasure. I take my other hand and wrap tightly around the base of his cock. He instantly thickens in my grip. His balls tighten and his hips jerk forward as he comes, shooting torrents of scorching hot semen on my tongue and down the back of my throat. I swallow and lick, and I'm still pumping him when he pulls from my mouth still coming, releasing whatever he has left on my breasts. He hovers, and I pull every last drop from him onto myself. His breathing is still fierce. He sits back and wipes his hand through his essence, smearing the warm cream across my breasts and stomach. "Mine," he declares. I look down at my sticky body, seeing the red marks he has left on my breast, no doubt on my neck too, marking me as his. I am under no illusion that tonight was about anything else.

I wake to an empty bed and just when I start to think that perhaps my erotic dream was only a dream I smell the aroma of coffee wafting in from my living room, followed by the equally delicious sight of Daniel in his tight boxer shorts carrying my liquid breakfast. I sit up and feel the tight stretch of my skin on my breasts and tummy. Looking down I now see my error in judgement regarding foregoing the late night shower in favour of sleep. I'm gross and flaking, I look like a lizard. I quickly pull my covers to my chin.

Daniel laughs as he passes my coffee. "I thought we'd passed the 'being shy' stage?" He raises his brow and shuffles in beside me.

"Oh, we have. We just haven't passed the 'I'm going to gross you out' stage." I smile, but a flash of heat in my face highlights my embarrassment.

"Ah…regretting the shower decision?" He chuckles at my discomfort.

"Just a bit. What time is it?" I sit up to check my clock and slump back down in the pillows. "Fuck!" I exhale.

"What? It's not early?" He lifts his arm for me to crawl under but I am still swathed in the sheet. I shake my head.

"No, it's not. Which means I have to run the gauntlet of showering with an army of horny kitchen porters, dying to catch the show." I pull my covers further over my head. I feel the mattress dip and hear my front door close. Five minutes later he returns with a triumphant smile. He leans down and kisses my nose.

"All yours, baby. You have 20 minutes, so move that sexy arse before I have to pay for a time extension." His lips curl casually around his cup.

"What did you do and don't tell me you went into the kitchen like that?" He is glorious, but he is also nearly naked.

"I sent everyone for breakfast, so you've got twenty minutes, and, yes, I went like this." He wrinkles his nose like I'm being ridiculous. It would be cute if I wasn't so mortified.

"Oh, my God!" I cringe.

"What's more important, your personal hygiene, or them all knowing you've been, how did you so eloquently phrase it?" He grins. "Oh yes! 'That you've been riding my enormous cock.'" His laugh is infectious and makes him seem really young. It's such a lovely sound. "Besides." He adds as I grab my towel, still wrapped in my bed sheet. "It's a small price to pay. There is no way anyone catches this show, except me." He whips the sheet from my body, and I squeal as he wraps me in his arms and dips me back into a dramatic embrace with the sweetest kiss.

Daniel is ending a call as I return fresh from the shower. His eyes are heated and instantly hungry as I close the door behind me with a click. He stalks toward me, towering, predatory, and he places his arms on either side of my body, caging me in with his frame against the door. Despite being hugely turned on by this animal display of dominance, I am suddenly completely freaked out that he got into my apartment in the middle of the night in the first place, and I push his chest and wrinkle my forehead in anger.

"Mmmm." He dips to suck on my neck. "I kind of like a little resistance." He pushes his arousal hard against my stomach.

"How did you get in here last night?" I try jabbing my pointed finger into his pectoral, but he is unmoving and just looks more dangerous.

"Mmm? How... how what?" He heard me. He's just trying to distract me with his wickedly playful tongue, which is flicking and sucking the soft spot below my ear. I'm starting to melt, his hard body preventing me from pooling in a puddle on the floor.

"Daniel, I won't feel safe unless I know how you got in here. What's to stop someone else doing the same?" My words may be breathlessly spoken, but they are enough to halt him.

"You're completely safe. Well, completely safe would be living with me, but you are safe here, too. My security company did the upgrade and fixed the shower door, too!"

I let the 'living together' remark slide, as I'm sure it was a joke, but the other bit is news to me. "Ok, and you may have to speak slowly, because I am not sure how the two are linked?" I narrow my eyes; I know exactly how the two are linked and I'm starting to feel a little bit violated, and not in a good way. He has the grace to look sheepish at least and he stands back a little to gauge my mood. His hands move protectively in front of his groin. He may well have to protect parts of his body if I lose my temper, but I'm not stupid. I'm not going to hurt him there, that would only hurt me more.

"I have a key. It drove me crazy the other day when I couldn't get to you. I need to know I can get to you. I need to keep you safe." He wants me safe, not 'crazy stalker in my basement safe'

I hope, just safe, and part of me is overwhelmed that someone cares so much about me, but then there is a part of me that thinks this is setting a dangerous precedent regarding privacy.

"That's sweet but also really wrong, you know that, right?" He nods but has a wickedly sinful gleam in his eyes indicating no remorse whatsoever. "And you'd give me back that key if I asked?" He nods again slowly, grinning. "Because it's not your only copy, is it?" He shakes his head. He may be a crazy stalker, but he is *my* crazy stalker.

Daniel joins me at the gym with Marco. Although he sits on the bench at the side to watch, he occasionally leaves to take a call. He returns just as Marco throws me hard on my butt, falling swiftly onto me with his knee in my chest and straddled over me. But only briefly before he is knocked clean off me and onto the mat. I catch my breath, which has been knocked from me with my fall, and look to see Daniel straddling Marco with his knee at his throat. I jump to my feet and push him off Marco. He doesn't resist. "Fuck! Daniel, what are you doing?" He stands and wraps me in his big strong arms, squeezing hard before he releases me and starts to turn me, checking for blood, I presume. My brow is wrinkled with confusion and amusement. I hear Marco snicker. Daniel shoots him the filthiest look and growls.

"Don't you think that was a little excessive, Marco?" His voice is deep and angry. I bite my lip to stop the rising giggle.

"No! I think that was payback!" Marco narrows his eyes at me, and I stick my tongue out. "You weren't here when she pulled the same move on me. Are you gonna kiss me better, too?" He turns to pull his sweats down, and I laugh loudly, but Daniel is not laughing. I feel bad that he is even worried about this, and I cup his cheeks and kiss him lightly.

"Hey, it's fi…" I quickly change what I was about to say in response to his scowl. "Daniel, I do this every week, and most weeks I kick his arse." I nod my head toward a grinning Marco.

"He does go easy on me, look at the size of him, of course he does, but there's no point if it's too easy. I'm pretty sure an attacker isn't going to be so considerate." His teeth visibly grind at this.

"Look, dude." Marco comes over to me. I don't think he has warmed to Daniel, but he is super protective of me, so I am not surprised. "I would never hurt her. Ever." He leans to pick up his towel, kisses my cheek, but as he walks away, he adds, "Can you say the same?" He swings the gym doors wide and leaves us.

I look in Daniel's eyes, worry, love, and lust all mix together for a lethal intensity. He grabs my butt and lifts me, so my legs wrap around his narrow waist. He notices me wince at his grip.

"Tell me again how this doesn't hurt?" He squeezes a little tighter, and I bite my lip and try to smile. He is right on an emerging bruise. "And, baby, I'm just dying for you to lie about this, knowing exactly where you'd be taking that punishment." His smooth voice is dark and sensual, his veiled promise searing a heat through me.

"It doesn't hurt." I giggle and grind my hips into him, hot with desire.

"I'm so fucking hard, I want to fuck you right here." He is looking around, and my eyes widen in panic. No, he isn't serious. "But I have to get you changed. We have someplace to be." He takes my hand and leads me from the building, not allowing me time to check on Marco or chat to anyone else. He mumbles something about private lessons before securing me in his car.

Back at Daniel's apartment I am freshly showered, changed, and pouring myself a coffee from his space station kitchen appliance with integrated coffee machine, when I hear him raise his voice on the phone. I'm not eavesdropping, he is shouting.

"Fuck, Mother, you had no right… But I'm really angry about this…I was bringing someone…No, I haven't asked her yet, but I was just about to. Hardly the point, mother, it was my decision… Fuck!…No, of course I'll accompany you, I just don't have to be happy about it." He hangs up abruptly and is still cursing when I walk into the room.

"Problem?" I walk to him, the tension visible in his shoulders. I reach up to try and massage it, but it's really not the right angle. So I take his hand and pull him to the sofa. "I heard you on the phone. I wasn't eavesdropping," I add quickly. "But you were shouting and…" I squeeze his solid muscle that has no give, "you do seem a little tense." I laugh lightly and kiss his cheek.

"Yes, well… My mother has just managed to piss me off and ruin my surprise." He grumbles.

"Ooo, I like surprises!" He turns swiftly and sweeps me into his waiting lap, stroking my hair from my eyes.

"Well, thanks to my mother, this surprise I'm not sure you're going to like." His frown deepens.

"Okay?" I wait for him to explain.

"There is this charity Gala tomorrow, and I wanted to take you, but my mother gave her ticket to a friend because she assumed she could come with me."

"Oh." I let out a breath. I don't know what terrible surprise I was anticipating, but I'm clearly relieved. "Well, really, that's not so bad. I can't blame her, and I'm sure she would really like to go with you, anyway. God, I bet you look smoking hot in a tux." I say wistfully.

"Lucky you're not the jealous type." He kisses my nose.

"Yeah, lucky." I may have to revise that position. "Anyway, I don't have anything to wear. Even Sofia's wardrobe is limited in the Gala outfit wearing department."

"That's what I wanted to do this afternoon, take you to get a dress." He seems shy. It's sweet.

"Oh." I'm stunned, so he does want to take me out, show me off at a Gala. I know that's not going to happen now, but it's the principle. I also know a small part of me should be affronted at the notion of being 'shown off', but unfortunately that small part is fighting a losing battle against my other insurmountable insecurities. So I am warmed by this development. I know I'm to blame for allowing the doubt Kit raised to have any oxygen to breathe, but I am thrilled that this was his surprise to begin with.

"So, no need to go shopping. I guess we'll have to think of something else to do in the meantime." He wiggles his brow suggestively, and I push his chest.

"You're a monster, a sex fiend," I tease.

"Takes one to know one." He covers my mouth, and his lips swallow my screams. "So what will you do tomorrow? I have to go to my mother's before the Gala, some family drinks."

"Sofs probably, although I should maybe invite Marco, too. After your alpha display today, he's probably a little pissed. He's my best friend, and it would help if you two got on a little better." I plead my case.

"Then he should stop beating up my girlfriend." He is deadly serious, so I decide to drop it.

"So, shall we go out tonight?"

"Oh baby, do you mind if we don't? If I'm out all tomorrow, I just want to bury myself in you, and when you crash I can work; it's perfect. We'll get take out -- anything you want. There could even be a bath in it for you?" I need to not let this eat at me. He was going to take me to a Gala, it's not like you can wear a paper bag on your head to those things.

I laugh. "You had me at bath." He leans to kiss me lightly, but his hunger for me consumes him, and he is delving deep with his tongue and thrusting his hands in my hair, pulling me tighter to his body. We both sag when we hear his entry phone ring.

"Expecting company?" I tease as he eases himself from beneath me.

"No, and it better be fucking important to interrupt me from doing what I have planned." His stern voice disappears into the hall as he goes to answer the phone. I lay back into the warmth, which is fading from the sofa at his departure, and throw my arms over my eyes. I hate that Kit has raised suspicions in me that simply weren't there before. I hate that she makes me doubt myself and makes me doubt him. I hear his tentative steps, his voice is soothing.

"Hey, baby, we've got a visitor." The hairs on my neck stand at attention, and I take a calming breath. I know who's just 'popped by', and I need to not be the crazy one right now. I move my arm and swing my legs round, standing in a smooth graceful movement with a huge smile, which I grip to my face with a gritted jaw.

"Kassandra." I notice Daniel's warm smile at my response, and I die a little inside. "It's really nice of you to stop by, and," I draw in a steadying breath as I feel the bile rise in my stomach, "I am sorry for my outburst. It's, well… it's just all been sickening." I'm sure her brow would raise at my choice of words, but her face is chemically frozen. She's only just twenty-six, and I think a line or wrinkle would be too scared to dare attempt finding a home on her face.

"Bethany." She sways toward me, and I panic at the thought that she might actually try to embrace me, and I know my instant reaction would be a take-down, followed by a swift elbow in the face. I move to the side and toward Daniel, with a half-smile at my violent fantasy.

"Kassandra, would you like something to drink, tea, coffee?" I ask her kindly, as I walk toward the kitchen, whispering, "Hemlock," under my breath.

"I'll have a beer, please, baby." His eyes are deep blue and sparkle. His smile dazzles me.

"Oh, no, I won't intrude." I return with a beer for Daniel and a bottle of water for me. I'm a little dehydrated from my class, and I start to drain the bottle as I sit opposite Kit, who is sitting next to Daniel; her knee touching his. "I have to say, I am rather pleased you have chosen to wear more clothing this time, Bethany." She laughs at her funny little remark.

"Any clothing is too much clothing," Daniel's voice rumbles low, and he moves with stealth across to my sofa. With a predatory glimmer in his eyes, he scoops me into his lap and dives his nose into my hair inhaling deeply. He strokes my body as if we were alone, and he sends tingling sparks where his fingers touch my skin. It would seem 'polite host' Daniel has left the building, and with his massive erection pressing through the thin fabric of his sweats and the thinner cotton of my dress, I am not entirely sure he even knows Kit is still in the room. But then she coughs and stands, brushing the creases from her dress, well, caressing the creases and fondling herself in the process. It's a move that is wasted, though, if only Daniel was looking.

"I only wanted to check you were okay, and I can see that you are, which warms my heart." I bite back 'like you have a heart to warm' with all my self-control, I am super proud of myself, and I give *me* an internal high five for not having a melt-down. "Bethany, may I have a private word." She walks toward the hall, and Daniel reluctantly lets me go and adjusts himself discreetly. I laugh, not *that* discreetly. She turns and steps close, so her face is hidden by mine, and her voice is too soft to be heard. Her eyes narrow to tiny slits. "I think you are so very cavalier with someone so precious to you, and you are so very naïve to think I was bluffing." She leans in to air kiss my cheeks, pleased with the effect her words have caused. My face is now drained of the flush I'd felt from Daniel's attentions. "Good-bye, darling." She steps aside and back toward the living area. "And I'll see you tomorrow at your mother's. I understand you are her date at my table? It will be such fun, so glamorous. Anyway, do enjoy your cozy evening in." Drained and winded, like I said, I don't stand a chance.

I take a moment before I return to Daniel. I told Sofia I would fight for us, and the only way is to tell Daniel the truth. But how much truth to tell? I have no evidence, and I have already come across as crazy, unstable, and mean. I don't want to add vindictive, too, because I know Kit is a professional at playing the victim. Still, I have to try. Daniel is lying fully stretched on the sofa with his arm lazily drooped over his eyes. He looks relaxed, and his lounge pants are barely hanging on his hips, so he looks incredibly sexy, too. I walk over and slide to the floor on my knees beside him. He lifts his arm and grins with a raised brow.

"Oh, baby, I like where you're going with this." He goes to

sit, but I place my hand on his taut stomach, and he sinks back down.

"Daniel…I need to tell you something." I can feel my mouth dry.

"Anything, baby…you can tell me anything." His hand stretches to cup my neck, and the warmth and love I feel give me much needed courage.

"It's about Kit…Kassandra… She left me, Daniel, but she didn't just leave me. She left me with my mum and all the bills, too." I swallow hard. His face seems to darken, and he draws in a deep frown.

"She didn't leave you, baby…She would've come back if she knew how…I know its hard-"

"-Daniel, she sold my home and took all the money for herself…She is the reason I work two, sometimes three, jobs." The pitch in my voice is starting to rise, and I take a steadying breath.

"Is that why you didn't look for her? You were angry?" I drop my head, because his eyes look…I don't know. They look sad, but I don't know if that's for me or Kit. "It's understandable, baby, but she didn't know. How could she? You can't keep blaming her. We all made mistakes in our past. You have to be able to forgive her, baby. I need to know you can forgive her past." His voice is almost pleading, and his face flashes with something I don't recognize, something distant, but then it's gone.

"I don't trust her, Daniel." I try one last time.

"And that's okay. That is completely understandable. It will just take time, that's all, and I'll be right beside you all the way. She's not expecting you to let down your guard right away. Well, she probably is, given that she feels abandoned, but she'll understand. She just wants to be a part of your life. Is that too much to ask?" His warm palm caresses my cheek.

"You'll be with me, always." He nods and sweeps to capture my mouth with his hot possessive kiss. It *is* too much to ask, too much for her, but for him, for us, it isn't too much at all. If he is beside me, it's Kit that doesn't stand a chance.

Chapter Eighteen

"YOU JUST LET him go? Knowing she is going to be there, drooling all over his Armani-clad arse?" I am nestled between Sofia and Marco, comfy, clad in our onesies, sharing a huge bowl of popcorn as we settle in for an eighties fest of John Hughes movies. Marco is not in a onesie.

"Well, I could've gone fatal attraction crazy, and he looked sorry enough to make him squirm, but that's not my thing and I scored major brownie points the other day being super mature." I smile and try to seat curtsy as she looks on impressed. "He didn't look happy that she dropped that bombshell and walked away. Also he didn't look convinced when I said she couldn't have known he had wanted to take me, and it can't *possibly* have been intentional." Sofia scoffs. "I have to let her mess up. I have no proof that she was who she was when she was young. It's not like I kept a scrapbook of my slutty sister's extracurricular activities. She didn't get arrested after she turned eighteen, so all her prior nasty activities would've been expunged. It's my word against hers and *I'm* the unstable one, prone to visiting the dark side. Oh, I love this bit, he's so angry, so tortured." Sofs looks at me, and we both say, "So hot," and fall together, giggling. Judd Nelson in 'The Breakfast Club' has just thrown a mad temper and climbed the outside of the staircase in the library, where he sits all angst ridden, moody and hot.

Marco is quiet ,but then he asks, "Why are you even pretend-ing to like her, Boo? Why are you pretending for him? He should just trust you. He should just believe you." He puts his large com-forting arm over my shoulder, and I adjust to fit in the crook.

"Yes, he should, but he hasn't known me that long, and, like I said, I have no evidence that she isn't who she pretends to be. Whereas me? I am definitely the uncaring sibling, who gave up looking for her sister and then was hostile and unforgiving. I can't stand the thought that he might think this is about me be-cause of her lies." He squeezes me and plants a kiss on my head. Sofia has reached over for her laptop to check her emails, Paul was supposed to come over after work, but he hasn't shown. It's not unlike him to be asked to work through, but it is unlike him not to let her know, and I know she is worried. I grab her laptop when she sees she's had no new emails. I decide to Google the Gala for red carpet pictures, hoping this will act as a distraction. I click on the images page and start to scroll the famous and not so famous faces, sparkling and glamorous. It seems this is a really big event held in The Dorchester Ball Room with many hundreds of guests raising millions for the charity. I stop on his image, Wow, I was right, he is smoking hot in a tux. I fan myself and sigh elaborately. This is enough to make Marco go in search of more liquor. "Oh my God, Sofs! I didn't see him before he left, look, I mean look! No one looks like that! He looks like he has a full on body filter." She leans closer to me.

"Oh yeah, he does scrub up well." She nudges me, and I scroll further down. The next picture he is walking beside his mother, judging by the striking family resemblance; they share a similar eye shape and colour. Her hair is styled in a sharp elegant dark bob. She is tall and slim and looks stunning in a floor-length dark blue evening gown with a chiffon wrap. The next picture is not so palatable. Kit has her arm threaded through Daniel's. There is no space between them, and she is wearing a demure smile as the caption declares Daniel Stone with partner, beautiful widow, Kassandra Shaw. Her bright red dress has a plunging neckline, and it clings so tightly, it leaves nothing to the imagination. But she does look good, and sadly they look good together. I close the laptop and pass it back to Sofia. Mission accomplished, I am very distracted. Marco returns with a fresh bottle of wine and some chocolate. I am going to have to go for a marathon run to work off the guilt of eating all this tonight. There is a knock at the door, and Sofia leaps, shouting that Paul must have lost his key, but instead of the normal noise associated with Sofia greeting Paul, there is silence. Then there are mumbled words, and then there is a heartrending cry.

Marco keeps squeezing my hand, trying to get some sort of response from me, but all I can do is look out across the waiting room in the intensive care unit at St. Mary's hospital. I am devastated by the sadness in the room. Sofia's mother is holding Sofia's head in her lap, trying to soothe the sobs, which are tearing Sofia apart. Paul's parents sit quietly, holding each other's hands, his mother's face stained with tears. Sofia's dad has gone to fetch drinks that no one will drink, but he is unsuited to sitting around waiting; and that is all we can do, wait. Paul's car ran through the central reservation, and it was only because the roads were unusually quiet that he has even made it to surgery.

The longest night of my life turned into the longest day. The surgery had gone well, but the next twenty-four hours are critical. Once he is stable, his family can see him. Sofia's parents left to get a change of clothes for their daughter and bring her back some food they desperately hope she will eat. She looks so pale, and with her hair scraped back into a pony tail, she looks too young and fragile to handle this, but she is not alone. Marco has his arm around her shoulder, and she is holding my hand in hers when the surgeon enters the room. Sofia is unable to move, but raises her head to meet his eyes. Paul's parents stand instantly and are shaking the surgeon's hand. The information filters in and is processed slowly in my head. Paul is in recovery and has just woken . He looks a lot worse than he is, but it could've been a lot worse than it is. He has some internal bleeding that they managed to stop in surgery, three broken ribs, a broken collarbone, and lots of bruising to the face, but no head injury. He should make a full recovery. He will be all right. I don't realize I'm crying when Sofia turns to me. She is still swallowing down her sobs, but I think from the relief that fills her eyes they are now sobs of joy.

Paul's parents take Sofia with them to see him. They aren't gone long, but their relief is abundantly evident, not just in their expressions, but in the way they walk and hold themselves. They enter the waiting room with smiles and purpose. Now they can set about getting him better and getting him home. There is a whole different energy in the room. Not for Sofia, she is still very much shaken as she walks over to me. The sadness in her eyes has been replaced with worry and fear. The police told her that Paul's car had been shunted into the central reservation, they are looking at CCTV footage, but where the incident occurred was on a part of the street that is not fully covered by the cameras. I hold her hand and pull her into my arms. She is so very precious to me, I whisper in her ear.

"No more. I'm so sorry, Sofs." I pull back with my hands on her soft pale cheeks, my determined eyes fixed on her sorrow-filled ones. "I am ending this, now." She never said she thought the same as me, when the police said that it hadn't quite been an accident, and that they were looking for someone. She didn't need to, and she didn't tell me *not* to end it, either. I just hope she can forgive me for not ending it sooner.

I leave Sofia with Paul's parents, knowing her mum will be back soon, and Marco catches a cab with me back to the restaurant. I feel sick with guilt. This is my fault. My sick twisted 'family' has infected Sofia's. I can't tell Marco any of this, because I know he'd kill for his family, he'd kill for me, and I have brought enough of a shit storm on this family. I can stop this. I can give Kit what she wants, and I can even move away, if it will keep the people I love safe, keep my real family safe. I'll do anything to protect them. Silent tears slip from the corners of my eyes and Marco pulls me tight to his side and kisses my hair.

"Hey, hey, he's going to be all right." He gives me a warm smile as we pull up to the rear of the restaurant, and I roughly wipe these weak tears.

"Yes." I say determinedly. "Yes, he will."

It's early evening before I get around to switching on my phone, which instantly starts beeping angrily at me, with twenty plus missed calls from Daniel, a similar number of texts, and one text from Kit.

HOW WAS YOUR EVENING? WE HAD A FABULOUS TIME. SEE YOU SOON I THINK. XXK.

I don't feel sick or angry anymore. I just want it to end and I want her out of my life. I scroll to open the messages from Daniel:

Sunday: 11.30

PICK UP YOUR PHONE!

11.45

ANSWER THE FUCKING PHONE BETHANY!

11.50

I'M SO FUCKING MAD, YOU SAID I SHOULD GO, I DIDN'T WANT TO GO, I WOULDN'T HAVE GONE IF I KNEW YOU WOULD BE LIKE THIS – FOR FUCK SAKE ANSWER THE DAMN PHONE!

12.00

I'M COMING ROUND!

12.20

WHERE THE FUCK ARE YOU? WHY AREN'T YOU AT SOFIA'S?

Sofia's parents were out last night but must have come straight to the hospital from their friends' house, once they heard the news about Paul, or they would have seen Daniel fuming on their doorstep. His last text is just after that.

I'M IN THE MAIN WAITING ROOM BABY IF YOU NEED ME TO DO ANYTHING, ANYTHING, LET ME KNOW. I'M GOING CRAZY THAT THEY WON'T LET ME GET TO YOU.

I wonder if he was still there when I left with Marco. I sigh heavily. It doesn't matter now, all that does is that 'this' ends; now. I dial his number.

"Bethany." His deep rich voice is calm, revealing none of the anger or relief he must have felt last night, but it is also strangely cold, too.

"Daniel." I don't bother to explain where I was, he knows where I was, and I also sense that something is wrong. "I would like to see you tonight. We need to talk." My hands are shaking slightly, and I can feel my throat tighten.

"I'll send my car; be ready in fifteen minutes." He hangs up. That was cold, brief and cold. I think that might make what I have to do easier, if he is angry and distant. Kit's words haunt me, but I need them, too. That he ever loved me was nonsense. It will help if I know it's only *my* heart that is going to be broken tonight. I swipe my fingerprint at the side door and wait for the green light and slight click of the lock releasing.

"Good Evening, Ms. Thorne." The cheerful tone greets me.

"Good Evening, Eric. How are you?" Eric is the guard and doorman for the building and seems to always be on duty. He must be in his sixties, close to retiring, I would guess.

"Oh, I'm well. Catching up on my reading. It tends to be a bit quiet here." He chuckles.

"I love reading, when I get the chance, although it's mostly coursework at the moment. Anyway, Daniel is expecting me, so I'll go on up." I continue to the lifts.

"You know you don't need my permission, you've got clearance, my dear." He smiles kindly and gets back to his reading.

I turn toward the lift. "For now," I sigh. I have a nervous, sickening feeling growing in my stomach. The lift doors open, and I notice his door is open, too. I step inside and hear her laughter; I am not surprised she is here. I guess she wants to make sure I go through with it, but I only have to close my eyes, and I see the pain in Sofia's.

Her laughter stops as I enter the living room where she is sitting next to Daniel. She looks very comfortable, at home even. She leans forward and pours more wine into her glass, her facial expression changes to a more somber mask.

"Daniel." My voice instantly catches. "Kassandra." This is going to be so hard. I grip my nails into my palm and try to focus on that small pain instead of the much larger one growing inside. "Daniel, maybe we should talk privately?" My voice is soft and as steady as it can be.

"Oh, Really?" His face is impassive, but his tone is ice cold. "Is that what you want?" His manner is openly hostile, and I wonder what she could have possibly said to cause this reaction.

"Well…" I falter. "Yes… I think…" I hesitate when he stands and walks toward me. He takes my hand, his grip more rough than firm. I try and resist being maneuvered into the room, but he is far too strong. "Look, Daniel," I will just say it and leave, rip the band aid and quickly, leave them to it and leave me to bleed. "I only came here because I didn't want to break up with you with a text." His head snaps to mine, his eyes narrow and dark.

"Break-up? Now why would you want to do that?" His cold voice has more of a sneer, and I feel I'm missing some vital bit of information. Kit's amused expression vanishes when she sees Daniel look her way.

"I… well, I just can't see you again. I don't want to see you again," I confirm. I don't want to make up horrible excuses to hurt him, but then again he doesn't look hurt, he just looks angry.

"Don't you love me?" His tone is cruel, and a quiet sob escapes my throat. His narrow eyes don't leave mine, as I prepare to say the words that will break my heart and delight my sister.

"No, Daniel, I don't love you." My hand reaches for my hair, but I rub my neck instead. The tension has set like a rock across my shoulders.

"You know, Bethany," he pauses as he looks at my fingers pulling on my hair, "I believe you." The quickness of his acceptance is like a sucker punch, and I fold a little at the invisible blow. "Shall I show you why I believe you?" Oh, my God, he hasn't finished. He leads me numbly to the coffee table before Kit, where there is a pile of papers face down. He leans over and picks up the papers. He still has a vice-like grip on my arm, but he releases me and hands me the papers. I turn them over, and I am confused by the image on the first page. It is a large grey photograph of me. I am standing on the steps of Marco's flat, and he is hugging me.

"Daniel, darling." My sister interrupts. "You must know I did this for my protection, being in my position, and Bethany, well, being in hers, I had to know who she was before I could let her into my life. I had no idea what I would uncover." She dabs her eyes and stifles a sob.

I am still confused as I look at the next picture. Marco and I going through his front door. The next sequence of photographs I can only slightly focus on, because my tears have built and are heavy in my eyes, causing a dream-like distortion. Marco and I are in his living room, and the next one shows a heated embrace, the next in a state of undress, the next in his bedroom, my naked back held in his arms, my legs wrapped around his waist, his hands gripping my bottom. The last one he has me pinned against the wall, and my head buried in his neck, and him buried deep in me. Only in the first picture you could see my face because only in the first picture it is me, but I know what this is supposed to be, and Kit did say she had something that would facilitate the break-up. I am desolate, and I look at Daniel's eyes, and briefly I see that he is, too, but it is quickly replaced with steely anger.

"Did you ever love me, Bethany?" His voice holds nothing.

"Oh, God!" I double up as all the air escapes me, and I stumble, dropping the photos on the floor. "Do you believe…" I can't finish my sentence, it hurts too much to think what he now believes to be true, that I'm a liar and a cheat.

"I believe what I see, Bethany." His mask is a fixed, impenetrable stone.

Kit stands to offer her hand in comfort, and he takes it. I feel dizzy and flushed, and I will faint if I don't leave right now. I turn to leave, but Daniel steps to block my way. He bends to pick up the photo, the one in the bedroom with my naked back.

"Please… do keep this one, Bethany, it's my particular favourite." I shiver at the hatred dripping from his words, but still my body feels conditioned to obey him, and I reach for the photo. I take it and walk away. As I reach his front door, I hear Kit's closing statement. "I'm so sorry, Daniel, you don't deserve this…I'll stay as long as you need me to." I run the last few steps to the lift and fall inside. I press the ground-floor button manically and try to stop myself from throwing up in the lift with deep breaths through my nose. I can't see for the haze of tears falling. The pain in my chest is like a saw, slowly inching its way around the soft tissue of my heart, until it falls unaided from the bleeding open cavity that is my chest. The lift reaches the ground floor, and I am grateful there is no one waiting to get in, because I am not going to make it outside. I dash to Eric's desk and swing my head around the corner to the waste bin, where I dry heave and deposit any remaining liquid from my stomach. I'm so embarrassed. I'm fucked-up, brokenhearted, and embarrassed.

"Oh, God, Eric, I'm so sorry." My vomiting has momentarily stopped my crying. I am relieved that my body is clearly unable to control that many excretions at the same time. "Eric, let me clean that up. Where are the toilets? I'm so sorry and so embarrassed."

"Ms. Thorne, it's fine. Don't worry. I'll fix it. Now, are you all right? You do look upset." His concern is only going to fuel the tears once more.

"I'm fine. I just witnessed something rather tragic, that's all. I'll be fine."

"Oh, what was it? Was it on the discovery channel?"

"No." I shake my head as I try and think of the words that

would aptly describe the last twenty minutes of my life. "It was a train wreck." I go to lift the bin and take it to the caretaker's room, which must be here somewhere, when there is a buzz indicating the entrance phone of the penthouse.

"Eric, Escort Miss Thorne from the building immediately!" He disconnects. I can add humiliated onto that previous list. I just want to go home. I smile tightly, and Eric looks embarrassed now.

"I'll go, Eric. I'm really sorry for everything." I feel like that is the understatement of the year. Daniel's driver is waiting, and he goes to open the door, but I shake my head.

"Really, Ms. Thorne, Mr. Stone was quite insistent I drive you."

"Maybe on the way here, Peter, certainly not on the way back, but thank you. Take care of yourself and--" I swallow my tears "--take care of Mr. Stone." I walk home in a numb trance, still gripping the photo, which damns me.

The restaurant is closed, but a few of the kitchen porters and Joe are still doing the final clean down. I don't want to be on my own right now, so I go into the kitchen and pick up a cloth and start polishing the silverware. "Hey, girl, you don't need to be doing that." Joe's heavy arm thumps down on my shoulders and gives me a little shake.

"Actually, Joe," I can't help the deep sigh that escapes my lips, "this is exactly what I need to be doing right now." I continue to mindlessly rub the knives, removing any traces of water marks and making them shine.

"Let me make you something, you are looking really pale, girl." He doesn't hide his concern in his voice.

"I can't tonight, Joe." I'm struggling with the sadness that's welling deep but rising fast and I plead, "Please."

"All right girl, whatever you say." He turns his back and carries on putting ingredients away. It's after midnight, and I must still be running on adrenaline and pain to still be awake after the last twenty-four hours. I lock the door after Joe crushes me in a bear hug and says goodnight.

I enter my bedroom and see the stack of deliveries of expensive beautiful lingerie, which have continued to arrive daily. They make an impressive tower in the corner of my room. My mind flashes to eBay. I couldn't wear anything he bought me without having him with me, inside me, and I need to stop thinking about him. I crawl into bed. It's too late to call Sofia, but I want her to know she doesn't have to worry anymore, and selfishly, I want her to forgive me. I send her a text that she will pick up first thing.

HEY YOU, ALL SORTED NO MORE WORRIES. I'M SO SORRY SOFS PLEASE FORGIVE ME. XB

My phone rings moments later.

"Hey sister." I greet her with our usual greeting. I just hope we can be normal again. "I didn't want to call you so late, but I wanted you to know you're safe, and Paul's safe." I'm silent while this sinks in but I need her so much I have to ask, "Can you ever forgive me, Sofs? I'm so sorry...I..." I am sobbing quietly. I am desolate.

"Shhh, sweetheart, shhh, there's nothing to forgive. I didn't actually believe the crazy bitch, so I'm just as much to blame for not taking her threat seriously." I can hear her own regret.

"But none of this would have happened if it wasn't for me. I think maybe I should move away, just to make sure, you know." This came to me tonight while I was polishing, that they would all be safer if I wasn't around, if I moved to another city.

"Oh, there you go, flight instinct kicked in quick this time, No! I am not losing you. She's got what she wants, that will be it. Won't it?" I can hear the uncertainty in her voice, so I try to reassure her.

"Yes, that will be it. Really, she was very clear. She just wants Daniel, and now she's created enough of a reason to disown me, she won't rear her ugly head again. I know he was keen on a big family reunion, but I don't think that's the case, anymore." My feeble laugh falls flat. "So other than my last lecture with him next week, I won't be seeing either of them again." I am saying this to reassure her, but I think it's the truth.

"Back to normal, then, eh?" She sounds relieved.

"Yes, normal." I'm not touching that one. I am a long way from normal.

"What happened? Why would she disown you now?"

"You know, it's not important." I try to sound disinterested.

"Bets, I'm sorry, too. I'm sorry you had to choose; it's fucked up. This whole thing is fucked up." She is sounding more like Sofia the angrier she gets.

"It was never a choice, Sofs. He's been in my life five minutes; you guys… you are my life." My chest hurts, and I press my fists hard against it to relieve the pain.

"But it only takes a minute though, doesn't it?" Her voice is soft.

"Yes," I sniff back a few stray tears that are tickling my nose, "it only takes a minute, but it doesn't change a thing."

Chapter Nineteen

I T'S BEEN ONE week, one tortuous week. I haven't heard from Daniel, and a sad reflection of my current state of esteem, means I am not surprised at this. My brave face is more a passive neutral mask, but luckily the only people who would probe to see beneath it are either at the hospital, or in Marco's case, have taken some time off to visit some old school friends who are working a ski season in the Alps. I had one text from Kit the day after, which said:

YOU'RE WELCOME XXK

But I have heard nothing else. At least her apathy toward me means I am not going to get petty updates or gloating.

I picked my shifts back up at the restaurant, and I have reverted to my pre-Daniel timetable. I have spoken to Sofia every night this week, and I know Paul is much better. He is being discharged tomorrow. Marco flew in early this morning and may come over with Sofia later. I'm feeling a little apprehensive, as the last time we were together like this seems a lifetime ago and not just in the sense of time, but in what has changed, too. I open a large bag of chocolate buttons and pour them in a communal bowl on my coffee table, grab a couple of glasses, and start to open the wine. I hear the back door open and the sound of Marco and Sofia laughing as they climb the stairs. I instantly relax, maybe we're not so changed. They burst through my door.

"Hey, Boo!" Marco rushes and squeezes me tight, lifting my feet clean off the floor, and I yelp as the wine bottle almost slips from my hands - almost. He plants an aggressively affectionate kiss on my cheek and slumps onto my sofa. Sofia's embrace is a little more sedate but just as loving. I put the wine on the table and go to fetch another glass.

"What is this you're listening to?" Sofia's tone is accusatory, and she raises her judging brow. "No, wait, I think I have this album. Is it volume one or two of 'Music to hang yourself by'?"

"Ha, ha, you are so funny. It's just a playlist, with a slightly morbid bias, I admit, but it just fits my mood of late, and I find it strangely comforting," I defend.

"Well, wallowing is definitely better than running," she quips, but her tone is almost a warning.

"Who's running? Why would you be running? This isn't about Daniel the Dick, now, is it?" Marco pours his wine and grabs a handful of chocolate.

"I'm not running-" I'm interrupted.

"Damn right, you're not!" Marco and Sofia chorus with the exact intonation, it's spooky.

"I'm not running. I might be wallowing… a little. And he's not a dick, well, he might be for believing her shit, but I can't really blame him." I walk over to my desk and pull the crumpled photo from the drawer and throw it on the table next to the wine. Marco sits instantly and shoots his mouthful of wine all down his front, hitting the table and the bowl of chocolate.

"Oh, gross, Marco, I was going to eat those," Sofia reprimands her brother, because she hasn't yet noticed what caused his reaction. He wipes his mouth and the droplets from his shirt and jeans before he leans to pick up the photo.

"Bets?" He looks shocked and confused.

"What the fuck!" Sofia grabs the photo from Marco's hand and studies the image. Marco is looking at me and then back to the photo.

"Bets, what is that? No, wait, why do you have that… no,

wait, just explain all of it." They both look at me. Their eyes are identical, but Marco's are confused, while Sofia's are all concern.

"It's one of a set, but this one was Daniel's favourite, and he wanted me to have it," I say with exaggerated affection. I explain the sequence of the other photos, the train wreck that followed, and sit dejectedly in my armchair. Sofia squeezes next to me, it's a tight fit and I laugh, because I don't think she realized it would be this cozy. We are practically nose to nose.

"You know that's not you, right?" Marco's ridiculous observation makes us both bark out with laughter.

"Yes, I'm pretty sure I know that's not me." This tragedy has momentarily morphed into a comedy.

"That's Rose, but I don't understand. She has a massive tattoo on her arse; I mean it's massive. A massive rose tattoo." He repeats dazed. "She's the right build, and her hair kind of looks the same as yours, so, yeah, she looks a little like you." He catches my eyes. I'm still chuckling. "And don't get freaked, I'm not harbouring any latent desires for a round two, sorry, a round one with you, Bets. Rose is really into me, she's fit and feisty in the sack." He holds up the photo. "Exhibit A, I believe. But that doesn't explain her disappearing tattoo?"

"No, but Photoshop would." Sofia adds.

"He believed this?" Marco's voice is sterner, and I can see his jaw start to grind.

"He believed what he saw," I sigh sadly, remembering his exact words.

"He's a fucking idiot, and she… she is a fucking bitch." He is openly angry now, and I tense. "Why the fuck are you letting her get away with this?" I feel Sofia tense beside me.

"I have nothing, other than her birth certificate, which I doctored to get my place at Uni. I have nothing that proves she is anything other than what she pretends to be. She has completely, and successful, rewritten her life, and I now have the starring role of 'villain'. She destroyed everything from her life before. I remember the bonfire in the garden, her fresh start. Everything went, photos, school reports, diaries, clothes. She left with the clothes on her back and a big fat cheque." My voice has been slowly rising, so I take a calming breath. "I think she did me a favour with the photos. He was so quick to believe her. I think… no, I know he didn't love me, not like…" I feel a rush of tears that I hold in my lids and a tingle in my nose. I let out small puffs of air to prevent my free fall, and Sofia puts her arm around my shoulders awkwardly, pulling my head into her neck. We are just too close for this to be comfortable, but I take comfort from the gesture. This is just bearable, believing Daniel didn't love me, and it will mean that Marco won't need to be fighting in my corner anytime soon.

"Look, I have nothing to gain from trying to expose her. It might be different if …" I hesitate, it wouldn't be different, because she is clinically insane, but if Marco knew about her threat, well, I physically shudder at that thought. "If he loved me." It's a perfectly plausible reason to let *it* go, and Marco seems appeased with my reasoning. Sofia doesn't say anything, but she holds a well of sadness in her face. She still has this misguided romantic world view where she truly believed Daniel loved me, and for that she is a little heartbroken, but for her I will be made of stronger stuff. I kiss her cheek and whisper, "I'm happy with my 'no-more,' Sofs, and I want you to be, too."

"Yeah, you sound happy." She nods toward my iPod speaker, and I laugh.

"God, Bets, Sofia is right. I'm on a freaking high from an awesome holiday, and even I want to hang myself," Marco moans.

"All right, all right, I'll change the tunes." I lever myself from the armchair and pick up my iPod and start to scroll. "If you're looking for upbeat I can offer you a whole play list of Disney Film soundtracks."

"What are you, seven?" Marco grabs my IPod and throws it on the sofa promptly replacing it with his, and it's a mix of Killers, Arctic Monkeys, and Muse. Perfect. "So are you going to ask me about my trip, or is it all about you girls tonight?" He pouts and pours another glass.

This is the last of Daniel's lectures and I am again sitting high, toward the back of the theatre with Mike and Sam on either side of me. I am all nerves and excitement, which is really stupid. I haven't been eating too well, either, but made sure I had at least consumed a granola bar and some juice. I won't be fainting again, no matter what stunt he might pull. The room falls instantly silent as his powerful presence emanates across the room. My body responds like the traitor it is, with a flush of prickles covering my skin and an increase in my heartbeat. I only brave fleeting glances toward the stage, but each time it is clear Daniel's focus is on his notes and the screen. His lecture is brilliant, and there is only one moment when his eyes meet mine. The bright dark-blue eyes reflect no recognition, no acknowledgment of any prior intimacy, and I am consumed by an excruciating pain in my chest at his obvious indifference to me now.

"Looks like you're off the hook this week, Ms." Mike nudges me and smiles.

"It would appear so." I offer quietly. I look at my empty page. I have taken no notes, despite the rich material offered and Sam looks at my page.

"Not like you, nerd?" He nods to my page with the query across his brow.

"Oh, don't worry, it's all in here." I tap my temple and start to pack my bag. Everyone around me has started to shuffle and make their way to the exit, but I decide to sit until the room is clear, and then wait a bit longer. I can fool myself that he might not have seen me in the room full as it was, but an up close and personal encounter, I know I won't fare so well. I have to wait a while for the room to clear as Daniel takes his time with the overly keen students vying for his attention. I rest my head in my arms and close my eyes, a huge mistake. I am awakened, I don't know how much later, but there is definitely a little drool in the corner of my mouth, by the kind face of my course leader. He is gently shaking my shoulder as I re-orientate. I discretely wipe my mouth and smile. Wow, I am embarrassed.

"Sorry Mr. Wilson. It's very warm in here, and I must have been a lot more tired than I thought, sorry. I didn't fall asleep in the lecture." I add quickly, hoping he wouldn't think me that rude, and he laughs.

"Well, it wouldn't be the first time a student has, my dear, but I believe you. I was just coming to lock up and saw you. Lucky I did, or you might've been here all night." He laughs again. Really, I'm so exhausted I probably wouldn't have woken before morning, anyway.

"You lock up the rooms?" That didn't seem right. Surely that is more a job for security than for a Head of Department.

"When I'm asked to." He still hasn't moved to allow me to get up. "Bethany, I wanted to check how you are doing? You seem a little pale, and, well, you just don't seem like yourself. Some of the Lecturers have commented, and I wanted to make sure you are okay?"

My face flushes red with this level of concern. Again I think this is outside his remit as course leader. "Oh, that is very kind. I'm fine, really. I love the course, but I have been working a few extra shifts, and I just think it's taken its toll on me, but nothing to worry about," I insist. "I'm fine." I smile, but my stern tone I hope will fend off further personal questions. I go to move, but he still makes no indication that he is about to join me in leaving the theatre.

"You don't seem fine." Okay, so maybe I need to work on my stern 'don't ask me any more questions' tone, but he looks so sincere and kind, there is no way I can get cross at his insistence.

"My mother died recently." I know it was mean to use this excuse and make him uncomfortable in the process, but it does have the desired effect.

"Oh, I am sorry, Bethany." He reaches for my entwined hands and squeezes. "I had no idea. I understand how traumatic that must be. If you need anything from me, you know you only have to ask." He pushes himself up out of the seat, and I follow him along the row. "We better get a move on, or we will both get locked in, and that *will* have tongues wagging." He gives me a cheeky wink, any awkwardness vanishes, and we both laugh.

It is dark across the Quad, and there are only a few students left. I decide to walk home. I know it will take me a good hour, but I am in no hurry to be alone in my apartment. Besides, I love London at night this time of year. The Christmas decorations are up, and the luxury arcades along Piccadilly look spectacular, festive and magical. The window display in Fortnum and Mason is decadent and luxurious, with mountains of mouth-watering Christmas fare, arranged in a feat of gravity-defying art; glossy glazed fruits, rich dark chocolates, and cinder toffee. Thick mince pies and delicately iced Christmas cakes. My tummy rumbles as I step foot on the Piccadilly road in anticipation of passing these windows.

I reach the corner of the street just after Fortnum's when I notice Daniel's driver standing at the back of his car. He waves me over. I look around. I don't know who would be following me, but I still want to check. I don't recognize anyone.

"Hey, Peter." I greet him cheerily. "Christmas shopping on the clock?" I quip. "Don't worry, I won't tell the boss; us 'staff' have to stick together." I snort.

"You were never staff, Ms. Thorne," he tells me quietly.

"I think you'll find I was." I'm still smiling, it might hurt like fuck, but there is no reason for everyone else to know that. "Anyway, how are you doing?"

"I am well, Ms. Thorne, and you? Are you keeping well?" His voice is tinged with concern, and I wonder how much he knows. Probably more than I would want, but his eyes are kind.

"Really, Peter, Bethany is fine. Actually Bets would be much better, and, yes, I'm fine." I wonder if I am using that description more because I know how much Daniel hated it. I smile at this. "I'm fine, anyway, it's freezing, so I'll maybe see you around."

I turn to leave.

"May I please drive you home? As you said, it's cold and it's still some distance from here."

"Oh I don't think that would be a good idea," I say in a gravely humorous tone. "If you're not in trouble for Christmas shopping, you'd probably get the sack for giving me a lift, which is not worth the risk, my friend." I laugh. "It's not that far through Green Park."

"I can't let you walk through the park Ms.... Bethany." Bless him, he is struggling with the informality.

"Don't sweat it, and, no offense, Peter, but it's not your call. Thank you all the same. See you." I turn and head off at a brisk walk. I decide not to go through the park. The streets are busy, and the roads are gridlocked, but when I turn to cross the road, I notice Peter is slowly following me in Daniel's Bentley. The traffic is moving no quicker than my walking pace, so he is pretty much on my heel the whole way to Knightsbridge. We even pass one another several times, and I wave. He looks exasperated at my stubbornness, but he'd not thank me if he got the sack just before Christmas. I remember painfully that I was escorted from Daniel's building. He would throw a shit-fit if I was using his personal driver for my own convenience.

The kitchen is busy with the final orders of the evening, and Joe tries to tempt me to eat a little of the special, a venison meatball spaghetti, which I'm sure is delicious but would be way too rich, given my limited intake of food recently. I do agree to a small bowl of the tomato and basil soup, which I carefully hold in my hands as I tuck my legs under me on the sofa. I knew I was hungry, but I didn't think I would be able to actually keep anything down. The soup, however, is sweet, and the basil tastes so fresh, I finish the whole bowl. I suddenly feel so tired, and I lie down on the sofa. I don't know where it comes from, but I am soon heaving with such sadness, my shoulders are shaking uncontrollably, and my tears are free-falling, drenching my face. I thought I was coping. I knew I wasn't, but I can't believe this pain, it hurts so fucking much. I can't believe I miss him so much and I'm so fucking angry. How could he believe those pictures without question? How could he believe her, believe I didn't love him? How could he look through me like I was nothing? Because to him, you are nothing, you're a fucking idiot! I then hear some lyrics float from the kitchen below about 'sharing all my secrets and all my fears, but the hardest part not having you to hold' and it feels like my heart has been ripped from my chest because 'I can't bear to let him go.' This crippling pain is me *not* bearing it, and I don't know what to do, I don't know how to survive Daniel Stone.

I don't know how long I release my sadness into the sofa cushions, but my eyes are now dry. They are empty, at least, when I hear my bag vibrate. My body feels unbelievably heavy, and with herculean effort I push myself up and retrieve my bag. Rummaging to the bottom, I notice it is the phone Mags gave me that is vibrating. I just hadn't gotten around to sending it back. I'm amazed it's still kept its charge. Expecting the call center ID to be flashing, I almost drop the phone when I recognise Daniel's number flash across the screen. My heart, which had been bleeding on the floor, now leaps to my throat, and I stare at the phone for ages. I shouldn't answer it, but it just keeps ringing. Why is he calling me on this phone? I guess I could ask him? I press the button and tentatively hold the phone to my ear like it might explode.

"Daniel?" My voice is barely a whisper. Silence. "Daniel, why are you calling me?" The line is quiet, but I can hear his gentle breathing.

"Lola?" His voice is smooth. My senses are instantly on high alert. I wait a moment, the silence palpable.

"Sir."

"Lola, good evening." His voice is smooth and commanding.

"Sir? I…I," I stutter.

"I said good evening, Lola." His dominant tone is very clear, and I shiver.

"Good evening, Sir," I acquiesce.

"Good girl." His deep sigh is sensual and captivating. I know Sir is Daniel, but I don't know what he wants. What I do know is that my body is programmed to obey him, and it starts to tingle with anticipation. "Now… how have you been? I think it might be worth mentioning now about my view regarding lies, Lola. They won't be tolerated, and you will be punished."

"I should be punished."

"Really? Why would you say that? Have you been bad?" His tone is serious, and his voice is dark.

"I must have been very bad, Sir." My voice is shaky. "I don't think anyone could suffer pain like this who hadn't done something so terrible to deserve every bit of it. So, yes, I think I must have been bad, and maybe in a previous life, too. Maybe I was Genghis Khan's mother."

His laugh rumbles through the phone, and the light sound makes me smile. All this pain, and I still glean some much needed warmth from his voice.

"I am going to help you, Lola," He states as a matter of fact.

"Sir," I sigh at this futile conversation, "that is kind, but I don't see how that's possible."

"Did I ask you what you thought?" He is dismissive of my reservation. "I want you to get changed into one of my gifts to you, and in ten minutes there will be a taxi waiting to bring you to me."

I gasp. "Da-" I don't get to finish his name.

"-LOLA!" He shouts down the phone making me jump.

"Sir, I can't see you. I can't come to you. I'm sorry, I just can't." My panic is evident in my rushed objection.

"You can and will," He growls his demands. "Lola, you will come to me, and I will make the pain disappear. I will make your pain disappear. Now, you can do as I say, and you will be brought to my flat, *not* my apartment, or I will come and get you. Do you understand, Lola?" Oh, fuck, I can't let him come here, but at the same time, I do want him to take my pain away. I really want the pain to go away. I am so scared. I can't help a small sob from reaching my mouth. "Lola, I won't let anything happen to you that you don't want to happen." His voice is pure sin, but he adds in a softer serious tone, "You will be safe, and everything that is important to you will be safe." He is adamant, his voice is reassuring. But then I worry that I just think it is reassuring because I need it to be. "Don't overthink this… ten minutes." He hangs up.

Fuck! Fuck! Fuck!

My head is spinning. What the fuck? I can't risk him coming here, that is just a no, but if I'm to get a taxi, then that means no driver to tie back to Daniel. Also not going to his apartment, and the fact that he won't answer his name is all good, I think. I don't really know what to think, but as it stands at this moment I am Lola, and Lola is taking a taxi somewhere to meet *Sir*. If I wasn't so scared shitless, I would be hugely turned on by the dominance of his request and this clandestine rendezvous. I run into my bedroom and dive on the boxes in the corner. It is pretty easy to differentiate which garments came from Sir and which came from Daniel, and I quickly identify a black and emerald green corset and matching silk panties, with black seamed silk stockings. I slip my black suede knee high fitted boots and pull a simple grey jersey dress over the top. I don't own a Mac type coat or any smart long coat for that matter, so I push my arms through the sleeves of my army green Parker. Not quite the image I was hoping for, but it's bloody freezing out there now.

I hear the horn of the taxi, and my heart ratchets up in speed. I put my keys in my bag and make my way outside. I keep telling myself I don't have a choice, because I can't risk him turning up here. At the same time, I am curious to know what he wants from me, or how he plans to help me. I can't sit still in the taxi.

"Do you know where you're taking me?" I ask the driver.

"Yes, Miss." He smiles but says nothing more.

"Do you mind me asking who paid for the booking?"

"You can ask, Miss, but I can't tell you. It was a cash booking. All up front, so I'm afraid there is no way of knowing, same goes for your return trip." He hands me his card. "Just call me when you need picking up, I'll be outside, anyway, but I can pull up right by the door if I know you're on your way."

I take his card, "Oh, okay, thanks." I feel stupid for being so paranoid, but then I have pretty good reason to be, and now I can't help thinking this is such a stupid thing to be doing. What if… Oh God. "Look." I address the driver, "Umm, I think I've changed my mind. Can you take me back?"

"Ah, sorry, love, my instructions are to take you to the destination and escort you into the building. If there was any change in the plan, I was to wait at the destination for the other party to join you to bring you back here. So I guess I can take you back but …"

"No." I sigh. "No, it's fine. I thought for a moment that this was my choice." I mumble. I feel my phone buzz with a text.

ENTRY CODE: Z78423P FLOOR 18 FLAT 181

My mouth is suddenly dry. The driver turns a corner to a complex of buildings I recognize and pulls up outside Paul's apartment block. I am really confused now. Paul was discharged yesterday, but I know he is staying at his parents' house in Notting Hill for a while. Also his flat is on the fourteenth floor, so I know I'm not going there. The driver walks around to my side, but I have already opened the door and stepped out of the car. He walks beside me until we reach the side entrance with the entry keypad. I press the numbers and say goodbye, but he waits until I am fully inside, and the door has clicked locked. I wave, and he finally turns to leave. I wonder if he is expecting me to change my mind and walk back out, and as he leans against his car still looking at me, I realize that's exactly what he is expecting me to do. Or at least what he has been warned I might do. I wave again and turn toward the bank of lifts. My hands are a little shaky, and as the lift ascends, it is not just the sudden weightlessness that is making me feel nauseous.

I stand outside flat number 181, my body is trembling, and I pull my head tight to one side to stretch my neck and release some of the tension with a loud crack. I let out a large puff of air, and I think this must feel like a combination of stage fright and entering a boxing ring for the first time. Although he has already done the TKO on me, so I am thinking the former analogy is more appropriate. I take a quick peek down beneath my dress and catch my costume; definitely stage fright. I lightly knock on the door, and moments later, it opens. Oh, he takes my breath away. He stands to one side with his arm high on the door; he is wearing the same black suit trousers he wore in the lecture earlier this evening and nothing else.

Chapter Twenty

I NOTICE HIS FEET first. They are bare, but his ripped body soon draws my eyes up his stunning frame. His is taking deep breaths, his chest rises slowly, and his muscles flex and ripple with the small movement. His lightly tanned skin is stretched smooth and taut across his firm, flat abdomen. The tension sizzles between us, and I can feel the instant heat burn deep inside me, but it pales significantly when I'm scorched by the glare of his darkly dangerous blue-black eyes. 'Wow', I think to myself, then gasp when I realize the word did, in fact, escape my shocked mouth. I snap my lips together and feel a flash of heat spread across my face. His face is impassive, although there is the slightest flick in the corner of his mouth, it could be the beginning of a smile, but it could equally be the start of a snarl. Only his eyes would give that away, and at the moment they are revealing nothing except a dark desire. I would be shocked if my eyes were any different.

"Lola." His deep voice is raspy, and he pushes the door a little further to allow me to pass under his arm and into the flat. I walk on legs I hope are not visibly shaking, although they feel like jelly. Passing close to his naked torso, I feel a palpable current race between our bodies. I wonder if it's only me who feels it, and as I try to suppress a moan at being this near to perfection, I can see his jaw tick and know he is struggling with something,

I just don't know what that is. His cologne is different, rich and musky, and on him it smells like sin. My skin is alive with instant prickles, and my heart is beating with the speed of hunted prey about to be devoured by something wild. I suddenly remember Mags telling me I was a natural submissive, what seems like a life time ago, and outside of everything Daniel and I have been through, I am here as Lola the submissive. It's the only reason I can be here, because tonight I am Lola and he is…

"Sir." I turn to face him. The corridor is narrow. We are not too close, but tonight, his size, and general aura of power and dominance, I find intimidating. I lower my head and refrain from meeting his eyes, and I get a sensual tingle all over when he steps to me and lightly lifts my chin with his finger forcing me to meet his eyes.

"Good girl." He is right about one thing. I am not thinking about the pain in my chest. I am now only thinking about the burning need for release rising between my legs. He passes me and tells me to follow him. I would have, anyway, but with his demanding tone, I am now beginning to understand that tonight is different from any other encounter we have shared, very different. I stand in the living area. Tt is an open space with three large white leather sofas and a small coffee table. The far wall is completely covered with a built in ultra-glossy black storage unit, which has some shelving for personal items, though there are none, and a sleek sliding door, which hides a small bar. The floor is polished white marble, there is no colour in this room. It is cold and impersonal and very different from Paul's apartment four floors below. He has fixed himself a drink and is walking back toward me. My mouth is dry, and I lick my lips for moisture.

"Mmmm, Lola." His voice is deep. "I want you to take your coat off." He sits slowly on the edge of the sofa, which has no arm rest and is more like a rounded off seat. His legs are wide, and he leans forward with the ice in his glass clinking the sides as he swirls the golden liquid around. I can feel his scorching gaze on me, but I won't meet his eyes, not tonight. I take off my coat.

There is nothing seductive about a parker, and I am glad to be rid of it, I am burning up and not from the temperature in the flat.

"Take off your dress." I inhale a quick sharp breath, but almost instantly pull the hem of the stretchy grey material and lift it over my head. He has his hand out, and I pass the dress to him. I wish I could see his face as I stand there in the sexiest lingerie I own --corset, stockings and stiletto boots, but I do hear him inhale deeply. I hear him move and step my way. He is right in front of me, and he places his large hand on my chest, palm flat, just above and between my breasts. His touch scorches me like a branding iron, and my breath hitches. "Your pain is here?" He is forcing words through his clenched jaw. His tone is deep and angry.

"Yes," I whisper. He waits, because I am distracted by his touch, I forgot, but then quickly add, "Sir. Yes, Sir," I exhale. I have to remember to breathe.

"Tell me about the pain, Lola?"

"Da-"

"ADDRESS ME LIKE THAT AGAIN, AND SEE WHAT HAPPENS!" His voice booms so close to my face, his sweet minty breath rushes my face, but the volume makes me jump back, and I stumble. He grabs my arm to prevent my fall and growls in anger. "The pain, Lola, tell me about the fucking pain." His voice is calm but no less demanding.

"I... I..." My voice is quiet, tentative, but that is mostly because I don't know how to say this. It is so raw, and although with anyone else, it is just as easy to lie, I know I won't have that luxury with him. "I never knew there could be pain like this, Sir." My voice starts to break, and I suck in a steadying breath. This isn't a cry and cuddle session, so I need to not cry. "Mostly I am numb, but sometimes I just can't stand it, Sir."

"This pain consumes you?" It is a statement and a question.

"Yes, Sir." I can feel the tension in my own jaw as he forces this excruciating admission from deep inside.

"This pain you can't handle?" He pushes, relentless, oblivious.

"No, Sir." I swallow the sudden sob but he notices.

"Then I will give you pain that you *can* handle. Do you understand, Lola?"

"No, Sir."

"The pain I can give you will be a pain you can handle, a pain you can focus on to get the release you need." His deep breath exhales across my sensitive skin.

"You are going to hurt me?" My voice is quiet as I try to understand the implication of what he is suggesting, when he all too quickly replies softly.

"You hurt me." But then he adds louder more forcefully. "Yes, I am going to hurt you, but no more than you can take and no more than you need."

"You think I need this pain, more pain?" I am struggling with *this* concept.

"No, I know you need this pain, and I know you need the pleasure too." His voice sounds so wicked, my core clenches, and I squeeze my legs at the thought of this pleasure.

"Will I need a safe word?" I can't believe I am asking this question. The Daniel I trusted I could say stop to, but this feels different. The trust is there, but there is also a darkness.

"Oh, you know, Lola, I think you might." His voice is seductive, but he speaks with a clenched jaw and repeats, "I think you might." I get a chill across my skin that makes me tremble, and it is then I realize that this is just as much for him as it is for me. I need to focus on a different kind of pain, and so does he. "So what is your safe word, Lola?" My mind has gone blank, not only can I not think of a suitable safe word, I can't think of any words. It feels like ages before I manage to speak as my mind tries hopelessly to think of something that isn't no, don't, or ow.

"I'm sorry, I don't know, I can't think of anything." I still have my head lowered, but if he could see my eyes, he'd see my vacant expression.

"A colour perhaps. Red is standard," He offers as a suggestion. It helps.

"Blue!" I fire at him abruptly. "Blue is my safe word." Blue is not an angry colour, it doesn't bleed or break. It is calm, safe, and cold.

"Good, let us begin." He puts his drink on the coffee table, takes my trembling hand, and leads me into the bedroom.

"I like what you've done with the place." His warning glare silences any further comments. It's only because I'm nervous, a little out of my comfort zone, a little out of any of my zones. I'm not in Kansas anymore.

This room is very different, the walls have a dark silver silk wall covering, and the carpet is a thick dark grey. The windows are covered with a rich, deep red velvet curtain, but it's the furniture that is the most surprising. The bed is easily a super, super king and has four posts, which reach up from the corners, but don't join each other. There is no comforter or blanket, although there are several black pillows and the sheet is also a dark silver silk similar to the walls. It is the padded bench with cuffs and chains at the end of the bed that has my heart racing. So do the ropes and ties on each of the four posts of the bed. There is also a rather ominous looking black briefcase next to the bench and a small whimper leaves my throat followed by a louder swallow. Unexpectedly, I receive a small hand squeeze in return, and the gesture is enough to settle me.

"Are you happy with the choices you have made, Lola?" His deep voice brings me back from my assessment of the interior design of his bedroom.

"I don't have choices, Sir," I snort.

"Really? All right. Are you happy with the decisions you have made?" Whether he is referring to saving my family or coming here tonight, the answer is the same.

"Yes, Sir."

"Very well. What we are going to do tonight." He clears his throat, his voice is deep and raspy. "What I am going to do to you tonight, was always inevitable with us. It's just that *your* decisions have made tonight more of a 'baptism of fire' as it were, rather than a more gentle introduction, which would have been the case had you behaved differently." He is standing directly behind me, gently scraping his fingernail up my arm, tracing a line all the way up my neck, and then down my spine to the top of my corset. A trail of sparks follow his touch. It is very distracting, as I try to understand what he is saying.

I think I understand from my limited research that a Dominant/submissive relationship would involve whatever he has planned. He's a Dom, he does what he wants. I clench at the thought, and I can feel the liquid heat at my core building, my pulse is racing. I am so fucking turned on right now. But he is saying he would have taken it slow, and now that is no longer an option. I didn't have a choice in this. There wasn't a choice with the decisions I made, it wasn't him or them. It was them. He doesn't love me. He thinks I'm a liar and a cheat who gave up on her family. I am angry, in love, and in pain, and he has promised to help. I hurt him, and he needs something from me, and I think this is it. If he thinks his 'baptism of fire' speech is going to have me running for the hills or crying out my safe word every five minutes, he doesn't know me at all. He may hear me cry out, but he won't hear my safe word, not tonight.

He walks to the bag and removes some more cuffs. He then turns to face me, and he takes one of my hands. "I had these made for you. The leather is very soft, like your skin. It will constrict you, but it won't hurt." He fastens the cuffs on each of my wrists before kneeling and doing the same with cuffs on my ankles. He stands and places his large hand around my neck; his hold is firm. "Your pulse is racing. Do you trust me?"

"Yes, Sir." My response is an exhaling breath. I must stop holding my breath, or with my blood rushing around my body at this pace, I am likely to pass out. He takes my hand and leads me to the bed where he sits in front of me. He pulls me roughly across his lap, my hands reach to the floor and my feet are on tip toes. I can feel his hot arousal through the material of his trousers, hard against my side. He holds me with one arm across my back. His hand is on my hip, and his other hand pulls my panties down over my bottom to my knees. I feel more exposed than if I was completely naked, certainly more vulnerable. He rubs his hand in circles smoothing the skin creating a gentle heat, and I feel a deep rumble vibrate through his chest. My head shoots up with a cry at the first strike.

"This is your warm-up, Lola. It will help you prepare for your punishment." He warns.

"I'm being punished?" I whisper.

"Ask me another question, Lola." His voice is husky, and I can hear his grin. "Please, ask me another question." Three hard rapid strikes follow his words and I grip my lips together to prevent another question. He rubs his hand over the area, alleviating the sting, but the heat generated is intense. I can't get enough purchase from my toes to move at all. I can't wiggle or dip away with his strong arm holding me in place. He continues a steady relentless rhythm of spank, stroke, spank. My head is dizzy, and my butt is on fire, but then he moves lower and strikes his palm against the sensitive skin below my bottom, on the very tops of my thighs. I scream out; fuck, that hurts. I squeeze my eyes tight, and all I can see is the colour blue, bright blue and bright blue piercing eyes staring into my soul, but I grit my teeth and focus on the pain. I alternate panting and grinding my teeth, but the individual strikes no longer register, just a burning, stinging sensation that I happen to know has me dripping wet.

"You have no choice, Lola? Why is that?" He growls his question.

"I have no choice, Sir," is my only response.

He helps me to stand, and I have a momentary head rush, where my eyes are glazed, and I am light headed. He stands and leads me over to the bench. I am still a little dazed when he pushes me over to lay my tummy flat across it with my bottom over the end. He clips the cuff on my wrists to the chains stretching my arms over the other end. He stands behind me and pulls my panties all the way off my legs before he clips the ankle cuffs to the chains at the bottom. My legs are spread, not wide but I am again exposed. He runs his hands up my legs and over my burning backside. His hands aren't rough, but they feel like sandpaper against my now raw and ultra-sensitive skin, and I can't help but tremble. I have an urgency and desperate need for release. I know if he was to touch me, even slightly, I would come. I am so on edge, I don't feel any of the pain in my chest, and I don't feel any of the pain from my spanking; I am just alive with sensation.

"You know you glow for me, when you're aroused, when you're wet." He swipes his finger along the length of my sensitive folds and lightly touches my clit. I buck and jerk, instantly consumed with uncontrollable spasms sweeping my body. A violent explosion takes me completely by surprise with its speed and intensity and leaves me panting for air. He tries to suppress his groan, releasing a sexy primal noise from the back of his throat. "Mmmm," I hear him lick his finger. He moves back and again reaches into the bag. I can't see what he has retrieved, but I don't have to guess because he walks slowly around the bench to where my head is facing and carefully traces the tip of the riding crop down my cheek and across my moist lips. His fingers follow the crop and tuck the stray hair that has fallen across my face behind my ears. "Look at me," he demands quietly. I obey instantly, I can't deny the way my body responds to him. I love this feeling of giving him total control, and now I can see his eyes. I love that this clearly pleases him. too. "You have a safe word for a reason." He clears his throat. "Understand?"

I catch a glimpse of the strained outline of his erection in his trousers, and I am pleased he is as affected as I am. And although I have had my release, my body is clearly building again, and I try to press into the bench for some friction. He very lightly taps my bottom at this movement, and I still. "Yes, Sir, I understand." My anticipation has my voice on edge.

"Tell me, Lola. Why is it you have no choice?" His repeated question makes me angry, so he gets the same answer.

"I have no choice, Sir." I snarl my response.

"Mmm lying and impolite, let's see how that works out for you, and let's see how long it will be, before you safe word on me, shall we?" He sounds so fucking smug. He stands to the side and strokes my bottom with the length of the crop; I clench with tension and anticipation. I hear the whoosh of air and the loud crack against my backside. The instant slice of pain causes me to scream loudly, and my whole body to jolt. The chains, which hold me, are pulled tight and the cuffs bite into my skin with the force I have pulled at them. Oh, Fuck, that hurts! My tight eyelids are awash with the colour blue, when I jolt again with another swipe. I whimper, but I feel another and another.

"Why do you have no choice?" His voice is raised above my loud panting breaths.

"I have no choice." I spit out again followed by a 'fuck you' in my head. More strikes follow, I don't know how many. He pauses, allowing me to catch my breath, before he repeats his question. He gets the same response, and I can hear his frustrated, angry breaths, but he continues his strikes moving the crop across every inch of my bare backside. I can feel my skin flame and rise in welts, but rather than tense, I find my body relaxing. A warm blanket flows across my skin, and I sigh; the tension evaporate, and I rest my head. I no longer count, my hearing is muffled, and I can just make out his voice.

"Safe word, Lola. Use your fucking safe word!" His demand sounds desperate. He is furious when I shake my head. He asks again with gritted teeth. "Why do you have no choice?" His voice is angry; he is angry, and I am calm.

"There was no choice," I sigh, and he has stopped to hear what I am whispering. "Because you don't love me."

"Fuck!" He throws the whip across the room. It takes only a moment, and all I can feel is heat, an unbelievable inferno across the top of my thighs and my backside. This heat is quickly replaced by the reality of unbelievable pain. Now this is a pain I never knew existed, and it takes all my focus to concentrate on trying to control it. I focus on small breaths, holding the pain tight, and then releasing it with each tiny breath. I do this a few times, while I am aware that my cuffs are being loosened. I find I am in control of this pain, I can hold it, absorb it, and release it, and I feel better for letting it go. How fucked up is that? How fucked up am I? I let out a small laugh and wince at this tiny movement. Oh, fuck, this is going to hurt. I feel his warm hand on my neck and he rubs his fingers into my hair and leans in to whisper.

"Don't move, I need to get some cream. I had no idea you'd take it that far." He sounds upset; he gently kisses my ear. I can't have him being sweet and tender, not when I've gone through that to have a level of pain I can cope with. He leaves the room, and I push myself up and stifle my tears, and I bite a little too hard on my lips, causing them to bleed. Tiny cries are kept silent in my mouth, and I walk out into the living room before he returns from the bathroom. Every step causes a thousand hot needles to race across my skin, and I continue to focus on my breathing; it's effective, and if I didn't have to move so much, it would be a perfect distraction. I just manage to pull my dress over and down my body when I hear him.

"Fuck! What do you think you are doing? You need treatment; your skin needs treatment," he scolds.

"Yes, Sir, and I will treat it when I get home." He is about to argue, but I continue, "You were right; I did need the pain and the release." I swallow quietly. "Thank you, Sir." I go to pick up my coat but struggle with the bend, and he rushes forward to hand it to me. Our hands touch, and I snatch mine back at the painfully familiar spark.

"I should be taking you home," He grumbles angrily.

"You should, but you can't," I confirm, and for the first time tonight, I look into his eyes, which are the deepest blue and swirling with anger. Mine are filled with regret. I am strangely grateful for tonight, but it doesn't change anything. "Good night, Sir." He walks to the door, but before I walk out I add. "Don't call me again."

"Good night, Lola." He closes the door.

I have the most uncomfortable taxi journey of my life, as I try to hold my body weight hovering above the seat, my arms shake with tension, and we finally pull up outside the restaurant. The driver has enough tact not to ask why I can't sit down, I don't need to add embarrassment to my already painful night. I ask him to wait a minute while I take my boots off in the taxi, I have to crawl onto my knees and pull them awkwardly off from behind but they are killing me, too, and it's just a few steps barefoot to my door.

"Thank you." I grab some money for the tip and hand it through the window. "I'm all good here, you're okay to go home now. Thanks for waiting."

"My pleasure, love, take it easy." He winds his window up and pulls away, as I rummage through my bag for my keys. My fingertips just touch the metal when I am forced with brutal strength against the wall, my face pressed hard and my cheek being ground against the rough brick. The stench of warm stale smoke fills my nose, and the attacker's breathing is laboured. His lips are at my ear, and his big strong body has me pinned immobile. His fingers are pressed around my neck. Why can't I think of what to do? My heart is panicked, and my head is screaming, but I can't make out what it's trying to tell me. I am just frozen, terrified.

"There's my little whore. What kept you so long? Eh? Who have you been fucking tonight eh?" His dirty laugh makes me shiver, his filthy fingers are caressing my neck, squeezing a little too tight, making my pulse race in fear. "It doesn't matter. After tonight no one's going to want to fuck you again. I'm to make sure no one wants you after I've finished with you." He grinds roughly into me, pushing my hips hard against the wall, and his other hand tries to grab the hem of my dress under my coat. His nails claw at my thighs trying to grab at panties that aren't there; they would still be with Daniel. "Ah, fuck, you are a dirty whore, wouldn't know it to look at you, but, look…" He paws my bare arse, and I scream as he scrapes the tender skin. He pulls me back toward him, and I instantly try to fold forward, the stiff curve of my spine making it impossible for him to get me on my back and drag me that way. He picks me up as if I weigh nothing and throws me with his weight against the wall. I hit hard, winded and feel a crack in my back or might be my ribs, and I fall in a heap on the floor. I flinch from the shooting pain from landing on my backside, but I am quickly lifted by my throat, my feet dangling as I fight for every breath. My head is spinning. What are you doing, Bets? Stop trying to fight him, look at the size of him, think! For fuck sake, think!

I push my arms up in between his, which have a front choke-hold on me. I press with all my strength against his elbows enough for him to release a little of the pressure on my throat, so I can grab some desperately needed air. I manage to jab my thumbs into his eye sockets. I feel the jelly liquid tissue give under the pressure, and although I don't have long nails, I can feel them sink into something soft. He curses and drops his arms a little, giving me enough room to pull back and throw my head full force at his face. I crack his nose hard, and he curses again, but still hasn't let go of my neck, and I feel dizzy from the impact of my head on his nose. I pull back again and throw my head forward. I misjudge and hit my nose full force on his iron strong jaw. I feel an instant blinding pain like an ice-pick through my skull and a loud crack. Blood pours from my nose, and large black spots float in my eyes, but he has let me go, and it's enough. I hit the ground running. I can hear him cursing, and he starts to run after me. I only have a slight lead, my head is pound-ing, blood is streaming from my face and I'm barefoot, having dropped everything at my door.

It's central London, I know it's late, but why is there no one around? I realize that I am running the route I take when I go for my morning run. Is that what my subconscious thinks, that I'm out for a jog, because I know my conscious state knows the last place I need to be is running around one of the Royal parks this time of night with a psychopath chasing me. I can hear him gaining, and I know I have run over something sharp because I can no longer put my weight down on one foot. Blood is gushing from my nose, and I try to wipe the excess away from my mouth as I gasp for air. I see Daniel's apartment block ahead. He is probably still at the flat, but there might be a guard who recognizes me. I run toward the door, my heart beating so fast, it's just pushing blood from my body at a speedier pace, and I feel dizzy and lightheaded. I bang on the door and press my face against the glass. No one is at the desk, but I can see a cup, so it might mean they are just doing a walkthrough. Maybe they will be back any minute. I can hear the footfalls nearing, and I think that maybe I don't have a minute. I rush to the side entrance and swipe my finger, silently praying that Daniel hasn't removed me from the code five clearance. Nothing, the red light blinks at me, mocking me. Did I really think, after having me escorted from the building, he wouldn't have had my access removed at the same time?

My head falls against the glass. The blood from my nose is still falling in large drops down the surface. My hands are sticky and warm from trying to clean my face. I look at the finger print pad and I can see my blood smearing the screen. I grab the cuff of my dress and rub frantically at the screen cleaning the blood while I suck my finger and pull at my dress finding a clean bit of material to dry it. I breathe in shakily. I swipe my finger, and I can hear him right behind me. I go to turn, when the door clicks, and I quickly push and slam it shut. I look through the glass of the door to see who was following. Try to see who did this to me, but I don't see his face, I don't see any face, I see a very bright light, then nothing.

Chapter Twenty-One

THE LIGHT IS really bright. I don't think I'll open my eyes just yet. I don't know where I am, but I'm warm, and I feel like I'm swathed in the softest fluffiest blanket, and it feels wonderful, but my arm itches like crazy. I could go back to sleep if this itching would stop. My arms feel really heavy, like they are moving in slow motion as I try to lift one to scratch the other.

"Hey, hey, sweetie, don't do that." Hey, that's Sofia... her voice. Sofia's with me... Oh, that's nice. I can feel her take my hand, and she squeezes it, but I need it to scratch this itch. It's driving me crazy, and I try to pull it from her hold. "No, don't, sweetie, you need it in. It's helping with the pain." She sounds sad, why is she sad? I don't feel any pain. I try to open my eyes, but clamp them shut instantly. It feels like I'm staring into the sun.

"Lights." My voice is hoarse, and it sounds muffled in my ears, but I am obviously understood, because the brightness of the light is dimmed. I try again to open my eyes, and they take a little while to focus, but I have spent enough time in similar rooms to know straight away I'm in hospital. My head feels thick, and I look at the source of my itch and see the clear IV and needle sticking out of the crook in my arm. That would explain the lack of pain, and my thick dazed head. I look at my hand and at the

294

beautiful face looking intently at me. "Ooo, Sofs, you look like shit." She looks tired, but I'm guessing I look worse, as I start to recall why I am here. She laughs out loud and sighs in relief.

"Yes, sweetie, I'm sure I do, but let's not go swapping mirrors any time soon, okay?" She is laughing lightly, but she has some tears falling down her face.

"That bad, eh?" I croak and try to smile, but my lips feel too puffed up to crease, like someone went crazy with the fillers. I try to shift up the bed, but she stops me and presses a button, which allows the bed to do all the hard work. "What time is it?"

"It's just after seven in the evening." She is stroking my arm. It tickles but feels nice.

"Wow, I must've been out of it to sleep right through a whole day." I keep trying to smile, but my face just won't play.

"It's Thursday, Bets. You've been unconscious for three days; you lost a lot of blood." She starts to sob, and I move to pull her to me. Everything I do is in slow motion, but she feels the extra pressure and moves in for a semi-hug.

"But I'm okay now, right?" She nods. God, she looks sad. "Obviously I won't be winning any pageants at the moment, unless there's a category for sexiest hospital gown model." I manage a small smile and feel really pleased that my face is making progress to react appropriately, but my tiny smile disappears, when I see Daniel stride into the room. His face is impassive, his eyes are dark, and I can feel the tension radiate from him.

"What?" I look to Sofia.

"Daniel called me. You were found outside his building. The guard from the building called the ambulance, but you didn't have your bag, so he didn't know who you were." Daniel steps closer, and I jump and press back into my pillow; I can't have him near me. He freezes, and his eyes flash with a look of pain. *Join the club.*

"What do you remember?" His voice is cold and commanding. He steps back into the corner of the room. It hurts to frown, but again I am pleased I am having some normal facial responses as I try to think of what happened.

"A man attacked me from behind, threw me against the wall, he tried to…" I take a sudden gasp of air. "He… he… I stuck my thumbs in his eyes, and he let go a little. I head-butted him, but caught my nose." I raise my hand to my face at this painful recollection, and I feel the enormous swelling that no longer resembles the shape of my nose, but more like that of an aubergine. "I ran. I just ran… I'm sorry, I went to your building. There was no one around, no one to help. I…I just ran." My face stings, as the salt from my tears soak the grazes on my skin, and I close my eyes. Sofia is right at my side, her gentle lips kiss my hair, and she continues to stroke my arms at the one part of my body that isn't bruised. My whole body tenses violently at her voice, and the sound of her heels clicking across the floor in my room.

"Oh, darling. Oh, Boo… are you all right?" She gushes. "I came as soon as I heard." If she doesn't recognize the look of hatred in my eyes, she must see Sofia's.

"Back up there!" Sofia snarls. "She doesn't need an infection, too!" Kit halts her advance to my bedside.

"How?" My voice is barely audible, but I want to know. "How did you find out?" She looks confused.

"That's not important. I'm just glad I'm here to take care of you now." She steps closer and takes my hand loosely. "You know I forgive you, when I heard, when I thought I might lose you, I realized, you are my family, and I forgive you."

I know it could be the drugs, but I feel really dizzy and sick.

"Were you raped?" She asks, as if she were asking if I'd like some coffee.

"What the fuck, Kit! What kind of question is that? What the fuck!" Sofia shouts, incredulously.

"I just want to know. You know she might need extra support." If she's trying for compassion, she is way off.

"No, she wasn't raped!" Sofia spits out. "And she has all the support she needs. She has me, and she has my family, so you can fuck off!" Her anger is justified, but Kit wouldn't be here, if she didn't want something. Kit gives a tight smile, and it's then she notices him. She looks shocked and a little panicked. Her face is doing a quick calculation to see if she has revealed anything she shouldn't have, but she relaxes when she is happy that she is still portraying the injured sister, more so because of Sofia's open hostility.

"Daniel, darling, what are you doing here?" Her voice changes, her tone chills me. "Are you? Is she, the two of you?" He steps swiftly across the room and wraps his arms around her waist, shaking his head at the very thought. It's no good. I reach for the grey card bowl and heave, only liquid. I clearly haven't eaten, but the small amount of liquid is torn from my stomach with violent heaves that rip the acrid material up my throat, burning as it leaves my wracked body.

"She was found outside my building. I don't know why she was there." He sounds angry when he adds. "Do I look like a man who needs to settle for sloppy seconds?" I hear Sofia gasp, but before she can jump to my defense, Daniel is thrown across the room. My sister stumbles from his hold as Marco charges, hitting Daniel side on, driving him into the wall. Before he can throw a punch, I have leapt out of the bed, knocking my IV stand and dragging it across the room. The drugs must be strong, because I still feel no pain. I pull at Marco's arm, screaming, but it is not my screams that stop all the activity, it's Sofia's.

"What's that? Bets, what happened to you? Look at your arse!" I crane my neck and see the gaping hospital gown revealing my welt-covered arse, red and bruised. Fuck! I twist the gown to cover my exposed bottom.

"I was thrown against railings, Sofs. I guess they are railing marks." She raises her eyebrows, and I shake my head for her to let it go. I wobble and grab onto Marco's arm. He lets Daniel go so he can scoop me up and carry me to the bed. It is then that the doctor walks in.

"What are you doing out of bed?" He reprimands me, not the two who caused me to jump out of the bed in the first place. I look contrite. "Bethany, you have to be more careful. You have two broken ribs, you broke your nose and lost a lot of blood. You need to take it easy, no drama." He looks around the room and both Marco and Daniel have the grace to look sorry. The doctor takes my chart and sits on the edge of my bed. He smiles kindly, ignoring the tension in the room. "I think you will be able to go home tomorrow. Do you have someone to take care of you? Your sister, perhaps?" I snort. I know that's rude in front of a stranger, and again, it makes me look bad, but I figure I can't look any worse.

"She can stay with me. I'll look after her." Marco volunteers, and I can see Daniel's jaw ticking, but frankly, after the sloppy seconds comment, I don't even know what he is still doing here.

"Oh, honey, that's kind, but you can't look after yourself, and we both know I'd end up looking after you and I'm not up to that yet." He kisses my hand, because he knows I'm right.

"She'll be coming home with me," Sofia informs the doctor. "Mama was very clear on the subject. In fact, you might have a fight on your hands about ever getting back to your place." She grins.

"All right, then, that's settled. Now I would suggest some rest, maybe a few less visitors. I know it's a private ward, so there is a little flexibility, but that doesn't mean you don't need to rest." I frown, I know I don't have private health care, but he is right. I do need my rest, and I feel exhausted. I need to clear the room, and in more than one way. I look at Daniel, his eyes dark and intense, it still sends a heat of prickles to my core, but I can't make out his expression. But you know what? It doesn't matter. I am done.

"Daniel, thank you for coming." My voice is clear, calm and determined. "You made your feelings toward me perfectly clear, always good to know where I stand. Thank you for our time together, I will treasure it, but I'm done, really, it's enough, no more. And you," I turn toward my sister, she has her head tilted and has a strangled smile awkwardly plastered to her face. "Well, you… you got everything you wanted and then some, I would say, so you can just…fuck off! I don't want to see you again… Ever!" I hold her glare as she huffs, indignant, grabbing Daniel's arm to leave the room. She turns for her last word; I knew she would, and I sigh. "Please, do go on, say what you need."

"I am so sorry, Boo, but I can't forgive you. I can't forgive this." She wipes her stray tear and turns away, resting her head on Daniel's shoulder. I don't know if he looks back at me, because I keep my eyes tightly shut until I hear their footsteps fade.

"I know." I let out my breath and close my eyes. Only to snap them open when Sofia squeals.

"Yeah!" She punches the air. "Oh, my God, Bets! You should take this more often." She grabs my IV tube and shakes it lightly.

"Yes, I definitely need to be smacked off my tits to deal with this shit and that bitch." I laugh, and it's the first time I feel a little relief.

"Seriously, Boo, you rock!" Marco agrees. "I know it's your battle, but I have wanted to tell her to fuck off for a while now, and I can't understand why you just wouldn't do it sooner?" Marco is holding my hand tight.

"It doesn't matter now." Sofia interrupts, stopping that line of inquiry. It really doesn't matter now. I know I won't see my sister again, and I know I won't see Daniel, either, and I have a shit load of other pain to keep me distracted, for now.

Sofia and Marco leave me shortly after and I fall into a dream-filled sleep. It feels so good, and I am smiling so wide, no restriction from the swelling. I lean into his warm hands holding my face; turning to kiss his palm. His minty breath feathers against my cheek, as he whispers to me, "I'm so sorry I didn't keep you safe, I didn't know. I needed to know, and you wouldn't tell me." He sounds so sad.

"Ssshhh, baby, it's all right. It's all right. I tried to, but I don't blame you, baby, I don't blame you." I nestle into his hand as his scent consumes me. "Mmmm, you smell so good. I loved you so much, Daniel, and, and it's okay, I'm okay, and you helped me.

You know, you really helped. I think I will survive you." I kiss his hand again, but he pulls it away, and I see his dark dangerous eyes, and the heat scorches through my soul.

"I don't want you to survive me. I love you. You're mine." He kisses me fiercely, sparing no consideration to the deep bruising on my mouth, my breath hitches, and my lips part welcoming his demanding tongue. God, that feels so good. It is urgent and passionate; stealing my breath as I moan with need. My pulse is racing, I can hear a rapid beeping noise, my shoulder is shaken gently, and a nurse fills my vision as I open my eyes.

"Hey, Bethany." She is still shaking me. "I don't know what you were dreaming, my dear, but if you keep setting your pulse racing like that, the doctor won't let you go home tomorrow." She smiles and I know under the bruising my face is bright red. I may have been projecting in my dream, but, God, that was hot!

I spend the first few days recovering in the guest room at Sofia's parents. I catch up on all my reading, and Mr. Wilson was kind enough to get all the Lecturers to email their notes and assignments directly to me. It was like having private tuition. I spoke to Mags, I felt bad for not having spoken to her sooner, she must have known I had stopped taking calls; she probably wanted her phone back. She didn't, and she was really sweet, told me the phone was prepaid and still booked until the end of the month, so to keep it and maybe pop it back next month, because she'd really love to see me and catch up. I know it didn't really work out, but she didn't make a big deal about it, and sounded like she really wanted to see me, so I promised I would pop round next month to do just that.

I have been at Sofia's parents' house for a whole week, and, really, I feel much better. The bruising on my face is a nice greenish yellow, and I still have two black eyes, but my nose is back to its normal size; though it is very tender . My ribs are the same shade as my cheeks and are still bound with strong sports tape and the cut on the sole of my foot is healed. It's not those injuries that has Sofia's judgemental brow raised, as I lift myself from her bed and head to her bathroom. The welts are now thin red lines, and they peek out of the bottom of my pyjama shorts.

"So, Miss, you gonna' tell me about those railing marks?" she quips.

"No." I shoot right back and shut the bathroom door to take a pee. She bursts right in as I take a seat.

"Sofs! A little privacy here! I've been prodded and poked with no chance at modesty for almost a week, so now I'm home, I'd like to regain a little of my dignity," I huff.

"You can ask for privacy with your arse looking like the rear end of a Grand National winner?" She has a point, but I don't know how I would begin to explain *that* night, because it would mean explaining Lola, and that I am perhaps a kinky bitch. I know she's my best friend, but I don't think that means she needs to know everything about me, especially when *I* don't know everything about me.

"You know Sofs, I think I can, and I think you should let me have it. All you need to know is, I'm okay." I look dead into her eyes and see that she is only worried about me. She doesn't really want to know the gory details—well, maybe she does--but she really just wants to know I'm okay.

"You sure, it's important, Bets. You sure you are okay? You're not just saying that?" Her need for extra assurance is why I love her so much. She really cares enough to ask the awkward questions even if I don't want to give her the awkward answers.

"I'm sure, promise." I cross my heart and blow her a kiss, and she walks to me, when I hold my hand to stop her. "Wait right there, Mrs.! I am not cuddling you while I'm sitting on the loo!"

"Right, right." She laughs, still not leaving. My eyes widen, unbelieving that she doesn't know I want her to leave. "Oh, sorry." She scuttles back into her bedroom and I laugh. She has no shame, but that doesn't mean I don't, either.

Sofia's mum has cooked the most amazing meal. I look at

the table, and I am sure there must be at least another ten people joining us, with the amount of food piled in the center, but no, it's the six of us: Sofia's mum and dad, Sofia and Paul, Marco and me. She has cooked a roast, and I know that's because it's my favourite non-Italian meal -- roast lamb stuffed with rosemary and anchovies, crisp roast potatoes, rosemary buttered carrots, cauliflower cheese, spring greens with leeks and broccoli. My eyes are definitely too big for my stomach as I pile my plate with the delicious smelling food. Sofia raises her glass of wine for a toast. I'm still on pain medication, so I have water, but I raise mine all the same.

"To family and no more hospital food." There is a light laughter, and we all chink glasses. I am so grateful to this family that literally saves my life on a daily basis. We all begin to eat.

"How have you been, Paul? I mean you look well." I ask, as I try to slow down shovelling food into my face like I haven't eaten in a week.

"I am all good, sweetheart, good as new, eh, babe?" He nudges Sofia, and she instantly blushes. It's sweet, but Paul quickly carries on when he sees her father's scowl. I chuckle. "I'm back to work, I mean." Nice recovery. "I'm sorry I didn't come to see you. My doctor said I should avoid hospitals, you know avoid possible infections, but if you look like this after nearly two weeks, honestly, I am glad I didn't get to see you then."

"Paul!" Sofia elbows him in the ribs, and he winces, but I laugh.

"What? What did I say?" He looks affronted, but then it sinks in what he said. "No, Bets, it's not that you look like shit, it's just you know-" Marco interrupts.

"You want a shovel with that, Paul?" he snickers, and I can't stop laughing as Paul squirms with embarrassment.

"Take no notice, Paul." I shoot him my sweetest I'm-not-offended smile. "I'm glad you're all fixed. Anyway, enough with the drama. What else is new?"

"Well," Sofia's dad joins in. "The restaurants are all coping without you, Bets, so there's no need to hurry back, you just take your time getting better." He reaches and grabs my hand, his hands are massive and completely cover mine, and holds it. "You're very precious to me, to all of us." I can feel tears building, and he senses this, too, and quickly continues. "Marco has some news." He nods to his son, and I turn to look next to me as Marco puts the largest potato in his mouth, whole. He grins. We all stare at him while he chews and swallows; he loves the attention.

"Oh, yes, yes, I do. I'm moving." He seems really pleased, but I hope he isn't moving too far.

"Really, where?" I sound apprehensive.

"Not far, two streets over, a little nearer to the restaurant, actually, and it's bigger, has two bedrooms."

"Ooo, fancy! That's great, though, nearer to the restaurant, not that it's much of a commute, but still, an extra five minutes in bed is not to be sniffed at." I nudge him, and he puts his arm around my shoulder and hugs me. I decide now is as good a time as any to mention going back to my place. I am much better, and as much as I love being here, I do miss my own space. "I was thinking, I would head back to mine tomorrow. It must need a bit of a cleaning by now." The table falls silent, and I look at all the faces staring at me like I had just suggested we eat babies for dessert. I press on, regardless. "I am much better and-"

"You're not moving back there." Sofia's dad informs me, and it would seem it's the consensus of the entire table with the general head nodding.

"Oh, okay. May I ask why?"

"Sure." It's Marco's turn to join in, and I turn to face him.

"Why?" I direct this specifically at him.

"Oh, right, because we said so." He narrows his eyes as a challenge.

"You know you can't keep me here, right?" I am a little irritated. I hate decisions being taken unilaterally, but Sofia's mum speaks and takes all the irritation away.

"Bets, honey, I don't want you living there alone. I won't sleep again if you go back there, but I also know you can't live here, either. Not that we don't want you, because you know we do. So we were hoping you would move in with Marco now, since he will have a bigger place." Her smile is warm and loving, and I can see the genuine worry in her eyes. I don't want her to worry. I don't want any of them to worry, but living with Marco? He doesn't have a flat, he has a shag pad. I know I've seen the pictures! I look at him skeptically with my brows raised, hoping he knows where my thoughts are right now.

"I'll tone it down a bit if you move in, Boo, you know I will." He wiggles his eyebrows and flashes the cheekiest grin, which makes me laugh. "Beside, I'm going to need help with the rent now; the landlord's a real ballbreaker." He nods in the direction of his father, who is scowling, but with a huge smile.

"Oh." Now I understand the whole set up, and I couldn't love this family any more if I tried.

"You would be doing me a huge favour." Sofia's mum's voice is soft and kind. "Keep an eye on my baby." It's Marco's turn to blush, and like his twin, he also has no shame, so this is a rare occurrence, and it makes me laugh even harder.

"Mum, enough!" He grumbles and picks up another potato.

"It's really kind." They all look my way, obviously expecting me to decline. I'm not so great at accepting hand-outs, but this time I want to. I want to share with Marco, because I think I need to feel safe for a while. "I'd really like that." My voice is quiet and is quickly drowned by cheers and raised glasses. Wow, they really thought I was going to say no. "When do you move in?"

"Oh." He finishes, his mouth full. "Next week; it's just being redecorated, so you get to pick a bedroom colour, but I'm choosing the living room, none of that pink shit!"

"Marco, language!" His mother clips his head with her palm. He is lucky he is down her end of the table; his dad is not so gentle when dishing out his discipline.

"That's fine by me. I wouldn't do pink all through the place."

I giggle, because I probably would. "I'll go to mine tomorrow and start packing." I lift my glass and suggest another toast.

"To family." My eyes well as we clink glasses again.

The next day is Sunday, and it's late evening when Marco drops me at my apartment to begin my packing. I have been at his place all afternoon, supervising his packing, and I got so excited that I wanted to make a start on my own. He dropped me before heading over to Rose's for the night. I promised I'd call Sofia or her dad to pick me up when I'm done, ensuring I wouldn't work too late. The flat really isn't big enough for it to take too long anyway, but it is always surprising how many boxes you accumulate when you start putting everything you own in them. I start in the living room with the easiest items, my university books and files. I have been steadily packing for half an hour, when I hear my door bell. I run down, thinking that maybe Rose wasn't in, after all, or maybe Marco was so consumed with guilt for leaving me to pack on my own when I had been helping him all day, that he returned. I laugh at that thought and open the door without looking. My reaction's far too slow to shut it and prevent the heavy boot from kicking it back open. I fall against the corridor wall as Kit walks past followed by her ape with the big boots, but that's not what makes my stomach drop to the floor and my heart sink. It's the bruising around his bloodshot eyes and the smell of stale smoke.

Chapter Twenty-Two

I LOOK AT MY hands and can see them tremble. He stands at the bottom of the stairs waiting for me to follow Kit up. I blow out the breath I had been holding to avoid gagging on the stench of his breath and make my way up and into the living room. She is sitting on the sofa, her expression failing to hide her distain at being in my home. She pats the cushion beside her, like we are going to have a nice little chat.

"Are you going somewhere?" She indicates the boxes.

"Um, yes, I'm moving, but I'm staying at Sofia's tonight." I don't want her thinking I am going to be here alone. Well, I don't want Clive the ape thinking I will be here alone. He takes a seat in the armchair his face a dark scowl. He makes my skin crawl.

She shakes her head, and a chilling smile spreads across her face. "Not tonight, you're not, you need to call her and let her know you are staying here tonight." Her tone is utterly chilling. "And, Boo," she snarls, "make her believe it. If she shows up, well, I can't promise…"

"Stop! All right, just stop. I'll call her, she won't come." I pick up my phone and dial Sofia.

"Hey, sister." Kit narrows her eyes and pinches her lips flat. "I'm staying here tonight. There is so little to do, I'll get it finished tonight…No, I know, but it's easier if there are no distractions. Besides, it will be nice to have one last night here. Marco can pick me up in the morning…Yes. Okay, I will, thanks, see you later. Love ya'." I end the call and slip the phone in my hoodie pocket.

"Oh, that's *sooo* sweet, love the 'sister' thing you two have, maybe if we'd…No." She shakes her head. "No, I can't even pretend, not even now." She sighs and waves her hand for my phone, and she takes it from me. "Can't have you calling the cavalry, now, can we? What is this?" She laughs, showing Clive.

"My brick, it's my phone." Obviously.

She snorts and throws it in her bag. "You're right about that. I'll get muscle ache carrying that thing around." She sighs and straightens her shoulders. "Right, I'll get straight to it. It would seem I need your help, *again*. I thought the attack…" She fixes her beady eyes on Clive, and he lowers his head. "Well, had it gone as planned it would've been enough for Daniel to walk away, just forget you, and see you as seriously damaged goods. You see, he still thinks about you, I know he does. He doesn't want you, but he won't move on, either, won't move on to me. He has just thrown himself into his work." Her voice is beyond irritated.

"He works hard." I quietly admit. "But I can't help it if he isn't interested, Kit. I've done everything I can." My hands are still shaking, and I have a terrible feeling growing in my stomach. I feel my other phone vibrate, and I dry heave into my hand.

"Don't you dare vomit on me! You're always throwing up!" She laughs acidly

"Yeah, well, you have that effect on me." I run, hand on my mouth, to the toilet where I continue to heave loudly while I answer the phone.

"What is your sister doing there?" Daniel's voice is low and calm, but he sounds worried, and I happen to think he should be.

"How did you know?" I whisper between pretend heaves.

"Not now!" He snaps. "Why is she there? Why is Clive with her?"

"How?" I can't keep myself from asking the question. I'm

completely freaking out.

"You've always known, Bethany." His voice is dark, and I relax a little, he's keeping me safe. I heave again. "Are you okay, Bethany? What's going on?"

"I'm heaving, and I don't know. I'm actually really scared. Clive's Kit's driver. It was Clive who attacked me. "

"I know." He sounds deadly cold and angry.

"You know?" I heave for real this time, emptying my stomach contents as sweat coats my face, and my skin feels sticky.

"The night of your attack…Something didn't feel right. I checked the photographs again, and realized it wasn't you. I can't believe I didn't see it straight away. I was just so…and you didn't trust me to tell me the truth, even after the flat! Fuck! Anyway, little things didn't sit right, but I wasn't positive, and I needed to know if there was a connection between the photos and the attack. I needed proof. I arranged to have a copy of the DNA from the hospital, but there was a delay, and I didn't bother chasing it, because I've been out of the country, and you were safe with Sofia's family. I got the results minutes ago. I called Sofia, and I checked your camera. Look, I'm on my way, I'll be forty minutes."

"No! Oh, God, no, Daniel, you can't, please! He'll kill you, please!" I am panicking my heart is crashing into my chest. "Please, you can't, you have to promise me. Promise. Give me your word." He is silent. "I'll get rid of her, just promise me! Call the police, but please don't come. Daniel, it will kill me, please." I sob.

"I promise." His voice is quiet. "Keep the phone on, don't hang up. I can see you but I can't hear a damn thing." He growls, more angry now.

I slip the phone in my pocket and flush the toilet, wiping my head and neck on the towel as I enter the living room.

"Gosh, Boo, you do look pale." She actually sounds sincere. Is she for real?

"Yeah? Well, I've been better. So how is it I can help you

now?" I sit resignedly.

"Well, like I said, Daniel has thrown himself into his work, I mean, I pop over for lunch and try and get him to engage. I've even asked his mother to invite us all over for dinner, but he won't set a date." I am grinning like a Cheshire cat on the inside. "Anyway, I started to think that he may need a little nudge, and really there is nothing like a little guilt to get someone to do what you want. I mean just look at how you looked after mother. If that wasn't guilt, I don't know what was." She has an evil laugh.

"Are you crazy? Guilt didn't make me look after mum; she was my mum, and I loved her." I can't hide my own disbelief.

"Right, of course." She starts to dig in her bag absently, clearly not understanding. She pulls out three bottles of pills, which she carefully opens, cracking through the childproof seal each time. She sets them in a row on the table and sits back; my eyes must be the size of saucers.

"Kit?" My voice is trembling.

"You've been through so much; you're just in a dark place. You are distraught that you have fallen so far. That you have let yourself down, that you have let me down, all the lying and cheating, well, it's too much, it's enough. You said it yourself 'no more.'" She pulls out a prepared note and pushes one of the bottles my way.

"No, Kit, you can't be serious. You're crazy!" But it's my voice that is starting to sound hysterical.

"Certified, but with money comes a clean bill of health, too, but really, darling, that's not what we are here for. Clive, get some water, would you?" She looks back at me, her eyes are dull, flat, lifeless. "So you will sign my little note and Daniel will feel guilty that I am alone and that he had a part in it, he won't be able to turn me away." She pats her hands together like a spoilt little child finally getting her way.

"But you said he doesn't want me. Why would he feel guilty?" I plead.

"Of course he doesn't want you, why would he?" She snaps

with venom in her voice. "If he wanted you, he would've taken you out in public, now, wouldn't he? Oh, I do love this little list; he would've taken you out to a restaurant even, you would've met his family, his friends, you were his dirty little fuck buddy, and you were staff." These words don't hurt, anymore, but she terrifies me.

"Yes, Kit, I know this, really I do. It's true, so it makes no sense for him to feel guilty about me killing myself." I breathe in some stilted breaths, as I realize that this is her plan; she is actually planning on killing me, but she wants me to do it.

"Well, he cares enough, and I can use that as my *in*." She smiles at her own brilliance.

"You're a monster." I cry softly. "You would let him believe he had something to do with this. He'd be devastated to think he caused something like this. How could you do that to someone?" I'm shaking my head in disbelief.

"Oh, I won't let him think he had something to do with this, I will let him know he *is* the reason behind this." She shakes the bottle and pours four tablets into her hand and passes them to me. I reluctantly hold out my hand, and my tears start to fall.

"Why?"

"You know why, Bethany? Yes, I am that shallow. I want money and him." She is dismissive and agitated.

"No. Why do you hate me?"

She laughs, and it chills my core. "This won't buy you time." She passes out more tablets and I put them in my mouth and swallow. "I do hate you. You are right about that. It really isn't terribly complicated. I was happy before you came along. We were happy before you came along. Then my dad left, and mum spent all her time with you, loved you, and I had to find my love elsewhere."

I laugh bitterly at this. "Wow! Don't believe your own press, Kit. Mum loved you fine, and she didn't make you into a slut. Fucking all the boys in the neighbourhood did that." She slaps the back of her hand across my cheek, her ring catching the skin, and I can feel the burn, and then the cool of the blood dripping down my cheek. I turn my icy glare back to her hollow eyes. "Mum was there for you, every step of the way, Kit. She always defended you, bailed you out of trouble countless times. She didn't make you steal, she didn't make you take drugs, she didn't-" Her bitter laugh interrupts me.

"-Yes, yes, she was a fucking saint and my dad left when she had another man's bastard, because she was such an angel." She sneers.

"What? What are you talking about? Our Dad left us both." My head is starting to feel thick, not sure if the tablets could be working so quickly, or this information is causing this dulling effect.

"No, you stupid bitch. MY Dad left because of you!" She laughs, and a cruel smile slowly covers her face. "But I did manage to stop *your* Father from ever finding you." I must look so confused. "Yes, this smart-looking man turned up one day, really posh car. I knew who he was, because you look just like him. He asked for mum and for you." She pauses, relishing this disclosure. "I told him you had died. It was tragic, think I even shed a tear."

"But he can't have just believed you? Why didn't he come back? What else did you say?" My speech is starting to slur.

"It was November 27th. Ring any bells?" Her voice is dripping with vile intent.

I gasp. "John's funeral, but I didn't go to his funeral. I couldn't... I just couldn't." My heart sinks, as I remember that day. It was all my fault, and I had let him down so badly, I couldn't face the service. I couldn't stand it, so I hid on the edge of the graveyard, watching until it was over. My mum took my place. "Oh, God!" I cry. "If he went to the church, he would've seen Mum, but...."

"Yes, stroke of luck he didn't actually try and speak to her, but I didn't think he would, after waiting sixteen years to make an appearance and then turn up too late."

"Did mum know?"

"No, why would I tell her? You're really not catching on with the 'I hate you thing', are you? If I'd told her, she would've pursued him, and you would've had your happily ever after. Well, fuck that!" She spits at me.

"Why tell me, now?" I draw in a breath that fails to clear my haze.

"Oh, I don't know, Bethany. How are you feeling right now? Angry and cheated? Hurt maybe?" She tilts her head with fake concern.

"No, Kit, you can't hurt me. That would mean I care about what you have to say." I try to hold my head a little higher, but it flops slightly.

"Really?" Her smile is pure malevolence as she pauses for effect. "You know he cried for you, he bled out in that cold alley, and you weren't there." Her eyes sparkle with malice and evil, and my body starts to shake as I slowly comprehend what she is talking about.

"You were there?" My voice is small.

"You never knew, and of course I was there. You know he kept saying you were nothing like me, so I told Dick to hit him, stupid fuck. But he died because of you, he would still be alive, if it weren't for you!" She takes a moment as I absorb this. "Daniel, well, if that is what happens to people you love, I don't think *this* is such a sacrifice. I mean it will probably save the lives of Daniel, Sofia, Paul, and Marco." I squeeze my eyes tight as the faces of the people she lists appear before me, she nudges my knee and points to four more pills, but I hesitate. "Take the fucking pills!" She shouts and makes me jump, but I am starting to feel sleepy. She stands and grabs her coat.

"You are leaving?" My speech is no longer my own.

"Ah, sweet, you want me to stay? Sorry, darling, but I have no intention of seeing the final show." She looks to Clive, who barks a nasty laugh. "No fucking DNA, Clive! She already got a skin full the other night; don't leave any here. Make sure you wear a condom, and that she is dressed when you leave. I don't need an investigation into this. Standard suicide, and move on, understand?" He nods slowly,not taking his eyes off me.

"Bethany, thank you for all your help. You've been a star, really." She leans down and kisses me on my head, actually kisses me. I am dazed, but I suddenly snap my head and stand up in her face.

"Seriously, Kit. What are you doing? This is crazy. Who does this? Who kills for money?" I sway a little. She laughs loudly.

"Oh, Darling, now you are just being naïve." She turns to Clive. "I'll drive the Range Rover, make sure you walk before you grab a taxi, and don't take all night." She walks out of the door, and I flop down on the sofa, my vision is starting to blur, and I feel really woozy, like I am starting to float, and my head falls back. I can feel rough hands on my mouth and some more pills put on my tongue followed by water, I swallow but then choke and spit. He curses and grabs my towel from me. I look at him, my eyes narrow, trying to focus on the fuzzy image. I can make out that he is taking his shirt off and sitting back. "I'm just going to leave it a little longer. I don't want any of that fighting shit from the other night. You nearly blinded me, you little bitch." I laugh at this, and I am rewarded with a much harder back hand across my cheek, a throb in my eye socket, and instant pressure in my head. My eyelids droop, but time means nothing; it could have been minutes or days when I hear his voice again,

"You look ready. I don't want to be fucking a corpse." I feel him lift me onto his shoulder, my head swinging like a rag doll. My whole body feels like jelly as he throws me on my bed with a loud crack. Not sure if that is my back or the wooden slats, because there are definitely no springs in my bed. He looms, large and ominous, above me; he has removed his trousers but has dark boxers on. He is kneeling over me, and he flips me onto my front and starts to pull at the waistband of my jeans. Stupid fuck should've undone the buttons before he flipped me. He is grabbing my hips, but his hands feel funny, smooth and slippery.

He sits back with a growl, and I hear a snapping sound. "Fucking latex, damn gloves, can't feel anything with them on, same goes for a condom." He starts again at my buttons and loosens them enough to pull my jeans down to my knees. He pulls my panties down too and I start to cry loudly; it's the only part of my body that seems to be responding. Inside I am screaming at my body to move, to fight, to run…nothing.

I can feel his weight. God, he's so heavy, I'm not going to be able to breathe. I'm going to suffocate. His face is pressed to mine, and I can feel his fingers trying to get between my legs. He is fighting his own weight as his own body presses my legs together, and he is roughly trying to get enough space to push into me. My eyes are tired, and I know I'm sobbing, angry at my useless body, my useless exhausted body. My chest is heavy, struggling for breath. I can't seem to suck in enough air. Everything is so heavy, my arms, my chest, my eyelids. Then all of a sudden I am floating, and it's okay; I can breathe, and a fresh gust of oxygen hits my grateful lungs. I can't move my arms or legs, but I can breathe and my eyes open, as I feel a sharp pinch in the inside of my arms. Fuck, that's going to bruise, and I frown and mouth, 'Ow'

"I'll do it again, if you don't keep your fucking eyes open!" I am being shouted at and whoever it is, is really angry. I snap my eyes open, only they don't snap, they glide slowly open, and the fuzzy image in front remains fuzzy, along with the ever-changing background of lights. The lights hurt my eyes, and I try to close them again. "Ow" I cry at the second pinch.

"Which part of keep your fucking eyes open didn't you understand, Bethany?" All right, so he knows me, but he is still being a prick, and he keeps pinching me.

"Fuck off!" I slur, it sounded much more forceful in my head.

"Do you think that's polite?" His deep voice causes an instant reaction, my eyes are wide, and my skin is tingling all over.

"No," I whisper. "No, Sir." He brushes the hair from my face and leans in and kisses the spot below my ear.

"Good girl," he whispers but I'm too tired to play, and I close my eyes again.

"Ow!" It really hurts, and my eyes spring forth with tears.

"I'm sorry, baby, but you have to keep your eyes open. We're nearly there, but you have to stay with me." He sounds desperate, and I try really hard to do what he says.

"I can't, I'm too tired. Keep pinching me, it's the only way." I close my eyes, and once more I feel the nasty pinch, and I sob but open my eyes. This happens every few minutes, from what I can tell, and every time I open my eyes, we are somewhere else, but Daniel is always there, pinching me. First the ambulance, then the stretcher, then the room. The room is so bright, and I can feel the rough tubing causing unbelievable pressure at the back of my throat. My head flops to the side, and I can feel his warm strong hands hold my head upright. That is just before I hurl myself forward, evacuating everything from my body. I just don't remember eating that much. I mean I don't remember eating that much in my entire life. My stomach is cramping with exhaustion, and yet I am still being flushed with liquid that I then spend the next hour hurling into a bucket. I lay my head on my arm on the edge of the bucket and gently close my eyes.

"Don't fucking... pinch me again...I'm not going any-where...I'm just exhausted." My words are breathless pleas. He must hear it in my voice, because there is no pinch, and there is no reprimand for being impolite either. The tube has been re-moved, but I still don't dare let go of the bucket. I don't know what was in that stuff they pumped into me, but the reaction it caused was scary explosive.

"The doctor said that anything you consumed in the last twelve hours including the pills should be out of your system now." Daniel strokes my back and is trying to reassure me.

I snort. "No shit, Sherlock... I happen to think anything I've consumed in the last twelve months is out of my system after that." I press my hand to my temple, I have the mother of all headaches starting. Daniel chuckles, then calls over a nurse. She gets the doctor, and she decides to start an IV for fluids, as the dehydration is causing the headache.

"I know you're tired, baby, but you can't sleep yet, and it's best if I can keep you walking and talking." His fingers are tracing patterns on my back that is sending me to sleep, but I don't want him to stop.

"I don't want to talk." I pout.

"I'm sure you don't. You probably don't want to walk, either, but luckily it isn't up to you." He states as a matter of fact. Once the IV is in, he slips a large cashmere wrap around my shoulder, puts some fluffy rubber soled spotted socks on my feet, and takes my arm.

"Shall we?" He flashes me a dazzling smile, unfazed by the fact that I have had my head stuck in a bucket for hours. We start our circuit of the hospital floor, and I am relieved he isn't planning on taking me outside.

"You lied to me." I tell him quietly, and he tilts his head as his lips curl in a grin.

"Well, pot, kettle! What did I lie about?" He smiles, but he looks as tired as I have ever seen him.

"You promised you wouldn't come. You didn't keep your word." My words are quiet, because it still hurts to talk at all.

"No. No, I didn't, and I'm not sorry. I am sorry for many things, but that isn't one of them," he adds softly.

"I only lied once, and you knew it was a lie at the time." I'm thinking about when I told him I didn't love him.

"I know," he confirms with no explanation. "Why didn't you tell me what she was doing?"

"I tried, but you thought it was this wonderful family reunion, and she had her story so well sewn, I had nothing to contradict it. I just came across... Well, you looked so disappointed." I stop to catch my breath. "Like you needed me to forgive her."

"I know." His expression holds a world of regret I don't quite understand. "Do you want to sit down?" He brushes my cheek with his knuckles.

"No, I'm fi-- I'm okay to carry on walking; it actually makes me feel less sick." His strong arms wrap around my slowly shuffling body and help in more ways than assisting mobility. "When I found out what she wanted, and what she was prepared to do, I didn't have a choice, Daniel, and she wasn't wrong about anything she said." My voice starts to break.

"Who's the shallow one now, Bethany?" His voice is loud and stern.

"I'm not shallow, Daniel, I'm a realist, and a little insecure and a lot scared shitless. Besides, you believed what you saw, where would we honestly go from there?" My eyes still manage to fill despite the dehydration.

"I did, but I didn't really look at the time. But when I did, I saw photos of Marco fucking someone not nearly as hot as you." He has a wicked grin, and I meet the heat in his dark blue eyes.

"But?"

"Do you honestly think I don't know every inch of this beautiful body, that I wouldn't be able to tell the difference?" His laugh is sexy as hell and has my skin prickling.

"Why didn't you?-" I am confused and a little bit hot, which is gross, because I must look like shit and smell like yesterday's sick. He interrupts.

"It wasn't until after the attack that I suspected anything at all, and even then I didn't want to believe it was Kassandra. She was always so kind about you, so curious and interested. It's why I liked being with her at all. I got to talk about you all the time. I had no idea, but why would I? I didn't know how you would so easily walk away, and you wouldn't tell me. Fuck, you just shut me out, and you just carried on. I could see you just carrying on, but when I saw you in the lecture I knew you were in pain. God, it killed me to see you like that." His hand cups my cheek.

"You'd never know." I snort.

"That's because you thought this--" he waves his hand "--was one sided. I thought I could help you with focusing on something else and get you to talk to me at the same time, but, God, you're stubborn." He growls. "Something we can work on, I think." He brushes his hand down my back and across the top of my bottom, and I clench with heat at the contact.

"It did help; it's strange and I don't understand it, but it did help. Would've preferred to not be attacked so Sofia had a good glimpse of my private life, but, hey…"

"I'll never forgive myself for not protecting you. I am so sorry I waited, if I had chased the results, none of this would've happened." His chest is rising rapidly, and I stand in front of him and put my hands on his face.

"There is nothing to forgive, Daniel. You did get to me." I smile and hold his heated gaze, filled with lust and desire. "I'm not going to kiss you, you know that, right?"

"I was really hoping you wouldn't." His mouth rises to one side in a smirk.

"But once I've brushed my teeth and don't stink, and maybe don't look like I've done ten rounds with Tyson, well, then, you're all mine, Stone." I wink and grip his shirt in my tight fists.

He laughs loudly. "Miss Thorne, that was never a choice."

THE END

If you fell in love with Daniel and Bethany, there is a treat at the end after the acknowledgement for you.
Oh and a Daniel POV chapter here if you subscribe:
http://eepurl.com/biZ6g1
xDee

Acknowledgements

My thanks and appreciation definitely falls into two camps and rightly or wrongly I am going to thank those how aren't necessarily closest to me but are without a doubt the reason this book is the first of a trilogy: My beautiful beta readers, Kymme and Lynn. I know I chose wisely when I asked you to read this story but you did and you not only were kind enough to ignore the roughness in the first copy but you saw the potential and encouraged me to continue. I love you for your enthusiasm and truly unbelievable support.

The second camp is wholly of the moral variety, given that my family are both horrified and proud in equal measure that I decided to write an erotic romance. I am happy with my genre choice but I am sorry that when I left my draft copy on the side your game of page roulette left you a little scared but hey, you're adults and you should know better! You know I couldn't do this without your support and love and for that I am grateful every day. Laraine for skirting around the content but encouraging none the less. To my mum, because even though you moved so far away I always know you're there when I need you and you're always on my side, I love and miss you every day. You are my most blinkered cheerleader.

Indirectly I have been given advice and encouragement from other authors, namely Kitty French, Pepper Winters, Ker Dukey and Jodi Ellen Malpas and I am hugely humbled that they take the time to respond and are kind enough to share their knowledge and support. It means so much - thank you.

My editor Philippa for agreeing to work on my book - you were so worth the wait. Also Angela for my beautiful cover designs which, when I first saw it, made me feel like 'Whoa! This shit just got real'. A HUGE thank you to my twelfth hour heroines; Joan, Kate (Stacey and Kitty again) copy editing is the devil's work!!And not lastly but certainly importantly the bloggers that have taken the time to reply to my review requests and have shown an interest in wanting more; THANK YOU :)

But mostly, I'd like to thank you, for choosing to buy my book and taking the time to read it - a huge, I mean really huge, thank you, you will never know how incredibly grateful and honoured I am that you have and I would be even more so if you are kind enough to leave a review at Amazon or Goodreads.

The People who make it all happen.
Dee Palmer - Author
Website - www.deepalmerwriter.com
Follow me here
www.facebook.com/Author-Dee-Palmer-995618753806518/?ref=bookmarks
www.facebook.com/groups/902682753154708/?ref=bookmarks
twitter.com/deepalmerwriter

Editor- Philippa Donovan -www.smartquilleditorial.co.uk
Formatter- Champagne Formats www.ChampagneFormats.com
Cover Design Angela - www.angieocreations.com

Choices Playlist

Take me to church—Hosier
Run—Snow Patrol
Make this go on forever—Snow Patrol
Changing -Linkin Park
Best of you -Foo Fighters
Halo—Florence and the Machine
The Only One -James Blunt
My Immortal -Evanescence
Focus-Emma's Imagination
Big Big World—Emilia
How Long will I love you -Ellie Goulding
Figure 8—Ellie Goulding
Tessilate -Ellie Goulding
I know you care -Ellie Goulding
(had a bit of an Ellie Goulding thing going on)
Wheels -Lone Justince
Heavy Cross -The Gossip
Stay with me—Sam Smith
Orbiting -The Weepies

About the Author

Dee Palmer hates talking about herself in the third person so I won't. My husband had my iPod engraved one Christmas with 'sing like no-one's listening' and I know my family actually wish they weren't listening because I am, in fact, tone deaf but it doesn't stop me and this gentle support has enabled me to fulfil a dream. This has been a truly brilliant experience, because I have written all of the books in The Choices Trilogy but need to tweak the others before I let them out alone, and it has undoubtedly been made possible by my incredibly supportive family. I know this is very much another acknowledgment bit but I know I wouldn't be writing even this single paragraph if it wasn't for them so this is about who I am, I am because they let me be.

Stalk me On Facebook, Twitter and Instagram

Always *a* Choice
The Choices Trilogy, Book Two

Chapter One

"BABY, WAKE UP. Wake up baby." His calm soothing voice filters into my subconscious moments before I am aware of his strong arms pulling my waist into the curve of his strong body. His lips are close to my ear and his words are barely whispered but they wake me, before I can recall where this particular nightmare was planning to take me. My heart is racing and I can feel the sheen of sweat covering my body chill as I am cradled into Daniel's arms and lifted from his bed. He kisses the top of my head, walks to the en suite and places me on my feet, leaving me for the briefest moment to turn the shower on. He carefully strips his t-shirt I am wearing, which is now soaked and I notice his gaze darken as he takes in my naked body. Even when we are both nearer to sleep than awake his look sets my pulse on fire. It has been the same for nearly two weeks, since I was discharged from hospital after my sister's failed attempt to force me to overdose on sleeping pills and three weeks since her driver, Clive, had attacked me. The bruises have gone only to be replaced by this unwelcome nightly routine.

"It feels very much like musical beds." I tell Daniel with softly sleepy speech as he lays me down in one of his guest rooms, into a freshly made bed after my quick shower and change. He climbs in on my side and folds his large body over mine. I am completely caged by his immense frame and I relax.

"Mmm I've not played that one but any game that involves you and a bed sounds good to me." His hand sweeps up my neck and his fingers spread into my hair while he kisses the nape sending a million shivers across my skin.

"Nancy must hate me for the amount of washing she's had to deal with?" Daniel's housekeeper is friendly, so kind and would never say that any of this was any trouble. But that doesn't stop me from being embarrassed that I am the cause of her work load tripling.

"I'd fire her if she did." He replied as a matter of fact. I twist in his arms with shock.

"You wouldn't!"

He laughs. "No, I wouldn't." He kisses a line from just below my ear to my collarbone. "Because Nancy could never hate you. She is actually quite fond of you and she's very fond of me, so how about you stop worrying about the laundry and tell me what you were dreaming?" Nightmares are not new to me. I have suffered with them on and off since John, my best friend, was murdered just after my sixteenth birthday. Typically only talking about them allows me to ever return to sleep and reduce their frequency but since the attack they have returned with a vengeance. Daniel however, has a knack of interrupting just before they manifest into anything I can remember, let alone analyse. I turn fully in his arms and look up into his intense blue eyes.

"You know you woke me before anything happened." I smile and lean in to kiss him. "You saved me, again." His lips are warm and soft, and despite his grumble at my comment he returns my kiss. He pulls back cautiously and I know where this conversation is going and I'm just too tired for it. "Don't please," I kiss him again. "You couldn't have known and at the time I sure wasn't sharing. You did save me." I place my hands on his face, his stubble scratches the soft surface on my palms. "Daniel, I wouldn't be here if it wasn't for you. I'm just sorry these fucking nightmares keep reminding you but they will get better, I promise." His brow is furrowed and I know he is struggling. He always maintains the utmost control in every aspect of his life and for a short period he didn't. I nearly died and he won't accept that there was nothing he could've done. But he did, in fact, save my life. It is exhausting. He lets a deep frustrated sigh escape into the darkness and gently kisses my lips. He has been treating me like I'm made of glass since leaving the hospital and for some reason tonight I have had enough.

I pull back, narrow my eyes, and before he can register my mood, I push heavily at his shoulders. He is much, much stronger than me and could easily have resisted but falls back onto the bed. I slip my leg over his hip and sit astride him. My naked heat on fire against him and I can instantly feel his erection pressing against the cheeks of my bottom. I pull his fresh t-shirt from my body and fix my eyes on his. His desire is fiercely reflected in his heavy lidded eyes and his chest rises as he draws in deeper breaths. I can feel his body vibrate with the rumble that escapes his mouth. He stares at my now naked frame; the room is dark and our bodies are all shadow and scent. I take his hands and place them on my breasts; he needs no further encouragement as he firmly squeezes the soft full flesh. He shifts the weight to lightly pinch my nipple but I grab his wrist before he can and I lean forward to put his arms above his head. I am not sure how this is going to work, he is so much bigger than I am and I have to stretch, shuffling my knees along the bed. I can see his grin and I try to manoeuvre him into position. He is being kind and helping, but I am now hovering with my breasts just above his face as I place his hands on the bed frame. I can feel his warm breath and despite the heat, my nipples are hard aching peaks, desperate for his mouth, but I pull just out of reach as he tilts his head and angles his soft wet lips.

Honestly, there is nothing I want more than to feel his lips and mouth suck and tease me but this is about getting him to react, to force him to react. I know I am out of my comfort zone trying to get him into his *zone*, but I miss him. I love when we make love but I love when he is hard and demanding too, pushing me, driving me insane with need and desire. But lately it has felt much too sedate and more like *Driving Miss Daisy*. I lean to kiss his jaw and he turns to take my lips, but I move back out of reach. I do this several times, all while gently rocking my hips just nudging the tip of his erection with my soft cheeks. I can see his jaw tick and his grip is all white knuckles, but he hasn't let go. I lean forward and sweep my tongue along his parted lips, dipping it in and dancing lightly with his tongue. I can't hold back the moan that escapes my throat and I sink deeper, demanding a similar heated exchange from his tongue. I drag in a deep breath, and sit up and arch my back holding my heavy breasts.

"Fuck!" He growls and his hips jerks tipping me forward slightly.

"What do you want, Daniel?" My voice is breathy.

"I want to make love to you." His voice is deep and strained. I can feel his tenuous control and I'm counting on its precariousness.

"Wrong answer." I moan out the soft words as I suck my finger and trace it down my torso. I am so turned on right now, I didn't realise I would enjoy being out of my comfort zone so much. Daniel's eyes narrow as they follow the line of my finger, not sure he is enjoying the switch in roles quite so much. My finger reaches the top of my sex and I lift slightly to give myself better access.

"Fuck, Bethany!" With lightning speed he sits and scoops his arms around my back and throws me on to the bed, his thighs have mine pinned wide. I am pure liquid heat and my body starts to tremble in anticipation. "I am responsible for your pleasure." I can feel the tip of his erection at my entrance, slick and hot. "Me... do you understand? Do I make myself clear?" He growls through gritted teeth. He pushes into me, only the tip and too gently. My core starts to quiver but it's not what I want.

"Maybe," I sigh and clench my inner muscles down on him. He grunts and throws his head back.

"Wrong answer!" He launches forward with the deepest down stroke, causing a high pitched scream at the back of my throat, but before he can temper his movement I scream again.

"Don't stop, please arhhh!" I catch my breath because he hasn't stopped not for a second. He thrusts and pushes me higher up the bed, grabbing my leg behind my knee he lifts and presses it into the mattress and continues his tortuously deep thrusts. The sudden shift and rotation of his hips sends me spiralling, gasping for breath, my hands gripping his back as his muscles flex and roll. Passionate urgency courses through our bodies, this is going to be quick, deep and dirty. Our slick bodies move together as one and he follows my release with a final push, and I am left trembling with my head buried in his chest. He rolls onto his side and pulls me into his embrace.

"Well, that won't be happening again." He firmly kisses my head as mine snaps up to question him.

"What! No! You've been treating me like I'm made of glass. Sometimes it's nice, but not all the time, you can't---" He laughs as he interrupts.

"Oh, that's what that was about. Well, Bethany, you have made your point. No more glass, girl. Got it." He kisses my hair, "But I meant no to you...topping me. That won't be happening again."

"Oh, really?" I pout and give him a cheeky grin, "I thought it was quite good, I mean I could probably use a few pointers but-"

"-Ha, you are funny!" He grabs my chin and fixes me with a serious and heated stare. "Not negotiable, Miss Thorne. You are mine. Your pleasure is mine and the next time you top me, *if* there is a next time, it will be because I have told you to, understand?" His tone is deadly serious.

"Not really." I snuggle into his unyielding muscular chest and feel him collect me tighter to his side. I sigh, I don't care, I got what I wanted and he didn't seem too upset by the whole thing.

"You will." His voice is seductively soft and I drift off to sleep encased in his warm strong arms. I know I won't have another nightmare. "Now, go to sleep." He squeezes me tight into his body. I can feel that his rock hard arousal hasn't diminished in the slightest and it's a testament to how these broken nights are affecting him that he is not capitalising on it. I think maybe it's time to mention my intended move to Marco's new place. Understandably shaken by recent events, I have quietly let Daniel take charge and I can't say it's not completely wonderful to feel so totally taken care of. But I'm fully recovered now and it's time to get some balance. My life, my decisions, and I have to be sure that they are my choices and I am not being completely overwhelmed and seduced by the completely overwhelming and seductive Daniel Stone.

I can feel his warm breath on my neck and from the sound of his relaxed breathing, I know he has fallen asleep, but now I am wide awake. That briefest thought about moving in with Marco has me thinking about the night I was packing boxes to move out of my apartment, just a few weeks ago. The night Kit tried to kill me. Although, I had kept my call to Daniel live, the phone was in my back pocket and he said he couldn't hear what she had said. My head was swimming with the drugs, so when I try to remember it is all very fuzzy. I keep trying to think; she hated me, that much she made pretty clear, and she blamed me for Dad leaving. No, that wasn't right, she blamed me for *her* Dad leaving. I can feel my head start to ache as I try and recall all the details. What had she said about *my* Dad? She'd seen him, she knew who he was. Why didn't I know who he was? Why didn't he come back? It's not like we moved around, we lived in that house my whole life. I lift Daniel's arm, which is a dead weight in his deep sleep state. I slip from the bed and make my way to the kitchen.

The milk is starting to warm in the pan and I smile when I see the fresh nutmeg next to the coffee pods. I had casually mentioned that warm milk and nutmeg helps when I can't sleep and low, there it is on the side. "So, think Bets, focus on the bits you do know." I give myself a pep talk. Kit could've just been fucking with me. A likely possibility, given her penchant for cruelty, but Mum did say something about my *real* Dad too. Just one time but-"Ahh!" I grab the handle from the heat just as the white foam reaches the lip of the pan, nice save. Mug filled and nutmeg grated I gently blow on the now too-hot-to-drink milk. What now? Where would I start looking for information? Kit has disappeared, not that she would be forthcoming, and Mum, well, she had been unable to remember much of anything for so long. Her brief lucid memory was just that, brief, and just before she died. I can't help feel a sudden flood of unbearable sadness wash over me. I have so many questions and no one left to answer them. I have never had a problem with being alone, but just right now I feel terribly lonely.

I walk back toward the living room when I notice the door to one of the other bedrooms open. It's where Daniel has put all my boxes from my apartment, waiting for me to unpack, probably. I flick the light and place my drink on the side. I know I have nothing that will shed light on the subject, but I do remember the care home giving me a small box with my Mum's personal belongings. I hadn't bothered to unpack it, after all it was me who had packed for her when she'd moved there. So it's unlikely there will be anything that I haven't seen already. I lift a few lids from the boxes before I see the one I am looking for, it's grey and light, slightly bigger than a shoe box. I sit crossed legged on the floor with the box in my lap and lift the lid, releasing a thick dusty smell of lavender and damp. Twenty minutes later and I am none the wiser. There are some letters to Kit's father, mostly begging for forgiveness. There are some photos, one taken on a beach somewhere. We didn't take holidays, so I'm guessing it was a day trip, I was still a baby and Kit must have been six. The next I do remember, Kit has her arm over my shoulder and we are both smiling proudly. That day had been really hot and we had spent hours clearing the garden shed, and then we had spent hours filling it with grass cuttings. Not just from our garden but also our neighbour's too. We were convinced that our Mum would get us a pony, now that it had somewhere to sleep. She didn't and she was furious. The next week Kit refused to help clear the mess we had made. I was so worried that I would get grounded, I spent the whole following weekend cleaning the rotting grass from the shed---God it stank. It was slimy and there were so many bugs. John helped but would tease me, because I hated the bugs.

I sip my milk, there are a few business cards and some trinkets, nothing of value. My great-grandmother's wedding ring, a gold heart locket, some hospital bracelets and nothing that is screaming, 'This is your dad!' with a big old X or an arrow. I feel the prickles on my neck just before I notice the door open. Daniel takes my breath away, stealing my thoughts from the past to the now. His feet are bare and his lounge pants are hung low on his hips, his naked chest is firm, ripped, and with clean cut lines of hard muscle. His hair flops messily over his eyes, which look tired. Now I feel guilty, again. He steps into the room and quickly sits behind me lifting me into his lap. His body is warm and sets mine instantly on fire, sweeping my hair from my neck he kisses and I can't help but moan.

"If you keep interrupting your sleep like this, Miss Thorne, I will have to chain you to the bed." His tone is stern and I shift a little at this.

"God Daniel, I'm so sorry I woke you. You do look tired. I just got thinking and couldn't get back to sleep."

"Shh, it's all right baby, it's a problem with a simple solution." His grin is wicked against my skin.

"Daniel, you can't chain me to the bed." I gasp, but my heart is pumping with the potential.

"Really?" He kisses my neck. "Think that, if it gives you comfort." His teeth graze my neck and he sucks hard, then bites down causing a red hot searing fire to spread to my core.

"Oh, God!" I cry, but he stops and chuckles when he feels my body deflate.

"Now, what have we here?" He points at the array of material spread before me.

"Mmm…What?" I struggle to come back from my Daniel in-duced daze, and he inhales as he digs his nose into the hair at my nape, not aiding my focus.

"Playing detective?" He removes his warm breath from my neck, tilts his head, and nods toward the messy pile before us.

"Trying to, but I don't think Sherlock needs to worry and I won't be giving up my day job just yet." I sigh in frustration. "I was trying to remember and I think because Kit and my Mum mentioned my 'real' father," I air quote, "that maybe there was something here that would help, but nada." I flop back into his chest. He picks up the hospital bracelets, two for me and one for Kit.

"What are these?" I take them from him to check the dates.

"These are mine and my sister's birth identity bracelets and this one is from when I was fifteen. I was pretty ill for a while and I guess mum kept it."

"Ill? How Ill?" His tone is firm and his deep frown is all con-cern.

"I was really anaemic but they thought it might be something else too. I remember there being a bit of a panic about donors but turned out I was just severely anaemic." I shrug it off because honestly it seems like a lifetime ago and I really haven't given it a second's thought, and still wouldn't if I hadn't been prompted.

"Mmm…" He looks thoughtful. "Would you like my security team to have a look through this for you? If there is any informa-tion here they will find it." I hesitate, not sure I want that level of scrutiny but then, Daniel knows all my secrets and all my fears. What else is there? He narrows his eyes as I take my time to consider his offer. "Are you hiding something, Miss Thorne?" I shift incredulous that he is serious given my level of disclosure to this man.

"I'm an open book to you, Daniel… you see me…all of me. I hide nothing from you. What about you? Are you hiding anything?" I fire back, and it's only fleeting but I notice the flinch and twitch in his jaw before his face is again impassive and he coolly interrupts.

"No."

All right, that wasn't what I was expecting. I thought this was about finding my Dad but now I feel my previous desire for some perspective has just become an imperative. "Sure, I'm getting nothing from this, other than an unpleasant trip down memory lane. I don't know whether I actually want to find him but I'd like that to be my choice."

"I am not sure he deserves to know you, but you're right that should, at least be your decision." He holds me tighter.

"What do you mean?" I twist around so I can see his eyes.

"Well, your mother said she wrote to him and he never acted on that. His loss, but still-" His frown is deep but I interrupt.

"He did, he did come but Kit told him I had died!" I blurt as if from nowhere.

"What?" His shock is as evident as my own, as the conversation I had with Kit hits me like a sledgehammer.

"Oh, God! I remember." I twist fully in his lap to face him. "Kit said she saw him, knew he was my father. We look alike but she sent him away. No… she sent him to John's funeral, where my mum was attending in my place. So if my real Dad had gone to the church he would've seen my Mum mourning." I shake my head as this all comes flooding back in a jumble of facts and lies mixed with the real sadness and loss.

"Oh, Christ!" He kisses my forehead standing with me as if I weigh nothing. "Look, leave it with me. Okay?" His eyes are intense and the comfort of his words takes a weight I didn't realise from my shoulders and I exhale a deep calming breath.

"Okay." I whisper as I gladly relinquish this burden to his charge. His lips cover mine and he sweeps his soft tongue over my lips, trying to gain access. I comply and hear his deep groan of appreciation.

"Now, let's see where I put those cuffs." I gasp as he strides from the room.

The blinds are still shut but the room is really bright for a winter morning so I know it must be late. That coupled with the rumbling complaint of emptiness coming from my tummy. I look over to the clock, start a luxurious first stretch of the morning and I feel the unfamiliar restriction instantly. My hands had been curled beneath my pillow and the soft leather is light. It is only when I pull against the material that I can even feel them, but I do now. Wow, he wasn't joking! I shuffle up the bed and investigate. The cuffs are the same or similar to the ones he used on me at the flat, but the chain that threads through the buckles is long and looped over a hidden bar, which slides the length of the headboard on the bed. There is a small but secure lock joining the ends of the chain and I give a little rattle just to check its integrity. *Yep that's secure.* I can't believe he did this; I can't believe I didn't feel him do this but mostly I can't believe he did this.

"Daniel!" I call out with mock sweetness, but the size of the apartment means with no response, I soon have to resort to shouting which is more reflective of my mood, I hear movement outside.

"Bethany?" A familiar female voice calls back. Crap! It's Nancy, what is she doing here on a Saturday? She stops just outside the door and I hold my breath. "Can I get you some breakfast, my dear?" My wide eyes are fixed on the handle watching for movement, I quickly reply.

"Oh, no Nancy, that's fine. You're not usually here at the weekend, so I'll sort myself, actually..." I feign a casualness I am not feeling. "I was just after Daniel, you don't know where he is do you?"

"Yes, dear, he is with his trainer. He said you needed to sleep in, that you needed your rest. Bethany, I hope you don't mind me saying but it is lovely to see him this way." Unfortunately, her sweet sentiment is a little lost on me this morning.

"Is it?" I grumble quietly but freeze when I see the handle twist. "Oh, Nancy, he is right. In fact I think I will try and catch a bit more sleep." The handle stops and slowly returns to its rest position. "Maybe you could get Daniel to wake me just as soon as he returns; you don't know when that will be by any chance?" The tone in my voice can't help rise with the uncertainty of my predicament.

"Oh, I don't think it will be too much longer, he asked me to fix brunch. It is sweet that you miss him, but then you two have been inseparable so it's not a big surprise. It's just lovely… anyway, I'll let him know when I see him." Her voice disappears. I throw myself heavily into the pillows in exasperation, lifting one of the pillows I squeeze it to my face and scream. I am not going to *miss him* this morning or whenever he decides to show his face, I am furious. I throw the pillow across the room with more frustration and I look for my bag. I will call him, there is no way I am going to wait here all day like some little slave. My bag is out of reach, so I slide the chain to the very edge of the bar. Slightly excited that I might be able to slip it over the end and free myself, but it just seems to be some continuous bar, damn. I stretch my body full length, pointing my toes frantically trying to grip the folded over handle of my courier satchel with my big toe. Every muscle is protesting at this extreme demand without a warm up, but I manage to curl the leather handle over my big toe and hook it securely onto my foot. I pull the bag to me and climb back on the bed. I give a little air punch at my small achievement but my smile disappears as I dial Daniel.

"Good morning, Bethany." His voice is smooth and deep, if a little breathless.

"Arsewipe." I reply sweetly and he laughs loudly but recovers.

"Now, that is not very polite, shall we try again? Good morning, Bethany." The command in his voice sends instant shivers across my skin and despite being furious, I still feel a deep desire to obey him but I don't have to be happy about it. I grit my teeth.

"Good morning, Daniel. Would you be so kind as to get your arse back here, now?" I may be trying for polite, but my jaw is clenched and my tone is clipped.

"Oh, Miss Thorne, now you're not even trying, I might think you actually *want* to be punished for your manners." I can feel the smile in his voice and I can't help the heat flame through me at his words.

"Exactly what am I being punished for at this moment, Daniel?"

"You're not." He sounds surprised by my comment.

"So I am shackled to your bed for my own good?" I can't hide the sarcasm.

"Mmm I do like the visual I now have of you shackled to my bed." His voice is pure sin, "But essentially yes... it is for your own good. You need to rest."

"For Fu... " I cry out but he interrupts.

"You might want to rethink what you are about to say. After all as you say you are shackled to my bed and you have already clocked up one punishment for your impolite greeting... two if I count the sarcastic tone." His is completely serious and I want that pillow to scream into once more, but I refrain from adding to this situation, which is out of my control. In the first instance I need him to come home and take these cuffs off, and then I'll be in a better position to highlight the crazy here, maybe. "Good girl, now I will be back when I am back. If you need anything call Nancy, but in the meantime, I would suggest more sleep. You are going to need it." He ends the call, luckily, because I think calling him a *motherfucker,* which is on the tip of my tongue, might also be considered impolite.

I hear the handle on the door and wake with a start. I am in a panic that it might be Nancy and irritated that Daniel was right, I did apparently need more sleep. I sit bolt upright. Daniel enters carrying two wonderfully smelling cups of coffee, my tummy makes an embarrassingly loud effort to be recognised and he laughs.

"Someone's hungry?" He is fresh from a shower, hair still damp, and he smells of citrus and spice, but he looks good enough to eat.

"Someone's starving," But in this rare instance I am not thinking of him. I am actually famished.

"Why didn't you get Nancy to get you some breakfast?" His innocent question has me taken back. Seriously. I slap my forehead, rattling my cuffs at the same time in an obvious display of why I hadn't done such a thing.

"Why didn't I think of that?" I reply with wide incredulous eyes.

"More sarcasm, really Bethany, you think that's a good idea?" He leans forward and pulls the chains so I am forced to slide closer. "I don't understand why you couldn't just ask for some breakfast. It is why I asked Nancy to be here this weekend." He leans down so his lips rest just above mine and I push forward to take a taste, but he grins and moves back out of my reach. I let out a frustrated sigh.

"Daniel, I couldn't let her see me like this? What would she think?" I exhale slowly.

"Sorry, do you think I would have a problem with anyone knowing that you belong to me?" He laughs and leans back in to nibble at my neck, his breath is warm and minty. "I won't dignify that with an answer." He sucks a little harder at a soft spot in the crook of my neck and my breath catches.

"Okay, but what about how I would feel?" My voice gets softer the more distracted I become and I'm trying to keep my focus.

"Same goes baby." His brows knit together like I am saying something incomprehensible. "You are mine... end of. I don't care who knows it, in fact the more people the better." He smoothly climbs above me pinning me to the bed with the covers, his strong thighs gripping me tight. "Don't you want people to know you belong to me?" His eyes are dark and flash with a slight flicker of sadness.

"Look, Daniel," I am trying to be calm, but I can feel an inner rage at his stubborn ability not to see that this might be considered a little over the top. "It's not that I don't want people to know, but how *much* they know,"---I rattle my chains for emphasis---"this is different, this is private and I am very new to it." The unpleasant thought that he is not new to this is an unwelcome distraction and I lose my train of thought.

"Hey." His warm finger traces smoothly along my jaw. "You are right…this is private." He leans down and covers my mouth with the hottest kiss that has me moaning into him as I try and arch up to meet him as he retreats. "But you know you could've just hidden the cuffs under the covers or pillows and asked Nancy to put your breakfast on the side." His smile is smug at this obvious notion, obvious now, that is.

"Oh, um yes… I could've done that." I return his smile and wiggle against his capture. "So we're good?"

"Oh, yes, I'd say we're good." His voice is dripping with lust, his eyes darken and my mouth goes dry.

"So, no punishment?" I smile weakly, and his laugh is rich and sinful.

"Now, what would have you draw that conclusion, Miss Thorne?" He pulls the covers down, rolls his t-shirt I am wearing up, and tucks it so that I am naked from my breast to my toes.

"Um that Nancy is here?" I try to argue.

"True, but that just means you'll have to be quiet because you know that I don't care." He pauses, his tongue lightly wetting his full lips. "So, can you be quiet, Miss Thorne, or would you like me to gag you?" His grin is wicked.

"What are you going to do?"

He narrows his eyes and draws his gaze the length of my body, sending a scorching heat across my skin. "Anything I fucking want to." His lip curls slowly to one side with his erotic declaration.

"Crap, you better gag me." I think I actually start to pant with eagerness. "I couldn't face Nancy if she hears me scream." My face is flushed and my heart is racing when his grin morphs and he flashes me his heart stopping smile.

"Yes, Ma'am." He tugs his fringe and I scoff at his mock servitude, like he ever does what anyone tells him.

Printed in Great Britain
by Amazon